Spa Girl

Spa Girl

Virginia Gray

Printed in the United States of America

First print edition, 2020

ISBN Print 978-0-9905236-7-3

ISBN ebook 978-0-9905236-8-0

cover: Toaster Shock Design

www.virginiagray.com

Contents

For Arthur

Other Books by Virginia Gray

1

The remote valley where I grew up was called Black Village, though no one remembers why. Each year, spring rains threatened to drown us, pouring water through our thatched roof as if it were a sieve, seemingly determined to muddy our dirt floors. The tiny slit windows welcomed summer's heat and biting bugs, and our clay walls did little to protect us from the cold. During harvest, I lay amid the golden rice stalks, wishing the surrounding mountains would become a great fortress to protect our farm, but they were nothing more than a teacup for my mother's tears.

As it had always been in the countryside, fathers wanted strong sons to provide for them when they grew old. Wives burnt offerings to their ancestors for luck. In my time, because the government had established a one-child-per-family policy, women prayed not just for boys, but for only one pregnancy.

Officials from the Organization for Family Planning often came to my village, searching for second pregnancies. When discovered, the women were forced to have abortions. To avoid trouble, neighbors reported on one another; no one went against our powerful government.

Out of fear, those determined to keep their babies often sought refuge in other villages until delivery; infants were allowed to live. My cousin was not so lucky. During her ninth month, the Organization hauled her away and tore the baby from her body.

I was one who survived, a second child, a girl. The year of my birth was 1983. My country was China.

2

Girl

My parents named my brother Ming. In Xiang dialect this means "bright light." When I was born, they called me Mei Zi, which means "girl".

With little supervision, I went everywhere. I ran across green yards and brown fields. I jumped from terraced rice paddies spilling down hillsides like great staircases. I splashed through murky pond shallows chasing jade frogs. I swung from branches like a forest monkey. I threw rocks. I laughed. Forever hungry, especially in wintertime when food was scarce, Mama's call for dinner sent me racing for home.

On one oppressive midsummer evening, it did not.

Her voice was clear and sharp as always, but I could barely move, much less reply. Baba's gruff voice was no more compelling. When others joined in, all calling my name, it seemed a burial chant. I closed my eyes.

Time had never meant much to me. The black rooster's crow meant morning, mealtime was when my belly grumbled, and the sun's last rays marked evening. I only knew that it was dewy and dark when my brother discovered me.

"Go away," I moaned.

"You wicked girl, hiding in here. Don't you know the whole village is searching for you? They've started draining the pond!" Ming growled.

Though draining the pond sounded wonderfully fun, I was too spent to care very much. I turned away from his torch flame, pressing my face against the chicken coop's cool dirt floor.

"Mama, Baba, I found her," Ming yelled irritably. I heard others relaying the message. Why everyone was so upset?

Mama picked me up and shook me hard, her voice frantic. "Mei Zi, why did you do this? Why did you hide from us?" If she was afraid, I knew I ought to be as well, but her trickling tears felt so soothing on my feverish skin. Coughing violently, I wilted in her arms.

Mama placed me on my mat and dabbed my forehead and body with damp cloths. I closed my eyes then and drifted into troubled dreams.

At first light, my parents wrapped me in a ratty sheet and set out to get help. With no paved roads, the area was impassible to trucks and cars, but Baba's bicycle had two seats. Leaning against Mama's shoulder as she and Baba peddled, my stomach lurched with every bump and drop.

Black Village had much land, few people, and no doctors. To reach the clinic, we rode for a very long time, past the pond where we fished and washed our clothes, past hillsides where sheep grazed, past the market where we sold our produce.

The concrete medical building, with its many glass windows, had an acrid smell, but the floor was white and shiny—until I vomited on it. Mama cursed under her breath.

"What's the boy's name?" the doctor asked. His coat was spotless, and I thought how wonderful it would be to own clothes not caked with dirt.

"He doesn't have a name," Baba replied.

The doctor's eyes narrowed behind his thick-framed glasses. No one in my village could afford such an extravagance—not even my grandfather. "Why doesn't he have a name?"

"We never gave him one," Mama quickly answered, her eyes darting to Baba's.

With my short hair and bare chest, I looked every bit the boy. Of course, when the doctor examined the rest of me, he knew differently.

"Is this your only child?" he asked.

Silent for a moment, Baba met the doctor's eyes. "No."

"Has this child been registered with the government?"

Baba looked away, but Mama said, "We are very poor."

"Ah. I'm sorry to hear that, but I'm obligated to record all patients. Is your first child a son or daughter?"

"A son, sir," Baba answered, exhaling deeply.

"Has *he* been registered?" the doctor asked, raising a gray eyebrow. My father nodded.

The doctor stared at me for a long moment and then at Mama. "I've seen you in the marketplace. And this child, too. You sell the best eggs of all the farmers." His face softened. "You are lucky to have this fine son to help you. Perhaps the government will not treat you harshly."

I wanted to laugh. This man was not as educated as I'd imagined if he still thought I was a boy.

Mama's hand shook as she held out her little gray money pouch. The coins made a tinkling sound as the doctor counted them. I knew this sound well. I also knew it was likely all the money we'd collected this season.

"If the boy has no name, then I will give him one. Hong Bo," the doctor said.

Now, this was a clever and kind thing to do. Hong Bo is a boy's name, meaning "Wave of Luck." Once the doctor marked my new name in his fat red book, he gave my parents medicine to help my fever.

郭

Two nights later, our door was nearly shaken from its hinges. "This is the Organization. Come out!" I was plenty old enough to know that if officials came to your house, it was a very bad thing.

"What do you want?" Mama yelled. Though the year was 1989, Black Village had no electricity. Our lantern's flame flared and flickered when the door swung open, casting wobbly shadows on the two uniformed men as they entered our house.

Their powerful flashlights danced over every surface of the dusty room, illuminating cobwebs and sending two brown rats scurrying in opposite directions. I wanted to follow them.

With a moan, Ming sat up on his mat and blinked his eyes. Wide awake but still feverish, I coughed loudly. Like hummingbirds, the beams jerked from Ming's face to mine, hovering there so long my eyes saw spots. I began to cry.

"Guo Meilin, you've broken the law," one of the men said zealously. "Pay the fine or go to jail." The penalty for having a second child was thirty-five RMB—a sum so enormous it could purchase a winter's worth of coal.

Mama bravely stepped in front of me. "We don't have money. We are farmers. Come back after the harvest."

"You know if you don't pay it, we can knock down your house," the taller man said, grinning. I curled into a ball and shivered at the thought. Crossing her arms, Mama stared stonily at them. "And your crops and your animals? We're authorized to destroy them as well. You don't want that, do you? Guo Meilin," the short one said, his tone suggesting he might enjoy that very much.

Still, my mother said nothing.

Looking at one another then, the men smiled cruelly. "We'll leave you with a reminder so you don't forget to pay."

"*Two* reminders," the other sneered. "And your daughter should watch, so she learns obedience."

When the short one grabbed my mother's arm, I screamed. Ming, who was twelve and very skinny, launched himself at the man, hitting him with his fists. The taller one sent him flying across the room, where he crashed into the wall.

My mother was no coward. She fought and kicked and threw our bucket at them. She hit them with our wok.

Relief washed over me when I heard Baba's angry voice outside. The men released Mama at once and disappeared. "Guo Boqin!" the men shouted. After a fit of yelling, we heard more ominous sounds.

Baba's face was painted with blood when he entered the house. Groaning, he slowly eased himself to the floor. My mother's eyes swept over him, and then Ming and me. She shook her head grimly. "We will not pay the fine."

3

A New Home

"We can't live this way," Baba whispered a few nights later, his voice ragged. "We need more money. I know some men."

Mama sighed sadly.

At first light, Baba left our village, and by week's end he'd set up a shop in Ningxiang. An hour trip by bicycle, it was a busy place with a factory and lots of people—or so Ming claimed. His middle school may have lain on the outskirts, but I doubted he'd ventured deep into the town itself.

It's very common for poor farmers to send their children into cities for work; the extra income is essential for their families' survival. Many of our villagers had done this. With our finances in question, I feared Baba would send me away as well.

My father was gone a lot after that, staying in Ningxiang most nights. This didn't bother me much because we started having nicer things; I got my first real pair of shoes, and Ming got a bike of his own. We had three bikes now! I couldn't believe how our fortunes had turned.

Mama began traveling to Ningxiang as well. Most nights she came home, but sometimes she did not; I minded that very much.

Since I was a girl and the daughter of her least favorite child, my grandmother refused to take care of me, or help my mother in any way. The chore of watching over me fell onto Ming's resentful shoulders.

In my dialect, the maternal grandmother is called *wai po*. My wai po was a proud woman who valued boys far more than girls. Because she'd married an accountant with lots of land, she'd been rich by village standards and never missed an opportunity to remind her neighbors of her good fortune.

When Mama was seven, my grandfather went blind. Unable to work, their finances quickly declined, and Wai po removed her young daughter from school to help care for all the babies she kept having; in the 1950s Chairman Mao encouraged large families, labeling one mother of eleven children a national hero.

Quickly becoming Wai po's second set of hands, Mama worked tirelessly, cooking for the family, cleaning, and even raising her blind brother, who Wai po had deemed defective. Of the eleven babies she bore, only five survived childhood, which further shamed her. But it was Mama's decision to marry the poorest man in the village that most humiliated her. In Wai po's eyes, this insult was unforgivable.

郭

In late summer, Ming's voice changed. Finding this wildly amusing, I goaded him whenever I could, just to hear it crack. Making him angry was easy enough to accomplish because, at this new and self-important age, he was irritable and impatient most of the time, often back talking to my mother, which only got him into trouble.

"What are you eating?" I asked, wandering into the rickety storage shed.

"Lotus root," he said with a loud crunch. "Want some?"

"You know we aren't allowed to eat that. Mama said it's too valuable to waste on us. It brings a good price at the market."

"Mama's not here, and I'm hungry." Then he smiled impishly, holding it up. "You sure you don't want a bite? It's very sweet."

I wanted that lotus root badly. Even the rotten one I'd once tasted had been delicious, but I shook my head no.

Ming shrugged. "Your loss. I'm going to eat a watermelon next. A whole one."

"You'll get a beating."

He smiled widely. "Worth it. Even green it'll be worth it."

My mother and I continued selling eggs and produce on market days as we always had, but with each passing week, Mama looked more and more haggard. It worried me, but what could I do to help her other than feed the chickens and pull garden weeds?

After the rice harvest, my parents announced we were moving to Ningxiang. This news was very exciting, of course, but frightening as well. Black Village was all I knew, and I couldn't imagine living without my Auntie and all of my cousins. Ming, on the other hand, was delighted by the news.

"I don't have to go to school anymore!" He sang, dancing around the room, picking me up and twirling me in his arms.

"You will go!" Mama said fiercely, banging her fist on our little table. "As soon as we earn enough to pay the government, you *will* go back. You must make a better life than ours. You must."

"What's wrong with our life now?" I sheepishly asked.

Kneeling in front of me, Mama's eyes softened. "There are better lives than this one. You are too young to understand such things.

One day you will. You and Ming can have things we cannot." She glanced up at Baba and then smiled at me. "We'll live at the business for a while. Be happy, Mei Zi, you are getting a new house."

"I like our house. I like our farm," I said, shocked.

"We'll still live on this very spot, only this house will be gone and a new one built in its place. You'll like it. More room."

郭

Whenever I asked Mama about the business, she explained that they bought and sold things. I often imagined all the exciting items they must keep in their shop. Well, they had lots of items. Lots of dirty, smelly items. It was a recycling shop, but only after seeing it, did I understand what that term meant.

"Lay your mats there in the corner while I make broth. Then we'll sleep. We must be up early in the morning to do the recycling. You're going to learn the business," she said. Her smile seemed forced.

The shop was dark and strange. All around us piles of junk—metal, paper, plastic bottles, and many other items I did not even recognize—rose up like great beasts. Though autumn, it was very hot inside this metal building, and the cloying smell of dirty oil and rust twisted my stomach.

I barely slept the first night, certain that at any moment, the towering golden Buddha statue watching over the town would leave its mountaintop perch, capture me with one of its many hands, and drop me into its smiling mouth. The street noises—groaning cars, angry motorcycles, and raucous voices—frightened me equally, and bugs bit me so many times that by morning I looked like a spotted egg.

"Today you earn your keep," Mama said. "Walk down every street and pick up any trash you find. Be careful not to break the bottles. They're worth a lot of money." Then she squatted in front of me and smiled. "This is a big adventure for you. A big responsibility for a small girl. Help your brother and don't stray from him. Do you understand?"

Carrying my bright blue sack, I obediently followed Ming. At first, searching for junk was like a great scavenger hunt, but as the temperature rose, the game was no longer fun. And when sweat ran down my legs, my bug bites began itching. Finally, I sat down in the grimy street and scratched them until blood oozed out.

"Get up, Mei Zi, before you're run over," Ming ordered.

Ming had been right: this town was far larger than Black Village. People were everywhere, but few took notice of two filthy children by the roadside. If we got in their way, however, men on bikes yelled at us with words I didn't know. My brother knew them, though, and grew angry.

One man tooted his car horn and then tossed a large brown bottle from the window. The smelly liquid splashed on my legs and burned my sores, but it didn't matter. Mama would be pleased.

When my stomach ached from hunger, and our bags were full, we dragged them back to the grungy building.

"Mama, we're hungry," I said, interrupting her negotiation with two men.

"Go inside," she hissed without looking at me. The quick but pleasant bartering voice she used when selling our vegetables had fled, replaced by something coarse and mean-sounding. I quickly placed my bag beside Ming's.

"Where's Baba?" I asked once we were alone.

"He's working on the house," she said impatiently, rooting

through our bags. "This isn't enough. Empty your sacks and go back out."

Recycling was hard and unpleasant work, and only now did I understand why Mama looked so tired all the time. That night, I didn't care if bugs bit me, or the floor smelled, or if the entire bronze statue army displayed on the plaza attacked. After picking up trash all day and then organizing it the way Mama had shown us, I was asleep before my head hit the floor.

This became our lives. Every day, Ming and I walked the streets of Ningxiang. Though he no longer attended middle school, we passed it often. If students were outside playing, he insisted we rest by the fence to watch them. Crossing the swinging bridge nearby was my favorite part of the walk because it meant passing the small theater and its forever-bulging garbage cans; it was easy to find bottles there. The little souvenir shops by the muddy river also had good trash, though who would visit this town, I had no idea.

One night, I awoke to hushed voices. Peering through a hole in the wall, I saw Mama talking with a man. I thought it strange to do business in the dark, but what did I know about such things?

After that, the man came regularly, bringing one item after another. Those strange-looking metal pieces sold very quickly.

Even as the weather turned cold, Baba stayed in Black Village. We went home on market days, selling any available produce we had. But with no place to live now that our house was gone, we made the long trek back to the shop at night, huddling around coal embers while Mama cooked.

We owned few clothes, and I had no coat, so walking the wet streets became unpleasant. Having already outgrown my thin-soled shoes, my cramped toes hurt constantly. I looked forward to snowy days when my feet turned red and I could feel nothing.

Very quickly our hands and faces chapped, and our skin began cracking. We couldn't afford lotion, so my mother boiled eggs and rubbed their reddish-orange yolks on our skin; a common practice in the countryside. I had never enjoyed the pasty feel of yolk salve—like smelly mud on my face—but it had always been worth the unpleasantness so that I could go outside and play. In Ningxiang, there was no playing. I missed home.

郭

Near the stinking factory, we always found good junk; there was trash everywhere. This became our first destination. The sooner we filled our bags, the sooner we could seek shelter from the biting wind.

There were always people hanging around outside the giant gray building. "Hey, little urchins, I have a gift for you," a man with rotting teeth called out. He lounged against the entrance's chain fencing nearly every day. He usually had a can for me, but on this occasion, he had a large clear bottle, which was something special. He also had an audience of people as filthy as he. "Come closer, little girl. If you sit on my lap, I will give it to you."

His friends laughed and began calling me to sit on their laps too, though they had nothing to give me. With its square shape and thick neck, the bottle was especially heavy-looking, and I thought Mama would be very pleased to have it, so I took a step towards him.

"Don't do it," Ming growled under his breath.

Confused, I looked at him. "But the bottle!"

"I said no, Mei Zi. Come here."

Though the men's cries grew louder, and some even whistled, for perhaps the first time in my life, I listened to Ming. Realizing I wasn't going to sit on his lap, the derelict who I thought was my friend threw the bottle at me. Bouncing off my arm, it shattered on the payment. With blurry vision, I looked up at Ming. "Ignore it," he said. "We'll find more near the guards."

The green-uniformed men were not friendly, but they didn't chase us away, like many of the shop owners did. And Ming was right; there were always bottles and cans near their station.

After we'd collected all we could stuff into our bags, one of the guards jerked his chin and said, "You missed one."

"Thanks!" I replied, scurrying to the foot of wide stairs. When I looked up, I saw a familiar face. "Hey, Ming, it's him. The one who brings Mama metal. Hello, sir!" I shouted, waving.

He glanced at me, tossed his cigarette on the ground, and mounted the steps.

I ran after him.

"Mister. Hey, man. You know who I am. You come to our shop at night."

His eyes flaring, he pushed me away. "Your mother may be a whore, but I am not your father, little girl."

The men congregating nearby laughed.

Dropping his sack, Ming launched himself at the tall man, ramming his fists into his stomach. "Don't call my mama a whore, you thief!"

When he slapped my brother's face, I hit the man as well, tearing at his yellow shirt. He gave me a swift kick, and I tumbled down the cement steps, landing flatly on my back. I gasped for air.

"Go home to your whore mama, urchins," he yelled and then disappeared inside.

Ming's face was like stone as he helped me up. Though I saw his lower lip quiver as we passed the derelicts once more, he did not cry. I cried enough for both of us. I cried all the way back to our shop.

To my surprise, when we told Mama what had happened, she scolded us. "Keep your mouths shut. Don't talk to anyone. Just pick up the junk and bring it home. That is your job. This is not Black Village, children. This is a rough town."

The hateful man did not come that night, and I was secretly pleased that we'd scared him off. The next morning, however, far worse people paid Mama a visit.

"Eat your rice, then go to work. Remember what I said. Don't talk to anyone."

Ming tossed a sack over his shoulder and left without a backward glance.

"Why did you call that factory man a thief?" I asked, running to keep up; it seemed his legs were growing longer by the day.

"Because that's what he is."

"How do you know?"

"Where do you think he gets all that metal? He steals it from the factory. That's what they make there. That's why it looks so new." I was amazed that my brother knew so much.

Not far from the shop, I spotted my first bottle. Certain it was a sign that we'd have good luck today, I scrambled down into the ditch to get it. Suddenly Mama shouted.

"Come on!" Ming shouted, tearing off down the road.

Tough-looking men in police uniforms were binding Mama's hands. Terrified, I clung to her legs with all my might. "Don't take my mama! Don't take her!" I screamed.

"Mei Zi, you must let go. Ming, get her," she begged. Wrapping his arms around my waist, he wrenched me away. Mama tried to smile, but there was real fear in her eyes. "Don't worry, children. Take my bike and go back to the village."

"But Mama!" Ming pleaded.

"Do as I say," she shouted as the police shoved her into their car. I didn't know where they were taking her. I didn't know if I would ever see her again.

Ming quickly locked the gate, and we hopped onto Mama's bike. He pedaled faster than I'd ever seen him go. Still, it took a lifetime to get home.

"Baba!" Ming and I yelled when our new house came into view.

Baba smacked the wide roof with his hammer. Wooden walls now wrapped the frame. I stared at it in wonder.

"Why are you here?" Baba shouted down.

"Mama's been arrested!"

"What?" he said, sliding down the long bamboo ladder. My uncles and Cousin Chen followed him.

As Ming told him the story, I cried all over again.

"Go to Auntie Song's and stay there," he said, plucking me from the bike seat as Ming slithered off. Dust rose in a great brown plume behind him as Baba tore off down the hilly road to Ningxiang.

郭

Save for a few scattered nights, I'd never been without my mother. I ached for her comforting songs, her goodnight kisses, her protective embraces. Even her stern scolding…I missed that as well.

In those first dark days back in Black Village, I was inconsolable. I barely ate, and sleep came only when I ran out of tears. I awoke screaming, my nightmares always the same—dark uniforms with shiny buttons, blue net bags, broken bottles, and Mama's frantic cries.

Ming suffered in a different way. I never saw him cry, but he kept to himself, often disappearing for hours once his chores were finished. No one said anything to him.

When Baba announced that it was time, we packed our few belongings and glumly crossed the frozen cotton field. Moving into our new house should have been an exciting event. It was certainly exciting for Auntie Song and her family, who continued caring for us.

"Look at all the room," my auntie remarked. "Isn't this a big house, Zhang Jing?"

My older cousin by two years shrugged indifferently. "It's not *that* big," she said, startled suddenly when her voice echoed down the hallway.

Unimpressed, I slid a rickety chair across the planked living room floor and listlessly mounted it.

"She has her own bedroom?!" Zhang Jing whined, stomping back down the hall.

"Staring out the window day after day, won't bring her home any sooner. Even with a different view," Auntie Song said, tugging on my knotted hair. "Come down, Mei Zi. Go chase your cousin."

Biting down on my trembling lip, I shook my head no.

After a few moments of watching me helplessly, she pulled me against her bosom and kissed the top of my head. "I miss her too," she whispered. "We all do."

Now that Baba was no longer needed at home, he returned to Ningxiang. Someone must run the shop, he'd explained. As one week bled into another and another, my loneliness consumed me. Relatives came and went in a steady stream; everyone wanted to see the new house. But relatives were no substitute for parents, and I soon stopped pretending to be happy.

In mid-February, Auntie Song began preparing for our New Year's celebrations. Rice must be cooked, vegetables cleaned, water and coal and wood brought in. In the past, this had been my favorite holiday, but without Mama, I didn't much care whether we celebrated it or not.

Leaning against the big glass-paned window, I spent hours on end considering prison. I wondered what Mama's room was like, if she had made any friends, if the food was good, if children were sent there—this I thought about a lot. Surely, a young girl who hadn't considered the consequences before broadcasting her mother's questionable associations would be a prime candidate.

But other than working hard to pay a government fine, what had Mama done to deserve such a fate? No one ever wanted to talk about it, especially Baba. I worried for him constantly. Would he go next?

A great billow of luminous fog crawled over the dismal mountains, devouring them. I watched in fascination as it shrank, rolled over upon itself, and grew once more. Onto the hill below, it suddenly spat out a dark moving shape that slowly became Baba's big bike. Both seats were filled!

Flying out the door, I tore across the barren field, yelling at the top of my lungs. Mama slid from her seat, and I launched myself into her waiting arms. Gathering up Ming moments later, she hugged us fiercely.

"Look at you both. So grown-up."

"It's barely been two months, Meilin," Baba said thickly.

"What was it like, Mama?" I asked. "Were there bad people there? Ming said bad people go to prison."

"Be quiet, Mei Zi," Ming growled.

"Speak only of happy things," Baba murmured in my ear.

Considering this for a moment, I grabbed her arm. "Come see the house!" Only now would I allow myself to be excited about it, only now could I celebrate this great gift. Only now, with Mama.

"Meilin!" Auntie Song cried out as we entered the dimly lit

kitchen. After tearfully embracing her sister, she appraised Mama's thin form and drawn features and then nodded curtly. "I'll feed you."

While she steamed rice, we showed Mama everything. Ming pointed out our new well and coal bin. Though the water was cloudy and didn't taste sweet like Wai po's, we were thrilled not to tromp all the way to her house every day to get it.

Skirting a large mud puddle and hurrying past the squat and stinking outhouse which supplied fertilizer for our summer crops, we towed her to the main house. Dragging her from one room to the next, I pointed out our three bedrooms, the stairs, the storage room, even demanding she try out each of our new mismatched living room chairs. We didn't have a fireplace, but Baba had recently rescued a ceramic heating container that we now used for burning coal and small logs. Set in the middle of the living room, I relished the faint heat it gave off.

"Mama, sit beside me and put your feet here," I said, circling my dirty toes around the warm rim. "It feels so good."

"Everything about our home feels good," she whispered thickly, pulling me against her.

4

Seeing Red

Lunar New Year is a very special time for the people of China, especially the children. For my poor family, it was the only time of year we had meat, which I really enjoyed eating.

Festivities begin on the first day of the first month of the Chinese calendar and end fifteen days later. Though the date changes each year, it always falls in winter. During our celebrations, my family prepared many traditional dishes; each was symbolic. For example, fish steamed with pickled chili sauce—the most famous dish in Hunan—we ate for prosperity. Pork, roasted chicken, beef stew, eel, animal organs, and, of course, spring rolls, which symbolize wealth, were also served.

Most people honor their ancestors on Tomb Sweeping Day, which is in the spring, but our family traditionally did this during New Year's. Offerings of meat, rice, fireworks, and alcohol were placed in front of the family crypts. We also burned fake paper money, which was great fun. These gifts were given to provide our fallen family members what they needed on the other side. In Back Village, burial sites were scattered along the hilltops; ours were behind my house.

Certain there were spirits wandering around there, I lived in fear of climbing to the tombs.

After performing the rituals, we returned to the house, hosting a feast to celebrate Mama's jail release. So many of our relatives attended that there was little room to stand, much less sit. My blind uncle, whose fortune-telling skills had made him a local celebrity, amazed us with his predictions. Gorging myself, I wasn't just happy to have food, I was happy to have Mama back.

Though I had my own room now, a wonder, yet a lonely place, I insisted on sleeping with my mother. She and Baba each had their own beds, which I did not at the moment; my cousins had taken it over, along with the entire upstairs. Sleep was difficult because every time I shut my eyes, the women—usually led by Auntie Song—exploded in peals of laughter.

Very late, when the house was finally quiet and Mama was snoring softly beside me, I awoke to find a strange woman standing beside the bed. Wearing the purple pajamas my auntie had just given me, she spun her body like a dancer. Frozen with terror, I helplessly watched her spin, her long beautiful hair fanning out to hide her face.

Only after she vanished could my arms and legs move once more. Grabbing Mama's shoulder, I frantically shook her. "Mama, wake up! Mama, I saw a ghost."

"Go back to sleep, Mei Zi," she mumbled. "It was just a bad dream."

"No, Mama, it was real. I could see her in the moonlight. She was in this room with us!"

"Hush now, or you'll wake your baba. You ate too many sesame balls. They're giving you nightmares."

Crushed that she didn't believe me, I could find no way to convince her. When she threatened to send me upstairs, I quieted, though I didn't sleep for the rest of the night. The following evening, after another banquet, I slept in Ming's room, surrounded by an army of cousins. I didn't eat any more sesame balls, and I did not see that ghost woman again.

郭

New clothes and red envelopes filled with money are traditionally given to children during New Year's celebrations. Because we were poor, our clothes were handed down from older cousins, who were also poor, and were generally worn out. And of course, the only money in our red envelopes was fake.

This year, however, my mother surprised us with new coats and sturdy shoes. I slipped my arms through the sleeves, glorying in the nubby feel of the wool; I had never owned anything so nice. The coat was the most beautiful shade of red. Hong, the name the doctor had given me, means both "luck" and "red" because red is the luckiest color. This made my coat all the more special.

"This is an important time in your life. You'll need this," she said, smiling.

"Why is it so important?" I asked, twirling around the room in a blur of red. It was so warm that I could barely feel the chill in the house.

"After your grandfather went blind, the family became poor. Any money we had was used for my brothers. I only got to go to school for three years. That's why I can't write more than my name and why I can't read."

Astonished by this revelation, I stopped twirling and climbed onto her lap. "You can't read?"

"Reading is one of the things you learn in school," she said, combing her fingers through my tangled hair." Your father can't read either."

At this, my jaw literally dropped. How could this be? My parents were hardworking and capable. This house and this very coat were testament to that.

"His family was in worse shape than ours, and after his mother died, he and his siblings had to fend for themselves. Your baba is a determined man with a strong will. See how he's taking care of us?" she said, patting the moldy brown sofa he'd recently rescued from a burnt down house.

"But you're smart, Mama. You can barter and count money."

She smiled sadly and then pulled me against her chest. "I may be a clever woman, but I'll only ever be able to make money farming or selling trash. It is a hard life, Mei Zi, but you will do much better. You'll go to school like your brother. You'll learn to read and make me very proud."

My grandmother had always been quick to point out a girl's lesser worth, that girls were only temporary family members—which I hoped I was not, that they were not useful for ancestral lines—which I didn't understand, and that they were only good for inside work—though every woman I knew, except her, worked in the fields. My parents were different. They'd always treated Ming and me equally, and I'd always felt loved.

Though I saw nothing wrong with my current life, if she wanted something different for me, then I would happily go to school. "I'll work very hard to make you proud," I said. "Harder than Ming."

"That won't take much," she said, snorting.

5

Fire-breathing Dragon

The night before I was to begin school, my mother bathed me in the large wooden bucket used for catching rainwater. She'd stopped cutting my hair the previous spring, so it was finally long enough to braid. She laid out my hand-me-down outfit, which she'd meticulously patched, and my glorious new coat.

"Ming, what will school be like? What does the building look like? Are the teachers nice? Are there lots of children to play with?" I asked, following him into his room.

Still angry that he had to return to middle school, Ming shook his head. "You won't like it. Now go away."

I knew differently. I would like it. I would like it very much.

The next morning, Mama handed me the latched tin box my father had brought home. She had fashioned a fancy bow with the string holding the lid shut.

"I've made a nice meal for you of rice and vegetables wrapped in a cabbage leaf. Yes, there are mushrooms," she answered before I had time to ask. Kneeling, she buttoned my coat and then tucked a loose strand of hair behind my ear. "Pay attention to your teachers. Do as they say."

Ming had already left for school; Ningxiang was in the opposite direction. Though disappointed that I wouldn't get to ride on his handlebars, I was glad I wouldn't have to spend every day in that horrible town.

Two of my cousins, Zhang Jing and Chu Hua, who also attended primary school, met me at the door. It was still dark outside, but Chu Hua carried a flaming torch that danced wildly in the damp breeze. Kissing my forehead, Mama's eyes shimmered with unshed tears. "Go learn to read and write. Do it for me."

"I will learn everything!" I said, running out the door.

Our primary school lay on the other side of the big purple mountain. From such a height—so great that even the clouds brushed its peak, I would finally be able to see all of China. Holding hands, the three of us sang songs as we skipped along the uneven dirt path. When the hill became steep, we walked and sang. And when the path seemed as though it was leading us straight to the sky, we trudged in silence.

Nearing the summit, perhaps an hour later, I sprinted to the top. Setting fire to the frost-tipped spruces, the sun's bold rays painted the blanketing mist pink. To my great disappointment, when I gazed at the glowing expanse, I only saw mountains. Mountains and mountains and mountains. Was China made of nothing else?

Zhang Jing pointed to a neat white building nestled in the jade valley below. Like ants, the schoolyard teemed with children—more than all the people in our village!

My teacher was old, her steel hair twisted into a tight bun at the base of her neck. Her clothes looked better than Mama's; not one patch.

A pretty girl in crisp blue pants seated herself beside me. "Do you want to be friends?"

Thrilled to have a friend who was not a relative, I immediately answered, "Yes!"

Another, who wore an elegant red ribbon tied around her wrist, said, "I like your hair. Do you want to be friends too?" Soon, I had so many friends I couldn't remember all their names.

The lead pencils and the crisp paper on which we wrote fascinated me. I struggled to hold the pencil properly—not like chopsticks, we were told—and though I couldn't read one character, the little books with their colorful pictures of birds and fruit were beautiful.

After lunch, I discovered my favorite subject: recess. The air was crisp in this mountain valley, and sun kissed our faces as we chased one another around the worn playground. A fast runner, soon everyone wanted me for their team. Surely this was the greatest day of my life.

郭

That first afternoon, I ran most of the way down the mountainside. "Mama, Mama, it was wonderful! I love school. I made lots of friends, and one of them—" I stopped suddenly and stared at the gaunt woman sitting in our kitchen. "Who's that?"

"This is Hop. She's from a village on the other side of Ningxiang. She'll be taking care of you."

"I don't understand."

"School is very expensive, Mei Zi," she said, reverently examining my red lesson book and then setting it on top of the others.

"Children are expensive," the woman added, shaking her head. "Very hard."

Mama nodded. "We need more money. I must go back to Ningxiang."

"No!" I cried, tears spilling down my face, painting dark streaks on my thin cotton shirt.

She knelt so she could look into my eyes. "Mei Zi, paying for Ming's schooling has been very difficult, and now we must pay for yours as well. Education is the greatest gift we can give you—greater even than money or land. It's very important that you behave and listen to Hop. When I come back this weekend, you can show me what you've learned."

Glancing at the dingy clothing bundle by the door, I hugged her waist. "Mama, don't go. Don't go back to jail! I don't need to read and write."

"You will do this for me!" she growled. The fire in her voice extinguished itself as quickly as it had blazed, and she smiled. "Besides, I'll be more careful this time." Winking at me, she slipped through the kitchen door.

Sprinting to the main house, I threw myself onto my bed, crying and screaming until my eyes were swollen and my throat sore.

"Just accept it," Ming said, banging on my wall.

The woman waited until I'd calmed myself and then knocked on my door frame. "Mei Zi, I made food for you. Come eat now."

"My name is Hong Bo," I hissed indignantly.

Laughing softly, she said, "You're teasing me. Hong Bo is a boy's name, and you are not a boy."

"Still, that's my name."

"Very well, Hong Bo, come now and wash your hands."

The woman could cook well—not as well as Mama, of course, but well. Picking at my onions and winter cabbage, I tried to ignore her.

"What mothers do for their children must be respected," she said. "She works so you'll have a better life. You must appreciate that."

This woman ate like a pig, shoveling so much food in her mouth,

I feared she might choke. It was as if she hadn't eaten in a month. Judging from her thin frame, perhaps she had not. Gawking, Ming glanced in my direction.

After dinner, I washed out my bowl and set it on the wooden cutting block beside his. After his last bite, Ming had vanished like lightning.

Wiping her hands on her skirt, Hop dragged our crude bench beside the stove's wood fire, and then patted the spot beside her. Her fingers were thick and knotted, the dirt wedged under the nails resembling marks I'd made with my pencil. She smelled of smoke and old sweat. "I've never been to school. Won't you tell me what it's like?"

After sharing my day with more enthusiasm than I'd planned on, she said, "Your parents are poor, but you have food and a dry house. Your life is better than mine."

"But what about your children?" I asked, thinking of the long and lonely winter I'd spent without Mama. "Won't they miss you if you're here?"

"My son was a soldier, but now he's dead."

"What about your husband?" I said, shocked.

"He's dead, too."

Suddenly, I resented Hop a little less.

"Hong Bo, you can call me Nainai if you'd like," she said warmly. *Nainai* means paternal grandmother in Hunan dialect. Though I'd never had a nainai, I was skeptical; the only grandmother I'd ever known thought less of me than chicken droppings.

"I'll think about it," I replied.

Over the next few weeks, I grudgingly grew to like Hop. She was gentle and patient, and soon I decided that she was the kind of nainai I wished I had.

郭

Spring brought the water necessary for our crops. It also brought mud. One morning, as I prepared to leave for school, the sky poured a waterfall over my village. We didn't have umbrellas or hats, so the rain soaked our clothes, and the mud seeped into our shoes. And because there was no pavement anywhere in our village, and certainly none up the mountainside, walking to school was very slow going.

Well before the path grew steep, my torch flame began flaring and flickering, finally dying with a faint hiss. I followed closely behind my cousins.

"Stop stepping on me, Mei Zi," Chu Hua whined.

"I can't see."

"Open your eyes wider then!"

School was misery. We couldn't go outside to play, and my feet were ice cold. When the teacher pulled our lunchboxes from the steamer, I hugged mine for warmth.

During nap time, I usually slept on mats with the others, but the floor was muddy and damp from our shoes. Instead, I lay on a bench.

I dreamed I stood at the edge of a high cliff. Below me, a thousand miles down, lay a glistening riverbed. Looking back, I saw I'd grown great bird wings. Spreading them wide, I soared over treetops and through sodden clouds, chasing imperial eagles and white-eyed buzzards. Suddenly, the roaring wind died away, and I tipped, flailing and flapping as I plummeted, finally crashing against the lumpy earth.

"You fell on me, Mei Zi. Say you're sorry!" Zhang Jing yelled, pushing me off her legs, then scrambling to her knees.

The name Zhang Jing means "quiet", though she rarely was. All the children awakened by her screaming began laughing at me. Even our teacher laughed, and she never laughed.

I didn't look forward to the walk home. Still mad at Zhang Jing for embarrassing me, I contemplated telling her mother, though I doubted it would do much good; my auntie spoiled her to no end. Though the rain had finally stopped, the afternoon was dreary, and the wind stinging; the shallow streams of water flowing this morning had become deep rivers of mud. Brooding and slipping often, I lagged farther and farther behind.

From the forest, a low, feral growl ripped through the silence. My cousins turned and glared at me as if I'd made that awful sound.

A large furry beast of a dog stepped out onto the stone ledge above me. His brown fur was matted, and drool dripped from his mouth. When he bared his teeth, they were long and yellow. We saw wild dogs often on this path, but I'd never seen this one before. When he snarled at me, I screamed and ran through the slippery muck. Though I was fast, that dog was faster. I flew past my cousins, who'd only just realized that the monster was chasing us.

"Climb a tree!" Zhang Jing shouted.

Desperate to get away from it, I leaped over the brush and scrambled up the first tree I reached. My scraped-up arms and legs throbbed in pain, but it was better than becoming a dog's dinner; let it have our lunch remains instead.

Zhang Jing was very brave. She pulled a torch from her bag and launched it at the dog. When it didn't run, she threw rocks at it before climbing a tree. My anger for her fled. When Chu Hua began growling loudly and shaking the tree branch above her, I followed suit. We stayed in those trees screaming until finally the dog had enough of our noise and loped away.

"You're late for dinner," Hop Nainai scolded. "Aiya! Look at your ripped shirt. Did you tangle with a dragon? All the sewing I must do. You make much work for me."

"I did tangle with a dragon, Nainai! A giant dragon with pointed teeth and fire shooting from its nostrils."

"Is that so?" she said. "A fire-breathing dragon? Why aren't you in its belly now?" Her face became one giant smile, and her small eyes twinkled.

"It decided we were too skinny to eat, so it flew away." I looked down at the ripped sleeve and my mud-painted pants. "Please don't be angry with me, Nainai. It was a very big dragon."

"Well, that's a very big story. Your mother will be home tomorrow. You can tell her all about your dragon. Maybe she'll believe you." At this news, my heart sang.

Hop Nainai set my clothes and shoes by the stove and poured water into the wok. Once warm, she helped me wash the blood from my hands and elbows and the dirt from my body.

The next morning, my clothes were dry but caked with dirt. Ming's looked no better, though I doubt he'd been attacked by a dog; his bike was too fast. Fat raindrops began pelting our roof and windows. We groaned in concert.

After Ming left, I said, "Nainai, can I take a second torch to school today? I may see another dragon."

"Only one for you, Hong Bo. You are mighty. Show your teeth and it will leave you alone."

My cousins and I spent much of our walk listening for growls and looking in all directions on our way to school. Even Zhang Jing held her tongue. To seem taller and fiercer, I waved my torch in the air as we walked. That is, until the rain put it out.

6

A Real Name

My close friends had always thought it funny that I had a boy's name yet wore pigtails. In my mind, Hong Bo was just my name and so it had never bothered me. But when my nipples swelled during fifth grade, and the boys began calling me Hong BoBo, which means "lucky titties," well, I quit liking my name completely.

Since the doctor had given me my official name, and my family had not seen fit to name me at all, at the wise age of ten I decided to choose my own name. I experimented with several, but none of them seemed to fit. Finally, because I missed my parents who were gone more often than not, I decided on a nickname that honored them. Both my mother and my father had the surname Guo; in a village as small as ours, this was not unusual.

"Hong Bo, wash your bowl. Why do you forget these things?"

"Nainai, I've told you my name's not Hong Bo. I have a new name. You can call me GuoGuo from now on."

"GuoGuo?" She snorted. "You change names every week. What will I call you next?"

"No, my name is GuoGuo. I'm keeping this one."

"So mysterious," she said, drying the wok with her skirt. "Now you have three names. You can trick many people this way. You can work for the government and have three faces."

My mouth popped open at her boldness, but then I shut it just as quickly; we were taught never to speak ill of the government. I liked it, though. I liked that Nainai said what she felt, even if it could get her in trouble. I wanted to be like Hop Nainai when I was older.

"So, do you like my new name?" I asked, refastening my school bag and setting it by the door.

"I like it very much. Your mother will also like it. Alright, Guo Mei Zi Hong Bo GuoGuo, go to bed."

郭

When school was dismissed for growing season, Hop Nainai returned to her own village. Though my parents continued working in Ningxiang most of the week, they still tended crops, and Mama and I sold them at the market on weekends. While I could haul water from the pond and pull weeds as well as the next person, I didn't like vegetable farming much and looked forward to the day when I could do something else.

My wish came true when my mother bought two small pigs and gave me full responsibility for them. I was no longer a vegetable farmer; I was a pig farmer, and that was much worse.

"These will make us money for your schooling, and we will eat well for Lunar New Year," she said, patting my head. I looked forward to the meat, but after shoveling stinking pig dung for the next two months, I wondered if the meat was worth the trouble.

At the end of each summer, my mother stayed home to supervise the rice harvest. We hired migrant workers who went from one farm to the next, gathering up the grains. These men were desperately poor, and owning no tools, they used their hands to gather the rice. We prepared two rooms for them in our house, spreading bamboo mats on the floor for beds. My bed was not much nicer than theirs—only a few pieces of hardwood to keep me off the floor, but it was mine, and I didn't have to share it. I also didn't have to share my new electric lamp, which filled my room with wonderful and unwavering light whenever we had generator fuel, which was not often.

During this time, my mother spent all day in the kitchen. Wiping her brow one afternoon, she said, "Mei Zi, you must learn to cook. It'll make things easier on me."

I'd always hated being dirty, and though I still had my pigs to tend, cooking would keep me out of the fields. At first, Mama taught me to cut the vegetables. We made a good team. But soon I graduated to more difficult tasks.

The following summer, Mama left me to tend the kitchen alone. During that harvest, I was responsible for cooking for fifteen people. I'd mastered ten different dishes by then, including mushroom noodle stir-fry and rice cakes stuffed with vegetables and chili peppers.

Many village women told Mama they wanted me to marry their sons because I could cook so well. In China, parents often arrange marriages at an early age—especially in the countryside.

"You'll marry soon," Wai po announced while picking mushrooms from her stir-fry. "I was thirteen when I married. You will be ready then."

"Mei Zi will not marry so young," Mama replied.

"Maybe you should let me decide. I waited too long with you, and you made a bad match with your sheep. His siblings are lazy, and his father sits on his decrepit porch, waiting for his children to bring him food. The only son who's made something of himself is the one who joined the military. At least he gets money from the government. What does Boqin do? He picks up trash and lets you go to jail for him. You are not as clever as you think, Meilin," she said, poking her chopsticks at Mama.

Wai po was right about my other grandfather. He only worked when he felt like it, and his other children—especially his youngest brother, whose birth had caused their mother's death, were no better. And though my one uncle received a small pension, he preferred getting free eggs and vegetables from us rather than buying his own.

"We're doing fine," Mama said with a sigh as she removed Wai po's plate.

My grandmother snorted. "You barely have money for the workers. You raise pigs to pay for Mei Zi's schooling. She doesn't need an education. I didn't go to school, and look at me. I married an accountant and have land to give to your brothers. Wipe the dirt off her face and she might not be so ugly. The doctor's son in the next village would be a good match for her. I hear he has a fancy new bike," she then said, nudging me with her elbow.

I knew all about this boy and his bikes; he received a new one every year. In primary school, he'd parked his shiny bike by the school entrance, so the children could admire it. All the older girls wanted to marry him so they could ride on his bike. I was glad when he went to middle school. I was not interested in a peacock like him.

Mama always cried after Wai po left; my grandmother knew just what to say to make her sad.

"Mama, if he was so poor, why did you marry Baba?" I asked as she tucked me into bed that night.

"Well, your father was very handsome. I used to watch him work in our neighbor's fields. He was skinny, but he had a straight back. And when he smiled at me, I felt warm inside."

"Did Wai po have someone else picked out for you?"

"Yes. Your grandmother wanted me to marry a pharmacist from Ningxiang. He was an educated man like my father, and because of his profession, she'd never have to pay for medicine if she became ill."

"Did you like him?"

She shrugged. "I'd never met him until the day he and his family arrived at our doorstep." She chuckled. "His mother inspected me closely. She liked my skin and decided I was pretty enough to give her attractive grandchildren. But when she introduced her son, I was surprised. He was short—shorter than me, and I refused to marry him. His family was insulted, and the matchmaker forced us to return the plump duck that they'd brought as a gift. But how could I marry one man when my heart belonged to another?"

I knew nothing of romantic love, but marrying a short man seemed ridiculous. "Why does Wai po call Baba a sheep?"

Throwing her hand over her mouth, she laughed. "Because growing up, Boqin had nothing to eat. When begging didn't work, and he could find no fruit or nuts, he ate all kinds of plants and even grass to sustain himself. People used to say he was like a sheep grazing in the field."

Giggling, I said, "Did you call him a sheep, too?"

"Of course not. It pained me to see him so shunned and hungry. When I was young, I remember my mother chasing Boqin and his screaming baby brother off of our porch with a broom. I felt so ashamed; we had enough food and milk to share.

"Many years later, while gathering mushrooms, I saw Boqin in the forest. I was a cook like you are now," Mama said, touching my nose. "Boqin's mouth was stained red from gobbling up berries. With no shirt on, I could see the ribs poking right through his skin. When he caught me staring, he dropped the fruit and turned to go, but I stopped him. How could I let him suffer so?"

Baba was a strong-backed, hard-working man, and I had trouble picturing the scene.

"Boqin was handsome, even with those red lips," Mama murmured.

Giggling, I said, "Baba had red lips like a fancy woman?"

"Yes, he did look fancy." Mama stared out the window, her lips slowly lifting into a smile. "I told him to meet me by that berry bush the next day. At lunch, I made two more turnip cakes than we needed and hid them behind our water bucket.

"That afternoon, we sat on a nearby log and talked. Well, he ate, and I talked. I took mushrooms home with me so my mother wouldn't become suspicious. Soon, I needed mushrooms for every dish I prepared." She shook her head and laughed. "My family ate a lot of mushrooms during that time."

"Is that why Wai po doesn't like mushrooms?"

"That's why."

"Next time she comes over for dinner, I'll cook my famous chili mushrooms," I said.

"Mei Zi, she is your grandmother. Show her respect."

I nodded to appease her. "So Baba married you because you were kind?"

"Perhaps. But I'd fallen in love with him, and though I tried for my family's sake, there was no falling out of it. One day I told him we should get married." Seeming lost in her memories, she became quiet. When I yawned loudly, her eyes found mine again, and her smile returned. "Boqin was shocked that a rich girl like me would marry such a poor man, but I told him that of all the faces in Black Village, his was the most pleasant."

"What did Wai po do?"

"She was already angry with me for refusing the pharmacist, and this only made matters worse. After slapping me and saying many things you're far too young to hear, she told me I was no longer her daughter."

"If Wai po was so mean to you, why do you give her eggs and vegetables? Why do we always cook for her?"

"Mei Zi," she said, lifting my chin. "It's important to forgive. Kindness makes your heart light, but hatred weighs it down. And when your heart can no longer carry the load, it spills out of your mouth."

"Is that why Wai po says such hateful things to us?"

"Maybe. But you can't let them settle on your skin. Shake them off like flies and keep smiling. One day she'll forgive me for being such a disappointment, and she will forgive you for being my daughter. I have to believe that."

7

Pig Money

Ming had never graduated from high school, but he was making good money driving taxis in Ningxiang. He still lived in our house, but I rarely saw him anymore. When he wasn't working, Ming chased girls. And as handsome as my father, he had no trouble catching them.

My parents' recycling business had expanded. Owning shops in two nearby towns, Baba transported junk between them in his little three-wheeled truck. He was already talking about his next venture: an auto parts store.

In January, Mama sold our pigs at the market. This particular year she sold three, which was more than ever before. Driving them down the muddy path, I smiled to myself; I'd been feeding them well all year—even adding rice to their meals when we had enough to spare, so they were big and fat.

Demanding an outrageous price, Mama dramatically waved her arms and shouted, negotiating harder than I'd ever seen.

"You got a lot for those pigs," I said on our way home.

Mama stopped her humming and smiled at me. "Mm hm."

We hired the butcher to kill our fourth pig—the one we'd kept for ourselves. After he finished his work, we cooked a big meal for his family, which was tradition, even inviting Hop Nainai and her sister to join us.

It's said that Chinese people eat anything with legs, except the table. My family ate a pig inside and out. Using its blood, we made soup. The brain, we broke up and scrambled with eggs—nothing went to waste. What we didn't eat immediately, we smoked, keeping some for ourselves, and selling the rest to our neighbors.

Life for my family was improving in many ways.

This New Year was the pig sign—my sign! Pig is the zodiac's last animal. Legend says that when the Jade Emperor called a great meeting, the pig was last to arrive. Some believe he slept late, others that he was slower than the other animals. I had my own theory. Having just filled my belly with delicious salted pork, I believed he was late because he didn't want to be eaten!

I got my usual coat. And while I was grateful for its warmth, Mama bought me the same style and color every year. I was so sick of red that I swore when I was grown, I would never own anything that color again. The best gift of all was my Mama's announcement during the third feast.

"We've been blessed with prosperity, and so I will leave the recycling business to Boqin and stay home with Mei Zi."

I was delirious with joy. Already grateful that Mama had been released from prison yet again—three was her lucky number—this was a dream.

My thoughts drifted to Hop Nainai. She'd become a real grandmother to me, and because her village was so far from ours, I would no longer see her. Plenty old enough to do all the things she'd once done for me, I hadn't needed a caretaker for some time, but her warmth and her willingness to listen and advise had been a great comfort during Mama's long absences. I wondered if she would now become a good nainai to another child.

On the fifth day of Chinese New Year, my father gave me a bike. Not just any bike; an adjustable bike.

"It's not new," he said gruffly. "And I had to replace the tires at the shop, so they don't match, but it will get you to school faster, and no more dogs will chase you, eh?"

"Not one," I replied excitedly; I'd accumulated too many dog stories over the years. Squeezing the brake handle. I marveled at the sparkling purple paint.

The last night of the New Year's celebrations, as my mother tucked me into bed, which I didn't need but loved nonetheless, she said, "Now I'll tell you about the pig money. We're sending you to middle school. It'll pay for tuition and books."

郭

Ningxiang Yunfan Experimental Middle School was on the outskirts of town. Walking from Black Village would have taken forever, but my bike covered the distance in half the time. Laughing into the strong breeze, I flew by my cousins, who were on foot.

When I arrived at my new school, I realized just how fancy my bike really was. Sure, there were plenty of them leaning against the long white wall, but only one other like mine: The Peacock's. Since he'd already been there two years, his latest bike was old news, so students came over to see mine.

Soon, everyone called me "rich girl," though that was a joke. I couldn't understand it; students either wanted to be my friend or they were jealous of me, all because of a bike my father had put together with used parts.

The middle school building had five classrooms. The high school wing across the courtyard had only three. My eyes traveled there often, watching the older students—mostly boys—taking notes. I knew some faces, but many of my primary school classmates were not there; poverty prevented it.

These middle school teachers were not pleasant and had far less patience for us. My primary instructor, Mrs. Woo, looked as though she ate bittermelon for breakfast, lunch, and dinner. Because I liked to talk, and because I had a difficult time paying attention, I quickly earned six strikes with a bamboo ruler and three ear pinches.

Mama had given me a little money, so after school, I bought my new schoolmates treats. Licking sugar off of our sticky fingers, we sat on swollen Weishui River's grassy bank, watching the boys jump off the swinging bridge into the icy water, trying to impress us.

Having friends had always been important to me, but I *needed* these kids. Perhaps the most unfortunate lesson I'd learned in primary school was that I was a terrible student. If there were fifty test scores, mine would rank forty-ninth. Ice cream and candy bought me homework and test answers. I didn't want to be an embarrassment to my parents, but what could I do?

"So, we have conferences next week," I mumbled at dinner one evening.

"Are your grades better than last quarter?" Mama asked.

I toyed with my turnip dumpling. "Well…"

Smiling sadly, she reached over and tucked my long bangs behind my ear. With so little education, she knew she couldn't help me with my studies. I think she was at least satisfied that I could read and write.

"Should I go?" she finally asked.

"Probably not," I said, unable to meet her eyes. "Could you pass the beans?"

郭

Only weeks after delivering that piece of bad news, the gods—or the ancestors, or whoever watched over naughty girls who didn't do their own homework, punished me. I had an uncomfortable stomach that morning. At first, I thought I'd eaten something spoiled, but I didn't feel sick in that way. During the middle of math class, a subject I was especially bad at, a strange warmth spread between my legs. Carefully scooting out my chair, I peered down and gasped; blood was just seeping out of me. Several friends glanced over, so I put my head on my desk, pressing my face into my folded arms, hoping my death would be a painless one. At the bell, I remained in my seat, fearing embarrassment even more than this affliction.

"Guo Hong Bo, you can go now," my teacher said.

Hesitating, I debated whether I should tell her, or simply stay in my seat for the rest of the day. As she walked toward me. I covered my bloody crotch and lowered my eyes. "I don't feel well, Mrs. Woo."

"What are you hiding in your lap?"

"Nothing."

Pinching my ear, she growled, "Show me now!"

When I lifted my hands, she let go at once, and her voice became unusually kind. "Is this your first time?"

"I don't know what you mean. What's wrong with me?"

"Nothing's wrong. You've just become a woman," she said, smiling.

"I don't understand."

She leaned against the desk across from mine. "During every full moon, after a girl becomes a woman, a portion of childhood seeps out between her legs. Only two things make it stop. One is when a baby grows inside of her, and the other is when she is so old there is no childhood left."

I looked at her skeptically. My parents had mentioned none of this.

"Get up before you stain the chair."

"I don't want the others to see me."

"Of course not. This is a private matter. Go to the shed and wipe yourself. Then you may go home."

The only bathroom at school was a white-washed concrete box a short walk from the courtyard. With no running water system and no toilets, students simply squatted, trying not to step on one another's waste. Having only one small window for ventilation, I gagged just walking past it. Often, I held my business in all day to avoid going inside it. On this day, I didn't want to come back out again.

The paper provided to wipe ourselves was scratchy and stiff, like our classroom stock. I didn't know what else to do other than stuff a crinkly wad inside my underwear and slip away when no one was watching.

Because Mrs. Woo's story seemed far-fetched, I wasn't entirely convinced it was true. But believing a lie seemed far better than admitting I was ill, especially to parents, who would surely have to sell their businesses to pay for medical care. Fortunately, my mother was a blue speck in the rice field when I arrived home, so I quickly scrubbed my underwear with hot water, and kept the matter to myself.

For the next few days, school was agony. Many times, I felt that strange warmth. Many times, I waddled like a duck to the horrible bathroom; this blood would never stop coming out of me.

"Mama, have you ever bled?" I asked, shelling beans on the roughhewn kitchen table.

"Of course, Mei Zi. Everyone bleeds. I scraped my knees almost as much as you when I was a girl."

"Have you bled from any place other than your knees? Any strange places?"

Setting down the sock she was mending, she narrowed her eyes. "What's this about?"

Glancing from the table to the rusty ceiling, I whispered, "When did you know you were a woman?"

Concern fled her eyes, and her expression softened. Scooting to the bench, she pulled me against her. "Mei Zi, have you started your cycle?"

"I think so," I said, resting my head on her shoulder; at thirteen, I was as tall as she. "Is your cycle when you bleed down there?"

"Yes."

"Does it mean I'm a woman?"

Smothering a smile, she said, "In a manner of speaking. It means you're growing up."

I sighed in relief. "I was afraid I was dying."

"Oh!" She laughed, covering her mouth. "When did this happen?"

"At school."

"That must have been scary," she said, smoothing my hair.

"And it won't stop." I wanted to ask why she'd never mentioned anything about bleeding, and how it might have been less terrifying had she, but my current condition was imminently important.

"How many days have you bled?"

"Five."

"Two more. I'll make special tea for you tonight to hurry it along."

I sighed in relief. "Will it come back?"

"Every moon it comes. Until you are old."

"Does Wai po still bleed?" I asked, rescuing a stray bean from my lap.

"I don't think so."

I pondered this for a moment, weighing my teacher's words. "That's why she's angry all the time. She has no childhood left."

Mama nodded, a sly smile forming. "Perhaps you're right. Now, go wash your privates. It's good to be clean during this time."

8

Blue Dress

Shortly before my fifteenth birthday, I finished middle school. High school was even more expensive, and since I'd barely passed my exams, my parents decided that it was a waste of money to send me. In all honesty, it was a relief; there surely wasn't enough candy in all of Hunan to get me through four more years.

Ming had recently left the taxi business to become a bus driver apprentice. I had no such apprenticeship waiting. Mama wanted me to have a better life, but my best skill was cooking. In a rural area such as ours, this was not a profession.

"I found a job for you, Mei Zi. A factory job," Baba announced one evening.

Factory work was certainly more interesting than plucking rice all day, but then I remembered my Ningxiang experience. "It's not the metal factory, is it?" I asked.

"A fabric factory. A tailor I know has a good relationship with the supervisor."

I raced around the table and threw my arms around his neck. "Thank you, Baba! I'll make you proud."

"We'll see," he said gruffly, shoving another bite of rice noodle stir-fry into his mouth.

郭

Yutanzhen, the small town where the factory stood, was only a short ride past Ningxiang. Plumes of billowing steam spinning lazily in the pale breeze blushed pink where the waking sun kissed them. Parking my bike beside what seemed a thousand others, I gawked at the sheer size of the structure—so much larger than the metal factory.

Workers flooded the stark courtyard, spitting, laughing, grumbling. A skeleton of a man, his cheeks standing out in sharp relief, furiously wiped a soiled rag across his sweating brow as he negotiated through the press of workers.

I fell in line behind two women my mother's age, who coughed and wheezed between cigarette puffs.

"Move, girl," a hunchbacked woman hissed, pushing past me as she made her way in jerking fashion towards the entrance.

Seated in a scratched plastic chair outside the office, I anxiously awaited Gui, my new boss. Because of Baba's connection, they gave me a quality control position in finished cloth.

With a loud bang, the door to the factory proper, swung open, filling the small lobby with sounds of metal clanging and random shouts.

Halting mere inches from me, a squat man said, "You Guo Hong Bo?"

"Yes, sir. And I'm ready to start."

He snorted. "I'll tell you when you're ready. Follow me."

Passing uniformed workers hovering over great vats of steaming liquid, I watched as their long bamboo poles stirred a foul-smelling cloth stew. Stepping over a confluence of colorful streams rushing across the floor and finally disappearing down a slotted drain, we passed a series of giant containers disgorging wet cloth in endless ribbons like icing.

"We determine which material gets the first quality rating," he said in a gravelly voice when on the second floor. "Ours is the most important job in the entire factory. Nothing goes out until we check it. Do exactly what I say, and you won't be fired." The large red mole on his forehead danced as he spoke, making it a genuine struggle to focus on his eyes.

A rush of heat escaped the jaws of a wide metal press, which flattened material until it looked as unperturbed as a pond's surface. I thought how wonderful it would be to work here in the wintertime if one could get past the biting lye aroma. The workers seemed oblivious.

Following Gui up yet another flight of stairs, I stopped to gawk at thread, like spiderwebs, spinning onto spools taller than me. My mother would be shocked by such a spectacle, I thought.

"We run the fourth and fifth floors," he announced once we'd gotten far enough away from the whining cutters to hear one another. "From now on, arrive at six, leave at seven."

"Well, at least I can sleep late on weekends," I joked, knowing our rooster would never allow it.

"No weekends off for you, I'm afraid," he said, laughing at my shocked expression. "We work seven days per week, no exceptions." I knew how to work hard, but not this hard. Suddenly, I wondered if Baba was punishing me for my grades. "Your skin is very smooth," he said, tucking a clump of loose hair behind my ear. "How old are you?"

"Almost fifteen," I said uncomfortably.

"So young," he murmured. "Too young to need beauty sleep."

郭

Under a relentless summer sun, the factory smoldered, and with so little ventilation the air was smoke made of fibers. The job itself was not so hard, and thanks to Gui, I learned to spot imperfections in short order. Feeling sorry for the frail workers, who wheezed and coughed and spat blood into stained rags, I was glad he did all the scolding. It took little time to recognize how privileged I was to have such a good position.

We were paid biweekly. After working so many hours, I could only imagine the riches in store for me. Taking my place in the snaking line that encircled our floor and inched down the skeletal staircase to the next, I fidgeted excitedly.

Gui pulled me aside and placed an envelope in my hand. "Now you don't have to wait like the others."

"You are too good to me," I said, flipping through the colorful bills; Chairman Mao's image seemed pleased by my hard work. My wage was seventy-five RMB, a sum far greater than the government fine my parents had once been unable to pay. I couldn't wait to show them.

Gui leaned against a cutting table and crossed his arms. "What will you spend it on?"

"I'm not sure."

"You're a pretty girl. You should buy yourself a nice treat. Red lipstick, I think." His eyes, glinting in the subdued light of early evening, hovered over my lips for a moment before looking full into my face again. "The shops stay open late on payday."

"What would I do with something so useless?" I scoffed. I may have earned more than Mama made at market, but certainly not enough for something so extravagant as a lipstick tube. And besides, the only ones that might appreciate red lips on my farm were the pigs. Folding the money, I tucked it away in my waistband. When I smiled up at Gui, a strange expression crossed his face, and he slowly dabbed his upper lip.

郭

The factory was filled with women, and in the evening, men often loitered by the front gates, hoping someone would show an interest in them. When I mentioned that a boy had asked me out, Gui, concerned for my safety, insisted on escorting me to my bike from then on. I thought this was very gentlemanly.

One evening, as we crossed the dusty courtyard, he said, "Those clothes make you look like a machine operator. You should wear dresses from now on. Here." He placed a small bundle in my arms. "This is for you."

I stared at the pale blue fabric, not sure what to think. Though clearly second quality, it was still very nice. Thanking him for his generosity, my thoughts drifted to the metal factory worker who'd sold items to Mama in the dark of night.

"You didn't steal this, did you?" I whispered.

He laughed loudly. "Why do you think so little of me after all I've done for you?"

"I'm just teasing you, Gui," I said, forcing a smile. "I know you're an honorable man."

"Of course, I am. Even my name means 'honor.' Now go home and make yourself something pretty."

郭

Mama and I spent hours on my dress, cutting and sewing the cloth. Too much a tomboy, I was not nearly the seamstress she was; her quick fine stitches were in perfect lines.

"What use are you to a husband if you cannot sew, stupid girl?" Wai po sneered from our moldy sofa. She then pointed a crooked finger at Mama. "A good mother would teach her daughter these important skills. Look how well you do it."

Mama's face colored, but she swallowed Wai po's words like rancid goat's milk. "Yes, Mama, you taught me well. I should be ashamed that I didn't share your wise teachings with my daughter." Mama worked silently until the dress was completed. I daydreamed about stabbing Wai po's beady eyes with my needle.

"What do you think?" I asked Gui, modeling the dress the following morning.

"Turn around and let me see the back. Ah, very nice," he said. "You're good at making clothes. Maybe you can open a shop one day."

Farmers rarely wore dresses, and I hadn't owned one since I was a child, and certainly never one made of such fine and airy material. Even with worn-out shoes, for once I felt pretty.

Smiling widely, I flitted from one station to the next, checking for mistakes. The women ignored me as usual, but men paid attention.

That afternoon, I dutifully followed Gui to the top floor. Sunlight spilled through the many rooftop windows, making mistakes easy to find. In such oppressive heat, I was sweat-drenched in moments.

"This is nice light for you," he said, dabbing beads of perspiration from his balding head. "It makes your dress almost white. We should come up here every afternoon." The woman whose work I was checking looked up, grunted, and then dropped her eyes again.

After only a short time, I became terribly thirsty. With no available water to drink, I wondered how these workers functioned; it was far hotter than in the fields. Wiping my brow with the back of my hand, I sought shade behind a girder.

"Hong Bo, check her work again," Gui ordered.

"It's fine. It looks good," I said.

"Do as I say."

Walking back to her station, I peered over the material again. "I see nothing wrong."

"Are your eyes not working? Look closer."

I bent over the table until my nose nearly touched the fabric. His words terrified me; blindness ran in my family. My eyes darting over the fabric like dragonflies over a pond, I still could find no flaw. My heart began beating wildly. How many other errors had I made?

Gui leaned over me and pointed to a spot. "Don't you see it right there?"

I nodded, though I could not.

Normally, when mistakes were discovered, he yelled at the worker, threatened her job, threw all manner of insults at her. I breathed a sigh of relief when he didn't scold this one.

"You can't make mistakes like that, Hong Bo," he said in a breathy voice. "I'd hate for you to lose your job because of carelessness." His hand grazed my bottom as he walked away.

"I'm sorry, but you'll have to cut that piece away," I said.

"Stupid girl, there's no flaw," the old woman hissed.

As I pedaled home that evening, I tried to make sense of the confusing day. This became my ritual, because over the next few weeks Gui found many flaws I couldn't see.

"Mama, when did Uncle Lou go blind?"

"Hmm, when he was very young. Why?"

"I think my eyesight is going bad."

Real fear crossed her face. Eye surgery was very expensive—too expensive to save my uncle's eyes. Gathering a handful of beans, she dropped them on the table. "Pick out all the bad ones."

I did as she asked, easily recognizing brown spots.

"Good. Now, pick out all the broken grains," she said, pouring out a small cupful of rice.

I'd been doing this all of my life, selling the best quality grains at the market, and keeping the rest for ourselves. When I finished, she said, "If you can see bad beans and broken rice grains, you are not going blind."

I felt much better about my eyes, and much worse about my job.

郭

"Another flaw," Gui said, shaking his head. "You are lucky I like you so much." He patted my bottom, as had become his custom when correcting me. His touching felt wrong, but I refused to shame my parents by quitting.

In the evening, once we'd completed our final check and the fabric bolts had been wrapped in plastic and stacked on wooden slats, everyone could go home. Certain that my eyes were not missing any flaws, I hurried through my work and kept my distance from Gui. He was becoming too familiar with me, and I liked him less by the day. I began sneaking past the smelly dye vats and out the side door before he could escort me.

Gui left to get our paychecks, as was his tradition. On this especially hot day, I was very glad not to stand in the long line of sweat-drenched people. Waiting on the sewing floor, I busied myself by replacing empty bobbins with full ones, ever impressed by the thick fabric stacks, cut in layers like so much paper money.

The paycheck line had long since disappeared, and I began running out of things to do. Still, there was no Gui. As the last of dusk's light faded from the windows, painting the endless dye stream spilling into the river below nearly black, the weak bulbs hanging from the ceiling came on, offering more shadow than light. With nobody milling about, the silence was unnerving.

Deciding I could wait until tomorrow for my money, I hurried down the steps towards the exit. Before I reached the heavy door, Gui's voice spilled down from the rafters. "Hong Bo, I need your assistance."

Torn, I could pretend I'd heard nothing and slip out, or climb to the top floor as he asked. I decided sneaking out was the best idea.

"I see you down there." I looked up to find him peering down the stairwell.

Taking a deep breath, I shouted, "I'm all finished and must get home. My mother's sick."

"I'm sorry to hear that, but there's no one left to help me. It'll only take a minute."

"Gui, it's getting dark and I have a long bike ride through the mountains. I really must go." Riding at night had never been a problem for me; I knew the path so well I could name every bump. Still, I needed some excuse.

"You don't want to get fired, do you? That would shame your sick mother," he said in the same tone as always, the same threats. "Besides, I have your money. Maybe you got a raise."

A bad feeling crept over me, and my heart beat like a trapped rabbit's. I slowly climbed the steps, floor by floor, until we stood across the room from one another.

"Help me lift these bolts," he said.

"How did they get scattered on the floor like this?"

"The stack fell. Didn't you hear it?"

"No," I replied. "I did not."

"Blind and deaf. So sad." His tongue clicking, he shook his head. He picked up two bolts and set them on the wooden pallet. Then he picked up two more. "What are you waiting for?"

Bending down, I lifted the one nearest me, placing it on top of his. It was hard work with so many bolts to stack, but I moved them as quickly as possible, all the while plotting my escape. Rising to my tiptoes, I groaned as I pushed the last one on top of the heap, wondering why he wasn't helping anymore.

Suddenly, his arms came around my waist, and he pressed himself into my back, pinning me against the wall of fabric.

"Stop it!" I yelled, my voice muffled by the cloth. I struggled to get free, but I couldn't turn around. He was larger, heavier, and much stronger than I.

"You're a naughty girl, Hong Bo. You stand in the sunlight every afternoon so I can see through your damp dress, and you rub your bottom against me all the time." He moved his hips in demonstration.

"No!"

His hand slid under my dress' hem and he began pulling and squeezing my bare nipples. He was rough with them, and it hurt. "Why do you do these things?" he growled.

As angry tears soaked the material in front of me, I tasted the bitter dye chemicals. My arms flailing, I blindly tried to scratch his eyes.

"Very bad girl!" Jamming his other hand inside my underwear, he pinched my private parts and tugged sharply on my fur. "You like that, don't you? That's what you've wanted all along," he mocked.

As he moved his pelvis, my skirt slid up and down in a jerky fashion. With cloth stuffing my nose and mouth, I thought I might suffocate. His breaths came hot and quick like a panting dog, and his hips began slamming into me violently. Suddenly, he groaned as though injured, which I desperately hoped he was, and then he relaxed his hold on me.

Pushing him back with all my strength, he tripped, landing on his side. Quickly grabbing the scissors from a nearby table, I threw them at him with all my might. Gui's hand shot up to protect his face, and they cut his skin deeply. He let out a curdling cry as blood poured down his arm. In that moment, I began liking the color red again.

I raced down the many flights and out into the street. Pedaling my bike faster than I ever had before, it didn't take long to get from Yutanzhen to Ningxiang. Though I could barely see through the veil of tears, I somehow found my way to the bus depot.

"Ming!" I yelled, jumping off my bike.

"Look, it's our pretty little sister," one of his friends said. "Did you bring us some dinner? We're starving."

"Where's Ming?" I demanded.

Realizing my state, he hopped to his feet. "What's wrong? Why are you crying?" Ming's other friends raced over as well.

I shook my head angrily. I didn't want any more boys around me. I wanted my brother.

"Ming!" I yelled louder.

Stepping out of the garage, he tossed his cigarette on the ground. "Mei Zi, why are you here?"

I launched myself into his chest and sobbed. After a few moments, he pulled me away. "Tell me."

"A man in the factory… he, he touched me. He hurt me."

Ming's eyes became cut coal. "What's his name?"

"Gui," I said, as fresh tears made rivers down my cheeks.

"Go home. I'll talk with this Gui."

I curled into a ball on my bedroom floor, wanting to be so small no one could see me. Mama saw me, though. She stood silently at the door for a long time.

"Do I need to send for your father?" she finally asked.

"No!" I hid my face in my hands. I couldn't imagine his embarrassment. He would lose face with the tailor. "I told Ming."

She nodded as if she were satisfied, and then disappeared.

Many hours later, Ming came home. He knocked on my door frame and then slid down the wall beside me. "I'm sorry to tell you this, Mei Zi, but you got fired."

I sat up, shocked, but then realized my brother was smiling. In fact, his smile was so wide I could see his molars. "You'll never see Gui again."

"Did you kill him?"

"Not completely," he said, laughing to himself. "Sleep now and forget you ever heard that name."

"But what about Baba?"

"Baba will thank me for saving him the trouble."

9

_____

Binlang

After a few days of feeling sorry for myself, I spread the ashes of my burnt dress around the pumpkin plants and set out to find a new job. I was capable and hardworking, and I'd inherited my mother's cleverness—or so Auntie Song always told me.

I rode my bike to Uncle Lou's house. Though his eyes saw nothing, his ears worked very well. I didn't ask for my fortune because his predictions about me rarely came true. Instead, I told him I needed to find a job that involved no men.

My uncle sent me to find Chen, the son from his first marriage who farmed his land. Chen liked to gamble, and because of this, he knew lots of people. He promised to ask around about jobs.

Two days later, while I was feeding the pigs, Chen tossed a folded piece of paper to me and then climbed back on his motorcycle. "You're welcome," he yelled as he disappeared over the hill.

Ming took me to Yiyang, a large city to the north. Seated behind him in the front bus seat, I thought myself important since he was driving. This place was a far cry from tiny Ningxiang. The paved sidewalks, flooded with well-dressed men and women parading in and out of banks and office buildings, seemed endless.

An acquaintance of Chen's had referred me to the owner of a dry-cleaning shop. This was how things worked in China; most jobs were gotten through connections.

I knew nothing about dry-cleaning. Having only ever washed clothing in pots or the village pond, I couldn't understand how one could accomplish this task without water.

Along with her other worker, I lived with the owner, eating and sleeping in her shop. The floor was no less comfortable than the one I'd so often slept on at the recycling business, only cleaner.

City noises that had frightened me as a small child delighted me now. Blaring car horns, revving motorcycle engines, and the hiss and clatter of lumbering buses meant I was in real civilization.

With its plate-glass window and shiny countertop, the front of the shop, where customers dropped off their fancy clothes, looked very impressive. Behind the swinging doors, the scene was much different. Hauling mounds of garments to our boss' grimy bathroom, we hand washed them in her bathtub. The majority of every day was spent soaking our skin in harsh, dry-cleaning chemicals.

We had no gloves to wear, so in short order, my fingers reddened and began peeling. Before the first week was over, my hands had swollen to the size of gourds, and it was torture sticking them into the tub. By the following Monday, I could no longer bend my fingers at all.

"Your skin will toughen up in time. Work harder and you won't notice," the owner told me when I complained.

My coworker was an old lady with no teeth. She washed clothes like it was her greatest joy to do so. Because we did nothing but scrub, I told her about my life; how I should have tried harder in school, and how I was determined to make my parents proud one day. She was an excellent listener, always nodding her head and smiling. Sometimes she hummed a tuneless song I did not know.

"Why do you talk so much when there is no one to hear you?" my boss asked one evening as we ate our rice.

I glanced at the old woman, but she didn't seem offended. She just smiled her usual toothless smile.

"I don't understand."

"She's lucky she's deaf, so she can't hear your whining."

On my ninth day at the dry-cleaning shop, my skin split open and began bleeding, turning the tub of chemicals pink. The old lady yanked my hands out with an expression of horror. Setting them on an old rag, she gently dried them. It was only then that I noticed she had no fingernails at all, and that the skin on her hands was gray, like boiled pork bones.

Though our village had no telephones, Ming's bus station did. Showing me how to use it before I left, he'd written his number on a scrap of cloth I kept in my small sack of belongings. Because this was an important place of business, it also had a telephone, which I used to call Ming when the boss was out of the shop. That evening, my brother came and got me.

郭

Burning through contacts too quickly, before I upset any more family members, I would secure my next job on my own.

I rode my bike to Longtian, an industrial hub for transporting goods to Hunan cities, including the dry-cleaning supplies I'd used in Yiyang. Though smaller than Ningxiang in population, I was optimistic that I could find a nice job there. And if I failed, there would be no one to disappoint but myself.

Dodging large trucks at every turn, I rode through the busy streets searching for job postings on shop doors. I tentatively stepped into the accountant's office to apply for an assistant position. The man looked about the same age as my grandfather, and since they shared the same profession, there was a chance the two had met. I considered telling him as much, but then realized he would expect me to be good at mathematics, which I was not.

Frowning, he scratched his head and said, "You look young. How old are you?"

I straightened in my chair. "Sixteen—almost, sir." Almost being nine months.

"I assume you don't have your high school certificate yet."

"I'm not going to high school," I answered.

Toying with his pencil, he narrowed his eyes. "What skills do you have?"

"I'm a friendly person and a hard worker." I smiled widely to prove this.

His frown deepened. "*Friendly* is your skill?" After a moment, he shook his head. "No skills, no certificate, no job."

"But—"

"Goodbye," he said, pointing to the door.

With similar experiences all over town, I was becoming frustrated. There had to be something for an enterprising young girl. Leaning against a Huangshan tree near the square, I unwrapped the rice cake Mama had packed for me; food was her way of saying good luck.

A man pushing a bike with a flat tire rolled it into the shop across the street. I'd watched Baba repair my tires many times; it wasn't hard. Marching into the store, I fidgeted, waiting for my turn at the counter. "Hey, are you hiring?" I finally said.

The bike shop owner shook his head no.

"Do you know anyone who is? I really need a job. I'll do anything."

"Anything?"

"Yes, I'm a very hard worker," I said, hoping his "anything" didn't involve men with busy hands.

"If you like hard work, try the binlang factory," the man with the flat tire interjected, laughing. "They'll hire anybody."

Binlang is a green nut resembling a large acorn. Hunanese are fond of chewing them, which is why so many locals have big mandibles. When guests arrive, a Hunan host usually offers the men hot green tea, binlang, and cigarettes. Binlang is highly addictive, so working in this factory would come with risks. Still, a job was a job, and I was determined not to return home without one.

Following the biker's directions, I rode several miles outside of town. Other than the large dust-caked truck that nearly ran me off the road, I saw no one on this remote mountain road. Deciding the man had played a cruel trick on me, I was about to turn back when I noticed two rough-looking armed guards leaning against a high and unmarked metal gate.

"Hey, is this the binlang factory?"

"Do you think we're standing in this blistering sun for no reason?" one snidely replied.

Considering myself a tough girl, I straightened my back and stared at them. I would not be put off by these men. "So, is this place hiring?"

"This place is always hiring," the second guard said absently, crunching a nut between his jaws.

Littered with trash, the packed dirt driveway was flanked on either side by thick forest. Just after it veered to the left, the trees opened into a vacant courtyard. Pressed against the stone face of a tall mountain, the dark factory behind it loomed.

By now I was used to being turned down, but in this particular case, at least I had experience. And though I would rather forget my previous factory job, at least I could apply what I'd learned.

Surely noting my confident smile as he glanced at me, the interviewer said, "Okay, you're hired."

"That's it?" I said, shocked.

Unearthing a walkie-talkie from his messy desk, he spoke into it. "Woman. Small."

A grim-looking lady soon appeared at the door, and I followed her deep into the cavernous building. The interior walls were even dirtier than the soot-streaked exterior ones, and the air smelled of unwashed men. Not a single worker looked up as we passed.

Stepping through a metal door near the back, I tripped over a soiled bamboo mat. Grunting in disgust, the woman picked it up by one edge and tossed it on top of the waist-high stack.

"You work out there, you sleep in here," she said, dropping a folded blue jumpsuit in the corner. "Change."

She delivered me to the packaging department supervisor, who placed me at the end of a long row of tables. After a cursory demonstration of how to run the machine in front of me, she returned to her perch behind us. Though there was an order to product assembly, to call this place orderly was a gross misstatement.

Shriveled workers with vacant expressions lined both sides of my unit, stuffing binlang nuts into cellophane bags. Smiling at the old woman across from me, I started to speak, but the supervisor hissed, "No talking. Just work."

For the next few hours, the only voice I heard belonged to the supervisor. "Eighteen per bag. No more, no less," she shouted out periodically, as if we might somehow forget.

Once a bag was filled, it was passed to me. I quickly fed the clear cellophane through the hot machine, which melted the edges and sealed them. The sour fumes smelled horrible, and by the end of the twelve-hour shift, my hair, clothing, and skin stank of it. With no place to wash even my hands, I woke up smelling the same as I had going to sleep.

The factory never shut down. Having arrived in the afternoon the first day, they'd assigned me the night shift. Under the dim lights, we lived in perpetual twilight, and without windows and prohibited from going outside, I only knew it was evening because they awakened me, fed me the poor-tasting food, and sent me back to my tedious job.

I noticed the man beside me slip a nut into his mouth. An hour later, he discreetly did it again.

"No binlang!" the shift supervisor suddenly screeched, slapping the man's face so hard the nut popped out and rolled across the table. With no emotion, the worker seated there added it to her next batch and then slid the bag to me for sealing.

Without any socializing—or even being allowed to go to the bathroom more than three times a day, it was as if we were criminals inside a jail. I felt a new kinship with my mother.

Relegated to silence, and with too much time to think, I began to realize how very fortunate I was. I had a family who loved me, a safe place to sleep, fresh healthy food to eat, and an education—a situation most of these people, who were poor beyond measure, could only dream of. This was not the better life Mama envisioned for me.

Pocketing my paltry wage, I marched out of that factory, mounted my bike, and rode home, breathing in the cool, clean, October air.

10

Mahjong

My family began worrying about my future; things were not working out as they'd hoped. Ming was doing very well in his bus business and now had several routes. While his successes left her with little to complain about, Wai po reveled in my failures; they gave her ample opportunity to blame my mother for raising such a stupid daughter. When Auntie Song suggested contacting the matchmaker, I became frantic.

"I can't get married! I'll work for Baba instead. A dutiful daughter should sacrifice for her family, right? It's tradition."

Ming, who was at home for once, snorted loudly. Glaring at him, he shoved a dumpling in his mouth.

"I did not go to prison so Mei Zi could pick up trash!" Mama hissed, slapping the tabletop. "She's not like us, Song. She has an education. She will do great things."

"The right marriage can be a great thing, Mei Zi," Auntie Song calmly said.

That weekend, Baba returned home with news.

"You will learn to cut hair, Mei Zi. This is good work for a girl, and maybe one day you'll own your own beauty shop. I've made arrangements with a woman who'll train you."

I met Mama's eyes, and she nodded.

Far more interested in racing boys than braiding hair when I was younger, I knew my skills were poor. But at this point, and especially if it made Mama happy, I was more than willing to try.

Baba accompanied me on the very long bike ride to Taojiang. Though no larger than Ningxiang, it boasted a host of tidy-looking shops and a pretty lake. I was immediately optimistic.

My one-year apprenticeship with Mistress Yao included room and board, reasonable hours, and the freedom to return home on weekends. Baba paid the hefty tuition fee, and I followed my new mistress to the salon's rear.

"Put your belongings in the back of this supply closet," she said, pointing, "then sweep the hair off the floor. Dandan, show her where the broom is kept."

When my mistress left for the house, which was above the shop, I asked, "Are you Mistress Yao's daughter?"

Dandan means "pretty", and though her face was not, her laugh certainly was. "I'm the other apprentice—when I'm not doing chores."

Mistress Yao taught us to cut hair, give facials, and perform massages, but only by watching her. Other than washing their hair or feet, it prohibited us from servicing clients. As Dandan had explained, doing chores was part of the agreement. As the newest girl, I inherited Dandan's assignments, which were cooking the family's meals, cleaning the shop and their house, and doing their laundry.

Cooking was fine, of course, but washing clothes and salon towels—this business dirtied a lot of towels—was my least favorite job. Dandan was promoted to babysitter, tending to Mistress Yao's seven-year-old son. Spoiled, he caused us nothing but trouble. After a few weeks, I decided I had the better job.

Our mistress was too cheap to buy cooking oil, and even though I could cook with the best of them, the food tasted terrible, and my mistress complained often. Dandan and I began bringing good oil back from our homes and hiding it in the supply closet. When I reheated the family's leftovers for our own meals, I threw oil into the wok with abandon.

"My parents didn't send me here to be a servant girl," Dandan groaned, carrying a tall stack of towels to the front. A city girl with a higher-class lifestyle than me, her litany of complaints was never-ending. I'd never been treated like a servant girl either, but compared to my previous experiences, I gratefully accepted the role.

Mistress Yao enjoyed the game of mahjong, often leaving us for hours while she played. If clients came in while she was away, we rescheduled their appointments for the afternoon. Returning in a good mood meant she'd won lots of money. Otherwise, it was bad news for us.

Because we spent most of our time watching her work, we weren't getting any real experience. Dandan and I quickly grew tired of not learning—well, Dandan had already reached this point. One morning when our mistress was away and a customer came into the shop, we decided to take matters into our own hands.

"I need my hair cut!" the woman announced excitedly. Panting, she pressed her pudgy hand over her heart as if she might die.

"Mrs. Yao is booked up until the afternoon. You want to come back then?" Dandan recited joylessly.

Peering around us to the empty salon, she seemed confused. "No, it can't wait. My mother-in-law is coming."

"You sure you don't want to come back?" she asked.

The woman grabbed Dandan's arm. "Did you not hear what I said? My *mother-in-law* is coming!"

I looked at Dandan, and she looked at me. Then we both smiled. "I would be honored to cut your hair," I said, bowing deeply for good measure.

The woman narrowed her eyes. "It must be perfect. Do you have experience?"

"Experience?" I laughed nervously before lying, "Mistress Yao lets me cut hair all the time."

"No, she doesn't!" her brat yelled.

Dandan pinched his ear. "Little boys shouldn't tell lies. You go upstairs or no candy." Tittering, she turned to the woman. "Boys are so bad. If you will sit here, I'll wash your beautiful hair."

Once wet and combed thoroughly, Dandan passed her to me. Rapidly discovering hair-cutting was not my strong suit, I fell back on my true specialty: talking. Every time another clump of hair fell to the floor, Dandan's eyes grew larger. Winking at her, I simply smiled and gave the woman another compliment.

When I had done all the damage I could do, Dandan dried her hair, and I used a hot iron to hide all the mistakes I'd made.

"You are good girls. Here's a tip for you," the woman said, smiling at her reflection. She did look pretty good from the front.

As soon as she left, Dandan threw her hands over her mouth and squealed. "We are in so much trouble."

"But now we have some experience," I replied, smiling. "And money for oil."

The next day we didn't smile so much; the woman came back to see our mistress. "Look at my hair! I have holes in the back. Do you know what my mother-in-law said? She said, with my terrible hairstyle, she didn't blame her son for taking a mistress. What kind of shop are you running here?"

"I didn't cut your hair," Mistress Yao said, narrowing her eyes. "You trying to get one for free, eh?"

"Your girls did this to me!" she shrieked. "You should teach them better."

My mistress grabbed our arms and yanked us in front of her. "These two cut your hair?"

"That one," she said, pointing at me. "The other girl just washed it."

Mistress Yao's face paled and then flushed. "These stupid girls are new apprentices. They've only been here one week." This, of course, was a lie. "You must accept my apologies and let me fix it for you."

"You fix it and give me my money back, or I'll tell all my friends, and you'll lose business."

Mistress Yao squeezed us so hard Dandan yelped. "Of course, I will give you your money back, and a facial to calm your nerves. The two will massage your feet. Hong Bo, bring this kind and patient lady my best green tea before you begin."

Her best green tea was no better than hot water, but I did as I was told.

The binlang factory smelled better than this woman's feet, and her sharp, yellow toenails bit into my skin like dragon's claws. "Make sure to work on my bunions. They're sore," she instructed.

"Of course. You have the loveliest arch. Doesn't she, Dandan?"

"So lovely," she said sweetly, glaring at me as she massaged the woman's hairy calves.

This was the longest afternoon of my young life.

11

The Peacock

His village on the other side, Chang rode past my house every weekend. His fancy middle school bike had magically transformed into a shiny, red motorcycle that sounded angry and powerful. This summer, whenever I happened to be in the garden, he slowed down to smile at me before speeding away. Though I'd never thought much of him in school, he'd grown tall and looked pretty good now.

Perhaps a month after he'd started flirting, he came up behind me as I carried eggs to the market. Baba had my bike at his shop, fixing its flat tire, but I was enjoying the long walk and the freedom that came with simply being outside.

"Hey, GuoGuo, do you want a ride?"

"Oh, it's you," I said, not bothering to turn around. Of course, I'd known who it was all along; neither Ming's nor Cousin Chen's motorcycles—the only ones in my village—were as loud as the Peacock's. I held up my basket. "Can't you see I am busy, Chang?"

"You can get to the market faster if I take you." His engine sounded like a lion as he revved it.

I wanted to ride on it very badly, but I remembered how spoiled he was. "No, I have better things to do than ride on your dirty, old bike."

"It's brand new. My father gave it to me as a graduation present. I just got my certificate. Now I can study medicine."

"I would never let you operate on me," I scoffed.

His smile widened, and his eyes twinkled with mischief. "If I operate on you, you'd like it."

"Go away, Chang, or I'll throw my eggs at you."

"Have it your way," he said, kicking up a swirling cloud of dust in his wake. I coughed and choked and thought mean things about him.

Sunbeams filtered through the lattice of foliage, mottling the ground with shadow and light, reflecting my confusion. I wondered what it might feel like to sit behind the Peacock on that long black cushion. I also wondered why he wouldn't leave me alone.

郭

"Do you sleep day and night and only come out on weekends?" Chang yelled from the road in front of my Mama's cabbage patch. Yanking a weed with too much force, I nearly toppled over on my backside.

"I'm not lazy like you. I'm a hairdresser's apprentice."

"Maybe you can give me a trim," he said.

"Oh, I would *love* to cut your hair," I replied evilly. "I'm very good. Maybe even better than my mistress. Also, I can shave off that caterpillar living on your lip."

His straight, white teeth gleamed in the sun. "I would like to see you try."

郭

"Why are you smiling so much?" Dandan asked the following Monday.

I clipped another toenail from a woman with swollen ankles. I would be the best pedicurist in all of China before my mistress' punishment was over. "There's this boy."

"Ooh... tell me."

Later that day, Dandan ran into the spa room. "GuoGuo, a cute guy is here asking for you!"

Tripping over the towel basket on my way to the front, I stopped dead in my tracks. "Chang, what are you doing here?"

"You promised to cut my hair."

"This is a very long way to travel for a haircut," I said, grinning.

"Is that a customer?" Mistress Yao shouted from upstairs. She'd returned from mahjong in a terrible mood.

"No. Nobody here but a lost delivery guy," I yelled back.

"Chang, huh?" Dandan purred, leaning against the counter. "I've heard a lot about you."

His face lit up. "You have?"

"You've got to go," I whispered frantically. "I can't cut your hair here. I'll get in trouble."

"Why?" he asked as I tried to push him out of the door.

"You lazy girl! Why have you left towels all over my shop?" Mistress Yao growled, walking into the room. "Customers expect clean towels, not dirty ones."

"I'll cut your hair this weekend. Go!" I hissed.

"Promise?"

Glancing back at my mistress, her sour expression told me everything I needed to know about my afternoon chores.

"Bye, GuoGuo," Chang said, winking.

"He is *so* cute," Dandan said, watching him zoom away on his motorcycle. "I especially like the mustache."

"He's trouble. But once you cut his hair, he won't ever bother you again," Mistress Yao said, cackling.

郭

The only pair of scissors my family owned were large, dull, and designed for shearing sheep's wool. My mother's one sharp knife was used only for cutting cloth and meat. It would be embarrassing to trim Chang's hair with either, and he would, as my mistress predicted, most likely end up bloody.

"Go see your grandmother. Maybe she has a pair you can borrow," Mama said, failing to hide her smile.

Well, I knew the answer to that before I bothered knocking, so I ran to Auntie Song's house instead. "Auntie, Auntie, do you have sharp scissors?"

"Why do you need scissors, Mei Zi?" Wai po grumped, snapping beans on the kitchen table.

"I need to cut someone's hair."

"Whose hair?" Auntie Song chimed in, smiling as if she already knew the answer.

"Just a friend's. Nobody important."

"You don't know anyone important, Mei Zi," Wai po said. Is it that doctor's son?"

In a village so small, there are few secrets. And the Peacock racing his loud motorcycle back and forth in front of our house every weekend was not one of them.

Mama expected me to show respect towards my grandmother,

which I rarely did when she wasn't around. But in this case, I really needed the scissors. "Yes, honorable Wai po."

"Daughter, bring Mei Zi your sewing scissors."

My auntie's eyes twinkled as she placed them in my hand. "Don't forget to bring them back."

"Thanks, Auntie!"

I didn't get to the door before my grandmother added, "Don't be a stupid girl. A doctor's son makes a good husband. Maybe you'll be wiser than your mother."

"I'm sure I inherited all my wisdom from you, Wai po," I replied far too sweetly.

I heard Chang's motorcycle well before I saw it. I'd already bathed and put on clean clothes. My hair was nicely braided and tied with red thread.

"Why are you here, Chang?" I asked meanly.

"You made me a promise."

"What? I made you no promise," I said, trying to look aloof and failing miserably.

He bent his head to one side and raised an eyebrow.

"Fine. Sit on that stump, and I'll cut it. But I'm very busy, so I can't spend much time on you."

"What are you busy doing?"

"I'm about to cook dinner."

"Everyone knows you're an excellent cook. Maybe I could see for myself."

"I'll cut your hair, but I'm not cooking for you. I'm no servant girl."

"He stays for dinner," Wai po interrupted, walking into my house with a large basket. "My daughter is making a special dish of squash, tomatoes, and green beans. Her specialty. You'll like it."

My face heated, but Chang smiled brightly. "Thank you, Gou Wai po. You're very kind to invite me."

Between her lack of subtlety and her fiery tongue, the thought of Wai po playing matchmaker gave me chills. Pulling the scissors from my pocket, I exhaled and tried to relax. "Okay, Chang. Whatever you do, don't move."

郭

Dinner was a quiet affair. Baba and Ming were both working, so it was only Wai po, Mama, Wai gong, my blind grandfather, Auntie Song, Uncle Bao, Zhang Jing, *her* husband, and her new baby boy...all crowded around our small kitchen table, all staring at Chang and me.

"So, Chang, I heard you got your diploma. Congratulations," Auntie Song's husband said.

"Will you follow in your father's footsteps?" my auntie asked, pouring him more tea.

"Yes, I will. I'm very excited to begin my studies."

"Mei Zi's good at chores. You'll need someone to take care of you while you're busy with school."

I glared at Wai po when she said this, she'd already embarrassed me twice. Chang stared at his plate, a smile painting his lips.

"A woman who can cook is a rare jewel. A pretty woman who can cook, even rarer. We're lucky to have such a jewel," Wai po continued. My eyes widened and my mouth fell open. It was the first compliment she'd ever paid me. "Unfortunately, *she* married a bum."

Zhang Jing choked on her tea, and her baby, whom she spat it on, screamed. Mama shook her head and looked away. I wanted more than anything to run into my room and hide, but I couldn't give her the satisfaction.

Chang smiled politely at Mama and then turned his attention to Wai po. "It's clear from this feast that Auntie Guo (which is how a younger person addresses a woman Mama's age) is an excellent cook, but I've heard GuoGuo is very good as well. Even people in my village say so," Chang replied, meeting my eyes.

I smiled gratefully.

"GuoGuo will be a successful hairdresser one day," he continued. "I'm certain she'll make an honorable grandmother such as yourself very proud. And GuoGuo is by far the prettiest girl in your whole village. It's clear that she got her looks from you. And GuoGuo…"

By the time Chang had finished saying all those ridiculous things about me, Wai po's face glowed with pleasure, and I sat trying to decide which of our prized chickens to cook for him next time he visited.

The sun was low when we finally stepped outside.

"Are you going to ride with me or not?" Chang demanded, glancing at the sky. "I know the best place to watch the sunset."

"If it will keep you from pestering me, I suppose I'll go," I said, sighing dramatically as I seated myself behind him. The black cushion was smooth against my bare legs.

"Hold on tight. I'm a fast driver," he said, turning back to me, his eyes twinkling.

He stepped hard on the pedal, the engine roared, and then we were flying. Hugging him tightly, I pressed myself against his back to keep from falling off. I loved the way the warm wind tugged at my braid. I loved the speed—even faster than Ming's bus. Even the road's miserable, mud-filled holes were thrilling to splash through. Chang smelled pretty nice as well.

He steered off the main road and onto the mountain path leading to our old primary school. Parking midway up the mountain, he helped me off the warm seat. Brushing past a rhododendron sapling, I followed him to an outcropping of rock wide enough for two to share. Chang offered me his hand, though I certainly needed no assistance climbing onto it, and we sat close to one another, our feet dangling over the side.

"When I was a little boy, I came here sometimes. I thought I was king of the world," he said.

"You *always* thought you were king of the world."

"You can be my queen then," he said, meeting my eyes.

My stomach filled with butterflies. No one had ever said such a thing to me.

Painting our faces and clothing the color of ripe peaches, the sun burnished the pond and rice paddies below. I'd never paid much attention to sunsets, and I was amazed by how our simple farmland could be transformed into such a spectacle. Chang scooted a little closer to me, his hand lightly touching mine.

"Do you see that yellow bird?" he asked suddenly, pointing to a tree on the other side of me. I followed his finger, but I saw nothing of interest. When I turned back to tell him as much, he pressed his lips against mine. I'd never been kissed before, and I wasn't sure what to do, so I sat still. His lips were smooth and soft as they moved against mine, and his mustache tickled my nose. My heart exploded like Chinese New Year fireworks.

I smiled shyly at him when he pulled back to look at me. We said nothing more until the sky was purple, and the mist heavy below.

The trip down the mountain went slower. Insects flashed in his bright headlight, the beam making ghosts in the pale fog. Once

Chang found the village road, he took his time, and I was happy to press my cheek against his back and feel the motor's vibrations.

"Will I see you next weekend?" he asked, leaning against the rusty fencepost by my house.

"Maybe you will and maybe you won't," I said tauntingly.

"I say, maybe I will," he retorted. "Besides, I might need another haircut."

"One is all you get." I hadn't messed it up too badly, but I didn't want to tempt fate.

"Goodbye, GuoGuo," he whispered, looking deeply into my eyes. Climbing back onto his motorcycle, he revved his engine and quickly disappeared over the hill.

That night Mama had a long talk with me about being virtuous, the importance of one's reputation, and that I should never give flowers to any man I wasn't prepared to marry.

郭

Every morning before Mistress Yao left for mahjong, she warned us not to cut anyone's hair. Lucky for us, she said nothing about spa services. I'd watched her for hours on end and knew it was no impressive feat to smear lotion on a woman's face. Eyebrow shaping was another story, but taking inspiration from Chang's kissing bridge, I soon discovered it was my best skill.

"Ooh, I like them," a particularly demanding client remarked, gazing into the handheld mirror. "This is for you," she said, sliding a generous tip across the counter after paying. "I'll see you in two weeks."

"I take morning appointments only," I said, winking at Dandan.

郭

"So, you'll come out riding with me tonight?" Chang asked, parking his bike by Mama's vegetable garden. The sunlight gleamed off the polished handlebars.

"My parents said I'm not allowed to ride with boys like you." I plucked a ripe tomato from its vine, turning it around in my hand.

"What? I'm a very nice guy—a gentleman."

I raised my eyebrows and then laughed.

"Fine. If that's the way it's going to be, we'll walk instead."

"Or…" I glanced back at my house. "We *could* ride your motorcycle."

"GuoGuo, you want to get me in trouble with your family?"

"Maybe."

"I'll park on the other side of the rice paddies. Meet me there when the sun sets."

I rarely disobeyed my mother, but I wasn't a child anymore. I could ride with whomever I wished.

That evening, Chang took me to his village's pond. At the pinnacle of the bridge's arch, we leaned over the railing, watching the moon write in white ink on the water's dark surface. The market's festive paper lanterns swayed in the light breeze, their bouncing and bumping reminiscent of distant drums. Forever the comedian, Chang never failed to make me laugh, and I returned the favor, telling him stories about my lazy mistress. When our lips touched this time, I was prepared, but that didn't stop the explosion of butterflies. It was a night I would never forget.

郭

"When you complete your apprenticeship, move to Changsha. There are plenty of spas there."

"When do you leave?" I asked, feeling pain at the mere mention.

"Soon. But I'll come back every weekend just to drive you around."

Chang kept his promise, returning every weekend for the next two months. We spent a great deal of time kissing on our secret mountain ledge, and he told me about his pre-med classes in subjects I'd never heard of. As my feelings for him grew, I thought more and more about getting a job near his university. Perhaps we would get married one day. Being a doctor's wife would probably please Mama; it would be a better life. The only downside would be Wai po's euphoria.

I took our eggs to the market, as usual, expecting him to race up behind me as had become his custom. Deciding he must have slept late after his big exams, I spent the afternoon fruitlessly watching for him. When the sun set, and he still hadn't come, I went inside and cooked dinner for the family.

"You're not eating much," Wai po said to me. "Boys don't like skinny girls."

My mind ran wild all night. Fearing he'd been injured in a crash, or something equally horrible, I resolved to go to his father's office and demand information. The morning seemed innocent enough when I set out for Chang's village. Only a mile or so into my ride, I heard the unmistakable sound of Chang's bike.

Letting out the breath I'd been holding since yesterday, I hopped off my bike. Failing to find a chiding comment in my sea of overwhelming relief, I simply smiled. Kiss first, scold later, I decided.

As his bike crested the large hill in front of me, I waved excitedly. Barely glancing in my direction, he tore past me.

"Chang!" I yelled after a stunned moment. "Chang!" I sped off after him, pedaling as fast as I could. When it became apparent that

I would never catch him, I went home. With a fat pumpkin as my stool, I spent the afternoon, thinking.

"I don't know why he acted that way, Dandan," I said, Monday while painting a woman's toenails. "I've done nothing wrong."

"Did you give him your flower?" the customer asked.

I couldn't understand why grown women talked so much about flowers, and moreover, why they thought men had any interest in them. Thinking back, when Chang had mentioned his mother liked chrysanthemum tea, I had given him a sack of our dried blossoms. Shrugging, I said, "I suppose."

"Ah, that's what happened then. He got what he wanted from you, and now he's gone looking elsewhere. Men do this all the time."

"I don't understand."

"You don't understand?" the woman said, raising her brows.

Dandan and I both shook our heads no.

"What mothers don't teach their girls," she sighed, clicking her tongue. Before leaving, she gave each of us a nice tip, even though Dandan had only watched.

Two Saturdays passed before Chang flew by my house again. Deciding I wouldn't wait like a fat pig to be slaughtered, I rode to his village. His father had given him the apartment above his medical practice as a graduation present. I rolled my eyes, thinking about how spoiled he was.

Working up the courage to knock, I paced back and forth in front of the white door, remembering my childhood visit to the clinic. Though Chang's father had probably had little choice but to report me to the government, I still blamed him for the devastating fallout. Allowing that bitterness to strengthen my resolve, I raised my arm and knocked.

Suddenly the object of my wrath stepped out, smoking a cigarette—something I'd never seen him do before.

"Chang."

"GuoGuo!" he yelped, jumping back. "Why are you here?"

"You know the answer. What have I done that you're treating me this way?"

"Nothing. I'm just busy."

"Too busy to stop by and explain. Too busy to even say hello? I don't think so." After a few moments of silence, I crossed my arms over my chest and said, "Well?"

"I have a girlfriend at school," he blurted out, looking away.

"I don't understand."

He huffed and kicked a rock. "What, do you think a guy like me doesn't have a girlfriend?"

"But what about us?" I said, flustered and hurt. "I thought I was your girlfriend."

"You were summer fun, GuoGuo. But I don't have time for foolish country girls now. I need an educated woman from a respectable family. I have to think of my future."

Rage, like hot oil, sizzled inside me. "You don't think my family is respectable? You don't think I'm good enough for you, Peacock?" Hauling off, I slapped his face so hard his cigarette fell to the ground. Seeming unable to speak for a moment, he rubbed his jaw. Finally, he turned and walked wordlessly back into his apartment. I followed him up the stairs, like a swarm of angry hornets.

"You can't treat me this way. You told me *I* was your girlfriend."

"I never said that," he shot back.

"How many times did you kiss me? How often did you suggest I move near your college, so we could be together?"

"Pipe dreams. It's not like they would ever come true." I hadn't begun searching for spa jobs near him, but I hadn't ruled it out either.

"Did you just want flowers? Does this girl give you flowers?" I shouted.

"What are you talking about?' he said. "Why are you acting this way? It's over. Accept it and move on."

"It is not over!" I heard my voice crack.

Sitting down on his bed, he lit another cigarette and then began reading an old newspaper. The longer he ignored me, the angrier I became. Jerking his closet door open, I began yanking his clothes from their hangers and throwing them at him.

"You don't just get a new girlfriend and hope the old one goes away. You are a coward!" I seethed, slapping him again.

"Stop it," he said, shielding his face by rolling onto his stomach.

"Cheater! Liar! User!" I screamed, hitting his back and arms.

I stomped all over the pile of nicely pressed pants and shirts, putting as much dirt on them as a foolish country girl could. Emptying his dresser drawers, I did the same to his socks and underwear.

With nothing left to destroy, I stood facing his prone body, my own shaking, angry tears spilling from my eyes. Finally, he turned his face to me. "Are you finished yet?"

I slapped his head once more and said, "I'm finished with you forever. I feel sorry for your new girlfriend. She doesn't know what kind of loser she's getting."

All the way home, I imagined what Wai po was going to say to me when she found out Chang had dumped me. I didn't care so much about her insults personally, but I knew she would find some way to blame my mother for it.

And I still didn't understand about this flower situation.

12

Tea and Cookies

Though Mistress Yao had not taught us particularly well, she did have connections. Dandan, who wanted a hair career, took a second apprenticeship with a salon near her home. Having little interest in hair, and even less in wasting more time trying to improve my poor skills, I took an entry-level position in a thriving salon in the bustling city of Zhuzhou.

Moving so far from home was a big step for me, but with Chang's insults souring my taste for country living, I wanted to reinvent myself in a place promising skyscrapers, traffic jams, and a population greater than Black Village's one-hundred-fifty.

The Lotus Leaf, an elegant salon and spa housed in a generous three-story building near Yan Emperor Square, hosted thirty professional employees, along with another twenty or so graduate apprentices like me. The spa, offering numerous services I'd never heard of, was every bit the same as college, and far more practical than Chang's biology classes.

The couple who owned the salon provided meals, and we were not expected to cook for the family, or do their laundry, or babysit their children. I was pleased beyond measure. Near the salon, the owners even kept an apartment for unmarried employees so we didn't have to sleep on the salon floor. Though pressed together in a single, crowded room, for the first time, I felt like an adult.

At least in the beginning.

I became fast friends with three other spa apprentices: Ting, Jin, and Yang. All three were farm girls like me, who yearned for big-city excitement and lives filled with more than pulling weeds and feeding pigs.

Ting, the oldest of our foursome by two years, had been working at Lotus Leaf the longest. "She's our *jiejie*," Yang whispered when Ting left for more steamed rice. "I've always wanted a big sister to watch over me."

In Xiang dialect Yang means "young", and though she was older than me, this name perfectly suited her personality.

"If you have questions about men, she's the one to ask," Jin said, dropping a pepper on my lap as she reached over me for more stir-fry vegetables. "She's got a boyfriend in Wuhan."

"Can you believe it? Another province! How exotic," Yang interjected, sighing.

"What are you whispering about?" Ting said, gracefully dropping to the floor. Tall, with elegant movements and long, fine hair, she reminded me of a willow tree.

"Your boyfriend," Jin answered. "What else do we have to talk about? The weather?" Jin's ready willingness to speak her mind reminded me of Hop Nainai. And if refusing to wrap her words in silk offended some, well so be it; I thought she was wonderful.

"He's coming in a few weeks. I'll introduce you if you'd like," Ting said dreamily.

"How did you meet?" I asked.

"Strangers on a train," Yang answered before she could. "Love at first sight. Right, Ting?"

Ting nodded, smiling radiantly.

The female owner's mother lived in the same Tiantai Road apartment building as we. In fact, her fourth-floor room was right beside ours. After work every evening, she served tea in her room. Though a pleasant enough person, few of us enjoyed going, because she always asked very personal questions. She asked us to call her Liu Wai po. Relieved to have left my wai po in faraway Black Village, I was in no hurry to acquire a new one. Still, we did as she asked.

When we left to go out for the evening, Liu Wai po opened her door and waved goodbye. When we returned, Liu Wai po opened her door and smiled at us.

"I don't trust that woman," Jin whispered into the darkness one night. "She gives me a bad feeling." We slept in a cluster in the back of the room, so we wouldn't get stepped on by those girls coming in late; Zhuzhou had much to offer, and none of us had anything better to do after work than to go out and enjoy it.

"She means well, I think," Yang said. "She watches over us like a good grandmother." Yang was an expert in forgiveness, looking past faults. This trait she shared with Mama, which was comforting. But unlike Mama, who missed little, Yang was very naïve.

"Oh, she watches over us alright," Jin growled. "I opened my eyes late last night and found her standing in the middle of the room, counting us."

"What?" Ting said, sitting up "Why didn't you say anything?"

"I just did."

郭

"Deep breaths," Jin said. "Ride through the pain."

"The wax is too hot!" Ting groaned.

"Do you want me to pull every eyebrow hair out with my tweezers? I will," Jin said.

"Just, just make me beautiful."

"GuoGuo will do your facial because she's the best. I've already picked out the perfect nail color. Your boyfriend is going to love it," Yang said.

"So, when does his bus arrive?"

"Six o'clock sharp," she said giddily. "I can't wait. It's been two months."

Ting left for the bus station, and we, after doing our own hair and makeup, hurried home. Karaoke had become our Friday night ritual. "Okay, let's have tea with the old bat, and then hit the nightclub," Jin said.

"We'll sound terrible without Ting's voice," Yang said as we filed into Liu Wai po's room.

"Yeah. She's the only one of us who can actually sing," Jin added.

"I can sing," I said.

Raising her eyebrows, Jin smirked.

"Where is Ting?" Liu Wai po asked sweetly. "She loves my cookies, and these are very special tonight."

Liu Wai po insisted we each have one cookie with our tea; it was the best part of going. Tonight, Ting's cookie sat alone on the plate. Until that moment, I'd never realized how clever she was at counting us.

"She hasn't felt well all day, so cookies won't be good for her stomach," I said.

Yang snatched it off the plate and shoved the whole thing into her mouth. She was a terrible liar and knew Liu Wai po could get the truth from her otherwise.

"She ate like a horse at lunch. She costs my daughter money, eating all that food."

"Ting's a grown woman," Jin said. "Why do you care where she is or if she goes out at night? It's not your business."

"So, she did go out, eh?"

"Only to get some herbs," I said. "For her stomach." I was the quickest and best at lying. Perhaps I shouldn't have been proud of this trait, but it had never failed me.

"I'll make her special tea. When she returns, I'll be waiting." Liu Wai po's smile was made of glass.

"What are we going to do?" Yang whispered once we'd returned to our room.

"Nothing," Jin replied. "We're not little girls."

Giggling as we tripped up the stairs hours later, Liu Wai po opened her door. "Ting's tea is cold. Where is she?"

"Maybe sleeping," I said.

Ting did not return that night, but every time another girl came up the steps, we heard Liu Wai po open her door and ask about Ting.

"Let's go upstairs one girl at a time," Jin said, as we returned from the steamed dumpling restaurant across the street the following night. "GuoGuo, you first."

I stomped up the stairs loudly. As soon as I rounded the last flight, Liu Wai po yanked open the door.

"Is Ting with you?

"She just passed us on her way out. Didn't you hear her?"

"I heard no one," she said through gritted teeth.

Jin waited a few moments and then stomped up the stairs. Liu Wai po questioned her as well. Then it was Yang's turn.

"Okay girls, time to go back out," Jin announced.

"You are so bad," Yang said, giggling.

郭

Ting glowed as she walked through the spa doors Monday morning.

"True love," Yang sighed longingly.

"Did you have a pleasant weekend, Ting?" the owner asked.

"It was fine, thank you."

"I heard you didn't come home at all. Is that true?"

"Of course, she came home. Where else would she go?" Jin challenged, balling her fists. "And how is it your business what any of us do outside of work?"

The boss stared at Jin for a long moment and then returned her attention to Ting. "My mother says otherwise. Who should I believe?"

"Perhaps Liu Wai po's eyes are not so good," I said. "She banged her door so often we hardly got any sleep. Maybe she's going crazy." Certainly, we cared about Ting's situation, but at this moment, Jin and I were both arguing about something even more important: our freedom.

"Watch your tongue, Guo Hong Bo. Many girls would like jobs in this salon. You don't like yours?"

"I like mine very well, and I work hard for you, but we are not your daughters. We are your employees."

"But my husband and I feed and house you. Do we not treat you like family?"

Thinking of my own wai po, I smiled prettily and said, "Yes, boss, you do treat me just like family. I'm very lucky to have such a mother as yours looking after me."

She narrowed her eyes at me and then cast them on Ting once more. "You will reimburse us for your share of food and apartment rent. It's unfair that I should pay so much for what you do not use."

Ting's weekend glow faded away. As trainees, we only made one hundred RMB per month, which wasn't very much at all, and she had spent all of hers on new clothes and a hotel room to impress her boyfriend.

"Yes, boss," she said, her eyes dropping to the floor.

I wanted to argue that since she was off this weekend, she hadn't eaten their food, but I was already in trouble. Jin met my eyes. She was thinking the same thing.

After a very tense evening tea, Jin tossed an apartment rental notice on Ting's mat. "Read this, ladies."

Snatching up the flier, Yang ticked off the positives. "Close to work, close to karaoke—that's nice, close to that dumpling place GuoGuo likes. Perfect."

"We're going to rent this apartment and leave Liu Wai po to bother the others!" Jin said.

"This will cost most of our salary," Ting replied, shaking her head. "After my weekend and our bosses' punishment, I have nothing left."

"We'll scrape our savings together and cover your portion for the first month. Don't you see? It'll be worth it. We're young, we need privacy, we need freedom, we need our own beds," Jin said, glaring at Yang. "You snore like a water buffalo."

13

Bank Robber

It was a wonderful time to be young and free. We walked to work every morning and sang karaoke at night. We spent days off picnicking at beautiful Tiantaishan Park, riding bikes by the silvery Xiangziang river, and dreaming about our futures.

Because we had no kitchen, we ate out all the time. On payday, we treated ourselves to nice dinners with the salon staff. When money got tight, we bought cheap ramen noodles from street vendors, sometimes splitting them four ways. Drying Yang's tears every time another guy dumped her became common practice; this happened more times than I could count. Jin and I hoped to find men as honorable as Ting's.

A handsome delivery guy, named Guang, regularly replenished our beauty supplies. Always in a good mood, his smile was the first thing I noticed about him. The only unattractive thing about him was the fact that he was related to the owner.

"Guo Hong Bo, take this box of lotions upstairs," my boss said.

"It's very heavy. I'll carry it for you," Guang quickly offered. Guang means "glorious" in my dialect. With his square jaw, wide shoulders, and bulging muscles, his parents certainly named him well.

Many girls leaned over the decorative iron railing to stare as he followed me up the wide marble stairs; I was not the only one attracted to him.

"You have a boy's name, but you don't look like a boy," he said, raising a bow.

"No, but I kick like one, and your arms are full. It would be a shame if you fell down the stairs and broke your neck."

Laughing, he set down the box. "I like a girl with spirit."

"You would like my friend, Jin. She has enough spirit for three girls." I winked at Jin, who was also watching. Rolling her eyes, she disappeared into the manicure room.

A giggle escaped Yang's lips. She'd had a crush on Guang since the first time she saw him.

"Or you might like my friend, Yang, here. She has a kind spirit. Probably too good for you, though."

"GuoGuo!" she hissed.

He smiled at her, then looked at me again. "Yes, too good for me. It was nice meeting you, girl-with-a-boy's-name. I hope to see you again."

郭

A tray of sweets waited on the lotion table the following morning. My bosses were far too stingy to provide such lavish treats, but no one else claimed responsibility. This mystery continued until the following Monday when several of us arrived early to open the shop.

"Are you a robber?" I asked, catching Guang at the foot of the stairs.

Seemingly stumped by the question for a moment, he then

laughed. "Yes, I'm a robber. Only I give things rather than take them."

"What have you given us other than a hard time?" I said, smirking.

"You don't think my cousin's been leaving you treats, do you? She's very cheap," he said.

"You're so kind to think of us," Yang said, batting her eyes.

Walking past Guang, Ting said, "Ladies, we've got chores to do."

"Here's the broom," Jin said, handing it to me with a snort. "Yang, come."

They had put me on sweeping duty for the third time that month; whenever Liu Wai po was around, I couldn't seem to hold my tongue. Guang followed me outside.

"So, Hong Bo," Guang said.

"It's GuoGuo, actually. Only your cousin calls me by my given name."

"I like it. So, GuoGuo," he began again.

"So, what?" I asked. The city was quickly waking, and I needed to finish this job before my boss arrived.

"So, would you like to have dinner with me?"

Other than Chang, who really didn't count since we'd done nothing but ride around our village, I'd never gone out on a date.

"I'll think about it," I finally replied.

"Think fast," he said, grinning. "I'm a hot commodity."

"Peacock," I muttered, sweeping dirt at him.

"Did he ask about me?" Yang said, bouncing on her toes.

"No. He asked me out on a date."

"Oh." Yang currently had crushes on three guys and didn't seem particularly crestfallen. "So, what did you say?"

"I said I'd think about it."

"Think about it?" Ting scoffed. "It's either *yes* or *no*. He's cute. Go out with him."

That evening, we were the last to leave—this time, Jin's mouth was to blame. Hungry, we tried to speed her chores along by sweeping for her, but when we heard Liu Wai po's tinny voice, Jin rolled her eyes and waved us off.

"Save me some noodles." The end of the month, we were out of money again.

"Hello," I said to Guang, who was waiting by the door, a small cake in his hand. I wondered how long he'd been standing there.

"This is for you," he said, smiling widely. "What time shall I pick you up?"

"What do you mean?"

"For our date. What time?"

"I haven't decided whether or not I'm going out with you." Clearing her throat, Ting pinched my back.

"Decide quickly," he said.

Smiling broadly outside the shop's entrance the following morning later, Guang pulled a napkin from his jacket. The word *Yes* was written on it. Though not my handwriting, I certainly recognized it.

"I think you've made a mistake," I said. "That must be from another girl."

A hand reached around the door and grabbed my arm. "Pick her up here at seven o'clock," Jin said, and then yanked me inside.

"You wrote that note! You go out with him!" I hissed.

"He didn't ask me," Jin retorted.

"Less talk, more work, ladies," our boss sang, clapping her hands. "I'm not paying you to gossip."

郭

"I have nothing to wear!" I whispered during lunch. It was true. I had two pairs of pants, three shirts, and one pair of shoes. All work clothes. All dirty.

"You can wear my new dress," Ting said, smiling. "But don't spill anything on it." Of the many gifts her boyfriend had given her, this was her favorite by far.

After work, one of the professionals did my hair, and Yang, who was very good at it, did my makeup. Ting's dress, which was white with a sweep of cherry blossoms running down the skirt, was a little too big, but lovely.

"You look beautiful," Yang said. "He'll fall in love with you."

"I don't want anyone falling in love with me. I'm not ready for that."

"She's hopeless," Ting sighed.

Guang arrived at the Lotus Leaf right on time. A taxi took us to a nice restaurant—the food was in all ways better than ramen noodles—and then another delivered us to my favorite disco.

"It's beer. You'll like it," he said, handing me a drink.

Though I was of legal drinking age, I rarely had the money for alcohol. Ting liked wine, so when we could afford it, that's what we drank. I found beer's bitter taste unpleasant, but light and happy after my second large mug, I changed my mind.

Dancing for hours, Guang and I had a wonderful time. I told him about my life on the farm and how I planned to be a successful salon owner one day to make my mother proud.

"I'll send you lots of customers. I'll tell everybody about you," Guang said loudly, spreading his arms.

After singing terrible karaoke together, he asked if I was ready to leave.

It was late, and I had to work in the morning. I wasn't sure where I stood on first-date kisses. Yang was all for them, but Ting suggested I be more reserved. Jin had no more experience than I.

Cowardness won out. "Well, thanks for a fun evening. I had a really good time, and maybe I'll see you soon," I said, turning to leave.

"Hey, where are you going?" Guang asked, laughing.

"Home. I live close enough to walk from here."

"*Please.* I'm a good date. I'll take you home." Flagging down a taxi, we climbed inside.

With its bright lights and sparkling riverfront, the city was lovely at night. A little chilled after sweating so much, I didn't complain when Guang put his arm around me. As we crossed the impressive Zhuzhou Bridge, he leaned over and gently brushed my cheek with his lips. My heart began racing. Perhaps I'd take Yang's advice on kissing.

"This isn't the way to my apartment," I suddenly said.

"You don't need to go home right away, do you? Let's take a ride." Guang's charming smile and silky voice were suddenly difficult to say no to. Besides, I was warm and comfortable in his muscular arms.

It seemed we traveled every road in the city, and I'd long ago lost my bearings. "There's somewhere I want to show you," he said, instructing the driver to stop.

"Why are we here?" I asked, staring at the scrolling Silver Lake Hotel sign. My fluttery feeling suddenly felt less fluttery.

"So we can spend some more time together. You know, play around," he purred, delivering another of his soft kisses.

"You want to play around?" I said, pulling away. "You want to go to a hotel and play around? I don't think so."

"We won't do anything you don't want to do."

"No."

"GuoGuo, I'm a gentleman," he said.

The taxi driver snorted.

"Come inside for a little while. Let me make you feel nice."

Jumping out of the car, I ran down busy Taishan Road, cutting through alleys I didn't know, hoping I was going in the right direction—though any direction taking me away from that hotel was just fine. I didn't know very much about boys, but I did know I didn't want these relations. Especially with a man I hardly knew.

Finally, and with great relief, I spotted Yan Emperor tower in the distance, its brightly lit spire a beacon to my apartment.

"Why are you out of breath? What's wrong?" the girls asked, crowding around me when I burst into our room.

"I, he...he tried to take me to a hotel room!"

"That's all men want. Sex, sex, sex," Ting said, rolling her eyes.

"My mother said I shouldn't have relations until I'm married." We'd had a more extensive talk about flowers after the Chang incident. Ting had since supplied the more graphic details.

"All mothers say that," Ting said. "They just don't want us running around and having abortions all the time."

"Nice boys don't want sex," Yang corrected. "They like talking and holding hands."

Jin rolled her eyes. "Yeah, right. Boys just want to hold hands."

"I don't know how to have sex, but I'd like to try it sometime," Yang said dreamily.

"It's no big deal. Just let the guy do all the work. It's over in no time," Ting said, waving a dismissive hand.

"You've had sex?" Yang said, her eyes bugging.

Jin shook her head and looked towards the ceiling.

郭

I was late to work the next morning; my head throbbed from too much beer and not enough sleep. A wave of whispers drew my attention to the top of the stairs where an enormous bouquet of flowers rested. My name was written on the card attached, a small heart drawn beside it.

"Ooh, GuoGuo has a boyfriend," several girls began chanting.

"I do not," I grumped, pushing past them.

"Who is he?" another asked.

"The same guy who brings us sweets every morning," Yang said. "Guang, of course."

"*Guang* brings those sweets?" a girl named Juan said. "He never used to bring sweets."

"That's because he didn't like any of us," Yang said.

"I wouldn't want him liking me," Juan retorted. "Sure, he's handsome, but too dangerous."

"Dangerous? What do you mean by dangerous?" Jin demanded.

"He's a gangster," Juan whispered.

"He's not a gangster. He's a delivery guy," I said.

"Oh, he's a delivery guy, all right. He delivers anything his boss wants."

"Like stolen goods?" Ting asked, suddenly concerned. She stepped beside me and protectively curled her arm around my shoulders.

"Yes, and he hurts people for money. Sometimes he cuts off their hands—or even their *head*," Juan said loudly enough for all the spa customers to hear.

"I don't believe it," Jin said skeptically, crossing her arms over her chest. "You're just jealous."

"Oh, look who's so smart. Go ask my brother. His friend didn't pay a gambling debt, and now he's missing three fingers. I'll bring him here to show you if you want."

"But Guang is so nice," Yang said in disbelief.

"He's nice until he cuts off your arm. Then you won't think so. You be careful, GuoGuo," Juan said, disappearing to the back.

I wore a path, pacing the plank floor of our apartment. Yang sat on her mat, wringing her hands. Jin stood in the corner, biting her nails.

"Dinner," Ting announced, walking through the door with four containers of ramen. "I splurged."

My stomach was in knots, I said, "I'm not hungry." I hadn't asked for this kind of trouble, and I didn't know how to get out of it.

"I spent the money, now you eat!" Ting said firmly. Then more gently: "GuoGuo, it's going to be alright. When you see him next, just tell him the truth. He'll go away."

郭

I didn't have long to wait, because Guang was leaning against the Lotus Leaf's big glass window the following morning.

"GuoGuo, we'll be right inside. Don't be long. You have a lot of work to do," Jin said, giving me a meaningful look.

My hands suddenly slick with sweat, I took a deep breath. I had no experience in this.

"I'm sorry if I scared you," he said. "I just like you a lot, and I want you to be my girlfriend."

"So we can go to hotels and fool around?" I said snidely.

"No, because you're pretty and funny, and I enjoy spending time with you. You had fun on our date, didn't you?"

"I had fun until you took me to a hotel! I don't want to be your girlfriend."

"Why not? I'll treat you really well. I promise."

"Look, Guang, that was the first date I've ever been on. It was nice, and I did have fun, but you want more, and I'm not ready for that."

"I know you're conservative, but you're an adult living in a big city. You're not under the watchful eyes of your family anymore. You can do whatever you want. Be my girlfriend, GuoGuo. You won't regret it."

When I didn't respond, he added, "I really am a nice guy."

Realizing he wasn't going to leave me alone, I shored my courage and said, "That's not what I heard."

He raised his eyebrows. "What did you hear?"

"That you're a gangster who hurts people for money."

I expected him to deny it, but after a moment, he just shrugged. "I have to make a living somehow. I'm a big guy. It's a good job for me."

A shiver ran through me, and I gasped. I hadn't wanted to believe it was true, and he was so casual about it. "That's a terrible job," I stammered. "You can't go around hurting people. That's just wrong."

"This isn't the farm, GuoGuo. Life is hard here, and people are cruel. Sometimes they must pay for their crimes. Think of me as a policeman—one who helps those who don't have government connections. If someone does a bad thing to you, I can bring them to justice."

I was a big fan of justice. My primary school nickname was "Justice Girl," because I always stood up to the mean boys who teased girls. I'd never hesitated to fight for someone who was being bullied, but Guang was not talking about that kind of justice.

"Gangsters don't help people out of generosity. Someone pays them. How do you even know the people you punish are guilty?"

"My boss knows. I do what he tells me to do. End of story."

"What if I become your girlfriend, and one day you get mad at me—or your boss does? Will you cut off my hand? What about my head?"

His face colored. "I would never do that to you. You'll always be safe with me."

"GuoGuo," Jin shouted from the upstairs window. "Time for work." When I glanced up, heads were poking out of every window.

"Look, Guang, I don't want to be your girlfriend. Please find someone else." Turning, I slipped inside.

Too many eyes were upon me as I climbed the stairs. Ignoring the whispers as best I could, I pulled on my black smock. Ting stood me in front of a lady awaiting a facial. "Madame, this is Hong Bo. She's our best facialist. She'll take good care of you."

Inhaling deeply to steady my shaking hands, I put on my warmest smile. "Good morning! Oh, what lovely skin you have…"

Ting kept me busy all day. As soon as I finished with one client, she dragged me to another. When business slowed, she even stopped in the middle of a job and asked me to finish it for her. This was a great kindness because it kept me too busy to think.

That evening, we hurried, my friends clustering around me like security guards. This time, it was Yang who went out for food.

"I brought cookies," she sang. If we didn't stop eating so extravagantly, we wouldn't have enough money to pay the rent.

To my relief, Guang was not waiting for me the next morning. Unfortunately, three flower bouquets had taken his place, each with a note: "I'm sorry", "You can trust me", "Give me another chance."

"Oh, this is terrible," I whispered.

Ting kept me even busier than the day before.

郭

I was both angry and a little afraid. I had said no, and I had meant no, but he was a dangerous man, and I needed to be careful.

"Did you like the flowers?" Guang said as soon as I stepped outside.

Gasping, I tried to gather my wits. "Um, they were very beautiful, thanks. But I still don't want to be your girlfriend."

"GuoGuo, we must hurry to our appointment," Ting said urgently. I smiled at my brave friends who stood nearby in a show of solidarity.

"Let me take you on another date," he said. "Maybe if you get to know me better, you'll see I'm no one to be afraid of."

"No."

"GuoGuo, why don't you like me?"

Noting Jin's worried expression, I scrambled to think of some way to prevent him from pursuing me. Clearly, no wasn't working.

"I don't like you because you are poor," I blurted out. An old woman passing by nodded approvingly. It was the most ridiculous thing to say to him, since cutting people's hands off surely paid well, but it was what Wai po had told Baba when he'd sought to marry Mama. And if anyone knew how to be unkind, it was her.

For a moment, he seemed stunned, but then he regained his composure and laughed. "You're not the kind of girl who chases after money. That's one of the reasons I like you. But if that's what it'll take to impress you, then I'll go rob a bank."

Now I was the stunned one. "Rob a bank? You can't just rob a bank!"

"Sure, I can. I've robbed banks before. It's no big deal."

"No big deal?" I threw my arms in the air. "Who does that?"

My friends' faces were white, and their jaws hung open.

"I really like you, GuoGuo. I'll do anything you want." Stepping closer, he gently gripped my arms. I pulled away immediately.

"If you'll do anything I want, then I want you to go away and never talk to me again."

Guang dropped his head, his bangs flopping in his face, and without another word, he turned and walked slowly down the bustling sidewalk. I flew back inside the shop, ran upstairs, and shut myself in the supply closet.

"GuoGuo!" Ting's voice rang out as she rapped on the door a few minutes later. "You can't stay in there all night."

"Yes, I can," I said, though the damp mop was soaking my pants.

郭

For the rest of the week, no flowers or sweets arrived, and Guang made no deliveries—at least while we were there.

"Jin, never set me up again," I said when she made a poor joke about Guang over lunch.

"Pfft. Next time I'll check him out first."

Because we'd been feeding our sorrows—mine, anyway—we were out of money. The landlord said we had to pay rent the next day or he would kick us out.

"We could always call Guang," Jin said sarcastically. "He could rob a bank for our rent money, *or* he could cut off the landlord's head so we wouldn't have to pay."

I threw my shoe at her. "You are a horrible human being."

"GuoGuo, you know what you have to do," Jin said in all seriousness. The other girls nodded with grave expressions.

"Unfortunately."

It seemed we ran out of rent money more often than not, so

we'd made a pact to alternate asking our parents for help. It was my turn, and I dreaded it. The more time I spent in the city, the more I understood what Mama had been trying to tell me all along; their lives were difficult, and making money was an unpleasant and sometimes dangerous proposition.

Too far away to travel alone, and because I was busy being my own person, I rarely returned to Black Village. Baba's Yuetang shop was only an hour bike ride away, however, and I visited it regularly, usually on the last Saturday of the month.

Negotiating the heavy traffic of Zhuzhou, where cars were as prevalent as motorcycles, and human life was of lesser value, I was glad when I finally turned onto the quiet country road leading to Yuetang. With little to do but peddle, I debated telling Baba about Guang, but feared he'd demand I move back home. I also thought about asking Ming's advice, but his hot-headedness would only make matters worse, and might even get him killed.

Baba smiled when he saw me. "How's my little lotus flower?"

"You're in a good mood today," I said, hugging him.

"Of course I'm in a good mood. I haven't seen you in weeks." Baba took the small sack of empty shampoo bottles, folded cardboard boxes, and bits of aluminum foil I'd salvaged from the shop's dumpster and set them by another sack of items ready to be sorted.

"I've been busy working. How's Mama?"

He smiled widely. "Ask her yourself. Meilin!" he called out.

"Mama!" I flew into her arms as soon as she stepped through the back door. When she wiped away a stray tear, a knot formed in my stomach. With Mama here, the task of begging for rent money would be all the more distressing.

Mama surveyed me from head to toe. "You're too skinny. You're not eating enough."

"I'm fine. I'm just a little short on money this month," I said, cringing.

"Did someone steal your wallet again?" Baba asked with a smirk as he walked by.

"Not exactly."

"That's good. It seems someone steals it every time your rent is due."

"People steal from you?" Mama asked, aghast.

"It's just part of city living. Things like that happen all the time."

"You should move back home. No one will steal from you there," she said.

"No, Mama. I love it there. I have friends. I'm doing well in my job."

"So, no one stole your money?" Baba asked, raising a brow.

"No, nothing so bad as that," I said, looking away. "Only my backpack got a hole in it, and all my money slipped out."

"That's terrible," he said, winking at my mother. "So now you need a new backpack, too?"

"Baba, that's so kind of you."

"Next time, maybe you should ask your grandmother for money," he said, grunting, as he dropped enough in my hand for rent and food. I shivered at the thought.

Baba returned to his sorting, and Mama took my hand.

"I don't have long," I said.

"You don't have time to talk to me?"

"I always have time for that."

"I brought rice cakes," she said, leading me to a stack of cement blocks behind the shop. After settling herself and unwrapping the small packet, she scrutinized my face. "Something's wrong, Mei Zi. You tell me."

My first impulse was to deny it, but Mama would have seen that for the lie it was. I sighed. "There's a guy."

"A boyfriend?" Mama asked, looking aghast.

"He'd like that, but I've told him no. Many times."

"And he won't listen?"

"I said something unkind, so I think he'll leave me alone now. I hope so, anyway."

"When men get ideas stuck in their heads, they become like water buffalo. You can't change their direction unless you hit them with a switch."

"I've never seen you take a switch to Baba," I said, laughing.

She pointed to her tongue. "I use this one."

郭

On payday, we ate our traditional nice meal with the other girls, and then bought candy from a vendor. With no more gangster encounters, and a city full of potential, life was good again. So good, in fact, that when we arrived at the disco, I decided to celebrate by buying my friends the first round of drinks.

Being a Friday night, the disco was packed, and there was a long wait for karaoke.

"We're not up for a while, ladies. Let's dance!" Ting said, pulling Jin and me into the crowd.

"I hope I see that guy I met last week," Yang shouted over the music.

"The one with the motorcycle?" Jin asked, turning in circles.

"No! The one with the mustache who works at the ice cream shop."

"He was cute," I said, bumping hips with another girl.

"Sixty-four!" the karaoke DJ called out.

"That's us!" Yang took her drink along with my arm and dragged me to the stage. Ting raced over to choose our song. Of course, it was always the same one, so there was no surprise when the music began playing. Jin, who'd been dancing in the middle of the crowd, swam to the stage and climbed onto it instead of using the stairs. She joined Ting at one microphone, and Yang and I shared the other.

Ting and Jin began the first verse. Yang and I always sang the second one. "GuoGuo, look!" Yang yelled into the microphone, pointing to the mustached guy she'd been looking for all evening. He smiled and waved at her. Unfortunately, the guy beside him was not smiling. Not at all.

Jumping off the stage, I pushed through the throng of people blocking the exit.

"GuoGuo, wait!" Guang yelled as I slipped out the door.

Turning right, I ran down the alley beside the club. My heart raced even faster when I heard the sound of heavy footsteps behind me.

"GuoGuo, let me talk to you."

Grabbing the back of my shirt, he stopped me in my tracks.

"Let me go, you brute!" I said, squirming to get away.

"Please. Just listen."

"No. We have nothing to say."

"Then use your eyes instead." He pulled a thick fold of money from his pocket and handed it to me. It was clearly an enormous sum—enough to pay our rent for a whole year with money to spare. "See, I have money now, so you can be my girlfriend. Come back inside and have some drinks. I'll pay for all your friends."

Stunned, I said, "Where did this money come from?"

He gave me a wry smile. "You said I was too poor. I am not poor anymore."

Shaking my head, I tried to give it back, but he held up his hand. "GuoGuo, use this money to buy nice things for yourself. I have plenty more where it came from."

Looking at the wad, I wondered what awful thing he'd done to get this money. I wondered how many people he'd hurt, if he'd really robbed a bank, if he'd killed for it. And yet, here was this very handsome, seemingly kind man—at least to me—standing before me with hopeful eyes. I didn't know what to think, except that I could be arrested at any moment just for being near him. This had to end.

"Whatever you did to get this, it was bad. It's dirty money."

"But—"

I threw the bills at him, watching them flutter to the damp pavement like paper butterflies. "Guang, I don't want your money and I don't want you. I can't stand to even look at your face. You are ugly!" It was such a lie—a terrible lie, and I hated myself for it, but his face was a mask of beauty covering something truly ugly.

Tears formed in his eyes. It was clear he'd been drinking, and I knew it was hard to control your emotions in that state. I wanted to cry, too.

"You don't know how lonely it is in my world," he whispered. "There's no trust. No honesty. You're the first shining star I've seen in so long. You're good and funny and beautiful. You say what you feel. You're a true person."

Tears streamed down my face. Nothing could change what he was, but I felt sorry for his sense of emptiness.

"There will always be a place for you in my heart, GuoGuo. And if you ever get into trouble or need a monster like me, just call and I will come." He gently ran his finger down my cheekbone. And then he was gone.

郭

"We need to have an important meeting," Ting announced, walking through the door with breakfast. She offered me tea, which I gladly accepted; another sleepless night.

"You know that my sister married a hairdresser last year, right?" Yang said, handing me chopsticks.

"Yes, so?" I said, confused.

"She and her husband have just opened a big salon in Changsha. She's offered to hire all of us. And not as trainees, but as professionals."

"This town is not good for us anymore. It's time to move on," Ting said.

"We would make so much more money," Yang continued.

"And it's not like you and I are getting raises anytime soon," Jin added, smirking at me.

Changsha was Hunan's capital and its largest city. It had an airport, a large train station, and no Guang. I momentarily thought of Chang, but he wasn't dangerous.

"I'm in," I said.

Yang clapped her hands. "I'll let my sister know. This will be so exciting!"

14

Mature Man

Moving to Changsha was both thrilling and bittersweet. Because Baba's Yuetang shop was now too far away to get to by bike, the only way to see my family was to take Ming's bus, which came only infrequently. But at eighteen, I was ready for a bigger life in a bigger city.

My friends and I moved in with Yang's sister, Annchi. Her Kaifu District salon was impressively large, and close enough to Nianjia Lake to attract wealthier customers. Ting, Jin, Yang, and I worked tirelessly winning clients for her; holding up signs outside her storefront, handing out fliers with discount coupons in Martyr's Park—anything we could think of.

Larger than Zhuzhou by far, Changsha had much to offer four wide-eyed country girls. Sleek glass and steel skyscrapers stood beside thousand-year-old ruins, zoos showcased panda bears and other strange animals, and hundreds of boats navigated the muddy waters of the wide Xiangjiang River, which cut through its heart.

To our disappointment, we soon learned that the larger the city, the more money it took to live in it. And though Yang's sister paid us decent wages, they weren't going any further. When we moved from Annchi's home to Juicaiyuan Residential District three months later, we were paying double our old rent for the same sized room we'd shared in Zhuzhou.

By 2002, computer access had become available to the residents of Hunan. Personal computers were extremely costly, but internet bars had sprouted up everywhere. For a little money, one could use a terminal to listen to music, play colorful games, and communicate with people from all over China. Because we couldn't afford to entertain ourselves any better than before, we visited these places often. And since I'd always enjoyed talking to people, I spent my time in chat rooms.

"So, I met this guy last night," I said to my friends, while painting seaweed cream on a client's face.

After wrapping a steamed towel around my client's wrinkled feet, Yang asked, "Is he handsome?" Always her first question about any man.

"How would I know? I met him in a chat room," I replied, pointing the clay infuser's steam towards her face.

"Why do you talk to those men?" Ting asked. "This guy could be a murderer like Guang. He could *be* Guang for all you know!"

"He could be perfect for her," Yang said, stretching her back until it popped loudly.

"Like the guy you dated last month?" Jin snidely asked.

"He told me he loved me," she whined petulantly, pulling another hot towel from the steamer.

"They all say that," Jin said, taking it from her, waving in the air several times, and then draping it over her client's face.

Neither Jin nor I were having much luck finding nice guys to date either. Even in this large place filled with single men, few were willing to put up with our candidness, and we were even less tolerant of their cheap lines.

"You never know," Yang said. "GuoGuo could have found an emperor's son."

"The emperors are all dead. Their sons are all dead. Wiped clean from China," Jin grumped, pushing too-long bangs from her eyes. Since we'd moved to Changsha, she'd already changed hairstyles three times.

"He could work for the government. That would set her up nicely," Yang continued, ignoring Jin.

"He's a businessman in Shanghai," I explained. "He said that I—*we* could start our own salon there, and he would help finance it."

Ting snorted. "And you believe that? Surely you are not so naïve." Ting's usual cheer had slowly bled away since moving to Changsha. Despite plenty of transportation options, her boyfriend visited less and less often. She still believed they would marry. I wasn't so certain anymore.

"I'm not moving to Shanghai," Yang said, shaking her head. "It's too far away from Hunan, and we're taking the word of a stranger. Even I see the danger in that. And what if he's not as handsome as you think?"

"*You* think," Ting said.

"What's this guy's handle? I want to check him out," Jin said.

"No."

郭

I became obsessed with "Mature Man," which was his handle, racing from work to Bayi Road's internet bar almost every night. I didn't know what he looked like—that technology wasn't available yet, but I was certain he was kind...and sincere...and, yes, handsome.

Fate has brought us together. It's destiny, and I want to help you, he wrote.

Having moved from rural Southern China to Shanghai, in just a few years' time, Fu—his actual name—had become very successful. And considering he was only a few years my elder, his story was inspirational.

Your words mean so much, I quickly typed back. *Tell me more about Shanghai.*

It's a shining city filled with very rich men who'll send their wives to the expensive spa you'll own, he wrote.

Fu had taken my simple vision of a small skincare salon and built it into a grand palace offering every conceivable service, and an army of workers to provide them. He said everything he proposed was easy in Shanghai, and that big dreams meant big money. My head filled with dreams, sleep often eluded me after our chats. And, of course, romantic fantasies sprouted from professional ones.

Businessmen like to pamper their girlfriends. Would you like to be pampered? You deserve it after the hard life you've had, he continued the following night.

Confused and wondering what he might mean, I wrote, *My life is good.*

Poverty is nothing to be ashamed of. I was poor once, remember? And look at me now. I know what it's like to be hungry, just as you've described it. GuoGuo, you deserve better.

I'd never met a rich man before, and this one understood me. We had so much in common. Other than coming from different provinces, our background was exactly the same.

Shanghai sounds wonderful, but I could never leave Hunan, I wrote.

My friends refuse to even consider moving there. They will only want a Changsha spa.

Changsha is a fine place if you never want much from life, he replied. *Shanghai is better. Shanghai is everything!*

Fu was awakening a desire for success I wasn't aware I'd had. *I'll tell them that,* I typed.

Tell them all you want, but they won't believe you. You're an excellent judge of character, and they wouldn't be your friends if they weren't nice girls, but they lack your ambition. Search your heart and you'll discover this. Was it always their dream to open a spa, or was it yours and they latched their hopes onto it? This happens sometimes.

Back in Zhuzhou, when I'd first shared my plans—how my mother had wanted a better life for me, how owning a spa would make her proud—they'd all been committed, Yang especially. But as time passed, they'd lost their enthusiasm. As I thought about it, I realized I was the only one who ever mentioned it anymore. Was Fu right? Had it always been just me?

If I left Hunan, my family would miss me terribly. My mother and I are close, I typed.

He replied, *Parents want the best for their children. They might not understand at first, but when you become a famous salon owner, your parents will be proud. With all of your riches, you can buy them things. I've showered my family and my village with banquets and gifts. The children run to my fancy car when I pull up to my parents' big house. The one I built for them.*

What he said amazed me. To buy my Mama beautiful clothes, a bigger house... To buy Baba a large truck for his recycling business—it would make him so happy. And Ming... Why, I would buy him a new motorcycle—or better, an entire fleet of buses! I would be so generous!

I was coming dangerously close to believing in this. And Fu and I... well, a match with a rich businessman would surely be one my family would approve of. Especially Wai po.

I have to confess something. I care for you, GuoGuo, Fu continued. *I know we haven't met, but I'm certain you are beautiful. I know who you are inside. Maybe better than anyone else. I really want to see you. Touch you... In person.*

Gasping, I pushed my chair back from the keyboard. He cared for me. He wanted to meet me! Oh, surely this is what love felt like.

"Are you crazy?" Jin said when I shared the news. "You don't love this guy. You don't even know him. What if he's misrepresented himself?"

"What if he hurts you?" Ting added.

"He's not going to hurt me. What kind of guy do you think he is?"

"That's just it. I don't know," she responded.

"You can judge him when you meet. I'm inviting him to Changsha!"

Yang threw her hands over her mouth to muffle her scream, then she grabbed my hands, and we danced in circles. I reached for Jin's arm, but she pulled away and sat down on her bed beside Ting.

"Why aren't you excited?" I said to them.

"This is a huge step, GuoGuo, and I'm not sure you've thought it through," Ting said.

"Fu means 'purity', and I'm certain his intentions are pure," I said crossly.

"Yeah, but look how 'glorious' Guang turned out to be," Jin said, rolling her eyes.

"I think this is a bad idea," Ting said gravely.

Jin shook her head. "Ting's right. This is a really, really bad idea."

My mind was so preoccupied with what I'd next say to Fu, that I rubbed warm massage oil on one client's face, and goat's milk facial scrub on another's feet. Though starving after work, I passed by the rice noodle restaurant without a glance, slipping through the internet bar door beside it.

Fu, I've been thinking about this a lot, and I want to meet you, too. My friends are worried that you aren't who you claim to be, but I only think good thoughts about you. So, would you like to come to Changsha?

I waited impatiently for him to respond. After a moment, I began biting my nails.

I'd like nothing more than to come to Changsha and see your beautiful face and meet your beautiful friends, but my business doesn't allow me much free time.

My heart sank, but before I had time to respond, another message popped up.

I think of you constantly. I dream of you. I must see you. Come to Shanghai. I'll wire you money for a train ticket and buy you beautiful things when you get here. Promise me you'll come.

Breathless, I wrote back, *I don't know. My parents would never allow it.*

You said you live far from your parents. We'll make this first visit a short one—just a few days. Your parents need not know. And if things work out the way I'm sure they will, they'll be happy when I finally meet them.

My friends won't like this, I replied.

They don't understand your heart as I do, and they're jealous of our love. They're jealous of your opportunity. If you tell them, it won't end well. Trust me. Let this be our secret.

Maybe he was right. Jin had never been in love, so she definitely wouldn't understand. Ting was jealous because her own relationship was crumbling. Yang would support me, though. She'd see it as I did. But a clandestine rendezvous seemed so romantic.

The Bank of China's Bayi Road branch was closing when I squeezed through the door. Fu had sent the money as promised, and I hurried to the internet café to make plans.

"Aren't you coming?" Ting asked as we left the salon the following evening. "It's karaoke night."

I shook my head. "I don't feel well. Go without me."

"But you love karaoke night!" Yang whined. "Who will sing your part?"

"Maybe try a different song. One for three people."

I turned away from their confused stares and bled onto the crowded sidewalk. Purchasing a yellow suitcase as instructed, I raced home and dumped everything I owned inside it. The door's slam echoed in the stairwell, chasing me as I flew back down the six flights.

Only in my wildest dreams had I ever imagined leaving Hunan, but the adventure of it all drove me almost as strongly as the love I felt for this man. As soon as the glass doors slid open, passengers flooded the train carriage. Lunging for a fourth-row seat the same instant as a grimacing old woman and a stocky businessman, the three of us wriggled into a space made for two. Suddenly, I was struck with the magnitude of what I'd done. My friends would see my flight as the ultimate betrayal, and my parents, if they found out, would lose their minds. But I was a grown woman, and this was my life!

The train lurched from the station before finding a steady rhythm. Sunset's dying embers ignited the city, my apartment building gleaming dully as we passed it. Sighing with relief; I smiled. My great journey had begun.

15

An Adventure

A horrible screech jolted me from sleep. Confused, I glanced around the compartment of placid faces coming to life after the many long hours. Sunlight fighting to penetrate the heavily fogged windows, I scrubbed a circle with my sleeve and peered outside. Shanghai was enormous!

Astounded by the great herd of passengers crowding the station—easily the size of Ningxiang's entire population—I stepped onto the cement platform, gawking at the skyline. So many buildings pierced the sky that it was a wonder it wasn't bleeding.

Jostled by those intent on getting onto my emptying train, I began searching for Fu. He'd instructed me to look for a tall man wearing a gray hat and red scarf. Many men wore gray hats, I discovered, and most looked tall to me.

From behind, a voice said, "Lady, look by your feet!" On the smooth, damp pavement lay a thick fold of money. "I can't reach it. Pick it up."

Quickly stepping on it so the bills wouldn't scatter, I asked, "Is it yours?" This seemed a lot of money for someone no older than me, a very skinny someone.

Offering a reassuring smile, he winked. "It is now. Tuck it in your pocket, and we'll find somewhere safe to count it."

"Maybe we should find its owner," I said.

The boy laughed loudly. "In this crowd? The first person you ask will claim it. Come on, no one will know."

"Move, girl," an old man behind me said, bumping me with his suitcase.

Having brought all my money with me, which was very little, I could use this. I glanced around. No one seemed to be searching for it, so I scooped it up.

"Here, your bag looks heavy, let me carry it for you," he said jovially. I followed him past the brightly lit kiosks and crowded ticketing office to the far edge of the platform outside the overhang. Taking the money from me, he began counting it. "Look at all this cash," he said, waving it in the air. "We are fortunate today. What will you buy with your half?"

My mind muddled from lack of real sleep, my body stiff from sitting for so long, and my eyes barely able to wrench themselves from the monstrous skyline threatening to devour us, I replied, "I really don't know."

"What's your name?" he asked amiably.

"Guo Hong Bo." I said, glancing at the mad swarm of passengers being disgorged from another train.

"Where are you from, Guo Hong Bo?"

"Um, Hunan Province," I replied absently.

"This is a fancy suitcase. Are you a rich girl?" My pants and shirt were no nicer than his, and I wondered how he could think such a thing.

"No. Not at all."

"Aw, I'll keep your secret. A train ticket from Hunan costs a lot of money. How much did you bring with you?" He seemed very excited all of a sudden, his speech hurried. "Are you alone?"

"Not exactly."

"Where are you staying?"

"I don't know. Can I have my share now?"

"Do you have family here?"

"Why are you asking me such personal questions?" I said, fully annoyed.

"What do you have in your bag?" he demanded, picking up my suitcase once more.

"Nothing of value. Hey, give it back!"

I reached for the handle, but he yanked it away. Stuffing the money in his pants pocket, he flung open the lid. Caught in a whoosh of cold air, my clean clothes scattered like dry leaves. Dropping to his knees, the boy began rummaging through the remnants, throwing things in all directions.

"Stop! What are you doing?" I yelled.

"You're not rich. Not worth my time," he spat, kicking my beautiful bag then disappearing into the crowd.

Hot tears dripped from my chin as I scampered around, plucking shirts, pants, and underwear from the filth and wiping them off as best I could. Here, I'd thought myself very brave for making this trip and certainly clever enough to handle myself in a city full of wealthy businessmen.

What if Fu thought I was a common thief like the one I'd just met; a girl pretending to be someone she was not? I hurried back to the disembarking area, searching frantically through the crowd for him.

Desperate to be seen, I climbed onto a bench and held my now scuffed yellow suitcase above my head. The woman seated by my feet yelled in some unintelligible dialect, but I ignored her. The relief I felt when I saw a waving hand and a red scarf waving in the breeze like a long kite tail was inexpressible.

I'd had so many dreams about Fu—his handsome and gentle face smiling down at me, his well-muscled arms pulling me against him in a loving embrace, his warm eyes full of intelligence and mischief—but nothing prepared me for the reality of finally meeting him. He wasn't handsome, which was fine, but he was ancient—at least my father's age. A petite eighteen-year-old, I must have looked like his daughter, rather than a girlfriend.

"GuoGuo, you are more beautiful than I imagined. What a lucky man I am." He opened his arms, and I hesitantly went to him, the scent of cigarette smoke and sharp male perfume stinging my nose.

"I'm lucky to see such a wonderful city," I said, swallowing my disappointment and smiling as brightly as I could.

"Sweet girl, you must be hungry after such a long trip. I'll take you to a special restaurant." Taking my bag, he led me through the grand glass-roofed station to the busy street outside, immediately hailing a taxi.

The restaurant was called McDonald's. He said it was American and very popular, though it didn't seem particularly nice with its uncomfortable seats and plastic trays. The pressed gray meat inside a coarse-textured bun that would have been better steamed, wasn't particularly appealing. Soaking his with soy sauce, Fu seemed to enjoy it very much.

Now that we were face to face, a wave of shy insecurity swept over me. Had he been twenty-five as he'd claimed rather than a sweating man with graying hair, I would have had no trouble making conversation. Instead, everything felt wrong; he'd lied to me. Though Jin had hinted at it, I hadn't considered this scenario, and I didn't know what to do—what I could do. The pittance I'd brought would in no way cover the price of a return ticket, and certainly my family and friends couldn't help me.

"You must be tired from your journey. Why don't we check into a hotel? We can spend some time getting to know one another." Wiping his mouth with a thin napkin, he grinned.

Well, I may have been a country girl, but I wasn't a stupid one. "I'm not tired at all. Where do you live? We can drop off my suitcase, and you can show me the city."

With a shrewd look, he said, "I'm sure you'd prefer a comfortable hotel room."

"You just want to have sex with me, don't you?" This was Guang all over again, only he'd been handsome.

Coughing, Fu looked away. "Well, I paid a lot for your ticket, and you chose to come. Surely you understood what kind of relationship I expected."

"I told you many times in the chatroom I was a good girl. I'm not looking for sex. I just wanted to meet you." I didn't tell him I had feelings for him—or rather the boy I'd spent so much time dreaming of. Taking another bite of my sandwich, I pondered how I might get out of this situation.

Squaring my shoulders, I said, "If all you want is sex, then please buy me another ticket so I can go home."

"You came to Shanghai to see the city and talk business. If you don't want sex, that's fine. We'll leave your case at the hotel, and I'll show you the sights. I feel strongly for you, GuoGuo. I want what's best."

郭

Shanghai was truly the place of dreams, and Fu was right; evidence of wealth was everywhere. Sidewalk masses engulfed us, and chaotic streets sang with car horns and motorcycle growls. Dizzying.

Fu ushered me through one shop after another, buying me shoes here, lychee-flavored candy there, a bracelet of woven cord. We devoured spiced skewered pork by the mighty Yangtze River and then toured a museum. And there were Westerners! I'd never seen a white person before in my life. With their round eyes and strange-colored hair, they looked so different. I wondered what Mama would think of them.

Fully exhausted and with feet aching from blisters, when Fu insisted on kissing me goodnight, I didn't argue. His lips were strong and demanding, and his gray stubble scratched me.

"Sleep well, sweet girl. I have a big surprise for you in the morning."

郭

It seemed only a moment had passed when a rap on my door wrenched me from sleep. "Get up, sleepyhead."

"I'm not dressed, Fu," I called back as my senses returned. "I'll meet you downstairs in a few minutes."

"Nonsense. You're safe with me."

"But I have no clothes on," I groaned, regretting the words immediately.

"A woman's body is nothing I haven't seen before. Open the door."

Quickly throwing on yesterday's wrinkled pants and stained shirt, I did as he asked.

"Good morning, sweet girl," he said, kissing my cheek. "Did you sleep well?"

"Yes, thank you," I replied, feeling anxious as his eyes traveled around the small room, finally landing on the bed, which was the only piece of furniture.

Setting a large suitcase on the floor beside him, he sank onto the thin mattress and patted the rumpled bedding. "Look, I brought hot tea for you," he said, raising a paper cup. As far across the room as possible, when I didn't move, he smirked. "Relax. I'm not going to attack you."

With great hesitation, I took the seat beside him.

"Oh, and there's a treat for you in my pocket." Spreading his arms, he smiled reassuringly. "Put your hand in and get it." When I looked at him dubiously, he said, "Go ahead, no snake will bite you."

Scooting closer, I slipped my fingers inside his suit coat, discovering a soft moon cake. Starved, I unwrapped the paper and took a large bite, savoring the preserves. All too soon, it was gone.

"Hm, I forget how much young girls eat." With an unsettling expression, he watched intently as I licked the sticky jam from my fingers.

"You have crumbs on your lip," he said, chuckling. "Here, let me get them for you." Before I could react, he trapped me in a powerful embrace and ran his tongue across my lips, finally pushing it inside my mouth. Chang had kissed me this way once, but his kiss had been hesitant and gentle. Fu's made me nervous.

"Mm, you taste delicious," he said, finally releasing me. "Like peaches."

Hopping up, I stepped away before he got any other ideas.

"I have another surprise for you, my little GuoGuo. I have meetings in a nearby town, and I want to take you with me."

"But I came to see Shanghai."

"This is better. And there's a spa at the resort. I'll introduce you to the owner. She'll be your first business contact."

Already so far from home, did it really matter if I went farther? Besides, I had no real choice.

"I'd like that," I said half-heartedly.

"Wonderful. Ah, but you can't wear those clothes on the train," he said, eyeing the ice cream drips on my chest. "I'm an important businessman. What would people think if they saw me traveling with a poorly dressed girl?"

I glanced towards my suitcase. The dirt-stained clothes inside weren't in any better shape.

With a knowing smile, he said, "I brought a gift to go with your new shoes." He placed his suitcase on the bed and opened it. I didn't step closer. "It's very nice, GuoGuo. You'll want it."

Withdrawing a beautiful silk qipao, he held it up for my inspection. Traditionally cut with fine embroidery, clusters of white and red blossoms spilled down the pink material like a great waterfall. I'd seen dresses such as this in expensive Changsha stores, but none so ornate. My face must have registered my joy.

"Yes, I thought you'd like it. Your figure will make it look even more beautiful. Put it on, sweet girl."

"Now?" I asked.

"Of course, now."

Without a bathroom or closet, there was no place to hide. "Could you step outside?"

"Change in front of me. I don't mind."

"But—"

Glancing at his watch impatiently, he said, "We can't miss our train. Put on the dress."

My insides shriveled. No man had seen me naked since I was a little child. I didn't want him watching me, but like this trip, what choice did I have?

Having hurriedly dressed with no thought of underwear, I was furious with myself for such an oversight. Bending down, I rifled through my suitcase for fresh panties, and then turned my back to him. Pulling the tight dress over my loose-fitting pants was an impossible task.

"GuoGuo, I am your boyfriend. Don't hide your body from me."

I was grateful there were no mirrors in the room. I would not have wanted to see my face after undressing. Goosebumps skidding across my bare stomach, I slipped on the dress as quickly as possible, struggling with trembling fingers to fasten the cloth buttons at my neck. I couldn't meet his eyes.

"Good girl. You look beautiful. Now, pack your bag."

郭

His business was taking us to Huzhou. I'd never heard of it, but China was a large country—larger than I'd ever realized. Though amazed by the river bordering Shanghai, when Lake Taihu came into view, I was certain it was as big as the China Sea.

We checked into a lovely hotel overlooking the lake. Never imagining a hotel room could be so luxurious, I gawked at a bed surely large enough for three people. Swimming through an ocean of colorful pillows, I crawled to its middle. The mattress was soft and very springy, and when I glanced at Fu, he nodded indulgently, the way my father often did. Squealing, I jumped twice and then bounced onto my bottom. My giggles stopped when I met Fu's hungry gaze.

"Such a nice bed," he said, sweeping away the many pillows as he made his way toward me. "You like it, do you?"

"Very much." Fearing the answer, I asked, "Where will you sleep?"

"It gets cold here at night. You'll need me to keep you warm."
His voice was that of a purring cat. "Besides, you can't expect an
important man like me to sleep on the floor, and I don't want you to,
either."

"I don't mind," I quickly said.

"You keep inching away. You are my girlfriend, GuoGuo. Let me
kiss you."

I didn't want his kisses, and I didn't like the way his eyes were
roaming over me. Suddenly grabbing my ankle, he pulled me
towards him. The hem of my dress didn't follow, and by the time I
was beside him, it was nearly at my hips.

"Such pretty legs," he said, running his sweaty hand over my skin.
He pressed his lips to mine, and as his tongue wiggled around in my
mouth like a snake, his fingers slithered inside my underwear. I tried
moving away, but he rolled on top of me, pinning me to the mattress.

Breaking from his rough mouth, I cried out. "I'm a good girl. I
don't want this."

"You'll like it. It feels very good, see?" He pushed his finger inside
me, and I gasped, clamping my thighs together.

"Relax, I know what I am doing. I'll teach you to be a woman."

"No!"

"Sweet GuoGuo, this is what people do when they're in love."
Pressing me deeper into the padding, he unbuckled his belt and then
pried my legs apart. "Let me show my love for you."

郭

Ting had been right; it didn't take long. When he finished his
bucking and panting, he rolled onto his back and zipped up his pants.

Quickly standing, I pulled my dress down and then gasped at the blood staining the sheet. What had he done?

Fu looked up at me, a gloating smile spreading across his face. "You've given me what you can never give another."

I cried after he left for his meeting. Regardless of his words, I hadn't *given* him anything. Staring through the window as I paced the generous room, I pondered my situation. In the short run, with no money, I was at his mercy. But of greater concern was the future. Conservative parents had raised me with traditional values, and I was like-minded. Fu and I had had relations. We would marry. I sighed, resigning myself to this fate. This was my life now.

When he returned that evening, he was buoyant and smelled of beer. I didn't bother fighting him this time, but I liked it no better. Curling into a ball, I slept in one corner of the bed, trying not to touch him, hoping he wouldn't want more relations, though I knew he would.

The following morning over breakfast, I said, "You'll like my father. He's a self-made businessman like you."

Grunting, he continued reading the Shanghai newspaper he'd brought with him.

"I'd like to get married in my village, so my whole family can be there. You said your family is from Liuzhou. It's not so far for them to come, is it? And I must meet your mother, of course. Do you think she'll approve of me?"

Collecting his briefcase, he stood. "I'll be gone all day. Stay out of trouble."

I hadn't left this room since arriving, so I wandered the hotel, admiring the gold lettering on the outside wall, the serene bamboo garden by the entrance, and the fancy upholstered chairs in the lounge.

"Excuse me, where's the spa?"

The reservationist raised her eyebrows and then shook her head. "This resort has no spa, but there's one in town. Would you like me to call a taxi?"

"No," I said, feeling even smaller. How could I have been such a fool to believe him? He was going to be a terrible husband.

Wandering down the long pathway to the sandy shore, I wondered if I should just drown myself now. The lapping green water at my feet faded to blue in the distance, becoming nearly the same color as the sky where they finally met. Though tight buds had formed on the cherry trees, the breeze was chilly.

Lost in thought, I watched a swan couple swim by; the female lagging well behind the male. Aware of voices whose words made no sense, I looked up to find two Westerners strolling by. Both men smiled at me, and one spoke, though I couldn't understand him. His blue eyes were so strange—as exotic as his sandy brown hair. I spent the next hours trying to mimic his words.

Needing certainty about our future, after sex that night, I asked Fu, "When do you want to marry? I was thinking maybe this summer when the flowers are blooming. It will be beautiful in my village then." Instead of replying, he rolled over, putting his back between us.

Fu was gone before I awoke and returned late that evening. With nothing to do but walk by the lake and flip through travel brochures in the lobby, I'd become desperately bored. I missed home, my friends, and the peace work provided. That night when Fu climbed into bed without touching me, I knew something was wrong.

"Are you unhappy with me?" I asked the next morning, forcing myself awake when I heard him open the newspaper.

"You could never do anything wrong, sweet girl. I love you," he said, taking a drag from his cigarette. "I'm just very busy with my job. Come sit on my lap."

Unbuttoning my shirt, he ran his hands over my skin, pinching and squeezing my breasts. Though I didn't enjoy it, I was becoming accustomed to his touch. "I have business in another town, and I'll be gone for several weeks. It's going to be boring for you, and we won't have much time to spend together. I'll buy you a ticket home," he said, unzipping his pants. "When my business is finished, I'll send for you. Then we can talk about marriage."

We had breakfast together afterward. Before leaving for the day, he slid a packet across the table. "Make tea with this. It will keep you from becoming pregnant."

I hadn't even thought about children, and I certainly wasn't ready for one at this young age. I drank three pots of that tea just to be on the safe side.

郭

"I'm getting married!" I announced as I walked into the apartment.

My friends swarmed around me. "We've been so worried!" Ting said, squeezing me tightly to her chest. "You disappeared without a trace."

"We thought someone had kidnapped you," Yang cried.

"Except that all your clothes were gone," Jin added snidely. "You went to see him, didn't you?"

I dropped my eyes. "Yes."

Jin put her hands on her hips. "And you didn't even think to leave us a note?"

"I'm sorry about that, but I was in a hurry. Besides, I was afraid you wouldn't let me go if you knew, and I...well, I needed to do this."

"We aren't your parents, GuoGuo," Ting said, stepping back. "We're your friends. We're your sisters. You should have told us this."

"I know that now," I said, feeling miserable on so many levels.

Jin finally pulled me into her arms. "You can be angry or you can thank us, but either way, we called your brother."

"You did what?" I gasped, unable to breathe.

"We thought you were dead!" Yang said, far too dramatically.

Sliding down the wall, I dropped my head into my hands. "What did he say?"

After a moment, Ting sighed. "He wasn't happy."

"He'll forgive me when he learns I'm engaged," I said, wanting desperately for it to be true.

"So, what's this Shanghai guy like?" Jin softly asked, sinking to the floor beside me.

I shrugged. "He's fine, I suppose." I glanced towards the window as a train rumbled by. "But you'll all be part of the wedding ceremony!" I said, trying very hard to look happy, to be happy. Jin simply raised her eyebrows.

"What was Shanghai like?" Yang asked dreamily.

"Enormous and very crowded. Fu took me to a resort with a lake so wide I couldn't see the other side."

"It sounds romantic," Yang said.

"Did you have sex?" Jin asked bluntly.

I felt my face turn red. "Yes."

"What was it like?" Yang asked.

"What do you mean, what was it like?" Jin snapped, glaring at her. "It's not like you haven't had sex before."

"That was a secret!" she hissed.

"From who? Everybody knows. Why do you think all those playboys keep sniffing around?"

"They aren't playboys. They're nice guys. It just... well, it never seems to work out for me," she whispered.

Turning back to me, she said, "So, you're in love then?"

"Well, no, not exactly in love. But we are getting married." I busied myself slipping off my uncomfortable shoes, not wanting to meet anyone's eyes, not wanting them to see my disappointment.

"So why d'you come back then?" Ting asked sharply, suddenly seeming angry.

"He's got a big business deal. He was worried I'd be bored. He'll send for me," I huffed, secretly grateful not to be cooped up in another hotel, no matter how pretty.

Yang knelt beside me on the red braided mat we used as a rug. Gently pulling back my hair, she looked at my earlobes, and then examined my fingers. "What did he give you for an engagement gift?"

"Nothing yet. But I'm sure it will be nice."

"He has money, right?" Jin asked, giving Ting a meaningful look. Ting dropped her reddened eyes.

I realized suddenly that she was still in her ratty sleep shirt. On weekends, Ting was the first one up, often back from the market before we realized she was gone. She never went back to bed.

"Are you sick?" I asked her.

Moaning, Ting rolled over and covered her face.

"She's not sick," Yang whispered. "Her parents just discovered her boyfriend comes from a poor family. They forced her to break up with him. She's been crying for days."

郭

Every evening, I rushed to the internet bar, hoping Fu was online. At first, I reminded myself of how busy he'd been at the lake, but anxiety was rapidly replacing understanding. I needed comfort and reassurance.

I didn't love Fu, but maybe there were more important things than love. Perhaps financial security, the opportunity to painlessly fulfill my spa dream, the better life my mother so often talked of... these things should be considered. We'd shared a bed together for many nights. I thought about that often. He'd made me feel special in his own way, he'd told me he loved me, and maybe I liked his touch more than I realized. Marrying Fu was the right thing to do, and I would learn to love him... in time.

I began leaving him long messages, relaying stories of my clients, and telling him more about my family—how Wai po would finally love my mother because I was marrying such a successful man, and how my father would appreciate his business advice. I told him what Ting's parents had done and asked all kinds of questions about his work. Since we'd spent far more time on sex than conversation during the trip, I believed these notes would help fix what we had lost, take us back to a time when we'd flirted and talked for hours.

Two weeks passed without a reply. Hoping he hadn't been in an accident and refusing to believe he was ignoring me, I stood in line outside the internet bar for more than an hour. Waiting in line is part of being Chinese. There are always too many people and not enough of whatever it is you want. I wormed into a chair as soon as a young guy stood. He said something unkind, but I didn't care. I had important business. My future husband may have left a message for me. Didn't he understand that?

Logging in, I immediately went to our chat room. A message

symbol popped up: a little envelope. My hands shaking suddenly, I took a deep breath and then clicked the mouse.

GuoGuo,

I've read all of your messages. You're a good girl, and I enjoyed our time together, but I do not love you. I have a wife, and I will not leave her to marry a girl younger than my own daughter. Don't contact me again.

-Fu

Devastated, I stumbled from the bar. Horns blared angrily as I crossed the street without looking. The choppy river of shoppers spilling from the market tossed me back and forth like a little raft.

With barely the strength to climb the many flights of stairs, I staggered through my apartment door, falling face-first on my hard bed. Overwhelmed by sadness and unable to eat or sleep, I lay in there for three days straight.

"You've got to get up," Ting said gently. "We've made excuses for you at work, but Yang's sister will fire you if you don't come in tomorrow. This will pass. See, I'm already smiling again."

Ting may have worn a mask of happiness, but her eyes could not hide her pain. I soon understood how she handled grief. At night, she sang karaoke with abandon. At work, she smiled too brightly and chattered all day—more so in the last weeks than ever before. It was as if she were floating in a pond, moving her arms and legs wildly just to keep her serene face above the surface.

I was not so refined as Ting, and not a good enough actor to mimic Yang's eternal optimism. I gravitated to Jin, who spat nothing but venom. Thanks to her, my sadness was soon replaced by indignation.

"He took advantage of you," Jin said, storming in circles around our apartment.

"Right!"

"He took advantage of your innocence and your inexperience with men."

"Yes," I seethed.

She flipped her bangs from her eyes before continuing. "He got you to tell him all about your life, and then decided you were a juicy country plum ready to be plucked and bitten into."

"Absolutely!"

Over the next few days, my anger grew to simmering rage.

"Jin, I have a plan," I said when we were alone.

"Yeah?"

"I'm going back to Shanghai to kill Fu."

She smiled widely. "That's the spirit."

What Jin didn't realize—what none of them did—was my sincerity. I really was going to kill that guy. The next day, I quit my job.

"What are you doing?" Ting asked, realizing I was packing my suitcase.

"I'm going home. I have to make lots of money so I can go back to Shanghai. Here's the rest of this month's rent. It's all I have."

"Are you crazy?" Jin said, picking up the money and pressing it back into my hand.

"Maybe," I replied, smiling. "Fu took something very precious from me, and he will pay for what he stole."

"But what about your plans for opening your own spa? You can't just pack up and move to Shanghai and forget all of that," Yang said. Her voice was thick with tears.

In a strange way, I think Ting understood. "Your heart will heal," she whispered, embracing me. "And then you can come back to us."

16

Gangsters

Ming's silver bus stopped with a hiss, and the many passengers filed out, hugging their bundled belongings. After helping several old ladies to the curb, he collected the tickets from his next customers as they boarded. I was beyond grateful that my parents weren't waiting when I stepped onto the bus; this had been my greatest fear. Nevertheless, it was a long tense trip back to Ningxiang. Though I sat right behind Ming, he barely acknowledged me until the bus was empty and parked behind his shop.

"Where were you, Mei Zi? Tell me!" he suddenly burst out.

"I was having an adventure," I said defensively.

"An adventure?" Crossing his arms, he glared at me. "Without telling Baba and Mama, without telling me, without telling your closest friends? You had them worried sick."

I dropped my eyes. "I feel bad about that."

"You should feel very bad." His eyes then flicked to my suitcase. "Who is he?"

"Who? What are you talking about?" My friends swore they hadn't mentioned Fu to Ming, and I had no intention of confessing.

"Young girls don't take all their belongings in the middle of the night and go on adventures by themselves. Men persuade girls to go on adventures. Trust me on this."

"You don't understand."

"I *do* understand. Your friends said you've been talking to people online. You don't know who you're talking to. You could be taken advantage of."

It was as if Ming was reading my mind. "I'm fine. I came back, and I am fine. I can take care of myself."

He snorted. "Next time you want to go on an adventure, you inform me first."

I needed to prepare myself. "You didn't tell Baba, did you?"

"No," he said, looking away, "but you should." Then taking my arm, he roughly escorted me from the bus and then drove me home on his motorcycle. I'd missed the smell of the countryside. I'd missed home and Mama's welcoming smiles.

That night was the first in which I'd slept well since Fu damaged my soul, and I awoke the next morning feeling lighter.

"You seem different," Mama said, tilting her head.

Too ashamed to let her know I'd had relations, I cringed, refusing to meet her eyes.

"You're tired of city life? You want to come home and be a farmer like me?" She began braiding my hair.

"No, I'm a spa girl. I'll live here and work in town. I'll also get a second job, so I won't be home much. I'm sorry, but I won't be able to help you with farming chores."

"Well, you haven't helped me for a long time, so nothing changes," she said, chuckling. "You're so skinny. Have you eaten nothing since the Spring Festival? I made congee for you."

Congee is rice gruel, into which people sometimes add vegetables and small bits of meat. It's usually given to babies, but for me, eating it was like coming home. Perhaps by cooking this dish, Mama was telling my stomach that she'd missed me.

郭

Yang's sister had been kind. Through her many connections, she'd secured a position at a small Ningxiang spa for me—yes, Ningxiang was slowly modernizing. Annchi must have told them I was an expert because they acted very grateful to have me.

I quickly found a second job as a nighttime grocery store stocker. Working so many hours between the two, I felt as if I were back in the binlang factory. At least in these jobs, no one slapped me but myself, and that was on the inside. I couldn't believe how stupid I'd been, believing in Fu. I would never trust another man with my heart.

Getting rich quickly was more difficult than I'd expected, but by eating at home and living rent-free, I was slowly accumulating the sum I needed to return to Shanghai; my vengeance money.

On Saturday nights, I spent time with my cousin, Chen, who gambled in the back of a Ningxiang butcher shop. I didn't care for the smell, but the chilled air felt wonderful during summer's reign.

Chen taught me how to play cards and promised I could make good money if I won. The game I liked best was called "Kill the Landlord." Three players were farmers and the fourth, the landlord. In this two-card deck game, if the landlord lost, he had to pay the farmers. If he won, they paid him.

Chen was a friendly and generous person, but he gambled with rough men. Many wore gold chains around their necks, and most spoke crudely, but they all had plenty of cash in their pockets. I couldn't risk losing much, so only a few people were willing to play with me. Even so, in time, I became fairly good. One Saturday night, several men—one of whom reminded me very much of Guang—convinced me to play with them. I think they assumed I was looking for a boyfriend, despite Chen's warnings that I was off-limits.

Clearly flirting, they let me win the first few games. In less than an hour, I had more money than I could've earned in a month at both my jobs combined. I was wise enough to know they'd want their money back if I kept winning, so I told them I had to go home to help my mother.

"Ah, you come back and play with us again. Maybe you'll not be so lucky next time," one said, laughing.

Waving back, I rode away, knowing I was that much closer to Shanghai. Unfortunately, things easily gained are also easily lost.

郭

With no local competition, Ming's bus business had been thriving for some time. Recently, however, a man named Xian had purchased a bus and started his own line. By charging slightly less, Xian began stealing Ming's customers. I'd not seen so for myself, but it was rumored that Xian never cleaned the interior and drove recklessly. Regardless, in China, saving money is everything.

Working in the grocery store late one evening, a boy ran in, shouting about a fight. In such a small town, with little to do for entertainment other than watch chili pepper-eating contests, the street quickly filled with spectators. Yelling back to the store owner, I followed the boy to the loosely formed circle's edge.

Over the commotion and shouting, I asked, "What happened?"

"Someone cut the bus driver's tires. He's accusing the other bus driver," the boy said, jumping up and down excitedly. I didn't need to hear anymore before pushing through the crowd.

Shouting and cursing had already escalated to shoving and kicking. Xian threw the first punch, hitting Ming in the shoulder. My brother replied with a fist to Xian's chest, causing him to stagger back. Ming was the taller of the two, and I'd seen him win plenty of fights, so I wasn't too concerned. Ming laughed when his next punch cut Xian's lip. "That'll teach you to cut a man's tires."

Xian lunged for Ming then, and soon they were rolling on the ground like weasels. Like many others, I was egging Ming on, until two of Xian's friends stepped into the circle. One pulled Ming's arms back, and the other hit him in the stomach. I knew that with three against one, Ming would be badly hurt, so I raced back to the grocery and called Chen.

"You must come now. Ming's in a fight, and I'm afraid for him."

Within moments, my cousin's motorcycle skidded to a halt, and he tore through the crowd, diving into the melee without reservation.

Strong from farming, Chen was also good with his fists, and the fight seemed to be turning in their direction. Suddenly, Xian pulled something from his pocket. With the flick of a finger, a shiny blade appeared. Someone yelled, "Knife!" and the crowd fell away. A good fight was one thing, a vicious attack was something else entirely.

Before Ming could defend himself, Xian's knife struck his head. Blood gushed down his face, dripping from his wet and matted bangs into his eyes. The cut was deep; white bone showed above a thick slice of skin, flopping like a piglet's ear. When Chen pulled Xian off my brother, the other men drew knives as well. Realizing this had become a life or death struggle, I jumped into the fray and helped my cousin drag Ming away.

With his arms draped over our shoulders, Chen and I jogged as quickly as possible to the nearby hospital. With so much blood loss, Ming's legs were rapidly losing their strength, which made carrying him very difficult. When he became too heavy to hold, I yelled over to Chen for more help. That's when I noticed the shiny blood on Chen's pale face.

Barely making it through the hospital doors before both men collapsed on the floor, I screamed, "Help, my brother's been attacked!"

"Do you have money?" the front desk nurse blandly asked.

In China, hospitals will only treat you if you can pay upfront. They will let you die like a dog in the street if you don't have the cash.

Though my revenge funds were safely stored in my room, I still had the winnings from last night's gambling game in my little pouch. Pulling it from inside my shirt, I emptied the contents onto the counter—every coin. The nurse took her time counting it while my brother and cousin lay bleeding at her feet.

"Is it enough?" I asked, staring helplessly at the scene.

"Barely," she replied after a moment.

郭

Terrified for my brother's life, I paced in the surgery waiting area, biting my nails. This situation was horrible, and I had to get word to my parents. Though it felt like hours, only a short time had passed before angry voices echoed from the lobby. Assuming there was another emergency, I casually peered down the hall. The emergency was of a different sort: Xian and his friends had arrived. With wild eyes, Xian repeatedly called out Ming's name. Sprinting to the operating room, I burst inside.

In the midst of sewing Ming's skin back together, one doctor glanced up at me. Ming's face was as white as his bone had been, and he was moaning, though I doubted he was conscious. Chen, who was lying on the table beside him, smiled and pointed to his stitches.

"Hey, little cousin, do you like my new look?"

"Stay still," a nurse ordered, struggling to bandage his wound; when my cousin gets excited, he flaps his arms about like a giant stork.

"Xian and his men are here!"

"In the hospital?" Sitting up immediately, his face paled. The nurse tried pushing him back down, but he swept her away.

"We have to hide Ming!"

Clearly, the surgeons were in no way finished with their work. One told us to be quiet. Though a yellow mask covered his nose and mouth, his eyes were ones I'd stared dreamily into for an entire summer.

"Chang?"

"GuoGuo?" He looked from Ming's bloody face to mine. "This is your brother?"

"Yes." The sting of his rejection had long passed, and under other circumstances, I would have enjoyed hearing about his life as a studying doctor. Instead, I said, "The guys who did this are searching the hospital for him. You've got to help us!"

"Draw the curtains around us," he ordered, nodding to the fabric folds beside him.

Before I could complete my task, the doors flew open, and Xian and his friends marched in, brandishing knives.

Chang and the other surgeon yelled at them to leave, but my stupid cousin, incapable of fighting though he was, began calling them names and threatening Xian. Anger further twisted Xian's features, and he lunged for Chen, punching him in the face. Blood spurted out of Chen's nose, and his stitches split open.

Several orderlies rushed in, getting between Xian and Chen, and a nurse shouted that the police were on their way. Only after hearing sirens did Xian and his friends flee.

I left to find a phone.

郭

Mama sat with Ming throughout the night, Auntie Song camped in the waiting room, a small ax in her lap, and Baba, gripping a large tire iron, guarded the recovery room door. They had given Ming medicine to sleep, but Chen, who was in far better shape, was wide awake.

"Xian knew he would lose. That's why he pulled the knife in the first place. He's a cheat."

"You need to rest," I said.

"If I'd just lunged to the right instead of left, I could have protected Ming. I'll make this right, GuoGuo. For the family. I vow it!"

When his litany began round four, I left to check on Ming.

Chang stepped out of Ming's room perhaps an hour later. After speaking to my father, he turned to me. "GuoGuo, I only have a moment, but I wanted to say that it's good seeing you. You look well."

I laughed. "I'm in an ugly uniform stained with blood."

He shrugged. "You still look nice."

"I heard you got married."

"I did," he said. "To that girl I met in school." I was tempted to say something scornful, but it seemed childish, especially after he'd cared for my brother. "Listen, I'm sorry about the way I acted that summer. I was young and stupid," he said softly.

"Mostly stupid," I replied, smiling.

He laughed. "Very stupid."

A nurse stuck her head into the hallway and called to him.

He reached out to touch my arm, but then stopped himself. "Take care, GuoGuo. I hope your brother heals quickly."

郭

They discharged Ming the following afternoon. Baba's bike fitted with a large flat cart, he and Mama wrapped Ming in blankets and loaded him onto it. The long trip home was challenging, and with every bump, Ming moaned. More family had joined us at the hospital and, walking or riding bikes, we followed Ming in a slow procession back to our mountain village.

For the next few days, it seemed someone was always at the door. Ming's friends came often, and Chen visited several times each day. One evening, he brought a group of tough-looking men—one with whom I'd gambled. Listening to them talk, I soon realized they were gangsters, and that Chen had enlisted their services. They were going to kill Xian!

In China, justice was both complicated and simple. If you had a powerful government connection, you could basically do whatever you wanted, especially in the countryside. You could kill a person and go unpunished. If you had no such connection, the same crime would see you sentenced to death. Xian's uncle worked for the government. Unfortunately, our family fell into the second category.

When Mama overheard their plans, she stepped in. "You cannot do this, Chen. If you're caught, you'll be killed. What will your father do then? Who will tend his crops? Who will feed him and his young stepchildren? Consider you may bring trouble to us as well."

One gangster laughed. "We do this all the time. We won't get caught." He sounded just like Guang, and I shivered; we had killers sitting under our very roof. I couldn't ignore the fact that my personal goal was to murder Fu, but that was completely different.

"Let us feed you dinner. We can discuss this with our bellies full. We have binlang," Mama lied. "Won't you have some?" Glancing at me, she jerked her chin toward the door, and I rushed to Wai po's; she had some. I then burst into our chicken coup, grabbing the first bird I saw.

I worked quickly, and soon delicious smells filled the house. We ate and talked late into the night. When a man pulled out cards, we played for money; I made sure to lose.

"You must be our guests tonight. Mei Zi is an excellent cook, as you can see. She'll make a delicious breakfast for you," Mama announced as they prepared to leave.

It took Mama three days to convince Chen and the gangsters not to go after Xian. I used all our best spices and oils, and she spent a great deal of money on beer, expensive cigarettes, and binlang for those men. I don't know what he traded to get them, but Baba even brought gold chains to thank them for their kind concern, though they really didn't know my brother at all. Ming wanted revenge as badly as my cousin, but for once, he listened to Mama, deciding mending a bruised ego was not worth dying for.

郭

It was Ming's season to get into trouble. Though healing well, he now had bigger problems. And those problems showed up at our door one evening.

Midway through dinner, with my grandparents and Auntie Song as guests, the sound of pounding fists interrupted us. Baba marched to the door and threw it open. "Who are you, and what do you want?"

After much yelling, a large group of men and women crowded into our little kitchen. Behind them, a timid-looking JiaoJiao cowered. My brother wasn't a playboy exactly, but he liked women very much, and I'd seen them together several times. She was older than him by four years, which I thought strange since men tended to prefer younger women. That thought took me to Fu and all the money I still needed to complete my mission.

When our eyes met, I noticed JiaoJiao's were rimmed in red, and her face was very pale. Ming's face had taken on a similar shade.

"Your son had relations with my daughter. They've conceived a child. He must marry her now," said the man I assumed was JiaoJiao's father. The rest of her family glared at Ming. Mama turned and glared at him as well.

My brother did not dishonor JiaoJiao by suggesting she'd been with other men. From the look on his face, he knew he was the father. Though plenty old enough, Ming was not ready to get married—he'd said so many times. Still, I gloried in the thought of a wedding celebration. Moreover, it was time for someone other than my mother to take care of him.

Weddings in the Chinese countryside are very exciting. Days before the ceremony, the bride and groom are separated. On their wedding day, the groom arrives at the bride's home with many gifts for her family. He then transports her to the ceremony in a decorated cart. For Ming's wedding, my cousins and I decorated JiaoJiao's cart with red material, colored paper, and flowers.

Sometimes, the bride's family and friends give the groom a hard time. JiaoJiao's bridesmaids would not let Ming into the house until he'd bribed each of them with red envelopes filled with money. Ming was then forced to kneel before JiaoJiao and sing the song, "I Will Love You For One-thousand Years." It would have been romantic, except Ming was not planning to love her for one-thousand years. He didn't love her now, and he didn't want to be a father.

Country people are poor and don't have nice clothes. Rather than elegant and coordinating bridesmaids' gowns, JiaoJiao's girls simply wore their best dresses. Since I was from the groom's family, I didn't get to participate in the ceremony, but JiaoJiao was kind and gave me a beautiful pair of white shoes as a gift. Though they fell apart a week later, I felt so honored to have them.

After the official proceedings have concluded, the father-in-law traditionally dresses up in a silly costume. Wearing women's underwear on his head or around his chest to symbolize that he's had an affair with the bride, he acts heartbroken that she's married his son. Baba, wearing Mama's bra and the bright red lipstick I'd borrowed from the spa, looked appropriately ridiculous as, in mock grief, he pulled JiaoJiao's cart to the reception.

郭

With each passing week, I felt more driven to return to Shanghai. In many ways, Ming's wedding had spurred me on, forcing me to dwell on my foolish assumption of marriage. I was grateful that I hadn't become pregnant like JiaoJiao. Unlike my brother, who had integrity enough to take responsibility for his actions, I was certain Fu would not have behaved honorably.

By summer's end, I'd made up most of what I'd lost paying Ming's hospital bill. Unfortunately, Ming had exhausted his savings on the wedding, and with a child on the way, there was nothing left for me.

"I'm sorry, Mei Zi. I feel miserable about this. I'll find a way to pay you back."

I shook my head. "Consider it my wedding gift to you and JiaoJiao, and an auntie present for the baby, who you'll name after me."

"I'll name him Guo," he said, smiling.

Leaning back against the pigpen, I rolled my eyes. "Of course, you will."

17

Big Dreams

Ningxiang's only internet bar was near the salon, and there I communicated with my Changsha friends often. I also visited chat rooms when I had time. In one of these, I met a Guangzhou farm boy named Chao, who worked in Shanghai. Unlike Fu, who'd also claimed to be from a farming community, I knew Chao was not lying because I quizzed him on crops and animals and things a city person simply would not know.

June peanuts taste best, don't you think? I wrote.

What? You don't harvest peanuts until their leaves turn yellow in late summer. Are you sure you're a country girl? he replied, to my satisfaction.

Chao never talked about love and romance, or how rich and important he was. Instead, he confided that he'd quit school and moved to Shanghai to find work and that he sent all his earnings home to care for his sick mother. This happened a lot; Southern China people are especially poor.

Chao seemed very genuine, even admitting that he was younger than me, which is not something a man trying to impress a woman would do. Slowly, I began trusting his sincerity.

I'm thinking of moving to Shanghai, I typed.

Oh, it's good here. Lots of jobs for farm people. I could help you. My factory is always hiring, and there's another one down the road.

Do you have connections? I asked.

No, I just work on a line. I'm not an important person. Want me to ask around to see which departments are hiring? He wrote.

Yes, I would appreciate that. I replied.

Great! I'll let you know tomorrow.

This was wonderful news for me. Other than Chao, I didn't know a soul in Shanghai, and because of this, I had little hope of getting a spa job. Fu had called Shanghai the city of opportunity. I knew his promises were empty, but he'd struck a match to my paper dreams and set them ablaze! And if I succeeded in my mission and wasn't arrested for murder, I would become successful to spite his ghost.

One afternoon, when I was feeling especially brave, I went to my father's Ningxiang shop; I was ready to buy my Shanghai train ticket. Chao's latest intel regarding his factory's job postings and his ongoing assurances that the wages there would be plenty ample to support me further bolstered my confidence.

"Baba, I've made a decision. I'm moving to Shanghai."

My father threw back his head and laughed. "You're funny today, Mei Zi. Hand me that wrench."

"No, I'm serious. I have a job waiting for me."

He set down the mangled piece of metal he was wrestling with and gave me his full attention. "How do you have a job so far away?"

"A person I know got it for me. I'm expected next week," I replied, squaring my shoulders.

"Who's this person? How do you know someone in Shanghai?"

"A friend. I met him online."

Baba snorted. "He's not a real person then."

"He is," I said, stamping my foot.

"What kind of job?"

"A factory one," I answered. "It's very legitimate."

"You're a trained spa worker. What kind of factory is this?"

"One that makes things," I said, biting my lip.

Leaning against the rusting pole beside him, Baba crossed his arms over his chest and raised his eyebrows. "What things?"

I wasn't sure about that. Chao had said he attached pieces of plastic together, but it had not seemed important to ask further. I remained silent.

"How much will they pay you?" he asked after a moment. I didn't have an answer for that either. When I didn't respond right away, he shook his head and picked up the wrench once more. "You don't have a job."

"I will when I get there. Baba, I'm a grown woman, and this is what I've decided!"

Suddenly, he threw the wrench across the room, toppling over an electric lamp base. "You are not a grown woman. You're a little girl, and you will get hurt. Big cities are dangerous. Have you not been paying attention? The SARS virus is everywhere! You're not going."

"I *am* going."

"How will you get there?" Baba demanded.

"I have money for a train ticket."

"Do you have money for food?"

"Not exactly."

"What about a place to live?"

I huffed. "Not yet."

"I will give you no money for this," he said, wiping his hands on his dirty pants.

I hadn't intended to ask him for any. Buying off Chen's gangsters had been costly, and the wedding had further bled my parents. What I'd wanted more than anything was his blessing, but we were cut from the same cloth of tempers.

"Fine. I'll starve to death. I'll sleep on the street like an animal. Is that what you want?"

"I'm your father, and I say you won't go."

"I'm my own person!" I seethed. "I have dreams. I'm doing this whether you like it or not."

His face reddened with anger. "If you go, you won't be my daughter anymore!" he yelled.

"Then, I won't be your daughter!" I yelled back. Though my temper came from him, my stubbornness came from Mama. We stood staring at one another for a very long time. Finally, he withdrew his wallet and emptied it; bills fluttered to the dirty cement floor and coins rolled in all directions.

"Don't come back here when you fail. You are not a Guo. You don't live here anymore." And with that, he stormed out, the sheet metal door quivering behind him.

Mama cried when I told her I was leaving. Though she begged me not to go—using the same arguments as Baba—I refused to listen. In her entire life, she'd never traveled farther than the shop in Yuetang. She didn't understand big cities as I did. And she'd made it clear, often enough, that she'd not spent all those years working for my tuition so I could pick beans and peanuts all my life. After cooking an enormous meal the following day, she wrapped up the leftover rice cakes and tucked them in my bag.

"Be careful in that place. Remember, you are a water pig sign—very trusting. This is your nature, and it's a good trait, but also your weakness. Here," she said, retrieving the money pouch she took to market. "It's not much, I know, but it's all that I have. Keep it safe with you and don't spend it frivolously. Use it for food. Use it for medicine. Use it to survive."

I threw my arms around her neck and hugged her fiercely. "Thank you, Mama. I'll make you proud."

"You'd better," she laughed, wiping her eyes.

Since Xian had destroyed my brother's livelihood, Ming now worked for Baba, who didn't bother saying goodbye. Climbing onto the back of Ming's motorcycle, we made the long trip to Changsha's train station.

"I'm proud of you, Mei Zi," he said, squeezing my arm. "You have Mama's strength and courage. You'll do well for yourself if you stay away from men and their promises. And no more adventures, eh?"

"No more. I promise this."

"GuoGuo!" my friends screamed when they saw me. Yang's eyes immediately flicked to my brother's.

"He's married now, remember?" I whispered in her ear.

"But he's so handsome," she sighed longingly.

"Won't you stay one night?" Ting asked after Ming shot out into traffic.

"Our new roommate can sleep on the floor," Jin added.

I shook my head. "I need to go. Someone's meeting me in the morning." Ting doled out a motherly look. "A nice person," I added. "A friend."

"Dinner then?" Yang asked.

I fished out my rice cakes. "No money."

"Our treat," Jin said. The other girls nodded.

郭

Chao was waiting for me as promised. Unlike Fu, he had not lied about his age. Tall and lanky, his eyes twinkled, and his smile could have lit up the entire city.

"Did you have a nice trip? Are you hungry? Why are all these people wearing masks?" he asked. I glanced at the many faces obscured by blue material; my train car had been filled with them.

"It's the SARS, I think."

"They look like gangs of robbers."

"They do," I agreed, laughing.

Chao carried my yellow suitcase through the terminal; I'd sold my qipao as soon as I'd gotten Fu's note but kept the bag. It had been expensive. This excited boy stopped talking only long enough to secure my belongings to the back of his motorcycle.

"There's the Bank of China," he said, pointing to a large stone building during his exhaustive city tour. "And there's the Agricultural Bank. And look, across the street, that's Shanghai Pudong Bank. So many banks. Lots of money here. I told you it's a good place," he said, suddenly cutting in front of a bus, and then nearly running over a man racing towards it.

"See the tall needle building? Oriental Pearl TV Tower. Beautiful at night."

"Oh," I said, amazed.

Crossing over a jammed Huangpu River bridge, Chao pointed out all manner of other buildings, from dizzying high-rises to expansive white stone monuments. My head swam as I stared at this city's skyline. Shanghai was even larger than I'd realized. It was immense!

"Okay, now I'll take you to see the factory."

According to Chao, the industrial area where he lived was on the outskirts of Shanghai, but the farther away from the city he drove, the more anxious I became. Vegetable fields and rice paddies soon replaced glass buildings and bustling sidewalks. His idea of the outskirts and mine were very different, and while I appreciated his kindness, I had not traveled so far from home to return to the countryside.

"This is Gujiabang," he said, waving at the little town's scant buildings and two-stall farmer's market. Far smaller than Ningxiang, it disappointed me to learn there was no spa, as I'd hoped. "That's the internet bar. It's cheap. I go there every night to talk to you. Now that you're here, I don't need it. You're saving me money!" Throwing his head back, he laughed.

Turning away from the market, Chao headed towards a giant box of a building seemingly dropped from the sky onto rolling farmland.

"What exactly do you make there?"

"Car seats. Vinyl ones. See that building over there?" Nearly a match to the one in front of us, its smokestacks were busily puffing billowy white clouds into the air.

"What do they make?"

"Medical supplies. You're smart. Eighth grade, right? Maybe you should work there."

Driving around the perimeter, I gasped when a vast compound of tents came into view. "And this is where I live," he announced, motioning towards it.

The air was thick with chemical fumes, and human excrement floated in the small stream running through its center. I coughed many times as we wound our way down a sunbaked path riddled with trash. Laughing and joking, Chao seemed utterly oblivious to the desperation which blanketed this place as surely as the fine layer of gray ash drifting from the towering smokestacks. I couldn't live this way. I couldn't. I fingered my little pouch of money.

"Are there *other* places to live nearby?" I anxiously asked.

He laughed good-naturedly—always laughing. "You're my special friend, GuoGuo. I wouldn't want you living here. I found a nice place for you that's cheap."

Past the medical factory, Chao turned right onto a winding gravel road, and we climbed the sloping hill until reaching a small, decaying farmhouse. After introductions, the farmer's wife led us to a sagging gray barn out back. Climbing up two rickety ladders, she showed me the attic which was for rent. Straw carpeted its floor, and bundles of bamboo, stacked against the far wall, nearly touched the rafters.

A large open window faced the farmyard, inviting in dust and animal stench from the pigpen below.

"What do you think?" Chao asked hopefully.

I didn't mind these conditions much; they reminded me of home, and the price she asked was low. "I like it just fine, Chao. Thank you."

At the break of dawn, I began my journey to the car parts factory. The pink sky soon faded to a beautiful shade of blue, and the warm breeze at my back made me smile; this was going to be a good day. Though my previous factory jobs had not been pleasant, with experience and an education four grades higher than Chao's, he was confident I'd have little problem securing a good position at his plant.

When the medical supplies factory came into view, I noticed a sweep of people crossing the field towards it. Realizing the walk had taken longer than I'd expected, and that I was probably already late for my interview, I hurried past it towards the tent village.

A long snaking line of workers wrapped nearly around the giant car seat factory building. It was shocking to think of how many people this factory could hold, and moreover that so many employees arrived at the same time. It seemed inefficient. After brushing errant straw from my shirt, I stepped up to the guard by the entrance. "Excuse me, I'm here for an interview. Do you know where I'm supposed to go?" Chuckling, the man pointed to the side of the building.

"Thanks!"

Scurrying past what seemed a thousand people, I rounded the corner. There was no entrance, just more people. "Excuse me," I said to an old woman, "I'm looking for the interview place. Do you know where it is?"

The old woman uttered something in a dialect I didn't understand, finally pointing behind her.

"No, I *need* a job."

"This is the interview line," a soft-spoken woman said.

"What?"

"I've been coming here for a week. This is the closest I've ever made it to the front. Maybe today will be my day," she said.

My shoulders fell as I took my place behind her, hoping it would be both of our days. I had to have a job.

Along with the old woman's strange dialect, I heard the more familiar Cantonese, like Chao's, and the Mandarin I'd studied in school. And while the surrounding people were optimistic about our chances, hours and hours in the fierce sun did not bring me near the factory gates before they closed.

"It was nice meeting you, Guo Hong Bo. Perhaps I'll see you tomorrow," the quiet woman said.

"How was your interview today?" Chao yelled from the barn's first floor. I waved him up. "Which department did you get?" he asked, his head poking above the ladder.

I sighed. "I didn't get anything."

"But why?"

"Too many people."

"The medical factory's bigger. Maybe they have more openings. There are always people leaving."

With nothing but pale moonlight to guide me, I picked my way down the gravel road the following morning, getting to the medical factory just as the sky was lightening. If anything, the line was longer—already. Did people sleep in that line? I wanted to cry.

Every day I stood in the heat with increasingly familiar faces, and every evening I returned to the farm unemployed. Though Chao made every attempt to buoy me with his eternal optimism, by the end of that first week, I was drowning in concern; my savings would only stretch so far.

郭

Chao visited me nearly every evening. Without a doubt, walking through the fields with him, talking and laughing were the only bright spots in this existence.

"Shanghai is beautiful at night," he said. "Would you like me to show it to you?"

I'd been in this place for two weeks now, seeing nothing other than factory smoke, long lines of dirty people, and pigs, so I was thrilled to go.

The warm autumn wind blew my hair around my face as Chao raced the country roads, passing stretches of farmland ready for harvest, and terraced rice paddies elegantly decorating sunset-kissed hillsides. I felt an electric thrill when Shanghai's glowing dome came into view.

Tooting his little horn and laughing, Chao dodged lumbering

trucks and blue, orange, and even green taxis diving in all directions for passengers. "I want to show you the river," he said, cruising past warehouses and quays crowded with small cargo ships.

Chao parked beside hundreds of other motorcycles, and we wandered a large park, mesmerized by the city's twinkling skyline dancing on Yangtze River's swiftly moving surface. Slowly meandering past vendor stalls selling anything one could imagine, we eventually found ourselves leaning over the wide boardwalk's metal railing, eating sticky strawberry taffy.

"I'll be right back," he suddenly said, diving into the great sea of pedestrians illuminated by every conceivable neon color.

Gazing up at the mountain of shining skyscrapers and tumbledown apartments, I wondered how on earth I was supposed to find Fu. He could be anywhere.

"This is for you," Chao said, blushing as he handed me a beautiful red rose.

"You are too kind," I said, looking into his hopeful eyes and wishing desperately that he wouldn't try to kiss me. He'd become a younger brother to me, and after three terrible experiences with men, I was in no hurry to have a fourth. I patted his arm. "I'm lucky to have such a good friend as you."

"I'm lucky, too," he mumbled.

郭

Not once in my life had I ever been truly full; hunger and poverty were brothers, but during my time here, I'd become gaunt. So afraid of running out of money, I only bought a few cheap vegetables at the market, stretching them out as far as possible. My stomach ached often, and while standing in the interview lines some days, I felt dizzy to the point of fainting. I thought about my father and how as a boy he'd eaten grass to survive. I would find a way to survive here, even if I had to do the same.

Recognizing my hunger, Chao began bringing me small bits of food—fruit he picked up on the roadside, or small portions of rice when he had enough to share. I soon realized what an extravagant gift that rose had been.

This evening he brought a handful of plums, and we returned to the familiar conversation about our futures.

"When I return to Guangzhou, I'm going to build my mother a very nice house with two bedrooms," he said, flicking a worm off his plum.

"She'll like that," I said, admiring him greatly for his selflessness.

"And a table for her to eat on. And a chair!"

"A chair would be good," I laughed. "My spa will have twenty chairs and a big glass window, so I can advertise to passersby as I work."

When not plotting revenge, which I had little strength for by this time, I spent those countless hours in line creating my dream spa, imagining which products I would use, how much money I'd make, what lavish things I would buy with it, and how happy I'd be. At least dreaming was free.

As we ate and talked, he sat in his usual spot on the windowsill. Carried on a gentle breeze, the strong pen stench wafted into my window.

"Little pig, you are smelly tonight," Chao yelled down.

The second-floor renter, who sat in his window most evenings as well, laughed. "You're right, my friend. Very smelly."

A quiet, middle-aged man, the renter was also a Guo from Hunan Province, though of no relation; Guo was a very common name. Like

Chao, Guo worked at the car seat factory, but his wages were higher, allowing him to live here rather than in the tent village. Also, like Chao, he was in no position to help me get through the gates.

Chao turned back to me, his eyes sparkling with humor. "When you open your spa, I'll bring all my friends. I may even bring that pig."

"Maybe you can come to work for me. You can cut the hair. The pig can do pedicures."

He tossed his head back and laughed. I was so grateful for his company and his kindness. The fruit he'd brought tasted heavenly, and as I laughed with him, sweet juice ran down my chin. When I turned away to wipe it off, his half-eaten plum rolled against my foot.

"What, you throw food at me now?" I stuck my tongue out at him, but he was not there.

"Chao!" I screamed.

Rushing to the window, I stared in horror at his twisted body on the ground below. The pig walked over and sniffed him.

"Someone help!" I screamed, racing down the series of ladders. Guo skidded into the pen right behind me.

"Chao, Wake up. Chao!" I cried, patting his face.

"See his chest? He still breathes," Guo said. "Maybe there's hope. I'll get the farmer."

A wide pool of blood slowly spread around his head, coloring the shallow puddle in which I knelt a muddy red. "You've got to get up. You've got to," I whispered. "Your mother needs you. I need you."

"We must get him to Gujiabang," the farmer said after checking him. "To the clinic there."

"We don't have money to pay," his wife moaned, wringing her hands. She looked up at my window and then back to Chao. "It will cost much."

From my knees, I looked up at Guo, but he shook his head sorrowfully. "I don't have it either."

With only four-hundred RMB left in the world and no job prospects in sight, if I gave it all to the clinic, I would immediately find myself homeless and starving—the very picture I'd painted for Baba. Though Chao meant a great deal to me, I dropped my eyes and said nothing.

"His uncle works in my division," Guo said, hopping up. "I'll get him." Tearing off across the barnyard, his head quickly disappeared below the edge of the steep sheep-grazing pasture.

It was nearly two hours before they took away Chao. Rocking his wet head in my lap, I'd sung to him—every song I knew, cried over him, recited a Cantonese nursery rhyme I'd once learned in school, and I'd wiped the oozing blood from his swelling face as my heart wept inside my chest.

郭

No news of his condition came for days. I didn't go to the factory to wait in line; I didn't have the strength for it.

I'd never hated myself before. I did now. I could have paid the hospital bill—or at least part of it, we could have gotten him there sooner. Surely, I would have found some way to survive. I'd been selfish and scared. Perhaps my father was right; I was just a young girl not ready to be on her own.

A soft knock pulled me from my thoughts. Guo stood in the entryway with his head bowed.

"No. No!" I covered my face and burst into tears.

"I'm sorry. It was too late. Perhaps if…"

Brushing past him, I slid down the ladders and ran blindly through fields, finally falling to my face in the tall grass. This wasn't supposed to happen. He was a sweet, kind-hearted, selfless boy—not even a man. All he'd wanted in the entire world was to care for his mother. She didn't even have a proper house! He'd deserved a wife, a child, a good life away from his factory's stench. He'd deserved ancestral mercy!

When I finally returned to the barn, Guo was waiting for me. "The farmer says you have no job here, and that Chao was taking care of you."

"That's true," I replied softly.

"Before he fell, I overheard him mentioning a spa. Do you have experience in this area?"

I nodded, scrubbing my face. "I'm a well-trained esthetician and masseuse."

"I may know someone who can help you," he said. "I'll contact her."

18

Lucky Jewel

Counting the floors of the magnificent high-rise building in which Shanghai's Lucky Jewel Spa was housed left me breathless. Unable to tear my eyes away, I slid off Guo's motorcycle, promptly tripping over the curb.

Guo had provided me a way out of a situation which, with sobering clarity, I'd come to realize I was incapable of finding on my own. I was shocked by this quiet man's charity, especially after the little I'd shown sweet Chao. My stomach knotted at the thought.

The mirrored golden jewel affixed above the entrance, and the slender shuttered-windows on either side of the black lacquered front door looked stately against plaster walls the color of goat's milk. Following Guo into the high-ceilinged foyer, I casually patted the jade frog statue in the corner for luck.

The spa's exterior paled in opulence to its interior. The walls themselves were formed of gray polished stone, and streams of water trickling down large slate slabs made tinkling sounds as they splashed into the pebble-filled trough below. I pressed myself against the wall by a black leather bench far too luxurious-looking to sit on, as we waited for the owner.

After a few long moments, a small, yet imposing figure glided into the entryway. Though much older than me, her skin was flawless, and her hair beautifully groomed; she had the most beautifully shaped eyebrows I had ever seen! I was mesmerized.

"Cousin," she said, nodding to Guo. "It was good hearing from you." Her eyes then traveled over me, a look of mild disgust on her face. With no mirror in the barn or farmhouse, I'm certain I looked like a dirty beggar. "What have you brought me?"

"This girl is a spa worker from Hunan. She needs a job."

"Is this true?" she asked in Xiang dialect, narrowing her eyes.

"I've had an apprenticeship and two salon jobs, one in Changsha. My specialty is facials and waxing, but I am proficient in manicures, massages—anything."

"What's your name, girl?"

"Guo Hong Bo," I replied anxiously.

"A Guo. Hmm. Where were you born?"

"A village near Ningxiang." I wanted to ask her the same, but that seemed inappropriate at the moment.

"I'm also a Guo, but you may call me Madame Li. I can use another worker in the salon. You can wash hair to prove yourself." I sagged in relief, and when she added, "You may eat and sleep here, if you wish," I nearly cried with joy.

When she snapped her fingers, the attractive girl behind the reception counter raced over. "This girl smells like a pig. Make sure all the filth is washed from her and give her an apprentice uniform."

Bowing respectfully, though I'd never done so in my life, I then threw my arms around Guo, who immediately stiffened. "You've saved my life. I will never forget you."

After Guo left, Madame Li ran her eyes over me once more. "Clients expect my workers to look good. I expect that. Throw your farmer's clothes in the garbage, Guo Hong Bo. You are in Shanghai now."

郭

I'd only ridden in two elevators: one in Changsha, and the other here in Shanghai during my first ill-fated visit. The shiny gold doors slid closed behind me.

"I'm Yuyu," she said in Mandarin. "As long as you work hard and stay on Madame Li's good side, you'll like it here." At this point, I wasn't nearly as concerned about liking it here as I was about having food and shelter. She pressed number three with her nicely manicured finger, and the car swooshed up.

Not nearly so fancy as the first floor, the third was tidy and very white.

"This is where the girls live," Yuyu said. "The kitchen is over here." Woks hung from hooks above the substantial stove, and a large container of cooking oil sat by a wooden chopping block hosting several long knives. It was the nicest kitchen I had ever seen. "We take turns cooking and cleaning. Which are you, a cook or a cleaner?"

"Oh, a cook," I replied in Mandarin, smiling. "My specialty is Hunan-style."

"Ooh. Spicy. I'm from Szechuan. I like things hot."

She led me through a room filled with narrow beds. "You can sleep by me if you'd like. Put your suitcase there and then I'll show you the bathing area."

The mirror's reflection made me gasp. It was a miracle Madame Li had allowed me past the vestibule.

"Use this soap and rag. Be thorough. You really do smell like a pig."

After so much time living over a dusty barnyard, feeling clean seemed the greatest luxury. After drying myself with a soft towel and brushing out my hair, which had gotten quite long over the summer, I twisted it into a knot at the back of my head like Yuyu's and slipped on the brown uniform she'd left on the counter. The tube of lipstick beside it was the loveliest shade of red.

When I entered the bedroom once more, I found Yuyu flipping through a beauty magazine. She looked up and smiled. "Much better. Come, I'll show you around."

The second floor's reception area was dimly lit. Beside two upholstered chairs, a tall table showcased a curved water dispenser filled with floating lychee fruit. The gentle sounds of wind chimes and falling rain drifted from hidden speakers, and the heady scent of jasmine hung heavy in the air.

"When you're on this floor, you must speak softly and calmly at all times," Yuyu whispered. "Appear serene no matter what you feel inside."

Past a series of illuminated cubbies displaying identical Buddha statues, we followed the long corridor to the back. Lightly knocking, she opened a lacquered door. Crystals like glistening raindrops hung from clear threads attached to the ceiling. A single purple orchid bloom seemed as if it had magically sprouted from the folded white bedding.

"Pinch me," I whispered.

"What?" Yuyu said.

"I need to be sure I'm not dreaming."

Giggling softly, we passed through a generous nail area populated by busy manicurists and clients reading magazines while their feet soaked in tubs. Glass shelving mounted to the walls displayed every conceivable color of nail polish.

"Excuse me, Yuyu," a technician sang, holding up a nearly empty polish bottle. "We're almost out of spiced plum. Can you ask Madame Li to order more?"

"Of course. This is Guo Hong Bo."

"GuoGuo," I corrected, shaking a hand softer than silk.

"Min," she said.

"We wear nail polish when not working in this area and always lipstick. We use the shade provided in the dormitory," Yuyu continued. "Madame Li likes us to look exactly the same. Now on to skincare."

Every facial station had its own room. I couldn't believe it! This was the kind of spa Fu had described: expensive, elegant, and filled with wealthy women in search of pampering.

Returning to the illuminated elevator, Yuyu brought us back to the first floor. After showing me the salon area where I'd be working, she said, "Now, I'll take you to Madame Li's office. Don't talk. Listen." Leaving me at the door, she added, "Good luck."

Poring over an enormous book on her imposing desk, Madame Li's narrow fingers gracefully manipulated her pen. She glanced up suddenly, though in no way surprised. "Ah, you look presentable now."

"Thank you for your kindness, Madame Li," I said, bowing once again.

Tilting her head to one side, she looked at me thoughtfully, then spoke in our native Hunan dialect. "You and I may have grown up speaking Xiang, but this is the last day you will hear it from my lips. You must learn Shanghainese, the city's official language. Listen to the other girls. If you are clever, you will pick it up quickly."

"Yes, Madame Li," I said.

"I will not pay you until you prove your worth," she added.

"I've been well-trained. You won't be disappointed."

She raised her eyebrow. "For your sake, I hope you are right." Her eyes then fell back to her book. "Close the door as you leave."

郭

During my life, I'd washed more heads of hair than I cared to count. Requiring neither thought nor skill, I listened carefully to the others while I worked, smiling, but not daring to speak until I learned this new dialect. Though they may have been given to me out of pity for my muteness, I received many tips that first day, which I was allowed to keep.

While in the residence, I quietly mimicked everyone around me, talking often to myself while bathing, something I gleefully got to do daily. Finally, I decided to test my skills. "Yuyu, am I ready to talk to clients?"

She cocked her head. "What did you say?"

"Do I sound like I'm from Shanghai?" I said, switching to my choppy Mandarin.

She giggled. "Not at all. You want to learn Shanghainese?"

"Yes, very much."

"There's a bar around the corner. The owner understands many dialects and loves to talk. You'll learn it quickly from her."

19

Nancy

The Dancing Tiger was filled with professionally dressed customers. I followed Yuyu inside, gawking at a boisterous group of Westerners seated in the corner.

"My dress looks good on you," she said smugly.

"Well, it was this or my uniform. Thank you again for loaning it to me."

"What are you ladies drinking tonight?" the tall bartender asked. Her short, fashionably cut hair had been permed and bleached brown, and her eyes twinkled when she smiled.

"Beer for me," Yuyu said.

I glanced at the drink menu and promptly choked; Changsha's high prices were cheap by comparison. If I wouldn't use what little money I had to help someone whose life depended on it, how could I justify spending it on beer? Still, I fished out my pouch and ordered a small glass.

"Nancy, this is GuoGuo," Yuyu said in Mandarin. "She doesn't speak Shanghainese."

"It's nice to meet you, Nancy. I understand you—"

"Wait, wait. I know this one." She tapped her chin. "Hunan!" she suddenly shouted, raising her arms above her head. Two men at the opposite end of the counter cheered.

"I told you she was good," Yuyu said, winking.

"Very good," I replied, amazed.

"GuoGuo wants to learn Shanghainese. I told her you were the one to see."

"I'm the master," Nancy said. "So, Hunan girl, do you work at the spa?"

"Yes. My boss says I must speak this language."

"You only need to say important things, like, 'You look so beautiful men will write songs about you'," she said, snickering. "Or, 'Your hair is so silky, I could weave a qipao from it'."

Yuyu squealed with laughter. "Oh, and don't forget, 'Please tip me. My boss steals all my money.' GuoGuo, you will definitely need to know that one."

"What do you mean?" I asked, genuinely concerned.

"You'll see soon enough," Yuyu said. "In the meantime, drink, learn, and be happy!"

郭

Neither Madame Li nor anyone else watched us, and those who came back very late—or not at all, were never questioned about their activities. I quickly learned that as long as I did my job well, I stayed out of trouble.

For the next few weeks, I spent nearly every evening at Dancing Tiger learning Shanghainese, often coming home past midnight and occasionally drunk. Unlike anyone I'd ever known, it took little effort to love Nancy, who taught me not only this city's language but its flavor and social culture.

The Pudong District in which we worked and lived was never dark, no matter the time. Neon lights glowed constantly, hovering street lamps mimicked the very moon, and the new Super Brand Mall on Lujiazui Road seemed forever open.

"Madame Li wants to see you," Yuyu whispered one morning. Her worried expression sent shivers down my spine.

I followed her to the back of the salon. "Am I in trouble?" I asked.

"I don't know," she whispered. "Madame Li's in a terrible mood today. She's called me stupid twice already."

Madame Li was a demanding woman, and many of my co-workers hid when they saw her coming. She reminded me of Jin because she said exactly what she thought, even if it was simply that you were stupid. And courtesy of Wai po, I'd heard that so many times I thought nothing of it. Tentatively, I knocked on her door.

"Come," she barked.

On her phone berating someone in Mandarin, Madame Li looked as composed and elegant as ever. I wanted to be her one day. Finally disconnecting, when she looked up at me, it was as if her anger had never been. "Guo Hong Bo, you're a hard worker and not as stupid as I first thought. You may stay at the Lucky Jewel."

I was overjoyed. "Thank you, Madame Li. I'm honored to be here."

"Of course, you are." She stood and walked around her desk. "You're hired as a junior pedicurist. Yuyu will give you a pink uniform."

Beside myself from happiness, I'd made it to the spa. "I'm grateful for any job you give me, but facials are my specialty. I'd like to be considered for a position in that department when you have an opening."

She threw her head back and laughed. "You could be the best

facialist in all of China, but until your skin looks perfect, I won't let you near those clients."

Her words surprised me. I used the same lotions as all the other girls, and my face was smooth and without blemish. "What's wrong with my skin?"

"Perhaps you don't know as much about this profession as you think. Dark skin means poor and uncultured. Pale means wealth and sophistication. With your tanned face and hands, you look like a farm girl plucked from the fields. You must lighten your complexion. There's a special product we use on our customers. It's very expensive, but if you want a facial position, you must use it."

Paying for my Shanghainese tutoring, one beer at a time, had depleted my funds to nearly nothing. "I'm certain I can't afford such a product."

"This is no problem," she said with a tiger smile. "I'll deduct the cost from your salary."

郭

With all the punishment Mistress Yao had doled out during my first apprenticeship, I'd become a competent pedicurist, and I focused all my energy on earning tips, which was my only source of income until I paid for my pale skin. Every night I suffered through the burn of the skin bleach, and every morning I stared into the dormitory mirror hoping I was a little lighter.

Madame Li floated into the pedicurist area one evening many weeks later, watching me closely as I prepared my station for the next day. "This is a famous city," she finally said. "Many foreigners come here. To get ahead, study English or Japanese."

Since I wasn't paying for food or lodging—*or* expensive facial products by this time, I'd begun setting aside a portion of my wages; my spa nest egg. The experience of living in true poverty had taught me frugality and the necessity of preparing for emergencies. These lessons I would never forget.

"I would love to study another language, but education is costly."

She smiled warmly and handed me the coveted purple uniform. "A facialist can afford such things."

郭

Not a night passed when I didn't think of Chao. With shame as my blanket and guilt my pillow, the image of his limp and bloody body haunted me. Fu haunted me as well, but in a wholly different way.

Now settled, I began looking for him in earnest. In chat room after chat room, I searched for his handle; there were countless places he could hide. Often, I fantasized that his wife would become my client. Once I gained her trust, I would follow her home and wait by her door. Perhaps she would invite me in for tea and introduce me to her faithful husband. And then… pow!

I grilled each customer. *Are you married? Is he a businessman? Do you have children?* Of course, in a city this large, many husbands were businessmen, and all of them had children—some two or three because they could afford the fine.

"Nancy," I said over drinks one night, "should I study Japanese or English?"

"Pfft," she replied. "Japanese is fine, but only one country uses it. Everyone speaks English—Americans, Brits, Singaporeans, Australians…" Suddenly she yelled out, "Who here speaks English?"

Nearly everyone in the bar raised a hand. "See? That's where you should devote your time. And pick an English name like mine."

In China, it was becoming fashionable for women, and even some men, to take Western names. Nancy picked out several for me, but none felt right. During a chat room session with my Hunan friends, I explained my dilemma.

I like Stephanie, Yang wrote. *It sounds musical.*

Ooh, I like it too, Ting added.

What does it mean? I asked.

Who cares, Jin replied. *Men sure don't. Speaking of men, have you met anyone yet?*

I'd followed my brother's directive and kept men at arm's length. *When you've found one, then you can ask me*, I replied to Jin.

"My new name is Stephanie," I told Nancy the following evening.

"I like it," she said.

"Okay, now for English classes. Madame Li recommended Joyy English School."

"I know that place. I think it's good."

"So, would you take them with me?" With a linguistic talent perfect for her profession, I knew Nancy had studied English.

"Sure, I can always brush up."

One night per week, Nancy and I studied English, practicing it at the restaurant next door, and then on any Westerner who dared enter Dancing Tiger. Yang had chosen a good name for me, it seemed because Westerners had no trouble saying it.

My life was perfect at the moment, which worried me. Whenever my *yang* brought brightness, my *yin* quickly shrouded it in shadow. I dreaded whatever was coming next.

20

New Eyes

It was getting harder and harder for me to see. I first noticed the problem in English class when the symbols began looking blurry, but as my sight rapidly worsened, nothing was clear. Remembering my mother's test, I purchased a small amount of second-quality rice. Though I knew there were many broken grains, finding them was nearly impossible.

Soon after, Madame Li called me to the front of the salon where my previous client stood fuming. "See what you did to her eyebrows? They're uneven. Are you suddenly a stupid girl?" Madame Li said, snapping her fingers in my face. "The money I refund her will come out of your salary. You are lucky I don't fire you, call the police, have you arrested!"

Mortified, I burst into tears. The financial cost of this mistake was relatively low, but the price for making my boss angry was astronomical.

"Please forgive me," I said after the customer left.

She waved her hand in the air, all anger gone. "That woman always complains. You'll do better next time."

"Next time" did not help my situation, and after several more mistakes, Yuyu escorted me to my boss's office.

"You were my most talented facialist. Now, you're not," Madame Li said with narrowed eyes.

I knew that as my eyesight worsened, I'd only make more and costlier mistakes. Quitting English school would provide the money necessary for a ticket home, but Shanghai was the most exciting place I'd ever lived, and I didn't want to leave it. Regardless, it was time to tell this woman the truth.

I sighed mightily. "Blindness runs in my family, and my vision is getting bad. I love working here and want to continue for as long as you'll allow it. I can give massages even without good vision. Will you let me stay and do this at least?"

She threw her head back and laughed. "Blindness is easy to fix. A doctor I know performs a special eye procedure using light. You'll see perfectly afterward. It's a miracle. We'll go there tonight to meet with him. You'll get new eyes, and I'll receive five percent in commission."

After the doctor checked my eyes with several instruments, he assured me that this LASIK procedure would fix my condition. I was so relieved I wanted to cry. Of course, I had tears of a different sort when I learned the cost; it was very expensive—more than I could possibly afford.

"I can't pay for this surgery," I said dejectedly as we walked the many icy blocks back to Lucky Jewel. If anything, winters here were harsher than in Hunan, and I could not afford to waste money on a coat.

"This is no problem," Madame Li replied with her tiger smile.

郭

Madame Li immediately moved me to the massage department, where I could do no harm, and on a January morning three weeks later, she accompanied me to my appointment. I'd never experienced surgery before but was far too excited to be afraid.

The procedure took little time, and after they placed patches over my eyes, Madame Li loaded me into a taxi and then guided me to the third-floor residence to rest.

My head throbbed when I awoke the next morning. Yuyu and several other girls whispered excitedly as Madame Li gently removed the gauze. The room's pale light hurt my eyes, and when I blinked, it was as if my eyelids were made of sand. I tried to focus on the faces hovering above me, but they were nothing but blurs of color. My heart began pounding wildly, and I felt as though I might faint; something had gone terribly wrong.

"I can't see!" I said frantically.

Madame Li's voice was calm. "You'll see better in a few days. By next week, you'll be my best brow-shaper again."

If only it were so, I thought, a tear slipping down my temple.

郭

My boss had not lied; the miracle surgery worked. Now, the finest hairs on my clients' faces were shockingly visible, reading the smallest print in the newspaper was effortless, and picking out broken grains of rice was nothing at all.

"Would you like to pay off your debt before you're old and gray?" Madame Li asked after I'd escorted my client to the foyer.

"Yes, Madame Li. More than anything!"

"I'll introduce you to Genji. She's a makeup artist who once worked for me. She needs a new assistant for her wedding business."

This thrilled me on many levels. If Genji could use Lucky Jewel to springboard her career, perhaps I could do so as well.

Friday after work, Madame Li took me to Genji's studio on the narrow Chuanyang river.

"Have you ever attended a wedding?" Genji asked in a gravelly voice as she circled me.

"Yes. My brother's. It was wonderful," I replied.

"She's from Hunan," Madame Li interjected. "What does she know about Shanghai weddings?"

"Shanghai weddings are fashion shows," Genji explained. "And brides are runway models, no matter how ugly. The women who book my services will change wardrobes four times during their daylong photoshoots. And with every wardrobe change, they will need different makeup looks, hairstyles, and accessories. As my assistant, you will help them—I assume she's good with hair?" she said, glancing at Madame Li.

"Do you not remember that I only hire the best? Otherwise, you'd still be unemployed," my boss retorted.

"I'm a master facialist," I added, hoping to impress her.

"Ah, good. I will give you the most important job an assistant can have: makeup removal."

"How much did you make on that Chen-Wong wedding?" Madame Li asked, flipping through a design catalog a little later. "I heard it cost one-hundred-fifty-thousand RMB."

Choking on my spit, I coughed violently. That was enough to sustain my entire village for many generations. It was an emperor's sum!

"Only four-thousand. Not so much."

"Enough to pay me a commission for a new assistant, eh?"

"Of course, Li. I owe you so much!" Genji said pleasantly—*too* pleasantly.

I began working for Genji on weekends. It was exciting to see all the beautiful dresses and Genji's exquisite makeup effects, and I imagined having enough money to afford such a wedding one day. Weddings made me think of Fu, for whom I had begun searching more aggressively.

21

Manhunt

Cherry blossom petals carpeted the sidewalks like pink snow, marking two years since I'd been so callously tossed aside. And as with last year, spring's arrival seemed tragic.

Nancy had become a sister to me, but I'd never revealed my dark secret. Through her business dealings, she knew lots of people and had many connections. Out of desperation, I finally asked for her help.

"Nancy, I'm looking for a man."

"Yes!" she cheered. "I've been waiting forever for you to say that."

My friend dated incessantly. Raised in this cosmopolitan city by liberal parents, her values were vastly different from mine. Forever declining men's invitations, I'd been vague about my reasons, only saying that my last boyfriend had bruised my heart. Yuyu was almost as frustrated with me as Nancy. Only Ting understood.

"No. I'm looking for a specific man. One named Fu."

She leaned in on her elbow. "Ooh. Tell me more."

"Fu was my…" I took a deep breath. "Fu was my last boyfriend."

"The reason you don't date?"

I nodded, taking a sip of my Snow beer.

"If he was so bad, why do you want to find him?"

"I just need to. I've been searching for him since I moved to Shanghai." Looking around, I cataloged the suited men in her small bar. "It's just really important that I find him," I said through gritted teeth.

After a long moment, she whispered, "Vengeance?"

Nancy was like no one I'd ever met. She understood people—how to read them. I couldn't hide my astonished expression when I realized she could read me just as easily. My lips began trembling. Fu deserved no more of my tears, and yet they came anyway.

Looking into my eyes for a long moment, her expression became grave. "I'll help you find this Fu."

郭

I hadn't forgotten a single detail about Fu; from the way he carefully folded his newspapers to the stinging scent of his cologne, yet painting a picture of him with words proved difficult. Worse, when Nancy asked for practical information, such as the type of business he was in, the company he worked for, and his position there, I could give her nothing. An innocent eighteen-year-old driven by love had no interest in such trivial details. Regardless, Nancy spoke to every man who ordered a drink, even the Westerners, slipping Fu's name into conversation; her distant cousin, her long-lost family friend, her former investor. Her stories were so clever.

Fu haunted my dreams—more so now than ever before, and I often woke shaking and drenched in sweat. Yuyu, whose bed was next to mine, had begun giving me worried looks.

Having occasionally done so in the past, I began regularly lurking in South Railway Station, watching for young girls meeting older men; there was an alarming number! My active imagination had me frantically pushing through crowds towards red-scarved men, only to be disappointed again and again.

Whenever I spotted a girl carrying a yellow suitcase, I followed her—sometimes for hours, weaving through crowds at the monstrous Grand Gateway Complex, hovering inside Shanghai Times Square boutiques, certain Fu had directed her to some clandestine meeting place.

With a small knife hidden in my sock, I regularly visited the unappetizing McDonalds where Fu had taken me, spending hours at a time sipping Coca-Cola, and wishing with all my might that he would walk through the door so I could stab his heart, gouge out his eyes, castrate him.

Nancy grew worried.

郭

"Do you like to gamble?" she yelled over the din of laughter and karaoke music one evening. Summer had filled Shanghai's steamy streets with tourists, and the Dancing Tiger with boisterous customers.

"Why? Do you want to give me all your money?" I yelled back, fanning myself with a limp paper napkin.

Shaking her head, she laughed. "Some guy invited me to play poker. You want to come?"

My mind went to Chen and his gangster friends, and from them to Guang. Could I sink so low as to ask him to find Fu? Had I lost my mind at last? "What kind of guy?"

Nancy shrugged. "A cute one. Are you in?"

Even with working two jobs, it had still taken half a year to pay off my surgery debt. Now free of that obligation, my financial situation was slowly improving. "Why not?"

Friday evening, Nancy left her bar in the hands of a trusted cousin, and we took a taxi to Siping Road Residential District. In Shanghai, there was every conceivable type of dwelling, from expensive high-rise apartments, like the one Madame Li owned, to disintegrating hovels no nicer than Baba's first recycling building.

The driver turned onto a tree-lined street in a quiet neighborhood. Two-story townhouses made of brown brick were pressed together in long rows. We walked the neat sidewalk looking for the proper house number, which turned out to be on the other side of the road. A very good-looking guy with short hair combed forward met us at the door. Wearing silver wire-rimmed glasses, he looked anything but dangerous.

We were ushered through a nicely furnished living room to a large kitchen table, around which a group of comfortably dressed men and women were gathered. Wisps of cigarette smoke floated to the ceiling, along with bursts of raucous laughter.

"Do you know how to play Shanghai Rummy?" the host asked me.

Nancy smiled. "Maybe you should show her how."

Sitting between us, he scooted closer to me. "Aces are high, jokers are wild. Let's play the first hand together, okay?"

Leaning back, I glared at Nancy, who innocently mouthed, "What?"

郭

Groggy after another late night of card playing, I sipped strong tea while setting up my make-up station. With six months of training under my belt, Genji had begun double-booking sessions, leaving me in charge of one bride while she tended to another. This promotion came with a higher wage, which was thrilling.

The bride could not have chosen a more beautiful location than People's Park for her first photoshoot of the day. A striking girl with long flowing hair, rosebud lips, and large perfectly shaped eyes, I'd chosen a subtle design to emphasize her natural features, while accenting the nineteen-twenties-style blue gown she wore. After serving refreshments to the respective mothers, and powdering the groom's face once again—summer's rampant humidity, a makeup artist's greatest foe—I turned my full attention to the bride, rubbing foundation on her pale skin.

Focused on my task, a swath of pink caught my eye. Glancing towards a lacy willow tree, I noticed a qipao the same shade as the lipstick I'd chosen. Wrapped in the arms of a familiar-looking man, its owner stared out over the romantic lotus pond. I smiled, thinking even strangers had dressed for this shoot.

Accentuating the bride's cheekbones with pale blush, my mind roamed. Had I not once owned a qipao that same color? I shook the thought from my head, selecting a cerulean colored shadow, and then dipping my brush into the creamy paste.

"Hold still for just a moment," I murmured.

"I'm melting in this heat," the bride whined.

"I said an outdoor shoot was unwise," her future mother-in-law tutted. "Not a smart girl."

"Mama," the groom groaned.

"Fan her again!" the mother demanded.

As I waved my arms energetically, my eyes drifted towards the couple once more. The man's hand slowly drifted from the young girl's waist to her bottom. When she tried to pull away, he leaned in and whispered something in her ear. Stiffening, she became a statue. I wrinkled my nose. What a lack of discretion on his part. At his age, a man should have more constraint.

"Applying eyeliner requires skill and precision, and no movement," I said, as the bride began fidgeting.

Who is he? Set to my task, I tried clearing my mind, but when my eyes flicked to his profile once more, my heart leapt to my throat. Fu!

"Hey, what are you doing?" the bride squeaked.

I stared at my handiwork in horror. A thick streak of black eyeliner stretched from eyelid to temple.

"Stupid girl!" her mother hissed. "We will not pay for this. Where is your boss?"

The lie sprang from my lips as quickly as if I were speaking to Wai po. "This is a brand-new design—an Egyptian look. We haven't used it on any other girl in the city yet. We'll hang your daughter's picture in our studio. She will be a trendsetter!"

The bride looked at me for a moment and then up at her mother, an enormous smile forming. "I want it, Mama."

The woman narrowed her eyes at her in-law and then at me. "Finish it then."

My hands shook as I applied a matching streak to the other side of her face. Wanting nothing more than to leap off this Japanese bridge, bolt across the wide patch of lawn separating us, and drown Fu, I hurriedly checked my ridiculous design for evenness, dusted the bride's face with crushed pearl powder, and then dragged her to the photographer's pedestal.

When I turned towards Fu again, he was gone.

"No!" I yelled.

"What?" the wedding party said in unison.

"I mean, no one has ever had more beautiful eyes. Perfection!"

I trilled. Then I tore off, covering the distance to the willow in seconds. The young girl could not have moved quickly in that tight dress, but I didn't see her on the other side of the pond, or on the path disappearing into the camphor forest. Choosing the forest path, I raced down the stone pavers, dodging families, baby strollers, and joggers, stopping only when I came to busy Xi Zang Road.

Kicking myself for choosing the wrong direction, I cut back across the lawn, my eyes sweeping over groups hovering around mahjong games and armies of shriveled elderly practicing tai chi. Running past the long series of potential-husband advertisements, I plunged into the bamboo grove and took up the southern path.

Shaking and sweat-drenched, once I'd canvassed the entire park, including the amusement rides, which seemed a silly notion, I returned to the spot where the bridal party had been. Nothing remained there except my make-up box and bag of hair accessories.

郭

"You are wrong, Nancy. I did not imagine it. He was there!"

Setting another beer in front of me, she shook her head. "Last week you accosted a man in front of Lucky Jewel, and the week before outside the internet bar you like. How can you be sure this man was him? You said you didn't see his full face."

"I didn't have to. It was the same dress!"

"GuoGuo, there are thousands of pink qipaos in Shanghai, and the pattern you've described is common. Why would he waste money on custom designs for country girls who'd never know the difference?"

I slammed my hand on the countertop. "I know it was him!"

"We've been at this for months. Over twenty million people live in this city, and ten times more visit it. You could easily spend a lifetime here without seeing the same person twice."

"I will find him," I growled. After years of searching, my hatred for Fu had not lessened, but intensified, its flames like an engine's furnace growing hotter with each failure. This fire had driven me on recklessly, just as my love once had, but I was burning out; becoming nothing but a black cinder. Nancy sighed and took my hand. "And what if his name isn't even Fu? Have you thought of this? Surely a predator such as he would not use his real name. Why would he be so foolish?"

I'd never once considered this—not in all this time. Nancy didn't use her real name, and when I practiced my English on Westerners, neither did I.

"GuoGuo, you aren't going to find him. You know this."

Tears spilled down my cheeks. "We can't give up, Nancy. We have to find him. I have to—"

Suddenly by my side, she drew me into her arms and rocked me against her chest while I sobbed. "What he took from you, you can never get back," she whispered. "And even if you do somehow find and destroy him, it will only blacken your heart and make it ache all the more. Don't waste any more of your beautiful life on someone who doesn't deserve it. Let this go. Give it to the wind and let it be blown away. This search is over."

22

Nose Job

Using all of my strength, I clung to Nancy's words as if they were a thick rope and forced Fu from my thoughts; I would not sink deeper into madness. I ceased stalking girls at railway stations, and I no longer searched for pink qipaos. From men in red scarves that autumn, I turned my face away. Slowly, a sense of peace I hadn't felt in years returned, and by winter I slept without dreaming of Fu.

January brought especially bitter winds, and on one particular day, many spa girls pressed their faces against the tall second-floor windows, gawking at the rare spectacle of snowflakes dancing through the air, transforming the busy sidewalks below into a parade of beautifully colored umbrellas. I'd seen snow all too often in my mountainous village and spent the late afternoon instead refilling lotion containers and humming to myself.

"Isn't it wonderful to see snow?" Madame Li said, floating into my room.

"Yes, it's very pretty. I look forward to seeing it in Hunan next month." Unlike the year before, which saw me so poor that returning home was an absolute impossibility, this Lunar New Year I could afford a train ticket back. I couldn't wait to see Mama.

"The flakes are so tiny, yet so easy for your repaired eyes to see."

"Yes, I'm forever grateful for your assistance, Madame Li."

"Taking a rich Shanghai fiancé back to Hunan would make your family proud."

"I suppose," I responded, taken aback by such a strange question. It would certainly please Wai po.

"Look in the mirror, GuoGuo," she then said, positioning me in front of one nearby. Confused, I did as she directed. "You're a smart girl, but your face is common. Wealthy husbands are hard to come by, and you'll never find one looking as you do. Surely you know this."

A wave of insecurity swept over me. "What is your point?"

"Now that your sharp vision has been restored, you can plainly see that it's time to fix your nose."

Many *Han* Chinese dislike their noses and eyes. Our noses are wider and flatter than those of most Europeans, and our eyes seem small because our lids lack folds.

"My nose is fine," I said. "It works the way it's supposed to, and I am not such an ugly girl."

"But you could be very beautiful with a different nose. One like mine."

Every girl wants to be beautiful, and I was no different. After our conversation, I spent a lot of time staring into that mirror. My nose was quite wide, but no more so than Mama's, and her face was perfect to me. Still, a sharper bridge would set me apart from other Hunan girls. And though I wasn't on the prowl for a husband at present, that would change in time.

According to Madame Li, the price for cosmetic surgery was six months' salary. This came as a shock to me, but many of my customers, whose daughters had this surgery as par for the course, thought the price quite reasonable.

Seeing was worth all the money I could ever hope to earn. Beauty was not. Besides, I'd just begun enjoying life. I'd purchased a new outfit, gambled more freely on Friday nights, and I'd started setting aside money for my future. I was not ready to give it all up so soon.

Unfortunately, Madame Li was relentless. She hounded the staff for two weeks straight; evidently, we'd all become extremely ugly.

"When the plastic surgeon comes next week, you must let him fix you," she said, storming into my facial room.

"No, Madame Li. Thank you, but no."

"This doctor needs practice, and he's paying me half his fee. I gave you a job when you had none, food when you were starving, sight when you were losing yours. You owe me this!"

I dropped my head into my hands. She was right on all accounts. Without her help, I might have been blind or even dead by now. But life beckoned, and I wanted to see my family. "I have no money for such an extravagance," I finally said.

"Of course you don't. But this is no problem," she replied, her tiger smile unmistakable.

郭

That night at my favorite internet bar, I slumped into a hard, plastic chair. I spent the first hour in our chatroom, railing to my Changsha friends about my manipulative, money-hungry boss. My second was spent composing a long-winded message:

Dear Ming,

I can't come home.

GuoGuo

Perhaps it was a cowardly thing to think, but I'm glad it was he instead of I who had to break the news to Mama. I would not have liked to have seen her face.

23

A Different Path

At twenty-two, I was no closer to owning my spa than the day I'd climbed onto Chao's motorcycle at South Railway Station.

"Why the long face, GuoGuo? This is not like you," Genji remarked.

Opening my case, I began dropping the weekend's dirty makeup sponges into soapy water. If anything, this summer's wedding season was busier than last. I thought of all the money Genji must make and sighed heavily.

"The cosmetic surgeon is returning. Fixing my nose wasn't enough, now Madame Li wants me to have my eyelids done."

Genji snorted. "It's always something with her. She gets richer while her workers stay poor. Why do you think I left?"

"But I feel I owe her so much."

"As do I. But if I ever wanted to become successful, I knew I had to find my own path."

"That's what I want. To be successful. I want to open a spa and make lots of money."

"Open your own spa, eh? Be her competition someday? To do that, you'll need an education and a name."

"I have an education—an apprenticeship, and I'm a master-level esthetician."

"You and a thousand others. You must attend the Shanghai Theatre Academy. You'll work with master makeup artists, famous actors, and when you graduate, customers will demand you. Why do you think I'm booked out a year in advance? Why do you think I can ask such prices?"

I had no idea such a program existed or that I, an eighth-grade graduate of a rural middle school, could ever hope to be considered for it. Unfortunately, I did have an idea about how this world worked. Bowing my head, I whispered, "I have no connections."

"This is no problem!" Genji said, winking.

郭

Though Jing'an Residential District was next to Pudong, I'd spent little time in it, and none wandering the cultural district. Genji smiled as our taxi meandered past the impressive Dramatic Arts Center. Moments later she murmured, "This is the Academy."

Set against a backdrop of towering high-rises, the short orange and gray buildings weren't terribly impressive at first. But as we passed an army of them, labeled with signs such as recording studios, production labs, orchestra complex, digital library, material design building, etc., I soon realized that what the campus lacked in height, it made up for tenfold in girth.

Following Genji through the administration building's foyer and up a generous flight of stairs, we made our way down an exterior walkway overlooking a private garden. Fidgeting with the peach skirt Genji had lent me, I nervously waited in a small lobby outside a series of offices until they called me.

"This is Feng Mian, Dean of Design and my mentor," Genji said. "She's agreed to review your portfolio."

The tall and imposing woman's dramatically painted eyes assessed me. I smiled pleasantly in return and then glared at Genji. I had no such thing as a portfolio. I wasn't even certain what that was.

Producing an envelope from her purse, Genji placed a series of photographs in front of the dean. I recognized them as pictures of brides under my charge this wedding season.

"Tell me about this one," Feng Mian said, pointing a long finger at an image that until last weekend had hung in Genji's studio. It was my first independent design.

After carefully explaining my choices and technique, and answering more questions than I thought possible, Feng Mian moved on to another of my designs.

"What did you think?" Genji asked as we passed through the enormous front doors once more.

"I have no idea," I responded, reeling.

郭

My thoughts whirling, I walked rather than rode the bus from Genji's studio back to Lucky Jewel. I'd had an only marginal interest in attending STA before visiting it; makeup seemed a wonderful way to make money in the short run, but it was only a means to an end. After exploring the campus with Genji and learning about the stage makeup program in detail, I wanted to attend this school. I wanted it very badly.

The next month gave me plenty of time to talk myself out of it. In truth, I had trouble imagining myself in such a place. STA offered countless majors—even Masters had Ph.D. programs; I could barely do math. I'd have nothing in common with my peers, and I'd still need an income for basic needs. Could I juggle school and a full-time job? I didn't think so.

No, the more I thought about it, the more at peace I became with my decision; the Academy was not the right place for me. Instead, I would begin searching for a new job—a spa where I could keep my earnings, a job pointing me in the direction I truly wanted to go.

郭

"When are you going to hear from that school?" Nancy asked one night. "It's taking forever, and I'm dying to know."

"Oh, the letter came last week," I said.

Her eyebrows shot up. "*And?*"

I shrugged. "It doesn't matter."

"Oh, honey, I'm so sorry. You were a perfect fit there."

"Come on, Nancy. I'd have been at least four years older than the other students, all of whom, by the way, would have finished high school. Even if they'd accepted me, I would have failed out in the first month, and we both know it."

"This is a makeup certificate, GuoGuo. Your six years in the beauty business are far more valuable than some run-of-the-mill high school diploma. And you're fabulous at what you do. What, you want proof? Just look at my brows. Perfect every time."

I wasn't sure this pep talk was helping as much as it was hurting. She was right about one thing, though; I ought to have more faith in my abilities.

Nancy offered me another beer, and we spent the next few minutes drinking in companionable silence. Suddenly, she banged her bottle on the table, foam spewing in all directions. "Well, to hell with them! They don't deserve you, anyway. Let's burn that letter. It'll be fun."

Pulling it from my purse, I held it up. I wasn't sure why I'd bothered keeping it. It seemed easy enough to let it go now. "Light the match," I said, laughing.

"Look, even the printing is pretentious," Nancy sneered. "I bet the letter's even worse, huh?"

"I don't know."

"What do you mean you don't know?"

"I never opened it," I said, shrugging. "I didn't need to. I know what it says."

"Well, I want to read it."

Nancy snatched the envelope from my hand and ripped it open. "*Dear Miss Guo, Shanghai Theater Academy*...blah blah blah...*prestigious*...blah blah blah...*highly competitive*...blah..." She stopped reading, and a slow but certain grin slowly unfurled across her face. Suddenly, her eyes met mine. "GuoGuo, you got in."

"What? No. *No*..."

"Yes. 'Congratulations on your acceptance. The deadline for payment is August 15, 2005'."

I covered my mouth in shock. "I assumed... I was so sure I wouldn't... I—"

"We're going to the Academy!" she squealed.

Disappearing to the back, she returned moments later with a chilled bottle of champagne. "I've had my fingers crossed," she said. "I'm so proud of you, GuoGuo."

Popping the cork, she filled two glasses and then in Nancy fashion, shouted out, "Everybody, raise your drink to GuoGuo!"

I covered my face, laughing, because, of course, no one knew why they were cheering or even who I was. Turning back to Nancy with tears in my eyes, I mouthed, "Thank you."

24

Loan Shark

August was screaming towards me, and I still hadn't come up with a way to pay STA's staggering tuition. It had been a far simpler task to convince myself that enrolling was the smart thing to do. This opportunity was a gift, a path to a better life, a huge career leap forward that would land me at the very foot of my dreams. But the cost...

For a split second, I thought of Guang, a man who had literally robbed a bank for me. I could sure use that money right about now. Of course, he was probably in jail or dead at this point. And if I sought his help, I might find myself right beside him. The thought gave me shivers.

There was only one man who truly had my best interests in mind—one who wanted good things for me in the right way. And that one I hadn't spoken to in two years. Loitering in the lobby, I waited for Yuyu to finish jotting down a reservation in the large appointment book.

"I need to call someone." Madame Li had strict rules about phone usage. Thankfully, Yuyu had her own policy.

"Is this an emergency?" This was the passphrase of sorts. If questioned, she could always cover herself.

"Yes. Life or death," I said, smiling.

"Make it quick," she whispered, glancing towards Madame Li's office. "She's in a foul mood."

"She's always in a foul mood," I said, giggling.

Ming had installed a telephone in the Ningxiang tire shop he'd taken over from Baba. I dialed the number, strumming my fingers while it rang.

"Ming, I need to talk to Baba. It's important," I said, without preamble.

"Are you okay?" he asked, sounding alarmed.

"Yes. I just need money."

"He's next door, sorting bottles. I'll go get him and call you back."

Waiting gave me ample time to relive our long-ago fight, and as the moments ticked by, I became increasingly anxious. Anxious and angry; he should have at least said goodbye when I left.

"Here he is," Ming said. "Good luck."

"Mei Zi?" Hearing my father's gruff voice after so long was a pleasant shock.

"It's me, Baba."

"Are you alright?"

"Yes. I'm great, actually. I have news. They've accepted me into The Shanghai Theatre Academy. I'll study makeup techniques."

Silent for a moment, he then said, "You're going to school? *You?*"

"Yes, *me*. This is a big deal, Baba. It's an honor just to be accepted."

"How will you work if you are in school? How will you make money?"

"I'll find a way. I'll figure it out."

"Why are you telling me this?" he asked.

This was not the reaction I'd expected, and it hurt. Could he not at least say he missed me? He had no idea what I'd endured to get to this place in my life, how lucky I'd been to get a nice job, how exclusive Madame Li's salon was. He hadn't even asked!

"It's a very famous school, but it's Shanghai, so tuition is very high. Seven-thousand RMB. Can I have—I mean, would you loan me the money? I know it's a lot, but I'll pay you back quickly after I graduate. I'll open my own business and make piles of money."

Baba's laughter drowned out further explanation. "Mei Zi, you've never paid back anything in your life. Why should I believe you'd repay this? This enormous sum?"

I wasn't a little girl anymore, though it was clear he saw me as nothing more. Perhaps if I demanded he rename me Nv Di, meaning "woman," he might think differently.

"You should have faith in me. You should support me. You should be proud of me!"

"You call after so much time and all you want is money. How does this make me proud? Tell me you're rich, then I'll be proud. No, I will not support this."

After a moment of charged silence, I said, "Baba?"

"He's gone, Mei Zi," Ming responded.

郭

I spent the next week cocooned in frustration. There was a great boulder blocking my path to betterment, and without Baba's help, I would have to trust a money-hungry tiger to carry me past it. With perfect vision, I stared at my reflection, touching the eyes and nose I'd lost a year of salary paying for. If Madame Li agreed to cover my tuition, she'd demand a lifetime of servitude in return.

Li had been good to me overall, and in her defense, she had sent me to Genji for help when I'd needed it. And if she were unwilling to loan me so much, perhaps she knew of others who would. Of course, when she learned I was planning to leave, she might simply show me the door. Could I quickly find another spa willing to hire me part time, yet shelter and feed me full time?

郭

The box was more tape than cardboard. Once I'd finally wrenched open the lid, I gasped. So much money! Untying the bundles of smudged and wrinkled bills, I quickly counted them. There was enough to pay tuition with a few RMB to spare. I unfolded the note.

Baba wanted you to have this. He said he would not deny his children an education, no matter how worthless it was. The other money is from me. It's payback for the hospital bill. Mama added a little, too, but don't tell Baba.
Get rich so you can buy me something.
—Ming

Sliding the empty box aside, Yuyu climbed onto the bed beside me. "Why are you crying?"

"It's just… my family. They are so kind."

"You're lucky," she said after a moment. "My family is dead."

The following afternoon, I escorted my last client to the front door and slipped out behind her, sprinting to the bus stop. STA's administration offices closed at five, and I had no time to waste.

Racing into the building, I couldn't believe it had come down to the wire. After so much trouble and angst, it would be heartbreaking to miss the deadline because of an overly booked schedule.

A helpful secretary directed me to the bursar's office. Bursting through the door without knocking, I pulled the wad of cash from my purse and slammed it down on his desk along with the admissions letter. "Here's my tuition. Let me in," I panted.

His eyebrows rose as he slowly counted the bills. "You shouldn't walk around carrying this much money. Someone could rob you."

"It's enough, right?" I said when he finished.

"Enough." He stamped my paperwork and handed it back to me. "Welcome to STA, Miss Guo."

Clutching the receipt to my chest as I stepped onto the sidewalk, I looked both ways and then squealed.

郭

Madame Li held up a finger when she saw me. "I'll fire you if you don't finish today," she screeched into the phone. "Fire you and destroy your reputation!"

Slamming down the receiver, she waved me in, the essence of calm quickly reclaiming her features. For the moment...

"Many customers have contacted me recently, praising your work," she said.

"Oh?"

Clients and their estheticians share a special bond. Women bring their trials and worries to our facial rooms, and we counsel them. Over the last few weeks, my regulars had taken turns counseling me.

"Would you like to tell me something?"

Unable to speak out of fear—or possibly shock, I was suddenly lightheaded. "Um, I've been accepted into the Shanghai Theatre Academy."

"And it took you this long to tell me?" I'd expected anger, not allegation.

"How did you—"

"Genji told me. Why would you hide such wonderful news?"

"I was afraid you'd fire me."

"Fire you?" She laughed. "I congratulate you. I'm very proud, GuoGuo. You've grown so much. STA is a prestigious school. How will you pay for it? Surely your family is poor. You came to me with nothing."

"Somehow they've found the money. I still can't believe it."

"If you leave Lucky Jewel, where will you live?"

"I don't know. I can sleep on my friend's floor for a while. Maybe Genji will let me stay in her shop. I'll figure something out."

"I've recently purchased commercial real estate nearby. One building has a first-floor bar. If you help with cleaning and bartending—for no pay—you can sleep there for free."

"Yes. That would be wonderful," I said, dumbfounded. "Thank you, Madame Li. Thank you so much." The thought of hugging this woman had never once crossed my mind, but at this moment, it took all my strength just to restrain myself.

"Gather your things, GuoGuo. You're fired," she said, winking.

25

Backstage Pass

A thick man, Mr. Li's gruff demeanor and country accent seemed at odds with his finely tailored suit. It left me wondering if Madame Li coordinated his outfits to match her urbane sense of style. I followed him through the bar area to a dimly lit storage closet. Stepping past a wall of boxes, he pointed to a mat in the back corner.

"You can sleep here and eat with the other employees as long as you work."

My mind drifted to dusty barn floors and factory mats stained with excrement; I'd certainly lived in worse places.

"Thank you," I said, placing my belongings on top of a box marked napkins.

Leading me to the front once more, he pointed to a shriveled woman with sharp eyes. "This is Chunhua. Do what she says." And with that, he left.

"My friend owns a bar," I said amiably.

"Do you cook?" she replied, poking a dangling lock of gray hair back into her bun.

"Yes."

"Good. You'll start tonight. Rice and leeks are beneath the wok stand in the kitchen," she said, nodding towards a small room off the hall and then handing me a mop.

郭

Moments of panic, joyful anticipation, and more panic marked my first day of school. I had no idea what to wear to a famous school, though my choices were admittedly limited. My transportation was limited as well, since taxis were a luxury well beyond my means.

The Huangpu River Bridge was so weighted with cars, it all but sagged. Traffic inched along like a fat worm in winter, the city bus driver in no hurry whatever to move with it. Did he not understand I was going to be late?

Jettisoned from the hissing hulk, I raced down the sidewalk only to stop short; where was I supposed to go? The image of a little girl lugging heavy books and a tin lunchbox to a single whitewashed building housing a handful of children popped into my head. On this day, I stood empty-handed, facing a vast network of multistory buildings steeped in a flowing river of students.

Grateful to find a discarded map, I joined the stream flowing into a modern building that seemed one house built inside the belly of another. Hurrying across an interior walkway that appeared to be suspended from a glass cliff face, I sorely wished I had a spare moment to take it all in. Following a long corridor ending in a wide staircase, I reached the third floor just as the floodgates opened, students spewing from classrooms in all directions.

What struck me immediately as I peered around at my soon-to-be classmates were their beautiful clothes—the types of ensembles displayed in Pudong's fashionable galleria shops. And though my hair was stylishly cut and my makeup applied competently, looking down at my plain cotton shirt and slightly wrinkled broadcloth pants, I knew in my heart I didn't belong here.

Girding myself for the humbling experience surely awaiting me, I slipped into my designated room wondering if my pen and small notebook were adequate for note-taking. My eyes traveling to the front where a chalkboard should be, they suddenly bugged out; this was like no classroom I'd ever seen.

Where tight rows of small desks should have been, makeup stations, mirrors, and mannequin heads stood instead. Taking a stool near the back, I selected an angled brush and nervously twisted it in my hands as if a pencil.

"Is this seat taken?" a stunning girl with large, expressive eyes and porcelain skin asked. For once in my life, I was at a true loss for words. I simply shook my head.

Gracefully lowering herself onto the stool, she set her expensive purse on the floor and reached out her hand, "I'm Xiao."

Before I could respond, a girl with short, unruly hair straddled the other stool, tossing her equally expensive purse beside Xiao's. I discreetly hid the one I'd found in a garbage bin under my chair.

"Did I miss anything important?" she asked.

Xiao and I shook our heads.

"I'm Ning, by the way."

郭

In our first class we learned about lip shades, and in the second, eyebrow shaping—a subject in which I excelled.

"Very nice," the instructor said when she viewed my work. Then she stepped to Ning's station and grimaced. "Start over."

"How did you get so good at this?" Xiao asked.

I shrugged. "I've worked in a spa for years?"

"Will you tutor me?" she said.

"I could eat a water buffalo," Ning announced when the teacher dismissed us.

Xiao laughed. "I've never even seen one of those."

"I've seen plenty," I said.

"In Shanghai?" Ning asked, raising her brows.

"No, Hunan. It's where I'm from," I said, somewhat embarrassed to admit it. Shanghainese generally thought themselves superior to and far more cultured than anyone outside their borders. This was a common message from my clients.

"I'm from Guangzhou," Ning piped up. "We're practically neighbors. Well, were, anyway."

"What do you mean?" I asked.

"After my mom died, we moved to Shanghai."

"I'm sorry," Xiao and I said at the same time.

Ning shrugged. "The Shanghai part wasn't so bad, but the horrible woman Baba married hates me."

"Surely not," Xiao said, looking troubled.

"My grandmother hates me," I offered.

"Sisters!" Ning exclaimed, laughing.

An orange brick building across a large lawn housed the cafeteria. Having little more than bus fare back to Pudong, I was planning on skipping lunch altogether, but trapped between my new friends, I felt I had to order something. Scanning the prices, I decided that I could just afford a small bowl of rice.

"Lunch is on me, ladies," Ning announced.

"That's very kind of you," Xiao replied. "But I have money."

"Well, I'm rich, and you are my new friends, so I'm treating." She raised a defiant eyebrow at Xiao. "Besides, the more of Baba's money

I spend, the less my stepmother gets when he dies. GuoGuo, what do you want?"

"Just rice," I responded, gaping at her.

"Rice? Are you on some strange diet?"

How could I tell these rich girls that I was nearly destitute? "No, I just don't want to take advantage of you."

"Three orders of braised pork belly," she told the server.

Xiao simply shook her head.

After lunch we walked to the performing arts building, joining the group gathered in front of a set of wide doors. STA was, of course, renowned for its theater program, and we learned, much to Xiao's delight, that this would be our stage makeup classroom.

"Working in the theater is my dream," Xiao excitedly whispered as we entered an impressive auditorium filled with row after row of velvet-covered seats. My eyes traveled up to the series of flat black speakers mounted to the ceiling.

"Backstage is magical," she continued. "When I was little, my parents took me to see *Teahouse*. The costumes, the hair, and the makeup mesmerized me. I wanted to perform. My parents even sent me to a theater camp. That's where I discovered I was a terrible actress and a worse singer." She shook her head, laughing. "I decided that if not destined for the stage, I could at least work behind it."

We passed by the wide, pale stage, where two students were rehearsing. A very attractive actor stopped mid-sentence and began serenading us.

"Beautiful makeup girls with necks like swans," he sang, altering the lyrics of a pop song.

Giggling, we hurried through a nondescript door into a well-lit room crammed with rows of hanging costumes.

"He was so cute," Xiao whispered.

"He thought you were, too," Ning said.

Xiao rolled her eyes.

"It's true," I said.

Chairs, mirrors, and scattered supplies cluttered the makeup room. Surveying the mess, our teacher grunted with displeasure. "Your first assignment is to prepare this room as if it were your own studio. Neatness and order should always be your goal."

While some girls seemed lost, I gathered handfuls of sponges and brushes and took them to the sink. Ning and Xiao followed me.

"What are you doing?" Ning asked.

"You must start with clean brushes, or the colors will mix and look bad. Why don't you know this?" I asked, perplexed.

"Well, I've never actually worked with makeup before," Ning said.

"Why are you in this program?" I asked. I did not intend to insult her, but her question seemed so odd.

"After failing out of college, Baba said I needed some sort of education. This sounded fun. I didn't know I'd have to *clean* anything," she said, wrinkling her nose.

Twice in as many hours, Xiao looked at her and then shook her head. I simply gaped.

When class was dismissed, we spilled back into the costume area. The actor who'd serenaded us was sorting through a rack. Glancing up, he smiled at Xiao.

郭

For the first time in my life, I loved being a student. Every day I looked forward to going to classes where math was counting brushes and writing was done on faces.

It took little time for my classmates to notice I wore the same outfit nearly every day. "Peasant Girl" soon became my nickname, which I laughed off. I could do little else, considering I lived in a supply closet and used bar tips to pay my bus fare.

"GuoGuo, I have an outfit that would look great on you," Xiao said as we left class one afternoon. "Do you want to borrow it?"

"I have one as well," Ning added too enthusiastically. "In fact, you can keep it. I don't even like it."

Though borrowing clothes from Nancy and Yuyu had become common practice, I felt embarrassed taking them from my new friends. Still, looking stylish might help me better fit in here.

"There's a party Saturday night. An actors' party. Zhxin invited us," Xiao sang. In a short time, Zhxin and she had gone from shy smiles in the costume room to kissing in public. "You two are coming. GuoGuo, want to borrow a dress?"

"Sure," I said.

郭

The year sped by. During the weekdays and on show nights, we made actors look beautiful, scary, old, or deranged. On weekends when I wasn't needed at Madame Li's bar, my friends and I attended parties, drank beer, and had a wonderful time.

Before we knew it, Xiao, Ning, and I stood on the grand theater's stage, not as actors or set designers, but as STA graduates. Grasping my diploma in June 2006 was one of the most satisfying moments of my life. It was the first time I'd truly accomplished something more than survival. Something I'd chosen for myself. Something difficult and challenging and absolutely rewarding.

I only wished Mama could have been there.

26

Mean Girls

I'd fully expected my STA diploma to land me nonstop jobs, and that money would pour into my pockets. This was not the case.

Photographers posted ads seeking make-up assistants for jobs. Partnering with anyone who'd take my call, I prepared brides for wedding shoots, models for print and television commercials—anything I could piece together. Genji called me whenever she needed extra help, and Madame Li occasionally threw me spa work—something I still loved. The most exciting opportunities, however, came from Xiao.

"Zhxin is performing tonight, and a stylist is sick. Want the job?"

A position at the Shanghai Dramatic Arts Center was the pinnacle of our profession. They hired only those with connections full-time, and even part-time work was impossible to get. Unless, of course, your boyfriend was starring in the show.

"Why do you ask such silly questions?"

郭

By fall, I'd developed a good relationship with several

photographers, who regularly called me before posting their jobs; I was making money. My landlord, so to speak, was not an easy person to get along with, and though Mr. Li didn't come by the bar all that often, when he did, we ended up in a disagreement. Our longest-running debate was over phone usage.

"My bar is not your business address, and my bartenders aren't your secretaries."

"I'm sorry, but I can't afford my own phone right now." By this time, all of my STA friends had cell phones. Of course, most also had rich parents subsidizing their expenses.

"I give you free room and board. What do you use your money for?" he said, his eyes flicking over my outfit. "Other than dressing like a fashion model."

"I have business expenses," I said. The ongoing cost of makeup, hair products, and accouterments was outrageous.

He snorted. "Buy fewer clothes. Get a phone."

"He's right," Nancy said, much to my dismay. "It's impossible to run a Shanghai business without one. But what you need more than a phone is your own apartment."

"I'll drink to that," I said.

郭

Nancy introduced me to an associate who owned several apartments in Pudong, one of which had a room available in my price range. The two-bedroom apartment came with two roommates. My thoughts immediately turned to Ting, Yang, Jin, and the wonderful time we'd had in Changsha. I looked forward to making sisters of Candy and Sugar as well.

Bedsheets like pale flags swayed on long metal poles poking from every window of the old French Concession building. Dodging great drips and sidewalk puddles, I passed by the first story's barred casement windows, finally entering the formidable stairwell at the far end. With no elevators, the higher the floor, the cheaper the rent; this was common practice in Shanghai. Grateful to have few belongings, I hoisted the box over my head and began the long climb.

It took only days to realize that my roommates and I had little in common. Candy waitressed at an American restaurant, and Sugar worked in a Western clothing store; both spoke fluent English. What little of that language I'd learned had been mostly forgotten by now. Though I was as friendly to them as possible, they did not warm to me.

The girls had had an arrangement with their previous roommate to split grocery and alcohol costs. Since I drank at Dancing Tiger and ate at the Li's bar, where I now earned wages, paying for supplies I did not use seemed ridiculous. My roommates saw it differently, and our relationship quickly deteriorated.

"She's a Hunan girl," Candy scornfully said to her friends, most of whom spent more time in our apartment than I. "I heard her last roommates were ducks and pigs."

"And she didn't pay for their food either," Sugar added loudly, banging on the thin bedroom wall.

Nancy's bar quickly became my refuge.

By the third month, living with my roommates had become unbearable.

"What have you done?" I screeched, storming into the living room, clutching my empty money pouch.

"Taking what you owe us," Sugar replied airily.

"I don't owe you any money. I paid my share of the rent last week."

"But not the food," Candy snarled.

"I. Don't. Eat. Here!" I yelled.

"We. Don't. Want. You. Living here!" they both yelled back.

"Fine," I said, slamming the bedroom door.

Wiping hot tears on my sleeve, I boarded a crowded bus, ringing the bell as soon as Nancy's apartment building came into view; her bedroom floor was perfectly fine for sleeping on. Besides, it was always better to be tripped over by a friend than kicked by enemies.

27

The American

"Nothing erases terrible memories like tacos and tequila," Nancy said brightly, pressing a short skirt in my hands. "Come on."

Pudong had several American restaurants, but only one Mexican place. Opposite Xigou Port, Cantina Agave was housed in a vividly yellow three-story. Neon lights shaped like spiky vegetables flashed in the windows.

After splitting a meal in the top-floor restaurant, we wandered downstairs to check out the gleaming bar. Against the entire back wall of a smoky room crammed with people, bartenders took turns juggling liquor bottles and pouring shots.

"You should do that in your bar," I said, pointing.

When the crowd started chanting, "Tequila," we joined in.

A male bartender climbed onto the glossy counter and yelled, "Arriba!" pouring liquor right down several customers' throats.

"Come on!" Nancy yelled, dragging me through the crowd to claim a spot upfront. Like baby birds waiting for Mama, we swallowed the searing liquid again and again. In no time, I was lightheaded.

"Bathroom," Nancy suddenly announced, pointing to the stairs.

"After you," I said, sweeping my arm dramatically and then nearly toppling down them.

"Ooh, beer," Nancy said, as we entered the basement.

"Ooh, dancing," I replied.

Casting snowflakes of light in all directions, a rotating disco ball spun feverishly above a pulsing dancefloor. Itching to join the writhing bodies, we looked for a place to set down our heavy, glass beer mugs.

"What about over there," I said, pointing to an empty booth immediately commandeered by a group of five.

"They should install more counter space," Nancy groaned.

Wandering over to a small table where two nicely dressed guys sat, I said, "Could we set our drinks here?"

"Sure. We'll keep them safe for you," the cute Chinese guy replied, his eyes sweeping over Nancy. "You want to dance?"

"Sure," she said, winking at me as she turned.

His American tablemate rose and held out his hand. I couldn't believe how tall he was. And those blue eyes... Smiling, I led the way.

He had good moves, but he kept trying to talk to me. I couldn't hear well over the throbbing beat, but it didn't matter; I couldn't have understood him, anyway. His Shanghainese was terrible, and my English was worse.

Late that night, after vomiting twice—once on our taxi's hood—I collapsed on Nancy's floor. And when the sun broke through her windows moments later, I decided I should just lie there until I died. An insect buzzed near my ear, and I slapped at it. When it made the oddly familiar sound again, I realized it was my new cell phone. Bleary-eyed, I stared at the screen.

"Who is this Dave person?" I asked an already dressed and alert Nancy.

Thrusting a cup of tea in my hand, she said, "I think he's that American guy from last night."

"How did he get my number?" I asked, squinting up at her.

"Did you give it to him?"

"I don't remember."

"What does it say?" she asked, peering down.

"It says, 'I like'—I don't know what this next word is—'with you long—no, last night.'"

Nancy snatched the phone from my hand and pressed the screen nearly to her nose. "It says, 'I liked dancing with you last night'."

"Oh. What should I say?"

"Say, 'me too'."

As soon as I sent it, I got a reply. Nancy read it to me. "Let's have dinner Friday night."

Gasping, I looked up at her. "What now?"

"Do you want to go?"

"I'm not sure. I don't know this guy. He could be a gangster."

Nancy sank to the floor, laughing. "A gangster? What are you talking about? He's a businessman."

"I don't know if that's any better," I muttered.

"He was cute, and you haven't been on a date since we met. Do it."

Taking the phone, I texted, *No.*

"What are you doing?" Nancy said, "Americans are rich. You shouldn't turn him down so quickly. Make up some excuse."

"Like what?"

"How about, I'm meeting friends?"

"That's good. You type it," I said, pressing my phone back into her hand.

When I returned from the bathroom and he still hadn't replied, I said, "Well, that's that. Now on to important matters. I need to find a new apartment."

"I'll get a newspaper," she said, lunging for the door.

Nancy and I pored over ads until we found a place that was very cheap. I made arrangements to view it that afternoon.

All the way up in Puxi Residential District, an old and densely populated part of town, the building was narrow, short, and looked as though it might tip over in a strong wind. Several rats scurried out of the vacant second-floor apartment when the landlord opened the door. The single room was small and square. There was no kitchen or plumbing of any kind, and the building's one communal bathroom was at the foot of the stairs below.

After fierce negotiation, the renter, who oddly resembled the building itself, accepted my offer.

"This place is shit," Nancy announced, setting down my box. "And what is that stench?"

"It's called death. The landlord said the man below me is dying, and I need to be quiet while he does it. He's been dying for a while evidently."

She gave me a stern look. "You should text that American back."

郭

Rats didn't bother me that first night because I had no food for them, but the couple above me fought loudly, and the man below continued to stink. The next morning, the American texted again.

Hi Stephanie, how are you?

I paged through my English translation book, searching for a proper response. *Fine. How are you?* I slowly typed.

I think you should go out with me.

Why?

I'm a nice guy.

Well, I had heard that many times before, and it was rarely true. *No, thank you.*

The next morning, I received yet another text from this Dave person.

Hi, how are you?

I didn't know what to think. What did he want with me? I certainly wasn't going to have sex with him just because he texted me a few times.

I must work.

What do you do?

I couldn't find the English word for cosmetologist or esthetician, so I texted, *I am a spa person.*

Leaving my building at dawn, I avoided the puddles of fermented liquid oozing from a clutter of trash bags and turned my eyes from beggars huddled against walls. I had nothing to give them at the moment, but unlike the many pedestrians who chastised them, I felt for their plight. Had I not been afforded the kindness of Chao, Guo, and Madame Li, I could easily have become one of those countless dirty faces.

Like a prostitute?

I deciphered his response while standing in the long bus stop line and then rolled my eyes at the stupidity of this American. There were two kinds of spas in China: whorehouses and places of beauty. Why would he assume the worst?

No! I make women's faces look good.

The young child beside me urinated through her split-pants. I stepped around the trickle and boarded the over-packed bus.

Oh. Sorry, he quickly replied.

The bus lurched forward and then listed to one side when the driver turned a corner. Losing my balance, I slid against the frowning man beside me. *I must go*, I typed.

The American texted every morning for the next month. He asked many questions, and each day I answered one. When he told me his age, I balked; he was sixteen years older than me—practically middle-aged.

"That Dave guy keeps asking me out," I told Nancy over Friday night gambling.

"You should go. Check him out. He was cute." Nancy tapped the table once, her eyes lighting after receiving the card.

"*You* should go out with him," I snipped, tapping the table twice.

"He didn't ask *me* out."

"But he's so old."

"He didn't look old to me. Besides, you want an older guy. They're stable and less stupid."

The guy to my left groaned, but the dealer smiled and nodded her head sagely.

"Did you really think he was cute?" I said, trying not to smile; I had a good hand now.

Nancy rolled her eyes, laid down her hand, and took the table's money. "Go."

郭

My STA friends and my Hunan friends agreed with Nancy, so I arranged to meet him for lunch. Lunch kept things very casual with no expectations.

Dave chose a dim sum restaurant. Dim sum is a Cantonese affair in which carts carrying an array of small dishes, such as wontons, sesame balls, or chicken feet, are wheeled around the room. The selections differ by cart, and you never know what they'll be. This was an excellent choice for a first date.

Dave and I had the only kind of conversation two people who speak different languages can have—lots of hand motions, choppy sentences, and smiling. He said many funny things in Shanghainese, and I laughed a lot.

"What's your real name? I know it's not Stephanie."

"It's Hong Bo, but my friends call me GuoGuo."

"We're friends, right? Can I call you that?"

Friends was a safe term, and after so many communications, I supposed it was accurate enough. "Okay, you can call me that."

He was as handsome as Nancy had claimed, and I blushed far too often. Unfortunately, by the end of our date, he'd only ordered three dishes for us to share. Dim sum dishes are generally inexpensive, and it left me wondering whether he was cheap, poor, or clueless.

After leaving the restaurant, we walked along the Yangtze River boardwalk. Small, white-tipped wavelets hurried to the banks, and seagulls, begging for scraps, squawked at us. The December wind was biting, and he offered me his jacket, which was very gentlemanly. As he settled it around my shoulders, he tried to kiss me. I decided then that our date was over.

That evening, he texted me, telling me he'd enjoyed lunch, and asking me out for the following Friday night.

"Nancy, what do you think?"

"Look, if you went to America, would you know how to order whatever they eat? He's been after you too long to be cheap when he finally sees you. If you want to know for sure, have dinner with him. Then you can decide. Either way, a cheap date is better than no date."

Nancy and I had different ideas about romance.

I wouldn't let him pick me up at my apartment. The guy below me still hadn't died, and it smelled even worse now. I met him at Dancing Tiger, and Nancy flirted with him until his cheeks turned red.

Climbing into a taxi, we headed for the Bund, a famous waterside area offering sweeping city views. After working a matinee theater performance with Xiao, she'd done my hair and makeup and loaned me a beautiful dress. When I entered the restaurant Dave had chosen, I was instantly grateful; it was the nicest place I'd ever seen. Dave ordered a bottle of white wine, and again we worked hard at communicating.

After a glorious and incredibly expensive dinner, he took me to a Western club with live music. The best musicians in Shanghai are actually Filipino, and this band was extremely good. We danced to many songs and drank more wine, and he behaved like a gentleman all evening. When our date was over, he didn't try to kiss me and didn't ask for sex.

Pleased that I'd given him a second chance, the next time he asked me out, I immediately said yes.

28

The Gentleman Test

Dave and I began seeing each other regularly, usually on Friday night. We dined in fancy restaurants, often attending shows or discos afterward. I hadn't eaten so well in my entire life! Though not uncommon to see Americans and Chinese interacting socially, we still got strange looks; I wasn't sure how I felt about that. But just like his texting campaign, his attentiveness won me over.

I decided that if I were really going to date Dave, I needed a better apartment—one with a shower and no dead people living nearby, one I would be comfortable showing him if it ever got to that point. I found an inexpensive unit back in Pudong, only six blocks from Dancing Tiger.

郭

"He is punctual," Nancy murmured, nodding as Dave's driver effortlessly parked the silver Mercedes against the curb.

Hopping up, I straightened my skirt, ever grateful to the many friends who regularly loaned me stylish outfits; I couldn't have afforded to date Dave otherwise.

"You ready?" he said, waving to Nancy as he opened my door.

"Where are we headed tonight?" I asked, scooting across the firm leather seat.

"I thought we'd go to my house for a change."

"Your house?" I said, hoping that in my flawed English intonations, he hadn't registered my anxiety. Though I definitely liked him, I wasn't ready for the next step.

Crossing what seemed the entirety of Pudong, the driver finally turned into a gated neighborhood filled with nothing but mansions.

"You live *here*?" I choked out, stunned.

He shrugged. "Corporate housing. Do you like it?"

All of Shanghai was piled on top of itself, yet these houses were like islands surrounded by grassy seas! "It's pretty," I said nonchalantly.

Passing one stately home after another, we finally pulled into a long circular driveway lined with short azalea shrubs, their leaves surely under some magic spell to remain green in this icy air. Taking my hand, he led me up the wide stone stairs and under the front porch. Waiting as he pressed in a long security code, I leaned against a fat white column to keep from collapsing of shock.

If anything, the interior was more elaborate than the façade, with its intricately patterned polished stone floors and curving staircase.

"I had the maid leave out dinner," he said, as I followed him to a large sunken living area. Handing me a glass of red wine, he motioned to a sleek and curving couch. The utter cleanliness of this common space struck me; his maid must surely be extraordinary.

"So, where is everyone else?" I asked, looking around.

"Everyone else who?" he said.

"The other people who live here."

"It's just me."

"This entire house is yours only?"

"It's pretty standard in American neighborhoods for everyone to have their own houses."

I was beyond shocked. I'd heard America was a rich and beautiful country—*Meigou*, the Mandarin name for America, means "beautiful country"—but this seemed obscene. And in that moment, I realized I could never invite Dave to my simple apartment, no matter how proud of it I was.

I called Jin as soon as I got home.

"So, let me get this straight," she said. "You went to his mansion for dinner, and he didn't hit on you?"

"I told him we were just friends, and he said he was okay with that."

"Uh huh," she scoffed. "No man is okay with a woman's friendship if he can have sex with her instead."

"He's just gone through a painful divorce. He moved to Shanghai for a fresh start. I think he's sincere."

"Pah!" she said. "Now you sound like Yang. What if he's lying about the divorce? What if he just feels guilty about betraying his wife and children back home? Maybe that's the only reason he's holding back. Think about it, GuoGuo. Why would a woman divorce a wealthy man for no good reason?"

"What if he's telling the truth?" I snapped, hoping she was wrong; needless to say, the thought had occurred to me. "He said his ex-wife was also a successful businessperson. Maybe she has her own money and doesn't need his."

"Or maybe he's a terrible person!" Jin retorted. Recently cheated on, Jin's opinion of men was not high at the moment. "And what kind of company is UPS? I've never heard of it."

Neither had I. He'd said he was a strategist—I'd made certain to get the facts right away—but I had no idea what that meant or what his company shipped.

"I'm sure it's legitimate, Jin. And he's always behaved gentlemanly."

"Eventually, he's going to want more than friendship. Before you give in to him, think about your future. Do you really want to become his plaything? Because that's all you'll ever be. I'm sorry to say it, but what else would a rich American want with a poor Chinese farm girl?"

郭

To test Dave's sincerity, Jin and I devised a plan. Spending time with him had cost me many Friday night card games. This week's meeting place was near Dave's neighborhood—if a half-hour bus-ride away counted as near.

"Our games break up really late, and since my apartment's on the other side of Pudong, I'd feel more comfortable staying in one of your guest rooms, if that's okay. There's been a lot of crime lately," I added. It was a flimsy excuse because I traveled late at night all the time, and in a large city like Shanghai, crime was as common as poverty. He immediately agreed.

When I arrived at his house, which I learned was a twenty-minute walk from the nearest bus stop, he greeted me with a warm embrace, gently kissing my cheek.

"I'm so glad you're here. Did you have fun?"

"Yes. I won big," I replied, smiling up at him.

After a drink, he gave me a tour of the house that eventually ended in a generous guestroom, its walls hung with beautiful paintings.

In Black Village, people decorated their walls with bicycle tires; our family room had three. Our worlds were so different it was laughable.

He had laid clean towels and an unused cake of soap out in the tiled bathroom. Once he showed me how to use the complicated shower, he kissed my cheek again and closed the door behind him. I texted Jin immediately. *Ha!*

In the morning, I wandered downstairs and found him seated at the dining room table, reading an American newspaper. With the sweetest smile, he said, "Good morning, Sunshine. Did you sleep well?" The enormous mattress had been so thick and soft, I could have stayed there all week.

"Like a baby's butt," I replied. Dave had been teaching me American phrases, most of which seemed odd.

He exploded with laughter.

"Did I get it wrong?" I said, my face flushing.

"No, you're doing great. Soon people will think you're American. Do you want something to eat? Eggs maybe?"

"Sure."

"Pang," he called out. "We'll have breakfast now."

"Okay, Mr. Wiseman," a voice sang from the kitchen.

In mere moments, a woman carrying a steaming teapot entered through a swinging door. Returning shortly after with more food than we could eat in a week, she laid out the dishes. Perhaps ten years my elder, the only thing she didn't offer me was a smile.

"I've got to go to the office for a few hours," Dave said as she cleared the plates. "I'd love to take you to lunch. Will you stay?"

Feeling very pleased with the situation, after he left, I locked the bedroom door and climbed into the lovely shower. Before I'd even rinsed my hair, the maid began banging on the door. Leaving a wet trail behind me, I peeked outside.

"What do you want?"

Scowling, she said, "Time to clean your room. Get out."

"Come back in a little while. I'm not finished showering."

"You shouldn't use so much of Mr. Dave's water," she snipped.

Well, after that comment, I can promise my fingers resembled shriveled plums before I finally turned off the spigot.

郭

As dusk approached, I told Dave it was time for me to go home. I'd canceled a makeup shoot, which I knew would hurt my standing with that particular photographer, but learning the truth about Dave's intentions had been worth it.

"I'll take you," he said.

"The bus is fine. Really."

"Don't be ridiculous. Besides, I get more time this way."

As we neared my apartment, I became nervous; I wasn't ready for him to see it yet. "Could you drop me off at the bar. I left something there."

"I can wait," he said when the car came to a stop.

"N—um, I'll probably be awhile."

"Oh. Well, I guess this is goodnight then," he said. "It was nice spending the day with you. Really nice." Leaning over, he touched his lips to mine. His kiss was gentle and undemanding, and warmth spread through me like thick honey. When he pulled back, my lips tingled. "Stay again next Friday night if you'd like—or anytime."

"I just might," I replied, surely glowing in the darkness.

郭

No ghosts had bothered me since moving to Shanghai, but on my third Friday night in Dave's guest room, that changed. I awoke amid a fancy party, the finely dressed women and men surrounding the bed soundlessly laughing and talking with one another; some smoked cigarettes, which I could smell!

Once the vision faded and my body relaxed from paralysis, I flew screaming into Dave's bedroom.

Wearing pajama bottoms and a startled expression, he hopped to his feet. "Are you okay?"

"The ghosts are here! They've followed me. They're in my room!"

Dave could not understand me, of course, because he didn't speak my native dialect. Instead, he wrapped his arms around my quivering body and gently rocked me against his hair-dusted chest. Eventually calm enough to speak, I told him all that I'd seen.

I expected him to laugh at me, but instead, he simply said, "Sleep here. I'll keep you safe."

This was not a ploy to get into his bed; had I wanted relations, I'm certain he would have happily accommodated me. Regardless, I was not going back into that guest room or any other.

After he returned from checking out my room, he eased his mostly naked body back into bed. With a slight shock, I realized how truly large he was. Chinese people are not big. With his six-foot-two-inch-height and proportionate frame, Dave suddenly seemed a giant.

A blush crawled up my cheeks. "I'll just sleep on the floor."

Pulling back the covers, he patted the mattress. "Climb into bed with me, GuoGuo. I won't do anything." When I simply stared at him, he shook his head, stifling a yawn. "You sleep on your side, and I'll sleep on mine."

Biting my lip, I reluctantly climbed under the sheets and then wedged my pillow between us so we weren't touching. The mattress shook with his laughter.

When I awoke in the morning, the pillow was right where I'd placed it. He hadn't touched me as promised, and other than his lovely kisses, I began wondering if he truly only wanted to be friends. Staring at his handsome profile, I wasn't sure how I felt about that anymore.

He stirred and then sat up. "Good morning, Sunshine." His strangely colored eyes were warm and kind, and I had the sudden urge to run my fingers through his mussed sandy-brown hair just to know what it felt like.

"Good morning, Dave."

"No more ghosts?"

"No more," I said. "Thanks for letting me sleep here."

A lopsided smile crossed his face. "You can sleep with me anytime you want."

Removing the pillow, I rose to my knees and kissed his cheek. His beard stubble scratched my lips, making them tingle. I lightly kissed his lips, and he wrapped his arms around me, deepening it.

We didn't have sex. But there are other ways to be intimate.

29

New Year

Lunar New Year 2007 was the pig year—*my* year. Though one's zodiac year is traditionally considered unlucky, I felt the opposite. I was not destitute; I'd earned a degree from a premier academy; I was making headway towards my dream job; and... I finally had a man in my life.

"Chinese New Year is all anyone at work is talking about. Parades, food. It sounds awesome," Dave said, his eyes twinkling in the candlelit.

"It's a very special time, and I haven't seen my family in so long."

"So, you're not staying in Shanghai then?" he said, looking disappointed.

"No. I'm going back to my village."

He was quiet for a moment, and then said, "I can drive you there."

"It's very far away. A thousand kilometers."

"Yep, that's pretty far," he said, chuckling. "I forget how big China is. Can I take you to the airport at least?"

"Thank you, but I'm going by train."

"By train?" he said, looking at me strangely. "Won't that take forever?"

"It's a long trip," I said, not looking forward to the cramped conditions and uncomfortable seats. Still, the price was right.

Then his eyes lit up. "Let me buy you a plane ticket instead."

A plane ticket was an extravagant gift, and the offer moved me, but we weren't far enough along in our relationship for me to accept it. "That's very generous, but I can't take advantage of you."

He laughed. "GuoGuo, you can take advantage of me. Trust me."

Taking a long sip of wine, I pondered how best to respond to such a statement. "That's not the kind of person I am. Besides, I've already spent the money, and my brother will be waiting at the station."

"How long will you be gone?" he asked.

"The holiday lasts fifteen days."

"Fifteen? Wow. That's... I'll miss you," he said earnestly.

"Me, too."

郭

The Olympics only a year away, it was as if Shanghai had bloomed after a warm spring rain. South Railway Station had bloomed as well, nearly tripling in size since I'd moved here. A good thing that it had, too, because, on China's most traveled day of the year, the cavernous space was at capacity.

Pushing my way onto the familiar platform, I swallowed a bitterness I feared would never leave me; Fu's living ghost haunted this place. And though two years had passed since I'd given up my fruitless search for him, I had not healed. The train doors opened, and I stepped inside.

As we pulled away from the station, a genuine spirit claimed my thoughts; Chao. Sweet Chao, and the choking sorrow of his loss.

Would his mother have meat to burn at his tomb on Sweeping Day? I wish I knew.

郭

"Ming!" I squealed, running towards him.

"Mei Zi!" he yelled, picking me up in his arms and swinging me in a circle. "Look at you, so grown up. No one will recognize you." Dressed in Xiao's beautiful castoffs, with a stylish haircut and skillfully applied makeup, I looked different—successful, I hoped.

Ming tied Ning's expensive red suitcase to the back of his motorcycle, and we set out for home.

Early morning sunbeams danced on the mountaintops, playing off the windswept clouds. As we sped down the highway, I shivered, but the thrilling sight of familiar farmland and the exultation I felt in simply filling my lungs with clean, country air vanquished my discomfort.

Over the motor's roar, Ming spoke of JiaoJiao nonstop—how resourceful she was, what a wonderful mother, what a skilled cook. He'd finally fallen in love with his wife. This news delighted me, but it was my niece I wanted to hear about. Mama was teaching her to cook eggs? The child was a prodigy!

Baba was puttering in the yard when we pulled up. "I'll tell everyone you're here," Ming quietly said, slipping off the motorcycle and disappearing inside.

Baba stood motionless. He'd aged far more than he ought to have in three and a half years. "Do you have my money?" he said in all seriousness.

Nonplussed, I simply gawked. Sure, I was making enough to live on, but I certainly didn't have thousands of RMB squirreled away.

"Um, well…" Glancing around the frozen yard, I wrestled with what to say. This wasn't exactly the reunion I'd envisioned. "See, the thing is," I said, meeting his eyes once more. Whatever nonsense I was about to spew died on my tongue. Baba was crying. I'd never seen him shed a tear; I didn't know he could. With a wavering smile, he opened his arms wide, and I flew into them.

"I've missed you so much," he choked out, hugging me hard.

"I've missed you, too, Baba!"

Letting go far too soon, he gruffly said, "You'd better go introduce yourself. Your mother won't recognize you."

郭

"Mei Zi!" Mama yelped when I entered the rustic kitchen. Unlike Baba, she was timeless. After accepting a brief hug, which I reveled in, she held me at arm's length, appraising me for a long moment. "You look different," she said, touching my nose. "What have you done?"

"Plastic surgery. It's what all the fashionable girls in Shanghai do, Mama."

"You're a Hunan girl."

"I'm both now."

"Mei Zi!" Auntie Song yelled, followed in short order by JiaoJiao and a parade of cousins. The sentiment nearly overwhelmed me, as did the barrage of questions. *Yes, Shanghai is wonderful, no, I'm not rich, a boyfriend? Well…*

"I have something for you," I said to my parents a little later. I'd brought them many gifts, in fact. A few were nice, most were cheap, but one was priceless—at least to me. Hurrying to my suitcase, which

Ming had left in my old bedroom, I returned just as Mama was setting out tea.

"Mama, Baba, this is for you both."

Mama opened the sturdy red folder and stared at the square parchment inside. The Shanghai Theatre Academy diploma looked every bit as prestigious as it should. Running her fingers over the embossed lettering, she seemed confused. "This book is very nice. What's this design?"

Baba plucked it from her, admiring it. "Beautiful. You can wrap a New Year's gift with this thick paper, Meilin." Gripping it between two soiled fingers, he started pulling it out.

"What? No! That's my diploma," I said, snatching it out of his hands. How could I have forgotten that they couldn't read? "This says I graduated from the Academy. I want you to have it. I need you to know that I didn't waste your money."

"Oh," Baba said, reverently taking it back. He traced each of the gold characters and then looked up with a twinkle in his eye. "We paid seven-thousand RMB for this?"

"Too expensive," Mama said, smiling through her tears.

郭

New Year's Eve, the most important day of the festival, celebrates family reunions. It's customary to set a place for those who couldn't come home. While stranded in Shanghai, I'd cringed each year on this day, knowing Mama would look at my empty plate and cry. But this year, Wai po had no reason to chastise her for raising such a neglectful daughter; I was here, with gifts for all.

My diploma made the rounds before dinner, and after gorging on dumplings, spring rolls, and all manner of lucky foods, I doled out trinkets. To my shock, once Wai po opened her small present—a cheap plastic comb I'd purchased from a street vendor, she immediately placed it in her hair.

"What fine jade," Mama said, winking at me.

"Shanghai jade," I said.

Suddenly, Wai gong, my blind grandfather, laughed loudly.

"And this is for you," I said, dangling a red silk pouch in front of WeiWei, hoping to lure my shy niece from JiaoJiao's lap.

郭

Dave called often. *Did you have a good trip? How's your family? Shanghai's dead!*

The fifth day of Spring Festival is called *Po Wu*, or "eat dumplings". The women in my family were packed into Mama's kitchen, assembling what seemed like thousands of them.

"More garlic," Auntie Song demanded.

"WeiWei, bring Mama another egg," JiaoJiao sang.

"Mei Zi, chop faster!" Mama ordered.

By this time, the novelty of my visit had completely worn off—"You're back, you're okay, can we eat now?"—so, no one paid any attention when my fancy cell phone's text notification sounded.

Guess where I am? It was Dave.

Shanghai? I typed.

Mama yelled out for another onion, and WeiWei dutifully pressed one into my hand; in my family, one is never too young to work. Snapping the phone shut, I set it by the chopping block and quickly removed the onion's crisp skin.

Hearing the ding again, I wiped my hands on my pants and flipped open my phone.

No. Somewhere far from Shanghai.

"I want to hold it!" WeiWei demanded, tugging on my sleeve. The Dancing Tiger remained open during the holiday because, in Nancy's opinion, money was money. To stave off boredom between customers, she and WeiWei had been texting gibberish back and forth all week.

"In a minute, pumpkin," I said, ruffling her hair.

Dave hadn't mentioned travel plans, and I was a little hurt that he'd chosen not to share them with me. *America?* I typed.

No. Give up?

Yes, I give up.

I'm at the airport, he typed.

Why are you at the airport?

Because my plane just landed. Hunan is beautiful.

"No!" I shrieked, covering my face.

"Mei Zi, has one of your ghosts come to help us?" Wai po said, cackling.

Looking around at the concerned faces, I said, "I have to make an important call."

"Here's your phone, Auntie," WeiWei said, poking into my thigh. "You dropped it."

郭

Like American Christmas, Lunar New Year is a time for family. It's inappropriate to invite someone you're casually dating to such a celebration. And in my conservative village, where customs were revered, bringing home a man I wasn't engaged to would spell disaster for my family. Though I would be far removed from the whispers, accusations, and criticism in Shanghai, my parents, especially Mama, would bear the brunt. Worse still, Dave wasn't even Chinese. To some, his light hair and blue eyes would be truly shocking.

Plucking the phone from my niece's little hands, I raced into the farmyard, my fingers shaking as I dialed his number.

"Hey, GuoGuo, I—"

"Why did you come here?" I hissed.

"I wanted to celebrate with you. Can you give me your parents' address?"

Walking in circles, my thoughts chased one another. On the one hand, his desire to spend this special time with me touched me. On the other, how could he assume this would be acceptable?

Thinking back to our failed dim sum date and Nancy's correct assumption that he simply hadn't understood our culture, perhaps this too was a mystery to him. After all, America didn't celebrate Lunar New Year as far as I knew.

Cultural differences quickly led my thoughts to financial ones. What would someone so rich think of my family's poor living conditions? I cataloged the puddles peppering the dirt yard, the pigs snuffling about, and to my horror, our stinking outhouse. Nightmare!

"Getting to my village is really complicated," I said. "You have to take a bus to a different town and then walk miles up a mountain road. Taxis don't even come here. And for an American who only speaks Shanghainese,"—*and not well at that*—"asking directions from people who barely understand Mandarin will be impossible. I need to think. I'll call you back."

The homey smell of dumplings scented the breeze. It would soon be time to eat a meal that traditionally went on for hours. This was very bad timing.

"Ming!" I yelled, marching into the main house.

"What do you want, Mei Zi? I'm busy winning right now." At a table pressed against the moldy couch, which had only gotten moldier over time, Ming was playing cards with Chen and two other cousins.

"I need to talk to you. It's important."

"What's so important that it can't wait?" Ming took another card from the deck; he had an excellent hand.

Pinching his ear until he stood, I thrust a young cousin into his chair and handed her the cards.

Chen smiled widely. "You will not be winning for long now!"

"Are you looking for a fight, Mei Zi?" Ming grumped, his face turning red. Exchanging ear for arm, I tugged him upstairs and into my room. "I have a problem."

"What's that got to do with me?"

"I'm seeing a guy in Shanghai."

Ming's eyebrows drew together. "Is he treating you well? Are you pregnant?"

"Yes—no, I'm not pregnant! That's not the problem. The thing is, well, he flew in."

"Why are you telling me this? Invite him to dinner." My brother had never been one to consider consequences.

"You don't understand. He's American."

Ming's face lost all expression. Then he began to laugh. Then he threw his head back and laughed and laughed until he could no longer breathe. "You're in so much trouble," he finally choked out.

"Listen, I need to go to Changsha. Can I borrow your motorcycle?"

He snorted. "I'll take you. I want to meet this guy."

"Mama, great news," I announced, breezing back into the kitchen.

"One of my Shanghai friends flew into Changsha. I'm going to go see them for a little while."

"Dinner is almost ready. Invite them here," Mama said.

"Boy or girl?" Baba asked, his arms full of fresh logs for the stove.

I glanced at Ming's grinning face. "A boy, actually."

"Then no dinner. Who is this boy?" Baba said.

Ming raised his eyebrows and nodded. "Tell him."

"He's American," I mumbled.

"What did she say?" Auntie Song yelled out over the sizzling wok.

"She said, he's American!" WeiWei's high-pitched voice rang out. Suddenly, everyone wore the same expression of horror.

Mama marched me to the pigpen. "How do you know an American?"

"He works in Shanghai. We're friends. I didn't invite him here," I added quickly.

"*Friends* don't travel across China to see women. Especially if they aren't invited."

"He doesn't know any better. He's unfamiliar with Chinese customs."

Mama glanced back at the doorway where Baba and Ming were locked in a heated discussion. "What does an American want with a country girl besides relations? You aren't stupid. You know this!"

This was not a topic I felt comfortable discussing with my mother. She looked even less comfortable. "We haven't had relations, Mama. We're not serious at all."

She grunted. "He thinks differently." Her eyes drifted to the tombs behind our house. From her expression, I imagined she was waiting for our ancestors to float down and admonish her. "He can't come here."

"I know that, Mama. Ming's escorting me to Changsha. He'll talk to him."

"You send him home," she growled.

"Yes, Mama."

郭

Ming was surprisingly cordial to Dave, and we spent the next several hours talking at the hotel's restaurant, which was miraculously open. Through my interpretations, Ming fired an arsenal of questions at him—some very personal. Once satisfied that his intentions were honorable, Ming called Baba, and late that night, we piled precariously onto Ming's motorcycle and traveled to Black Village.

"We may still have guests. Stay here," Ming said, disappearing inside.

"It's so quiet. And look at all the stars," Dave whispered, squeezing my waist.

"Yes, we do have those," I replied, grateful for the darkness blanketing our yard.

"It's okay," Ming yelled.

Leading him inside, I held my breath. "Baba, Mama, this is my friend, Dave."

Dave's eyes swept over our humble living room, the empty tables, the scattered chairs left after the feast. Then in poorly pronounced Mandarin, he said, "Hello, Mr. and Mrs. Guo." Baba shook the hand he offered, looking slightly unsettled. Mama just stared.

"What's wrong with his eyes?" she suddenly said.

"Nothing. He has American eyes," I replied, smiling up at him. The color of a crisp winter sky, his eyes had mesmerized me during our first date, and sometimes I still found myself lost in them.

Baba then said to Mama, "What strange hair. Like a water buffalo."

"And big," Mama added, her eyes flicking from head to feet. "Like a white tree."

I smiled at Dave, refusing to translate any of this and so grateful he didn't understand our dialect.

As the silence stretched, Ming finally said, "Do you play mahjong?"

"No, but I'd love to learn," he said in English.

After translating this, Baba said, "Mei Zi, teach him." Then to Dave: "Do you want binlang?"

"He doesn't want any, Baba. He doesn't smoke either," I said, pleased that he was at least being hospitable.

"Does he drink tea?" Mama asked, eyeing him skeptically.

"Yes," I said, stifling a laugh.

Dave picked up mahjong quickly, and the five of us began playing, Dave and I sharing tiles.

"What's your job?" Baba asked.

"I develop global strategies for a shipping company."

I didn't know any of the words he was using, so I said, "He's a rich businessman."

Baba nodded appreciatively. "Mei Zi tells us Shanghai is an expensive place. How's the recycling business there?"

"He wants to know what your favorite part of Shanghai is," I lied.

After Dave rambled on about the coastline and how it reminded him of the place where he grew up, I looked at Baba and said, "Dave says, you wouldn't believe the things people in Shanghai throw out. Bottles, tires, even appliances and bedding. You could make lots of money selling all that junk."

"Maybe we'll move there, Meilin," he joked.

"Have you had relations?" Mama demanded, pointing her finger at him. My jaw dropped open, and Ming fell back in his chair laughing.

Dave smiled, taking Ming's cue.

"Stop smiling and say no," I hissed.

"What did she ask?"

Mortified, I said, "If we've had sex."

"What?" Dave choked out, sputtering. He met Mama's eyes and shook his head solemnly. "No, ma'am. We have not."

"See, I told you we were just friends," I said brightly, dying inside. "Move this tile," I then whispered to Dave, desperately trying to redirect the conversation.

"Hmm. For a foreigner, he's not so bad at this game," Baba remarked, scratching his chin.

For the next three hours, my parents randomly fired questions at Dave, and I watched the tension slowly bleed from their faces. After many yawns, Baba stood and said, "He's an acceptable acquaintance for you. He can come back tomorrow night. Late."

Feeling as if I'd won a great victory, I sagged with relief.

"No one can see him. Do you understand?" Mama said, glowering.

"Of course," I said.

"Take him back."

郭

Because we couldn't return the following night until darkness shrouded us, I had to find some way to entertain Dave. After a brief nap in his hotel room, I said, "I want to show you Hunan."

"I'd like to see it," he said.

"First to Chairman Mao's childhood home in Shaoshan. It's a tiny farming village like mine."

Chuckling, Dave shook his head.

"What?"

"The way you dress, your confidence. I didn't actually believe you'd grown up on a farm."

"Why would I lie about something like that?"

He shrugged.

"Now you've seen for yourself. Do you think less of me?"

He looked surprised. "Less of you? I'm relieved. Women aren't always truthful."

I laughed cynically. "Neither are men."

The idyllic village, set against rolling hills that seemed a constant in my province, was a favorite tourist attraction at any time of the year. Swerving around several colorfully dressed old women, we followed the narrow street leading to the impressive memorial. Purchasing fireworks from a vendor, I handed them to Dave.

"People light fireworks in front of Chairman Mao's statue and also his house because they praise him as a god. I heard a story once—you know the azalea flower, right?"

Dave nodded.

"Azaleas bloom in spring and summer, but when his statue arrived, even though it was winter, the azaleas bloomed."

"Really?" Dave asked, smiling.

"It's also said that a python watched over the statue. Mao was born in the snake year," I explained. "The snake stayed nearby during the whole installation, but when it was finished, the snake disappeared and was never seen again."

"And you believe this?" Dave said, his eyes sparkling with mischief.

"Lots of people saw the snake! We learned it in school. My teacher also said that when workers tried lifting the heavy bronze statue by its neck, it wouldn't budge, no matter how hard they pulled. Eventually, someone suggested putting the rope around the Chairman's waist instead. This worked immediately."

Walking around the statue, Dave scratched his head. "Maybe it had something to do with the angle."

"And the man who'd tied the rope around the Chairman's neck died from a mysterious disease soon after."

"You learned a lot of interesting things in school," Dave said, smirking.

I laughed. "Maybe so. Now, light the fireworks before the snake comes back."

After touring the house and sharing more interesting facts, I took him to a local restaurant.

"Hong Shao pork belly is a famous Hunan dish," I said as they served our food. "You'll like it." Cooked in an aromatic sauce spiced with cinnamon and star anise, it was one of my favorites. Deeply inhaling, I took a large bit. "Hey, this is all gristle and fat," I said, forcing the wad of meat down my throat.

"It's not too bad," Dave said, chewing and chewing and chewing.

"No, these people are using cheap meat to trick the tourists. I'll make this for you when we return to Shanghai."

"You cook?" Dave asked, wiping his fingers.

"In my village, I'm known for it. Mothers want me to marry their sons so I can cook for them."

"Really?" He laughed. "But the sons want you because you're beautiful." A blush crept up my face as I met his eyes.

Dave took my hand when we left the restaurant, which gave me a secret thrill. In showing affection, Chinese people tend to be timid. It's rare to see men and women holding hands, hugging, or kissing in public. And though Mama personified this behavior—with a mother like Wai po, this was no surprise—my father had always been affectionate, pinching our cheeks, kissing us, telling us he loved us. Ming and I became students of his philosophy—what child doesn't crave physical contact, and I was glad Dave had been raised similarly.

We spent four days touring Hunan. I showed him all the places that had been meaningful to me while growing up, and we visited countless tourist sites. After waving goodbye in the Changsha airport, I felt oddly alone, and I realized with a shock that my feelings for him had deepened. The term "friends" didn't seem accurate anymore.

郭

Dave's smiling eyes met mine as I stepped off the train. After carrying my bag to the car, he opened the rear door for me; the heady scent of roses wafted out. Placing the beautiful bouquet in my lap, I said, "These are really lovely."

"I really missed you," he said, kissing me softly.

Self-conscious after spending the past fourteen hours on a dirty train filled with sweaty passengers, when we got to his place, I said, "I need a shower."

As soon as I turned off the water, he knocked on the guestroom door; though I refused to sleep there, the shower was not haunted as far as I could tell. "Can I come in?"

There were plenty of other bathrooms in this giant house, so I was confused. "I don't have clothes on."

"I was hoping you'd say that."

Wrapping a towel around myself, I padded across the room. His expression left no doubt about his intentions. "Dave, you can't see me naked."

"Why not?" he said, touching my lips with his. "I think you're beautiful."

I hadn't exposed so much as my midriff to a man since Fu. And though Dave's words weren't the same as his during that first horrible encounter, they still made me anxious. "I'm not comfortable with this," I said.

Dave nodded. "Then I'll give you your privacy. Find me in the living room."

Pacing back and forth for a long while, I thought about my situation. Unlike the young girl who'd been a helpless victim, I was a powerful woman now. And if Dave behaved poorly, well, I could march right out of the door and hail a cab. Moreover, I liked him—too much, maybe. Still, having sex was a big step. Mama's and Jin's warnings chased one another through my mind; I wasn't a stupid girl or a plaything. At least I hoped not.

He rose when I entered the room. Putting plenty of space between us, I stood at the opposite end of the sofa. "Look, Dave, I haven't had sex in a very long time, and that relationship ended badly. Plus, we haven't even stated our status yet."

His lips curved up.

"Why are you making that face? You think this is funny?"

"No. And I appreciate your honesty. But 'stated our status'? I don't understand."

"You haven't asked me to be your girlfriend. I don't know if we're exclusive or casual."

Crossing the space, he pulled me into his arms. "If I didn't consider you my girlfriend—my *only* girlfriend—I wouldn't have flown all the way to Hunan to see you. I really care for you, GuoGuo," he said, lifting my chin. "Please be my girlfriend."

I wanted this, I realized. Wanted him. I'd brushed off many men out of fear, and in doing so, I'd kept myself safe. It was time to bury my past and reclaim my life.

"Okay," I said after a moment. "I'll be your girlfriend."

Taking my face in his hands, he kissed me for a long time. Then he picked me up in his arms and carried me to his bedroom. "I'm going to make love to my girlfriend now. Is that okay with you?"

I nodded timidly.

Dave was nothing like Fu. Gentle and attentive, he took things slowly, letting me have him on my terms. And when it was over, he held me, kissed me, stroked my arms, and told me again that he cared for me.

In a single intimate act, Dave erased the ugliness of sex for me, and I began feeling clean inside, whole again. He might never understand the tremendous gift he'd given me, but I would never forget it. It was as if I were giving my virginity to him.

30

Haunted

I'd never had trouble speaking my mind, but I still had trouble doing it in English. Dave and I quickly realized that if we wanted a deeper relationship, we needed to better communicate. He began taking Chinese classes through work and insisted on paying for my English ones.

"My Chinese colleagues recommended Berlitz. It's supposed to be a really good English school. They say it's the best in Shanghai."

"How much is it?" I asked.

"Don't worry about it," he replied, smiling.

郭

Unlike STA, the simple classrooms lined with neat rows of desks laden with books, pencils, and practice sheets were all too traditional. The instructors were different too; predominantly American and Canadian men as eager to meet Chinese women as they were to teach. English was a hard language to learn. Sentences flowed horizontally, and the grammar and punctuation rules rarely made sense. Reading was particularly challenging for me; I wasn't all that good at it in my Mandarin language. And there was homework.

Dave found my assignments thoroughly entertaining, and he began helping me with them—or doing them for me. With him, bribing cost me nothing. Before long, they promoted me to a higher level, which was not a good thing at all.

"I'm going to fail this course," I huffed in frustration.

"You're doing great, honey. You just need more practice."

"I don't have time for more practice. Between work and spending time with you, I'm falling further and further behind. This is too hard."

"Then quit working," he said.

I burst out laughing. "Are you crazy? I can't quit work. How will I eat? How will I support myself?"

"You don't need to. I'll take care of it."

"What do you mean 'take care of it'?"

"I'll pay for everything. And you can move in with me. Pang does all the shopping, cooking, and cleaning, so all you'll have to do is study," he said eagerly. "It'll be great."

"No, I was right. You're crazy."

His offer was very attractive; who wouldn't want a leisurely with nothing to do but take language classes? And living in his big house? I'd feel like a rich mistress. He'd already been so generous, buying me nice clothes and expensive jewelry. This was just one step more. And living with him sounded very nice.

But I hadn't spent a year of training and another establishing a freelance reputation simply to walk away; that seemed reckless.

"And if things don't work out between us?"

"You mean if I drive you nuts?" he said, chuckling.

"Yes, that," I said. "I'd have nowhere to go."

"Keep your apartment, if that's the issue. Then when you need space, you'll have somewhere to go. What do you say?"

I felt like I was on the losing end of a business deal, except the downside was getting everything I could want.

"I need to think about it for a little while."

"Take all the time you need," he said.

I spent the next few days agonizing over the decision. Mama would certainly caution against accepting Dave's proposition. In fact, I was afraid to even mention it to her. Baba, on the other hand, simply wanted me to be rich. But living a wealthy lifestyle and being wealthy were two different things, and the money only lasted as long as Dave was in Shanghai.

"What are you going to do when he leaves?" Jin asked when I pleaded my case. Of all my friends, she was the most level-headed. "And he will, GuoGuo. He's not Chinese."

"I can start over, I suppose. I'll always have my diploma, and I'm really not making that much money being freelance." Of late, I was passing on more jobs than I was taking. I'd even given Xiao and Ning two wedding jobs so I could spend those weekends with Dave. One of my top photographers had stopped calling me entirely.

"It's taken a lot of hard work to get where you are, and you have big dreams. Are you willing to put them aside so easily? GuoGuo, Dave is the first boyfriend you've ever had. Is living with him worth losing yourself?"

Jin was not wrong, but neither were Xiao and Yang, who believed love justified any sacrifice. Nancy thought me a fool for even hesitating.

"Life is about money," Nancy said. "It feeds you and clothes you and puts a roof over your head. You were living in a supply closet last year, using bar tips for bus fare. Don't forget how difficult that was. What Dave's offering is better. You deserve better."

I'd been poor all of my life. To suddenly have anything I could want—a driver, a maid, a free education... It did seem foolish to forego these gifts. And though I didn't love Dave, I did care deeply for him.

"I've decided I will move in with you, but I will keep my apartment."

"Done," he said, picking me up in his arms. "This is going to be so great!"

郭

I moved in the following day, much to his maid's dismay. Sulking, she said horrible things to me when Dave wasn't around; I was too young for Dave; I was a bumpkin dressed in pretty clothes; I was a slob. Her jealousy was palpable, and though she fawned over Dave, I was more than a little suspicious that she was overcharging him for groceries.

Unlike the maid, the ghosts seemed very happy to see me, even coming into Dave's room at night.

"I can't stay in this haunted house," I said, burying my face in his chest after the third visitation in as many weeks. "They won't leave me alone."

"Then we'll move," he said simply. "Human resources will take care of it."

Dave's company assigned him to an immense glass and steel high rise in Xintiandi, an expensive neighborhood famous for foreigners.

"This is sweet," Dave said, whistling at the cavernous apartment.

"Let's check out the view." He led me to the living room's wall of windows. "Do you think the ghosts will bother you here?"

"They'd be too tired after climbing twenty-five flights of stairs."

"I'd die if I had to climb them," he said, kissing the back of my head. "Do you want to eat out or have dinner here?"

"I can cook," I said, glancing at the stunning kitchen. I couldn't dream of contributing financially, but I could thank him for his generosity with excellent food. "I'll do it from now on."

"No need. The maid starts tomorrow."

I was delighted—*more* than delighted—to learn that Dave's company was supplying a new maid. Auntie June was a friendly older woman and a talented cook—far better than Pang. We learned quickly, however, that if we complimented her on a dish, she would make it every day until we told her to stop.

It became our custom after dinner to stroll through the neighborhood holding hands. Sometimes, we shopped for antiques or clothing in the fancy shops. Other times, we bought fruit or dessert from street vendors and ate it at a nearby park. I couldn't believe how my fortune had turned. After living four months with Dave, the thought of ever moving back to my tiny apartment by choice seemed laughable.

31

Take A Hike

"Are you up for an adventure?" Dave asked, vaulting over the couch after work.

"Adventure is my name," I said, laughing. "You're in a good mood."

"It's Friday," he sighed. "And tomorrow, we're going hiking with Sam. You do like to hike, right?"

Hiking was mountain climbing, and in Hunan, where mountains were everywhere, climbing wasn't so much a "like to" as a "have to".

"Sure."

Dave's Australian friend Sam, a rugged, blond-headed jokester, was dating a pretty Shanghai native, who called herself Lisa.

Dave rented a jeep, and on Saturday, the four of us traveled to Hangzhou Park. After checking into the park's formidable lodge, we filled a small backpack with water bottles and snacks and then set out on a wide path leading to the giant waterfall the park was famous for.

The grounds around the lodge were stunning, with tea bushes stacked in neat rows along rolling hillsides. Before long, we entered a lovely and verdant forest. Sunlight peeked through a leafy lattice teaming with squirrels that hopped from one branch to another, disrupting songbirds. The walk was easy; the path's incline nothing compared to my village mountains. Content, I was in my element. Lisa was not in hers. Falling farther and farther behind, she seemed to enjoy herself less by the step.

When we stopped for a break an hour in, Lisa pulled me aside. "I've dated plenty of Westerners, and if I've learned one thing, it's that they like weak women. Watch this." Sinking to the ground, she said in a whiny voice, "I am too tired to go on."

Sam's eyes lit up, and he grinned. "Well, we can't have that." Scooping her up, he tossed her over his burly shoulder and began marching up the path. She squealed, beating him on the back repeatedly, and then she winked at me.

For the next few miles, Sam and Lisa did nothing but play. The more girlish she acted, the more he seemed to enjoy it. Admittedly, I had little experience with men, especially Western men, and wondered if I should follow her lead. Dave was a fun guy, but we never played like this. When I noticed him watching them, I took action.

Imitating Lisa was more difficult than I thought. Raised a country girl used to physical activity, and moreover a tomboy of sorts in my youth, I was anything but helpless. Nevertheless, I crossed my arms and refused to go on unless Dave carried me on his back. But unlike Sam, who spent most of his time laughing and chasing Lisa around, Dave became quiet. In fact, the sillier I acted, the cooler he became. Finally, he suggested we turn back.

"Did you have a good time?" I asked once we were in our room.

He shrugged. "It was fine. I'm going to take a shower."

Our hike Sunday morning was much the same as the day before, with Lisa charming Sam, and I mimicking her. From the Jeep's back seat, giggles periodically erupted on our way back to Shanghai. Unfortunately, the atmosphere in the front seat was quite different.

"Look, I've some work to do," Dave said, after dropping off the rental car. "Why don't you sleep at your place tonight?"

"What do you mean?" I asked, shocked. I hadn't returned to my place in weeks. Besides, he worked all the time in my presence.

"I could use some space. That's all."

"But—"

"I'll call you later," he said, kissing my cheek and then paying the taxi driver.

No call or goodnight text came that evening or the following morning. The bad feeling that had kept me from sleep grew life-sized. Finally, I took matters into my own hands, calling his office, or rather, his office's voicemail. When he finally answered, he seemed distant.

"Why don't you want to talk to me? What did I do wrong?" I blurted out.

"Nothing. I'm just busy right now and I just don't have time for distractions."

"Is that what I am?" I asked, stunned. But in truth, what *was* I to him? He was certainly more than a distraction for me. Jin's words buzzed around my head like a harpy.

Quiet for a moment, he then said, "I'll call you later, okay?"

Though he'd made no mention of the trip, I felt certain the distance he was putting between us resulted from it. Embarrassed didn't begin to describe what I felt about my behavior; I was no Lisa. When he failed to keep his word, I stopped reaching out. Instead, I threw myself into my coursework and tried to ignore my mounting anxiety.

It wasn't until Friday that he finally called. Still stinging from his rebuff and angry with myself for pretending to be someone I was not, I didn't answer the phone. When he called a second time, I turned off my ringer.

A few hours later, the knock on my door surprised me. I wasn't expecting anyone, Dave had paid my rent up, and Nancy was out of town. I didn't bother getting up. Soon the knocking became kicking and banging. I was already yelling when I threw open the door. Dave stood on the other side, looking very upset.

"I've been calling and calling. I was afraid something had happened to you."

"I've been here studying all week. Why do you suddenly care?"

"Why do I care?" he sputtered, running his hand through his hair. "Because you're my girlfriend!"

"You send me away, refuse to talk to me all week, and I'm your girlfriend? It feels like you're punishing me, but I don't know why."

"I was busy. I told you that," he said.

"So busy you couldn't text me? I was busy too. Do you think I waited day and night for your call? Do you think I can't live without you? I was just fine before we met. I don't need someone mistreating me."

"Look, I'm sorry. I should have explained," he said.

"You do it now."

"Fine, you want the truth? You were acting like Lisa last weekend, okay? Lisa is annoying, and she and Sam… well, I just wanted to have an enjoyable weekend with my girlfriend, not babysit a child."

Though sure in my gut that this had been the issue, I still felt small hearing him say the words. After a moment of awkward silence, I asked, "How did you get here?"

"My driver knew the way. Can I come inside?"

Drained by a week and angst and frustration, I didn't have the energy to be embarrassed. Shrugging, I stepped back.

He walked around the front room and then stuck his head into the other, which contained a single pile of folded clothes and my sleeping mat. "Where's the rest of the apartment?"

"This is the rest of the apartment."

"Where's your bed?"

I pointed to the floor.

"This is how you live?" He seemed genuinely shocked.

"This is how Chinese people live. What do you think, we all have million-RMB apartments like yours? That we all have balconies overlooking the city, shiny glass elevators?"

"You need a nicer place. We'll spend the weekend looking for one."

"I can't afford a nicer place. Without your help, this is what I can afford. I don't even have a job now. That's what you wanted."

"That's what I still want. I want you to have the freedom to go to school. I want you to have a nice, safe place to live," he said, staring at my bare walls. "I want good things for you."

"But do you want to be a couple?"

"Yes. Very much. I'm sorry for the way I acted. I was a jerk. Come back to my apartment. It's empty without you."

"You mean your bed is empty," I said coldly.

"No, I don't mean that."

"So, if I come back and sleep in the guest room, you won't have a problem with that?"

"I'd rather have you stay in my guest room than not at all. Here, let me get your stuff."

32

Saving Face

The next six months were wonderful. Dave rented a nice apartment for me near STA—a place I could never have afforded on my own. So large, it even had a guest room which Nancy made use of frequently.

Every weekend getaway, every candlelight dinner, every evening stroll through Taipingqiao Park brought me closer to the brink of love until one night I realized I'd already fallen. My days weren't complete without seeing him, and the rare nights I spent alone were agony. The love I'd invented at eighteen paled to this, but fear kept my heart hidden. What if he didn't feel the same?

"How's your grandfather?" Dave asked after I ended an unusually long phone conversation with Mama; along with electricity, telephone service had finally found its way to Black Village.

Stunned, I sank to the floor beside the couch. "Gone," I whispered.

"Oh, Honey, I'm so sorry," he said, kissing the top of my head. "I'll call the airline."

Wai gong's health had been declining for some time, and when I'd seen him during Chinese New Year, he'd needed help even using the bathroom. I'd trimmed his toenails while telling him stories of Shanghai.

In China, elder care falls solely on the family, and medical treatments are expensive. Since Wai gong could not work for much of his life, he and Wai po had little to spare—certainly not enough to pay for the level of care he required.

Wai po had tended to him as best as she could, but she'd never been a nurturing or patient person, and it came as no surprise that Mama and Auntie Song had ended up doing most of the unpleasant work. When Wai gong's back peeled from lying in the same position for so long, his wife abandoned him completely. Past her sadness, Mama had sounded exhausted on the phone, and I knew she'd need all the help I could provide in preparing for the funeral.

Dave booked an early flight for me the following morning. The only problem: he purchased a ticket for himself as well.

"What are you doing?" I asked as he placed a dark suit in his hanging bag.

"Which tie, gray or burgundy?"

"Dave, you can't come."

"Of course, I'm coming. I want to pay my respects to your mother."

"But she doesn't want your respects."

Looking at me oddly, he said. "It's a gracious gesture. She'll appreciate it." He held the burgundy tie up to the suit and then shrugged. "I'll just take them both."

"If you come to my house, the neighbors will see you."

Dave huffed. "I don't give a damn what your neighbors think. It's the right thing to do. Besides, what would your parents think of me if I didn't come?"

"No," I said.

He pulled several pairs of dark socks from the dresser. "GuoGuo, what's wrong with a guy supporting his girlfriend and her family while they mourn? It's completely normal in the US."

"That is not how it's done here. People won't understand."

"*I* don't understand."

Citing the need for family time, when I'd requested he stay in Shanghai this past Spring Festival, he'd been agreeable. Why could he not see that this was so much more important? That Mama needed me?

It was the first time I'd flown on an airplane. When it took off, I was stunned by a power and thrust far surpassing the sluggish and jerky onset of a train, or even that of a car's acceleration. My stomach felt as though I'd eaten dragonflies! And though the engine was a constant roar, we gently floated above the clouds and the mountains—even above the birds. This was a miracle.

I stared out the window for most of the flight, partly because I was amazed and partly because I didn't want to fight with Dave anymore. Either my English was too poor to explain the trouble his presence would cause, or he was too thick-headed to understand; I had my suspicions. Our cultural difference had never seemed so stark, especially when I found his funeral customs as strange as he seemed to find mine.

After landing in a thrilling and violent rush, I made reservations at a nearby hotel and then called Ming. Ningxiang, the nearest town to our village, didn't have any hotels, and whatever delusions Dave had about staying with my parents were just that. Keeping him in Changsha seemed the best solution.

"Should we bring flowers? Like an arrangement or a basket or something?" Dave asked as we passed an airport vendor.

"No flowers."

"We can't just show up empty-handed."

"You'll bring shame to my family if you show up at all!" I growled, turning on him. "My mother has just lost her father. She doesn't deserve to lose face as well. I told you not to come."

Dave and I barely spoke while waiting at baggage claim. In the taxi, I found a softer voice. "The ceremony takes days, and there is much for me to do. Please stay here, and when I have time, I'll return to check on you."

Once in our room, he unpacked his suitcase without speaking. When he finished, he turned to me, anger flashing in his eyes. "Am I not good enough for you?"

What was I supposed to say? I loved him and I didn't want to hurt him, but the truth was plain. "You're good enough for me, Dave. You're just…" I searched for kinder words but failed. "You're just not good enough for my family."

His face paled and then flushed pink. "I'm taking a walk. Now."

When I received Ming's text, I met him in the lobby.

"Where's Dave?" he asked, picking up my suitcase.

"Taking a walk," I said. "I told him he couldn't come."

"I guess he could stay with us if he wants. It would be easier for you to go back and forth that way."

Ming's auto parts store, where his family lived in the shadow of tire mountains, was barely an upgrade from Baba's old Ningxiang recycling shop. Sleeping on a dirty floor with Ming's family would not suit Dave. Moreover, they would be far less effective in keeping Dave from joining the grieving ceremonies.

"That's very generous, but he'd be happier staying in his business luxury suite."

Leaving Dave a note, I climbed onto Ming's motorcycle and raced home.

"It was very bad at the end," he said, negotiating the mud puddles forever plaguing our village road. "Wai gong was in a lot of pain. It was time for him to cross over."

Taking a deep breath as I scrubbed my tear-streaked face, I slipped into the kitchen.

"Mei Zi," she sobbed, gripping my arms.

郭

Chinese funerals are like large weddings; they go on for days. Caterers slaughter pigs and lambs and cook them for the family, their neighbors, and the guests. Families also hire professional criers. These people—usually women, for they are the best at it—cry day and night in front of the coffin. I was immediately pressed into service; securing the musicians, directing the cooks, setting up tables—anything.

They laid my grandfather out in our living room. Men, who specialize in preparing dead bodies, treated him with lime to retard the decay. After the villagers paid their respects, we held a private family ceremony to say goodbye. It was heart wrenching, and I felt for Mama—so much pain. Spiritualists then came to chant special words that would help my grandfather's soul cross over.

Once all the traditions were accomplished, the lid was sealed, and the coffin carried to the family crypt. Outside the entrance, my uncles placed a small house built of paper and wood. Mama arranged tiny furniture replicas inside, and then Auntie Song stuffed it with fake money and food. With a shaking hand, Wai po lit the little roof with a match, and we watched the smoke slowly rise. Now Wai gong's spirit would have everything it needed for the spirit world.

I was relieved when the funeral was over. Sleeping under the same roof as a corpse had been terrifying. Already too haunted for my liking, meeting Wai gong's ghost in the hallway would surely have been my undoing.

During the funeral festivities, I'd missed several calls from Dave. Too busy to offer more than a quick text, after the caterer's last dinner, I finally had time to talk.

"Dave, the funeral just ended. I'll be over in a little while," I said in the message.

When knocking on Dave's door left me staring at a stranger's face, I went to the lobby in search of answers. The desk manager handed me an envelope.

Gone back to Shanghai.

"That's it?" I said aloud, turning the letter over.

Expecting him to wait three days in a hotel room hadn't been fair, but what choice had he given me? Going home made the most sense. He had work to tend to. And honestly, torn between the expectation of entertaining him and the duty of helping my family, this news was in many ways a relief. I returned to Black Village, unfettered.

33

Panties

Nearly three weeks of helping my mourning mother and nursing a surprisingly devastated Wai po, who'd become all but despondent, had left me exhausted. Wai gong had included Mama in his will, leaving her a sizable piece of fertile farmland—a gift she'd never expected. Privately, I celebrated this victory; she deserved some real semblance of love.

Though I'd texted Dave several times, telling him I was finally coming home, he hadn't responded, and he was not waiting for me at the airport when I landed. Prepared to apologize for abandoning him, I stopped by my place to shower and change before going to find him. All in the world I wanted at the moment was to collapse in his arms and be comforted.

A large garbage bag blocked the entrance to my apartment, and I was instantly annoyed with Nancy for not taking it to the street. Kicking it aside, I expected to hear the satisfying rattle of cans and bottles. Instead, my foot silently connected with something soft and solid. Chills ran through me when I unfastened the stay and discovered my belongings from Dave's closet—all of them.

Hurrying to his building, I marched past the security officer without a glance, stabbing the elevator button repeatedly until it opened. Inside his apartment, I found him sitting on the couch, reading a book. He didn't look up.

"Someone could have stolen my clothes," I hissed, crossing my arms. "Why have you done this?"

Dave's ears turned pink, but he otherwise ignored me.

"Well?" I said, stamping my foot.

When he finally spoke, his voice was remote. "You seem to enjoy my world, but you won't let me into yours."

"My world? I have no world. I'm a poor farm girl."

"I'm not talking about money."

Kneeling beside him, I forced him to look at me. "You and I live differently. Our cultures are different. Mine confuses you."

"I'm not confused. I just don't understand what your parents suddenly have against me. We had a nice time before—"

"In the middle of the night!" I screeched, my voice echoing off the high ceiling. "If my village finds out about us, they'll judge my family. And if we don't marry, my parents will lose face. People will make fun of them. They won't be welcome in the homes of their own relatives."

"If we don't get married? That's crazy."

"That may be crazy to you, but not to my family. Not to my village. You say you understand, but you don't. This isn't America. What would your family think if you brought me home?"

He shrugged his shoulders. "They'd be happy I found someone who loved me." Then he turned and looked full in my face, his eyes hardening. "I just haven't found her yet."

"I do love you," I whispered, as panic set in. "I do." It was the first time I'd said those words aloud, and in crisis, a terrible time to do it.

Dave shook his head. "I wish that were true. I hope you find a man your village will approve of," he scornfully said, standing.

"But... no. No!"

"Goodbye, GuoGuo."

"I'll make a special dinner for you. We'll have nice sex. You'll change your mind. Please let me show you how much I care about you." I hated the desperation in my voice, but I was desperate. I didn't want this relationship to end.

"Don't make this worse than it already is. I don't want to see you again. Just... just go."

As if a knife had slashed it open, great pain ripped through my heart. I moved unseeing through the lobby and drifted into the crowded sidewalk outside, eventually finding myself by the Taipingqiao Park pond, where Dave and I so often walked. Sinking onto the serpentine wall underneath a graceful willow tree, I stared out at the neighborhood's reflection on the still water while quietly falling to pieces.

When my phone buzzed sometime later, I glanced at it with no intention of answering. Even with blurred vision, I recognized the number. My heart beating wildly, I hoped he'd changed his mind. "Dave?"

"I found a pair of your panties under my bed," he said lifelessly. "Do you want to come get them?"

Shocked and indignant, I screamed into the phone. "You keep them. *You* wear them! I don't care. I do the best I can, and you reject me. Then you want to know if I want my underwear back? Is this some bad American joke? I'm done with you!"

I was glad he'd said such a stupid thing. I was glad he'd ignited my rage. Just as a sudden breeze erased the pond's watery image, so I deleted everything on my phone: his contact information, all the pictures we'd taken together, every text he'd ever sent, his voicemails. Then I threw his spare key far into the pond. If he wanted that back, he could swim for it.

Once my anger had burned itself out and reality set in, I found my way home. For the next five days, I didn't leave my apartment, eating nothing unless friends forced it on me. Sleep brought only nightmares and sorrow. The heartache I felt was overwhelming; Fu's desertion had been nothing in comparison. After shedding so many tears at Wai gong's funeral, I should have run out by now, but it seemed I had an endless supply.

"You want me to find you a new place?" Nancy softly said, lowering herself onto the floor beside me one evening.

I hadn't considered that. He'd surely stop paying my rent, if he hadn't already. "Yes. I guess I'll be kicked out of here soon."

"I'll ask around at the bar."

Nancy quickly found a regular who had a cheap place for rent in Pudong. Glad to be back in a familiar neighborhood, I moved into the modest third-floor apartment the following week. Sure to run out of money soon, I needed a job. The thought of restarting my career gave me a newfound purpose.

In turning down so many makeup jobs, I'd dropped off everyone's call list; no photographer wanted someone they couldn't depend on. With few options for quickly earning money, I sold some of my jewelry to cover rent and began searching for spa jobs.

郭

"So, I met this guy," Nancy announced over a dinner of ramen noodles; I was eating as if poor again. "I like him, and he has a friend who wants to meet you."

"I don't want to meet any men."

"He's a very rich Singaporean. We'll all go out, and they can show us a good time. It's been a month now, and you need to move on."

"One month isn't much time, and I'm not ready." In truth, I wasn't sure when I'd be ready again. When love finds you, it doesn't leave your heart easily.

"Please? This guy is special, and he wants to help out his friend. You can do this for me," she said.

At dinner, I checked off all the ways Xing differed from Dave. He was short—shorter than me, round, and mostly bald, but highly entertaining. And while not as attractive as Dave, he was certainly not an ugly man.

"I like your accent," I said when he spoke English to the waiter.

"It's British."

"I don't know that one. Only American and Australian."

"British is the easiest, I promise. If it weren't, I couldn't speak the language at all," he said, laughing.

The men had chosen a very expensive restaurant, and when the bill came, Xing insisted on treating everyone. He did seem rich, which was convenient, and charming, but I knew I would never want more than simple friendship from him—no amount of money would ever make him taller than me or give him blue eyes and sandy brown hair.

After dinner, Nancy and her date went one way, and we another. Xing took me to a Western café that served American coffee and dessert, and we talked for hours. He'd grown up rich and had become even richer through his construction business. And because he was of no romantic interest to me, I told him all about myself without pretense.

Once Xing returned to Singapore, we began communicating by email. He believed it was crucial that I learn English; I simply couldn't succeed in the business world without it. He also went on and on about stocks; the market was screaming, whatever that meant, and I should take advantage of it.

I laughed outright. I would never have money to invest in such things. I wouldn't even be able to pay rent when I ran out of jewelry.

A few weeks later, when his business brought him back to Shanghai, Xing asked to see me again. Over dessert, he asked me to be his girlfriend.

"I'm flattered, but we don't know each other well," I said, more than a little shocked.

"Relationships are like construction. You build them one story at a time."

"But we have no real foundation," I said. "In fact, we don't even know the location of this building."

"Singapore, of course. You can live in one of my many apartments. I can make an enjoyable life for you."

His offer was certainly attractive, and I'm sure plenty of girls would have jumped at it—Nancy included. I just wasn't one of them. "Xing, I'm sorry, but it's too soon."

"Don't dismiss me so quickly, GuoGuo. Think about it for a little while. Talk to your friends."

When it became clear that Xing had no intention of losing this argument, I said, "You would make a wonderful boyfriend, but I'm recently out of a serious relationship, and I still have feelings for him. I wish it weren't so, but it would be wrong to pretend otherwise."

I didn't tell him I loved Dave with all my heart, and that I cried myself to sleep every night. Or that with each necklace or bracelet I sold, a small piece of my soul went with it. I didn't tell him that sometimes I dreamed Dave was beside me, only to wake and find an empty mattress. Those very private things I didn't share with anyone.

"It's difficult to find people you can really trust. I'm grateful for your honesty and for not leading me on."

A few days later, I received an envelope from Xing, containing ten-thousand RMB. I'd never seen so much money in my life.

"What does it say?" Nancy asked, peering over my shoulder as I read the letter.

"He wishes me a good life and good fortune, and he wants me to study English so I could better myself."

"How do you keep meeting all these rich guys?" she whined.

In his letter, Xing instructed me to use half the money for tuition and to invest the rest in the Hong Kong stock market. He even told me which stocks to buy and how to go about it.

So moved, I burst into tears where I stood. Though my heart was broken—or perhaps because of it, life was treating me kindly at the moment. But as is so often true, with Yang's warmth comes Yin's chill.

34

Obliteration

Less than two weeks after receiving Xing's extraordinary gift, my mother called, hysterical; what she said made no sense. I'd already paid my tuition and purchased the designated stocks, so I immediately sold some clothes and bought a train ticket home.

Destruction was what I found. Pure and utter destruction.

郭

In 2008, the government decided to build a road and public park where Black Village stood. It gave my parents, their neighbors, and all my relatives only hours to gather their belongings before the bulldozers arrived.

I found Mama and Baba huddled in a sheet-metal tent six miles from our home. Reminiscent of Chao's factory village, the rest of the villagers were living similarly, and, like my parents', their faces registered only shock.

I spent the night in Ming's drafty car parts store. After living in clean Shanghai apartments, the cloying stench of dirty oil and lubricant-soaked cement beneath my mat was nearly overpowering.

In the weak early morning light, Ming and I met Baba, and we traveled to the village.

At first, the place looked fully unfamiliar, but as I slowly pieced together my surroundings—the nearby mountains I'd climbed so often, the glint of the stream in the distance—I gasped in horror. *This could not be!*

The enormous hills behind our home had been flattened, and the valley in which I'd spent my youth filled with dirt. The pond where we'd washed our clothes and fished for food was as if it had never been. All the animals were gone.

Stumbling across the loose soil, we followed Baba to the site where he believed our house had stood. I was certain he was mistaken; there was no indication that any structure had ever been there. But then, to my utter horror, I saw skeletons.

Though the tombs of our ancestors were indiscernible, coffins and bones were strewn about like trash on a Shanghai street. The sudden dread of discovering Wai gong's corpse was a solid thing. I couldn't imagine his body's state of rot and decay. I wouldn't.

Lagging farther and farther behind, I finally stopped altogether and covered my head with my hands. Turning in slow circles, I surveyed this barren, wasted place, my soul silently screaming. Black Village was no more. Our past had been erased.

"Over here!" Baba shouted, waving.

Staggering towards him in a blank stupor, I watched him kneel in the dirt and gather up bones. He had come for this very purpose, I realized. Rooting through his pack, he tossed a large sack to each of us and pointed in different directions.

Picking through debris reminded me of our long-ago time in Ningxiang: two children collecting trash for Baba's recycling business. But instead of dragging bottles and cans behind us, we dragged ancestors.

The snow-flecked wind ravaging me, I squatted by an overturned slab of turf and unearthed another bone, not recognizing the body part it had once been. So disgusted and overwhelmed by my task, my icy hands shook as I scraped off the dirt and placed it in my blue sack. Tears streamed down my face, falling in fat drops from my nose and chin as I retrieved another. This horror was beyond words.

Stepping forward, my shoe caught on something hard, and I tripped, feeling the sickening crunch of bone beneath my knees. As I scrambled off the skeleton, my hand landed on its skull, the fragile bone caving in under my weight. Frantically scrubbing my palm against my pants, I jumped to my feet, vomit exploding in a violent gush. When I wiped spittle from my lips, I felt bone fragments clinging to them. Screaming hysterically, I ran toward Ming.

When I reached him, he grabbed my arms and roughly shook me. "Hold your tears, Mei Zi," he growled. "This ground needs no more of them." With mournful eyes and lips pressed into a thin, grim line, he found a kinder voice. "Pretend that you're pulling up onions. It'll make this easier."

Though shudders racked my body, I clung to Ming's words as I trudged onward. Unearthing pale onions was something I'd done all my life, something not unpleasant at all. When I stumbled on another bone, I forced my thoughts to farming, to warm summer days, to the comforting songs of grasshoppers.

Many villagers had joined us in this field of sorrows, searching for remnants of their own lives. I can't express the loathing I felt for my government at this moment, that we meant so little to it. But within earshot of others, I couldn't openly express these feelings.

Once our sacks were full, we dragged them to Baba's little truck.

I'm not certain any of the skulls I found belonged to my people, but it really didn't matter. Surely my ancestors saw that we had tried. As I climbed on the back of Ming's motorcycle, preparing to leave, I wondered where all the ghosts would go.

I didn't join my extended family at the mass gravesite they'd dug. I couldn't bear it. Instead, I crawled into Mama's tent and curled into a ball on the ground, searching for sanity.

35

The Future

Within the week, several truckloads of construction supplies arrived.
The villagers were given plans and explicit instructions to build a
series of identical apartment buildings that would become their new
home. Since the government had provided no land, the people I'd
known all my life would no longer be farmers. They'd have to find
some other way to survive.

When I was no longer needed, I returned to Shanghai. Though my
past was gone, I had a future to tend to. Raw and empty, I resumed
my English studies.

Leaving the school building a few days later, my arms laden with
books, I listlessly shuffled down the sidewalk. I didn't see the man
in front of me until he grabbed my shoulders. Existing in a constant
state of numbed loss, I no longer saw people as anything more than
obstacles to avoid. And if this person wanted to hurt me, well, I doubt
I would have felt much.

"You've forgotten what I look like already? I suppose I deserve
that."

Speechless, I stared up into blue eyes I could never forget, my heart
hammering in my chest.

"I've been looking for you everywhere," he said. "Your apartment is empty, and I couldn't get anything out of Nancy." Shaking his head, he stared at the pregnant clouds. "Finally, I thought I'd try here. How have you been?"

A sob escaped my lips as my books fell to the sidewalk. Launching myself at Dave, I clung to him, weeping for the us that no longer existed, for my home and everything my family had endured, for my uncertain future.

Dave lifted me into his arms and carried me to his waiting car, telling the driver to take us back to his apartment. As we wound through the dampening streets, Dave gently cradled my trembling body, whispering assurances.

"When's the last time you ate?" he asked, laying me on his sofa and tucking a thick blanket around me.

I simply shrugged.

"You're so pale. Have you been sick?"

Rain pelted his large windows, blurring the world outside, the mournful wind a tribute to my sadness. *Where on earth to begin?*

Dave plied me with cup after cup of hot tea, and we snuggled for hours, my story coming out in fits and spurts as he gently caressed my arms, my face, my hair. He seemed as genuinely shocked and outraged as I felt, unable to fathom that my village had been wiped clean away. And though he had only visited it twice, and then in the dark of night, he mourned for it as well.

After a long stretch of silence, he whispered, "I'm lost without you. Everywhere I turn, I see your face. In restaurants, I think I hear your voice, but when I look around, all I find are strangers. There's a hole inside me that only you can fill." He kissed the top of my head. "GuoGuo, I love you."

Never imagining I'd hear those words from his lips, I sat stunned.

"I've been in America for the last month," he then said. "UPS is transferring back."

And before it had time to swell, my heart shriveled again, its edges curling like dry autumn leaves. While I'd come to terms with the end of our relationship, the thought of his leaving China forever was too much to bear. I suddenly understood Wai po's bitterness at being given so much, only to have it taken away again.

"No," I said defiantly, shaking my head. "No. You tell your company no."

Taking my face in his hands, he stared at me solemnly. "I have no choice."

I thought I'd finally run out of tears—I'd shed thousands in these past months—yet I felt another slide down my cheek.

"Don't worry," he said, wiping it away. "It's going to be great. They're sending me to Atlanta. It's a nice city—kind of like Shanghai. The landscape reminds me of Hunan a little. There are mountains nearby. Farms, too," he said animatedly.

Though disappointment surely dulled it, I tried to smile. It didn't matter which city he was moving to or what the landscape looked like. This place might as well have been on the moon; the distance was the same. "I'm sure you'll be happy there."

"No, *we'll* be happy there."

I stared into his dancing eyes. "I don't understand."

"You have nothing left here—no village, I mean. And no job, right?" I shook my head, confused. "What I'm saying is, I want you to come live with me in the US."

I stared at him blankly for a moment, certain he'd just lost his mind—or I had. "You feel sorry for my situation, and this is your solution?"

"No, no. This is the solution to *our* situation. I've already looked into the paperwork. There's a lot of it," he said, chuckling. "And it'll take a while to get your visa approved, but I can't live without you."

"What about my culture, my values, how different our worlds are? What about those things that you said?" I hadn't forgotten his words or behavior. I'd replayed our argument a thousand times. Its sting had not lessened.

"I was stupid to dismiss your customs and traditions just because I didn't understand them. I'm such an idiot. Can you forgive me? Will you let me back into your life?" His words seemed so genuine that I wanted to believe them. And he was an idiot; this I knew. But what could I say to such an invitation?

"China is my home. And you don't want that part of me." Though I loved him, the thought of leaving my family and all that I knew for a man who could so easily break my heart again terrified me. And I would certainly not understand his village's customs and traditions any more than he did mine. I saw no way for this to work.

"I want all of you, GuoGuo. Every last bit. Tell me you'll think about it."

I nodded, though I had little intention of doing what he'd asked.

"I'll only be here another month," he then said, sighing. "Move back in with me until I leave. Be with me."

Knowing the relationship would end as soon as he left, I decided to afford myself this small bit of happiness—pretend that he'd decided to stay. "I'll live with you for now, and we'll see about the rest later," I said.

After we made love and he fell asleep, I watched his chest rise and fall. His lips formed a gentle smile after mumbling my name. I would spend this last month committing his face, his scent, his voice—all the little things about him—to memory.

郭

Our month together went by in the blink of an eye. He filled my bank account with tens of thousands of RMB—enough for me to live well on without the need to work. It wouldn't last a lifetime, but definitely for several years if I were frugal. He also put me in a larger apartment and furnished it completely. Providing for me seemed to make him happy, and perhaps it assuaged his guilt. I would not deny him that.

We filled our final ride to the airport with forced smiles and promises. I waited with him at his gate, our hands linked. He continued talking about my move to America as if he believed it might really happen. I was becoming a talented actor, I thought, pretending to be enthusiastic, excited about his dream. But that was all it was: a fanciful dream. Surely, he knew this.

"I'll miss you so much," he said. "Don't worry, GuoGuo, everything is going to work out. We'll see each other again soon. Promise."

I kissed him goodbye, luxuriating in the moment, knowing it was our last. He would find an American girlfriend soon, and I would become nothing more than a pleasant memory of his time in China, a simple distraction from being alone. I waved goodbye cheerily, and once he disappeared down the ramp, I folded in upon myself.

36

Shadow Of Doubt

I threw myself into studying, into partying with Nancy, into gambling—anything to keep my mind off my pain. But it didn't lessen, because Dave continued calling and emailing. And like a binlang addict chewing his nut, I savored each communication, all the while craving the next.

After completing another English proficiency level, I flew to Hunan. Where there had been refugee shacks, six rows of identical buildings now stood. My mother's family filled the one nearest the road.

Ming and Chen were busy converting the bottom floor into a hotel and restaurant. My brother would own the former, and my cousin the latter. JiaoJiao and my niece, who was growing up far too quickly, had moved in with my parents and now enjoyed the kind of comfort a salvage shop could never offer. JiaoJiao was pregnant again, and I wondered if I should spirit her away to Shanghai to deliver the baby there; China's one-child policy had not changed.

Baba continued running his recycling shops, and to my utter astonishment, Wai po had begun walking the nearby highway, collecting bottles and cans for him. Since my blind uncle had failed to predict the village's destruction, his fortune-telling days were over. To provide for himself, he'd begun a massage business in his apartment; he needed no eyes for that.

As there was no farmland to work, my mother made a small garden in the roadside ditch. Already, winter cabbage was thriving, and stakes had been erected for tomatoes and summer beans. She'd readied several patches of soil for herbs and the other vegetables Chen would need for his restaurant. I bought my mother several chickens, and Baba built a coop for them under their building. My family would survive this new life forced upon them. They had no choice.

郭

Dave suggested we try Skyping one another. When I returned to Shanghai, I discovered that this communication was available in internet cafes. Looking into his eyes as he told me silly things about the government paperwork was very pleasurable.

"The K-1 visa is what we want," he said excitedly. "It's a fiancé visa. It allows you to stay in the States for three months. Once you're here, we'll figure out the rest. I want you to have enough time to make sure you're happy."

I couldn't understand why he continued with this charade. He was a good-looking guy, and though painful to think of it, I was certain women in Atlanta were already chasing after him.

"Sure, Dave, I'll believe it when I see it."

I received an email the following morning, containing scanned copies of the forms he'd filled out. I had a case number, he explained. This came as a complete shock to me; he was serious.

Soon after, he began asking for personal documents, including my birth certificate, which his government needed, though why I didn't know. Considering the circumstances under which I was born, it was very difficult to produce such papers; Chen's gangster associates proved very helpful in this endeavor. I was also required to have a medical examination as part of the process.

Though costly, the lengthy exam went smoothly until I received the unfortunate news that one of my tests was positive.

"I have a shadow in my lung," I said.

"What does that mean, honey?" Dave asked, anxiety threading his words.

"They said I might have the tuberculosis disease. I don't know what that means exactly, but lots of people have it here, I'm told." Sighing deeply, I said, "My government won't process my papers until I can prove I don't have it."

"Are you feeling okay?" he asked.

"I feel the same as when I went into the clinic. They say it's very contagious. You'd better see a doctor, too." The thought of transmitting something fatal to him terrified me almost as much as the prospect of dying myself.

"I got inoculated as a kid and again before I came to China, so I'm covered. Want me to come over and console you?" he asked, his eyes solemn.

"Yes, very much."

37

Redemption

Spitting into a cup is something only a child enjoys, but to fulfill test and treatment requirements, I had to provide a saliva sample regularly over the next few months. I also had to swallow a large pill daily. When doctors explained the advanced symptoms of tuberculosis to me, I thought of those coughing fabric factory workers, whose blood-stained rags were their constant companions. Beyond my medical tests, I began coughing into a tissue every day, checking for the ominous red stain.

Dave visited when he could, but over time those visits came less frequently, and when he canceled his first trip, citing UPS budgetary cutbacks, I feared the distance and my stagnant visa application were degrading our relationship. His promise to make it up fell flat when he canceled yet another trip, saying his business plans had changed. Though I told myself not to worry, new fears sprouted; was there another woman?

Summer brought with it a renewed sense of hope when he promised to celebrate my birthday in person.

"Nothing's going to stand in my way this time, GuoGuo. I promise. And I'll stay an extra-long time, okay?"

Overjoyed by the news, I made reservations at our favorite restaurant, even booking a photographer friend to commemorate the occasion. But days before he was supposed to arrive, he began wavering.

First, it was, "GuoGuo, I'm really backed up at work and I might have to cancel." Then, "My boss wants me to go on a business trip with her. I'm so sorry."

Missing my birthday was not the end of the world, but the knot forming in my stomach seemed life-threatening.

"It's no big deal," I told him. "I'll just go to Hunan."

"I'm sure you'll have a good time," he said, sounding relieved. "Tell your family I said hello."

郭

After two refreshing days visiting with my oldest friends—Yang was pregnant and hoped the guy would marry her, and Ting had just gotten engaged—Ming took me to the complex. Since the ragtag village community lived near a scenic mountain highway, wealthy Changsha residents who took vacations to the countryside were booking Ming's rooms. The influx of money bolstering China's economy was finding its way into my family's pockets. I was so thankful.

Mama made congee for my birthday breakfast. I thought it ridiculous to feed a grown woman baby food, but it tasted like home. Of late, that had become an important thing—to remember my childhood, to fix it in my mind.

"Now you'll have a good day," she said, patting my head. Mama didn't smile so freely anymore—recent events had given her little reason, but on this morning her face was radiant.

Walking arm and arm through her little garden, we picked a few ripe vegetables and then collected eggs from the chicken coop. I wistfully remembered riding with her to market, guarding the produce which was our complete livelihood. Chen's restaurant was her only customer now, purchasing her garden's bounty. I thought only kind things about my cousin.

Explaining that he had to go into Changsha to pick up a package, Ming asked me to watch the hotel's front desk that afternoon. I assumed he'd forgotten to buy me a present, which didn't surprise me in the least. I played with WeiWei to give my very pregnant sister-in-law a break and answered the phone.

When Ming returned, his smile was as large as Mama's. "I have a present for you, Mei Zi. Close your eyes."

WeiWei was plucked from my arms, and then someone's lips touched mine. My eyes flew open, and my jaw dropped.

"Miss me?" Dave said.

Climbing right over the reservations counter, I threw my arms around his neck. Laughing, he swung me around in a circle and kissed me again. WeiWei, thinking this was a wonderful game, began turning circles beside us.

"I thought you couldn't come!" I said, wiping a tear.

"What kind of man would I be if I missed my girlfriend's birthday?"

Village mentality had changed little, so Dave quickly set me down when a neighbor stuck his head into the lobby to see what the commotion was about. "I would like one room in this very nice hotel," Dave suddenly announced in butchered Mandarin.

Ming replied at equal volume, "I have a special rate for American tourists. My sister will show you to your room."

A short time later, my parents knocked on Dave's door. Formally greeting them, he shook Baba's hand and even hugged Mama, who seemed confused by his behavior.

"Now you can become friends," Baba said gruffly. This meant we could be seen together in public, which made things a lot easier. "No touching," Baba added.

"No, sir," Dave replied innocently.

郭

Dave and I went everywhere. He tacked many vacation days onto his Shanghai business trip, and we used them to make up for lost time.

"I was reading about this amazing park. I know you don't like to hike, but it's supposed to be gorgeous," he said over dinner one evening.

"I like to hike," I responded, baffled.

He rolled his eyes. "GuoGuo, it's a very long hike."

Pain's sharp blade lanced me when I realized what he meant; the disastrous weekend spent with Lisa and Sam so long ago. Clearly, he hadn't forgotten my helpless schoolgirl act, and I hadn't forgotten his behavior in the aftermath. I might not be able to erase our memories, but I could certainly cover them up with new ones.

"I hope you can keep up," I said.

The next day, we boarded a train to Hua Shan in the Shaanxi Province. After a wonderful night together, involving very little sleep, we joined the hotel owner, and the thirteen other tourists signed up for the journey. I learned only then that our destination was a three-day hike away. Perhaps I shouldn't have been quite so eager.

"Don't worry. We can turn around whenever you get tired," Dave whispered in my ear.

"I won't get tired," I vowed.

Dave had only met the city-girl part of me—the one with spa-soft skin, the girl who enjoyed dancing and parties and nice dinners. He'd never met the other side of me—the factory worker, the farmer, the girl whose mountain climbing days had begun before the age of six. It was high time he was introduced.

Equipped with water and snacks, we set out. The mountains were stunningly beautiful but perilous. Often, the path skirted cliff sides so steep that falling meant certain death. Neither the difficulty nor the distance mattered to me, however. I planned to walk until my feet were bloody and my legs heavier than the rocks over which we climbed to prove myself to Dave.

That first day we walked for twelve hours. Several times during the night, people awoke screaming about leg cramps. By lunchtime on the second day, many hikers had quit, and by the third morning, only three remained: Dave, the head guide, and me.

Even though late June supplied very warm temperatures below, at this elevation the air was cool and crisp. When we finally reached the pinnacle of the mountain range, the guide took our picture and then produced three bottles of beer to celebrate. I couldn't believe the view; I felt as though I could see all of China. I also couldn't believe I'd made it all this way. Smugly, I ran my eyes over Dave's wilted form.

Surrounded by boulders and sheltering trees, the fabled lodge was small and secluded. Dave gave our guide a big tip and treated him to dinner. The meal was ridiculously overpriced, but when the waiter explained that workers from the valley far below had carried the food and supplies to the summit and that the eight-hour climb involved balancing on rickety ladders and edging along treacherous paths that switch-backed the face of the mountain, well, we were glad to pay.

There were others staying at the resort, and we discovered the next morning that for tourists, there was a five-minute-long cable car ride directly to the distant town below. Picking up both our backpacks, Dave began walking towards it. I did not.

"GuoGuo, you coming?"

I couldn't take my eyes off the breathtaking view. "No, I want to walk."

"Walk? We've been walking for three days."

"It's too pretty. I don't want to miss anything. Besides, if the villagers can do it, so can we."

It took us nearly ten hours to climb down that mountain, mostly because I stopped so often to take pictures. The sun was on its way to America before we found our next hotel. My legs shook under the table as we ate supper; forty hours of walking is a lot of walking.

"I'm so sore I'm going to die," Dave announced once we were in our room. He threw himself on the bed and moaned.

"Are you a silly schoolboy who can't take a little walking? You should have asked me to carry you on my back."

"You amaze me, GuoGuo," he said, pulling me on top of him. "I assumed you wouldn't make it past noon the first day, but four days straight? You're the strongest woman I've ever met."

I surely smiled the entire night.

38

Pretty Wrapping

Dave's next business trip wasn't scheduled until October. Restless and to keep my mind off my loneliness, I took on a variety of small jobs, the strangest of which was waitressing at an American restaurant called Hooters, where the girls wore provocative clothing and sang silly songs such as "I'm A Little Teapot." Though the male customers enjoyed this and tipped well, this experience made me extremely uncomfortable, and I quit after one week. Nancy fell over laughing when I told her.

The only real high points during this time were my friends' weddings.

Yang had had her heart broken so many times I'd lost count, but the man she'd said yes to was honorable, stepping up to take full responsibility for her pregnancy. Both handsome and kind, I could feel his affection for her. It warmed all of our hearts. With her entire village joyfully parading behind her, I thought, *finally* she'll have the life she deserves.

Ting's village wedding was not so different. She married a Changsha taxi driver. Though he wasn't a rich man, he was a suitable match for her. More importantly, her parents approved of his family.

During the ceremony, Jin leaned over and whispered, "It's just you and me now. Want to make a wager on who'll fall next?"

Jin had given up spa work and moved to Guangzhou. Through a family connection, she'd secured a job in advertising and was doing well. She was currently dating the chief financial officer of an insurance company. My eyes traveled from their clasped hands to his serene smile.

"Absolutely not!" I hissed.

郭

Two days before Dave's arrival, I squirmed on the medical clinic's padded examination table, awaiting my tuberculosis results. If they were positive, I wouldn't be allowed to travel to America. A negative result would breed its own set of problems.

Thousands of miles apart, this long-distance relationship was wearing on both of us. If my health mandated it, would Dave be willing to immigrate to China? I wasn't sure his company would allow him to do this. In fact, I wasn't certain my government would allow it. An equally challenging question weighed on my mind: was I willing to move to America for him?

Having goals to achieve and fanciful dreams to dream was a very fine thing, but reality was another matter. Except for Dave, everything I knew was in China, everything I loved. Was America a place that would make me happy? Could I thrive in that strange culture?

Seated in the airport's waiting area, anxiety gnawed on my insides. The medical report in my purse weighed a thousand pounds.

His smiling eyes met mine as he crossed the distance, arms open wide. "Oh, I've missed your face," he said, hugging me tightly. "Let's get out of here."

Our reunion was tender and wonderful; we'd been separated for too long.

"I have something for you," I said, reaching into my bag.

"A present?" he asked, his eyes lighting.

"I think so," I said, wondering how he'd respond. I searched his expression as he read over the translated report.

"Negative?"

I nodded. "Negative."

Sliding his chair back from the restaurant table, he lifted me from mine and hugged me to him, kissing my head. "I've been holding my breath," he said. "Have you told your parents yet?"

"No." In all honesty, I was afraid.

"Let's fly to Hunan," he said. "We can do it together."

郭

Dave checked into my brother's hotel, and I stayed with my parents. We decided not to tell them right away. Ming was a good meterstick of their response, however, so I tested the news on him. Besides, I needed an ally.

"You like Dave, don't you?"

"Sure. He's a nice guy. He seems to treat you right."

"He's invited me to come to America."

"America?" he said with a laugh. "It's too dangerous for you. Lots of murder."

"Dave says it's really safe."

Ming raised his eyebrows. "Our government says differently."

"Do you think Mama and Baba will let me go?"

Ming shook his head. "No."

This had been another fear of mine; upsetting my parents. Parents who hadn't traveled, parents with closed minds. What did they know of America?

"Ask Dave. He'll tell you the truth," I said.

Ming and Dave spent the evening together working on an old wreck he was resurrecting. With mixed dialects and hand motions, they'd developed an unusual and amusing way of communicating. Dave liked cars and was surprisingly handy—something I hadn't known about him, so the two bonded over tools, grime, and most likely, beer. The following morning, Ming announced that the family was having a special dinner in our honor. This seemed a strange thing since we worked hard at pretending to just be friends.

Chen's quaint restaurant was becoming popular with travelers. He'd even hired a local meatball maker, whose reputation extended halfway to Changsha. Chen's wife, Chynna, led us through the main dining area to a separate room typically used for parties. Most of my family was already seated around a large banquet table. When we entered, Wai po scowled at Dave.

My little cousins were an entirely different story. Crowding around him, they asked all manner of bizarre questions and then giggled at his attempted responses. He was good with the children, which warmed my heart, even tolerating precocious WeiWei, who climbed onto his lap to examine and then poke at his eyes.

Chen had evidently ordered a feast of local delicacies, including bean noodles, lamb stir fry, and, of course, meatballs. The moment these succulent dishes began parading in from the kitchen, all laughter ceased. After a full course of special desserts, I thought my stomach would burst. Wai po picked her teeth with a splinter of bamboo while Chynna and her small team of waitresses cleared the table.

Suddenly, Dave stood and tapped his glass. My family stared blankly in reply.

"GuoGuo, could you translate?" he whispered.

"What is wrong with you?" I asked, appalled.

"Just, please?"

Shrugging, I rose and stood beside him.

"I've known many of you for some time," I parroted. "It should come as no surprise that I cherish GuoGuo. So, I've brought her a gift."

When I gave him a questioning look, he winked at me.

Chen whistled loudly, and his wife entered, carrying a large box. With everyone gawking at me, their faces displaying a variety of emotions from scorn to delight, I felt shy and embarrassed. Tugging at the large ribbon, I removed the deep red wrapping, careful not to tear the beautiful piece of rice paper. I handed it to Auntie Song, who kept such things.

Inside the first box was another, this one wrapped in blue silk embroidered with a phoenix pattern. With each new box, my frustration grew in proportion to my family's laughter. By the time I'd gotten to the sixth box, my auntie had quite a collection of paper and cloth.

"This is a strange gift," I said. "I didn't know I needed so many boxes."

Finally, I came to a small box covered in red velvet. There was no ribbon tying it together, and the material would not come off. Dave took it from me and cracked open the lid.

I'd never seen a ring like it. There was wealth in Shanghai, and the occasional extravagant piece of jewelry, but seeing a diamond and holding it in my hand were two different things.

Dave's eyes shone with warmth and love as he slipped the gold ring on my finger. "GuoGuo, will you marry me?"

I didn't know what to say. In fact, I wasn't sure I could even speak at the moment. I'd always assumed the fiancé visa was just a ruse to trick our governments into letting me visit America. "Is this pretend or for real?" I whispered.

Looking both confused and indignant, he sputtered, "Of course, it's for real. I want you to be my wife."

My eyes found Mama's. Even though her face registered outright shock, a strange sense of peace settled over me, and I was certain at this moment that marrying Dave was the right thing to do.

"Are you going to say yes anytime soon?" Ming said. "I have to go to the bathroom."

"Okay, I'll marry you, Dave Wiseman," I said, laughing. "I will be your wife."

"I predicted this!" my blind uncle suddenly yelled out.

"Stupid girl," Wai po hissed, grimacing at me and then Dave for good measure.

"Mei Zi will be rich now, Mama," Auntie Song said, attempting to intercede.

"So, you're a rich girl now, eh? You're going away to be rich? What about being rich here and taking care of your own family?" Wai po said, pointing a gnarled finger at me.

"I'll take care of you all," I said, shocked. "I'll send money and gifts." I wanted to throw the Chinese customs she always needled us with back in her face. Traditionally, a wife was expected to care for her husband's relatives, not her own. But even saying this aloud would hurt Mama, and in truth, I would never abandon my family. Smiling up at Dave, who had no idea what we were saying, I would make sure he understood this before we wed.

"Lots of gifts," she muttered. "For me." After a moment, she went back to picking her teeth, and the rest of us went back to ignoring her.

郭

Mama and Baba sat in mismatched chairs in their small den, while Dave and I took the kitchen bench. Baba nodded to Dave and then looked at me.

"He doesn't have family in China. You will move in with us?" Baba asked.

After translating it for Dave, he smiled. "No, GuoGuo is going to move to America."

Mama hissed. "Is this true, Mei Zi?"

"We're talking about it," I said. "My paperwork hasn't been approved yet."

"What about a ceremony? They cost money and we need time."

"We're planning to marry in America," Dave offered. This was news to me.

Mama suddenly seemed satisfied. "It won't be official then. Not legitimate."

"When's the baby due?" Baba asked.

I gasped. "There's no baby!"

"Why else would you marry a foreigner?"

"Because I love him," I said, exasperated. "Mama married you out of love."

"I'm Han Chinese!" he thundered.

Dave looked to me for translation, but I shook my head.

"This man is not right for you," Mama said tersely. "He's water, and you're water. Too much flow to be a good match. I'm Fire to Baba's water. A very good match. Find someone else."

"There's no one else I want," I said.

"Then we call the matchmaker," Baba said.

"No! I'm moving to America and marrying Dave," I said belligerently. "That's my decision. You need to support me and trust my judgment."

Without a word, Baba stood up and marched out of the room. Mama followed. Dave raised his eyebrows.

"They'll come around," I said.

郭

The next two months were a flurry of paperwork and fee-paying, culminating in an interview with the United States Consulate in Guangzhou. Standing in long lines during the day, I savored the evening with Jin. Though we didn't see one another all that regularly, knowing we'd be twelve thousand miles apart was a painful thought.

"Are you sure you want to do this?" she asked.

"I'm sure," I replied, wondering if that was really true.

"I don't know if you're courageous or crazy," she said. "I try to imagine you living in another country, but I can't do it."

I wasn't afraid of moving to America—well, not terribly afraid. Flying across the world was certainly daunting and submerging myself in an alien culture even more so. But had I not blindly raced halfway across China to a city in which I did not speak the language for a man I'd never met? At least in the US, real love waited for me. And I knew the language—kind of.

"If things don't work out, they don't work out," I said, shrugging. "I can always come back."

"Can you?" she muttered.

郭

After a quick trip to Shanghai to bid farewell to my friends, I flew to Hunan. It was right to spend my last days in China with family, but painful not getting to spend any of them with JiaoJiao; she'd already been spirited away to her family's village for childbirth.

On my last evening, Mama said, "Come walk with me."

Throwing on my coat, I dutifully followed her outside. Past her hibernating garden, she stopped and gripped my arms. "Don't go," she said urgently. "Don't throw away your dreams for this man. Stay here and start your spa."

"Maybe I'll start a spa in America," I said without conviction.

"I wanted you to have a better life."

"I'm going to be a rich American wife. I'll live in a mansion, with maids to cook and clean for me and a driver to take me wherever I want to go. Baba's happy for me. You should be too." When all she did was look away, I said, "Mama, you know Dave. He's a good person. If I want to come home, he'll buy me a ticket. He promised."

"Don't be a stupid girl. Once you're his wife, you'll see a different face. He might beat you or starve you. What are you supposed to do then? His government will surely believe him over you."

"No, Mama," I said, pulling away. "My new life will be wonderful. You'll see."

39

Arrested

A sizeable crowd gathered around me at the Changsha airport. Ting, Yang, and their husbands bubbled with excitement, showering me with bouquets of wildflowers, beer, and cakes. Ming hugged me fiercely, and my father, his chin set, emptied his wallet into my purse. Mama gave me tears. Many, many tears.

Though I'd flown several times now, I'd never been in the international portion of an airport. It was a different experience altogether. Serious-looking people carrying briefcases flooded the wide walkways, travelers with skin colors I'd never seen before stared back at me, and there were many, many Westerners.

Brightly lit duty-free stores selling everything from liquor to expensive clothing lined the walls. My gate lay at the far end of the long concourse, giving me ample opportunity to shop. I bought Dave cologne and a large candy bar.

The airplane was enormous; it even had an upstairs! Dressed in neat blue suits, the Caucasian flight attendants smiled pleasantly, their hair elegantly tied back in knots, their eyes all manner of color. Cataloging them, it seemed my fiancé's features were not as unique as I'd thought.

Dave had booked a window seat for me so that I could see the world. Though certainly exciting, watching China disappear was both terrifying and painful. I discreetly wiped away my tears and forced myself to think of only good things, to imagine the future and the wonderful life awaiting me.

We chased the sun until it disappeared completely, but even in darkness, sleep was difficult. I watched movie after movie, ate strange food, and listened to hours of Western music through headphones. Finally nodding off, I was jolted awake by a flight attendant instructing me to buckle my seatbelt. Groggily, I stared out at the expansive city below, the slices of orange soil, and the great swaths of land surrounding the large airport. The neat row of concourses, each surrounded by long white airplanes, reminded me of animal spines.

Following directions to immigration, which were mercifully written in Mandarin, along with many other languages, I joined the snaking line marked non-US citizens. Anxious, I fidgeted as I waited for my turn to pass into the main airport.

"I've landed! I'm in the line," I told Dave, pressing the phone to my ear.

"Thank God. I've been holding my breath for hours. How was your flight?"

"Long, but very nice. America looks pretty good from the air."

"It's pretty good from the ground, too. I can't wait to show you."

We talked non-stop as the line inched forward. Exhausted, I barely remembered much of what he said, but it didn't matter. I was here; he was here. We would be united in mere minutes.

"I'm next in line, I'll call you back," I said, disconnecting.

With a big smile, I surrendered my burgundy passport and visa to the American immigration officer.

Looking them over, he said in English, "I need your I-94 form."

"I don't understand."

"Your form should look like this." He held up a sheet of paper that looked unfamiliar.

I thought I had everything I needed. "I don't have that."

"You'll need to fill out an I-102 then. Are you planning to stay in the US for over three months?"

"Yes. I'm moving here. I'm getting married."

"May I see your I-539?"

I had no knowledge of "I" forms, so again I said, "I don't understand."

He sighed. "Show me all of your forms, please."

My heart started racing. "You have all of my forms."

After a brief phone conversation, he handed my passport back. "Go through that door," he said, pointing.

"But my fiancé—"

"Will wait," he said curtly. "Next."

I stared at the ominous white door, terrified of what lay beyond. If my government was frightening, I could only imagine what the American one was like. My fingers shaking, I called Dave.

"Honey, calm down," he said.

"You don't understand. They're going to put me in jail or send me home."

"They're not going to put you in jail, GuoGuo. It's just some paperwork. We'll get through this together. I'll stay on the phone in case you need me."

When I stepped inside, I was expecting anything but a tranquil waiting room filled with frustrated-looking travelers. I smiled nervously at the woman seated behind a narrow window at the far end.

"The man outside told me to come here."

"Papers," she said.

I slid what I had under the glass. She studied first my passport and then flipped to my visa.

"Okay. Take a seat until we call your name."

"Have they arrested you yet?" Dave asked before I could speak again. The humor in his voice irritated me; this was far from funny.

A door beside the counter opened, and a uniformed man stepped out. He called out a name. A woman wrapped in a strange and colorful dress rose and followed him.

"No, but there's still time," I said brittlely.

"How many people are ahead of you?"

"Twenty or so."

"Oh, well, it probably won't take too long then. At least you're..."

"At least I'm what?" I said after a long pause. "Dave? What did you say?"

When I got no dial tone after trying to call him back, I sat confused for a moment. Finally, my sleep-deprived mind registered that my phone had died. Afraid of losing my charging wire, I'd packed it in one of my suitcases.

Scurrying to the counter, I said, "Excuse me. I need something from my bags."

"Your luggage is in holding. You can claim it once we have cleared you to enter the country," the woman replied. Morose, I drifted back to my seat.

A few minutes later, the door from which I'd entered opened again, and an elderly Chinese woman stepped inside. She looked as terrified as I'd felt—still felt. After receiving the same instructions at the window, she took a seat near me.

"Ni hao," I said, which means hello in Mandarin.

"Nay hoe," she returned in Cantonese.

My mind traveled to Chao and the trouble we'd had communicating so very long ago. A wave of sadness rolled over me at the mere thought of that sweet boy. My guilt would forever follow me.

The woman in the colorful wrap never returned, but the same official stepped into the waiting room and called out another name. A bearded man, his head wrapped in black cloth, looked nervous as he rose.

After hours of waiting, the officer finally called my name. Exhausted and hungry to the point of fainting, I hurried towards him, altogether forgetting to be afraid.

He escorted me to a small room, and the man inside invited me to sit. He began thumbing through a set of papers I soon realized was my K-1 visa application. He asked a lot of the questions I'd already answered on those documents and he wanted to know about the tuberculosis disease.

At some point, he must have decided I was who I said I was because he stamped a form and handed it to me.

"Give this to the immigration officer, and then you can collect your bags. Welcome to America, Miss Guo."

Left in the large immigration area where this nightmare had begun, I again took my place at the end of the long line, wondering if I would ever see Dave again.

40

Ta Da

Though neat and uniform from the air, Atlanta's airport was a giant rat's maze inside, and it took me another half-hour to find the correct train going in the correct direction to the exit where I would claim my suitcases, and far more importantly, my fiancé.

It had been early morning when my plane landed, but as I hurried past an observation window, the sky was colored the pink of evening. Clusters of people, holding up signs and brightly colored balloons, waited on the other side of a thick red line marking the floor. Dave's was not among the expectant faces.

I wove through the crush, searching for the man I loved, hoping he hadn't given up on me and gone home. On the other side of a glass partition, I noticed a large waiting area scattered with chairs. Seated on a green couch in the far corner, my future husband, dressed in a nice if not rumpled suit, flipped through a magazine.

"Hi," I said, sneaking up on him.

Dave's head snapped up, his tired and anxious expression melting into relief. He smiled hugely and then wrapped his arms around me, rocking back and forth for a long time. "It's so good to finally see you," he said. "It's been forever."

"Today has lasted forever."

Chuckling ruefully, he lifted a bouquet of wilted roses from the couch and offered them to me. "Yeah, these have seen better days."

"They're still beautiful," I said, beyond touched.

郭

"I bet you're exhausted," he said, rescuing my bags as soon as they were spat onto the conveyor belt. "Let's get you home."

Following him past innumerable cars, it disappointed me to learn that he'd driven himself. For hours, I'd imagined snuggling in his lap and kissing him all the way to his enormous house.

He'd told me several times that Atlanta was a large US city, and certainly it spread over a great distance, but before landing, I realized he'd been joking. Yes, there were some tall buildings here and there, but nothing resembling the great mountain of skyscrapers that housed so many of Shanghai's twenty-six million.

The Atlanta streets were wide and well lit, and though there were many cars—most much larger than those back home, traffic was orderly. In fact, no horns blared at all, which was a constant sound in Shanghai, no matter the hour. I found it equally strange that the roadsides were not littered with trash, and I wondered how people who recycled for a living survived here. My family would surely starve to death.

We drove for what seemed forever. In his excitement, I think Dave wanted to show me everything at once, but I caught myself nodding off several times.

The buildings grew fewer and farther apart. Eventually, Dave exited onto a smaller road, marked by squat shops and restaurants boasting enormous, well-lit paved lots. I wanted to laugh; so much space just to park cars.

Past a stoplight, he said, "We're almost there."

Dave pulled onto a quiet avenue, flanked by small, tidy homes with lighted entryways. We traveled less than a minute more before pulling into the driveway of a modest two-story structure.

"Ta-da!" he said, pressing a button above his windshield. The large door in front of us rose as if by magic, and then Dave did the craziest thing I'd ever seen; he drove right into the very house itself. I couldn't believe it!

Shutting off the engine, he smiled, his eyes bright with anticipation. "Welcome to your new home, GuoGuo."

郭

Dave led me into the warm house and down a short hallway. "This is the kitchen," he said, waving his hand at an open room, complete with a double sink and many cabinets. Through a homey dining area, we skirted an empty living room, and I followed him up a narrow set of stairs.

It wasn't a large building, certainly not the size of his mansion in Pudong, but America was a rich and most likely expensive place. Perhaps this was its equivalent. Swallowing my disappointment, I forced a smile. This house was still a dream. It was wonderful.

"Here's the master bedroom," he said, patting the generous bed. "And here's the closet." Opening a white door, he invited me to look. "You'll like this." The space, half-filled with Dave's suits, was larger than the storage room I'd once called home.

"I like it very much," I said, grinning.

After showing me a compact guest room and a sparse office, he said, "You probably want to freshen up. I'll bring in your bags, and then go get dinner."

I'd always enjoyed being clean, and after twenty-two hours on an airplane followed by a day trapped in customs, the well-pressured shower felt wonderful. And unlike the toilets in China, where rims were rare, his American toilet seat was wide and comfortable.

Wrapping myself in the big blue towel he'd left out, I padded across the softest rug I'd ever felt. Though lacking any sort of design, it stretched from one wall to the other, into the hallway and to the other rooms. I could easily have slept on top of it every night for the rest of my life. No, this was a very fine place.

郭

"You ready to eat?" Dave asked, pulling me into his arms.

My slumbering hunger reawakened. "Yes."

Dave placed several paper buckets with little metal handles in front of me. "I thought you'd like Chinese to start with."

Though smelling different from what I was used to, I scooped a generous portion onto my plate. Before swallowing my first bite, I knew Chinese people had not cooked this food. It wasn't bad, but the meat was heavily coated with bread and covered in a thick, sweet sauce. The rice, with so many broken grains, was second quality.

"The restaurant tricked you, Dave. This is not Chinese food."

He laughed. "It's Americanized. This is what every American-Chinese restaurant serves."

Wondering if his maid cooked like this, I said, "I'll cook for you instead."

Dave placed a folded cookie in front of me. "Let's see what our fortunes are." Cracking his open, he fished out a tiny piece of paper.

"Mine says, 'a new adventure is coming your way', and my lucky numbers are seventeen, six, thirty-two, twelve, and sixteen.' Well, at least I like sixteen," he said, shrugging. "And we're definitely having a new adventure. Now your turn."

I broke mine similarly and read the thin strip. "A home is happy if you are." I flipped it over. Along with a series of numbers were the words "Learn Chinese." The characters meant absolutely nothing, and I laughed outright. "If this is how Americans learn Chinese, then you are all in trouble."

Dave told me I didn't need to eat the cookie and then dropped his into the trash bag. Though the cookie itself was without taste, I ate it; a Chinese person would never consider wasting something as precious as food. Rummaging through the empty containers until I found his cookie, I ate it as well.

"You must really like them. I'll ask for extras next time."

Soon after, Dave stifled a yawn. "It's been a long day for us both. Bed?"

With so much food in my stomach and my body still warm from the shower, I knew I should be sleepy. Instead, I felt lightheaded and curiously awake. After making love, I finally drifted off, but when I awoke, it was still dark outside. Leaving Dave peacefully snoring, I crept to his office.

The computer was on, but deciphering his American keyboard and then finding an online translation program took time. Eventually, I emailed everyone to let them know I was safe, happy, and not to worry.

41

Company Perks

I wanted to cook a good meal for Dave's breakfast. Rooting through his refrigerator, I found a shriveled onion, two pink tomatoes, a bag of carrots, and several perfectly shaped white eggs. I was glad that at least these foods I knew. After a fruitless search for chili peppers and ginger, I settled on a bottle of hot sauce, which, after tasting it, wasn't all that hot. I couldn't find his wok, and I wondered if the maid brought her own each day. This seemed strange.

Dumping yellow oil into a large flat-bottomed pan, I turned knobs until a flame appeared; everything was different here. Dave had pointed to the microwave oven in passing, telling me it cooked things quickly and that I would like it. Placing the rice container inside, I pressed the button called start. A light came on and the oven whirred like wind before a storm. Soon, tiny lightning sparks began bouncing off the metal handles. It was very exciting to watch.

Smoke billowed out the back of the machine, as I assumed it should. Suddenly, a piercing scream filled the quiet kitchen. A startled Dave burst into the room, his hair sticking up in all directions.

"What's happening?" I yelled, covering my ears.

Reaching up, he removed a small white disc mounted to the

ceiling. The sound instantly stopped. He then glanced at the microwave and smiled ruefully. "I probably should have shown you how to use that."

"I was making breakfast for you."

"Good luck with that. I haven't bought groceries in a while. I thought we'd do that today." He walked over to the pan. "It smells great, though."

Sitting down at the kitchen table, he said, "Couldn't sleep, huh?"

"I slept a little."

"Jet lag. I have it every time I come back. Your body will adjust in a few days, and then you'll be on US time." He stifled a yawn. "Seeing the sun will help."

郭

Morning brought with it a lavender sky, and I was amazed to think that in China the sun was just setting.

"I have a full day planned, but first, let's take a walk. I want to show you the neighborhood."

Taking my hand, Dave led me to the neat sidewalk in front of the house. Filled with unfamiliar, yet pleasant scents, this January morning was far warmer than the one I'd left behind, and I began feeling more myself once the gentle sun hit my eyes.

"That's where I play golf," he said, pointing to a misty lawn behind a thin wall of trees. "I'll teach you how to play."

The sidewalk took us down another street where several houses were under construction, each with its own bulldozer.

In China, many buildings, sometimes very large ones, are constructed solely by manual labor. Though the government has plenty of bulldozers, companies often employ workers to dig up the soil and carry it away instead; people are much cheaper than machines. Men, and sometimes women, work day and night on a building site. It's a dangerous job, and occasionally people fall from the high ladders to their deaths. An education isn't necessary for this kind of labor, so construction is a good job for those who are very poor.

Past a set of exuberant fountains and an impressive iron gate, we stepped onto a wide street dotted with mansions on the scale of Dave's Pudong home.

"Why don't you live in one of these?" I asked.

He snorted. "Yeah, right."

When Dave's relatively modest house came back into view, I studied it analytically. Though not what I'd expected, it was certainly charming, and the thought of it belonging to me made me nearly delirious.

We spent the next portion of my first American day wandering an expansive grocery store. After filling a cart big enough to ride in with all manner of strange vegetables and fruits, we searched for the Asian section, which turned out to be only a couple of shelves. No matter. As long as I had rice, anything was possible.

Unlike the Asian section, the meat department was shockingly large. I so wished I could show it to my family. My mother would lose her mind! My only complaint was that everything was displayed skinless, boneless, and headless, making animals difficult to identify. Fish were not kept in tanks. Dave chose for me.

"Your cook will thank us for doing the shopping," I said, looking forward to teaching her my recipes.

Dave chuckled. "I don't have a cook."

"Why don't you have a cook?"

"GuoGuo, only rich people have cooks."

"But you're rich," I said, thoroughly confused.

"I'm not rich," he said, running his fingers through his hair. "Just normal."

"What about a driver?" I asked.

He smiled and shook his head. "Drivers, maids, and million-dollar houses were company perks for overseas employees. Back in the States, I don't get those things." He cocked his head. "I thought you knew that."

"How could I know that?" I said, feeling let down. I thought of my mother's warnings.

"Don't get me wrong, I make a good living," he said defensively. "I do really well. Way better than lots of people."

"I'm just trying to understand," I said wearily. "Can we go home soon? I need to rest."

郭

Within days, I began sleeping when Dave did and waking with the sun. Several times he went to his office. I didn't mind being alone; I needed time to think about this new life.

Friday night, I prepared a feast. Dave had been at work most of the day, and cooking felt good to me—natural. I steamed fish with chili sauce, cooked the fat noodles we'd purchased, and stir-fried green beans with garlic.

"Something smells great, honey," Dave said, pulling me into his arms.

"I made a special dinner for you."

After dinner, Dave set our dirty dishes in the sink. "I want to talk to you about something. It's important," he said with a gravity that made me uncomfortable. I didn't know what to think, except that perhaps I'd done something wrong.

Taking my hand, he led me to the empty living room. Other than his bed, desk, and kitchen table, there was no actual furniture in the house. This was common enough in China; my parents certainly had little in the way of furniture, and until Dave furnished my apartment, I'd never even owned a chair. He mumbled something about needing a couch and then tugged me back to the table.

"I love you," he said.

"And I love you."

"Are you happy here? Do you like America—what you've seen so far?"

"So far, yes, I like it."

He took a deep breath and let it out slowly. "I think it's important to discuss the terms of our marriage."

"Terms? What terms?"

"I want to make sure you're marrying me for the right reasons."

I had no idea what to say.

"What I mean is, I hope you're not just marrying me for my money."

My mouth popped open. "Why are you saying this stupid thing?"

He exhaled heavily. "I think it's best if we sign a prenup."

"I don't know that word," I said, though I didn't like the sound of it.

Pulling a crisp sheet of paper from his briefcase, he laid it on the table. "It's a document that says if you divorce me, you can't have my money."

Angry and hurt that he could think so little of me, I glared at him for a moment and then laughed. "You know what, Dave? I'm not going to marry you. I left everything I've ever known to move here, and now you ask me to sign this agreement? Especially when you don't even have a lot of money. I may be blinded by love, but I'm not stupid. I'm still young and can easily find another man. I'm going back to China."

Marching upstairs, I retrieved my suitcases from the closet and began stuffing them with clothes. Dave was instantly behind me.

"GuoGuo, please listen. When my ex-wife and I divorced, she took half of everything I owned. I...I just don't want that to happen again."

He pulled me against him, but I didn't want this contact. When he didn't let go, I beat his chest with my fists. "I'm not your ex-wife. I'm not the kind of person who would steal from you. You should know that by now." My heart beat wildly as angry tears raced down my cheeks.

"GuoGuo, stop hitting me and just look at me. I love you. I asked you to marry me because I love you and I want to live my life with you."

"You say you love me, but you don't trust me. That's not love."

Snatching up my luggage, I stomped down the stairs.

"I'm sorry. Look, forget the prenup. Forget I ever mentioned it." He raced over to the table and tore the paper in half. "I do trust you. I really do. Please...just stay."

"I'm going for a walk now," I said, dropping my bags and sidestepping him.

"Let me grab a sweater."

"No. Alone."

郭

I walked a different direction than normal. Rather than passing the rich houses, I went by the ones on Dave's street, waving back at a man as he drove by. I'd been struck by the smiling, friendly neighborhood people, some of whom even said hello from their yards as if they knew me. China was not like this; people there were too busy taking care of themselves to talk to strangers.

I thought about my mother, and how she'd begged me not to come. How, after Dave returned to America, she'd argued with me, ranted about his true nature, and what he might do to me once here.

I'd defended him because I believed he was a gentleman and a true person. This was the first time since our early breakup that he'd seemed anything but that. And while I didn't understand American divorce law, if I married him and things didn't work out, I would expect him to share some of what he had with me—enough for me to survive on at least.

He'd misrepresented himself, allowing me to believe him rich when he was not, never contradicting me once when I'd said so. And while his house was certainly nice in its own right, the life of leisure I'd painted for my family and friends was not this.

But what would I do if I went back to China? Living off what Dave had given me for the last year, I'd made little effort to earn any real money of my own. Starting over in Shanghai, or even Changsha, would be difficult, but certainly not impossible; I had connections in both places. But I'd come here to be with the man I loved, hadn't I?

And I still loved him. Very little could change that. He was tender and sweet, and I was certain that he loved me as well. My diamond ring glinted in the setting sun, and I stared at it. Surely, he wouldn't have gone to such expense and trouble to bring me here had he not truly wanted to marry me.

I decided finally that he, like me, was scared. And saying dumb things without thinking was nothing new for him.

By the time I returned to our block, I felt more at peace. Sitting on his front steps, he looked defeated. I smiled to myself. This was not the posture of a sinister man.

"Alright, I'll marry you," I said, stopping in front of him. "But I will not sign a prenup. If you can't live with that, then I'll go home."

"No prenup," he said solemnly, shaking his head. "I'll never mention it again."

He pulled me onto his lap, and we sat this way for a long time, staring up at the darkening sky. Stars appeared above the treetops, and other than the gentle sound of the breeze, it was quiet. This was a pleasant place to be. A good place. America would be my new home.

42

Purple

In China, our wedding ceremony would have been a village event. Here in America, it was a matter of a quick visit to a government building downtown.

My anxiety grew as we neared the courthouse. We'd moved mountains just to gain permission for a visit. Could acquiring something so much more significant be accomplished this easily?

To calm myself, I teased him. "Hey, are you sure you're not going to make me sign that prenup? You'd better think this through. Maybe someday I'll dump you, and you'll have to share half of everything with me."

Dave smiled and shook his head. "I'd share it with you, anyway."

Obtaining official papers was exactly as easy as Dave had promised; a few signatures, a glance at my passport, payment of a small fee—less than what we'd spent on dinner the night before—and we were officially married.

Dave wanted an actual ceremony, which pleased me; the process had been anticlimactic thus far. Because he hadn't lived in this city very long and worked long hours all the while, he'd made few friends. Of course, I had none.

"Will your family come?" I asked, wondering what they were like. Would I be good enough for his mother?

"Hm, well. Yeah, that's complicated."

"Won't they want to meet me?" I asked, confused.

"Eventually, sure."

郭

Four people attended our family room wedding: Dave, Jonathan—a guy I'd met only once, a government official called a Justice of the Peace, and me.

A great longing for my family and friends nearly overwhelmed me as I transformed myself into a bride. In another world, my friends would have designed my hair and makeup, and a professional photographer, like the ones I'd so often worked with, would hover about. There would be wardrobe changes, a giant feast—so many things. And Mama would be there...

Dressed in the traditional red qipao I'd brought from Hunan, I descended the stairs carrying a white lily, the traditional symbol for long and happy marriages. Dave and Jonathan, who were chatting with the justice by the fireplace, stilled when I entered the living room. Dave's expression was radiant.

"You look so beautiful, honey," he whispered, reaching for my hands.

Not sure what to do with the lily, I handed it to Jonathan, who quietly chuckled. After the justice spoke, we repeated words I didn't understand. As I said them, I looked into my husband's blue eyes and thought about how strange fate was, how I could never have foreseen this event, especially in a country so far from home and to a man who embodied the very opposite of my village's ideals.

Jonathan took pictures of us with my phone, so I could then send to my family. I wondered what Mama would do when she saw them. No, I didn't need to wonder; she would cry.

Once we thanked the justice and signed another official-looking document, Jonathan, Dave, and I went to a nearby hibachi grill to celebrate. The Japanese chef—who was actually Mexican—played all kinds of games with us as he cooked our meat and vegetables, even tossing shrimp into Dave's mouth and making a flaming volcano of onion rings. In honor of our wedding day, the staff sang at our table, while the other patrons cheered.

When we returned home, Dave swiftly scooped me into his arms.

"What are you doing?" I said, alarmed.

"It's an American tradition," he replied, carrying me through the door and up the stairs to our bedroom.

Our wedding night was beautifully romantic. Loving me tenderly, Dave made me feel so precious, and I was certain marrying him had not been a mistake. This was my life now. I was an American wife.

郭

"Okay, Mrs. Wiseman, it's time to make this house our home," Dave announced the following afternoon. He took me to several furniture stores so I could pick a style I liked. We then went to a hardware shop to choose wall paint.

"I can have any of these colors?" I asked, amazed by the hundreds of selections. In China, walls do not have color. Everyone uses white.

"Sure. Pick whatever you like."

"I'll have these then," I said, placing the stack of paint chips on the counter.

"*All* of these?" he said, laughing.

"Yes."

郭

Over the next few months, color spread to every room in our house, and furniture was rearranged often—too often for Dave's liking since he was the one doing the heavy lifting. I painted our bedroom deep blue, and once it dried, I added light blue stripes. Then, when the curtains arrived, I realized the blue I'd chosen didn't match them, so I painted the walls purple.

"What do you think?" I asked as soon as Dave got home from work one evening.

"I've never seen a purple ceiling before," he said, grinning. "I like it."

We also bought a large television, and I spent countless hours watching CNN from my new sofa. My initial shock in learning of all the terrible things going on in the world was quickly eclipsed by the fact that US stations were allowed to broadcast it.

Because my government controls all media, including access to the internet, watching Chinese television is like watching a royal wedding. Everything looks beautiful. Everything is perfect. From the outside, you'd think nothing bad ever happens there.

When Jonathan asked for my thoughts on Tiananmen Square, I said that it was very large.

"Yeah, but what happened there. I mean, how can you stand it?"

"Stand what?" I responded, perplexed.

"You know, how the government ran over protesters with tanks?"

"Are you crazy? That never happened," I said, shocked.

There were many things I didn't like about my government, not the least of which was what they'd done to my village, but plowing over livestock was far different than plowing over human beings. Besides, my teachers would have taught us this in school—surely.

"See for yourself," he said, pulling up a video on his phone.

"No," I moaned as I watched in horror.

Left shellshocked that evening, I searched the American internet for more information. There were so many things I didn't know about my country, and plenty of it written in Mandarin. It was as if my government had constructed a second great wall around knowledge itself; I'd always believed Chairman Mao was a great and honorable man.

43

A Fat Goose

Once I'd finished decorating our house, I had little to do each day until Dave returned from work; I could only handle so much world news. Used to seeing thousands of people in a Shanghai afternoon, at times the Sandy Springs suburb felt desolate. Those neighbors home during daytime hours were friendly enough, but they seemed to have trouble understanding me, just as I was stumped by their Southern dialect; Dave didn't sound that way. Evenings were my salvation.

Jonathan's visits became increasingly frequent, until finally, we saw him nearly every night. During the week, we went out to bars and restaurants, and on weekends we took trips—sometimes going as far away as Las Vegas, which, to a gambler like me, was especially mesmerizing. Soon, I decided I had two husbands.

郭

Every morning I walked the neighborhood streets, paying far more attention to people and cars than wildlife. However, on one of these outings, a loud honking pierced the quiet. I stared in wonder as a flock of big, fat geese landed by one of the golf course's ponds.

Chinese people eat nearly anything, and in my village, if someone saw plump birds like these, they would do anything in their power to catch one. Geese were delicious, and the thought of surprising Jonathan and Dave with a juicy bird for dinner had me running back to my kitchen.

Brandishing my largest knife, I crept across the damp field. When I was reasonably close to the flock, I dropped bread pieces onto the ground, coaxing the birds towards me. When a particularly adventurous one dove for the crust nearest me, I raised the knife over my head and launched it.

I was not a master knife-thrower, and my knife went wide. The goose honked at me and then flew a few meters away. Retrieving my knife, I threw it again. This time it hit the goose on the back before bouncing off. When the goose honked this time, the entire flock took flight, landing on the other side of the pond.

If I couldn't kill one with a knife, perhaps a golf club would work. Rushing back to our garage, I rummaged through Dave's bag, pulling out the one with the biggest head. I returned to the course, happy to see that the geese hadn't left.

Taking my time, I edged very close to them once more. Though I hadn't mastered golf yet, I enjoyed the driving range. Winding up, I swung the club with all of my might and hit nothing but air. The geese scattered, and I raced after first one and then another, swiping at them unsuccessfully. It was like chasing chickens with no fence. When the flock finally had enough of me and flew away, I surrendered in defeat. We would have chicken for dinner.

That night, after telling Dave and Jonathan what had happened, they laughed at me. In fact, Jonathan fell right out of his chair. Why they would laugh at free food was beyond me.

"I wish I could have recorded that," Dave said.

"If you'd ever eaten goose, you would not be so quick to judge."

"What do they taste like?" Jonathan asked.

"Like goose, of course. Tender and juicy and delicious."

"Didn't they eat a goose in *A Christmas Carol*?" Jonathan asked Dave.

"I don't remember. Something like that, I think," he replied, laughing all over again. "But I doubt it was a golf course goose." I slapped at Dave when he pulled me onto his lap. "Last week she tried to catch a rabbit. I married a crazy person."

郭

When I'd first arrived in America, the thought of living a life of leisure was alluring. But as the months passed, I became increasingly bored and lonely. I cherished my Chinese friends, and because of the time difference, I often stayed up late or got up very early just to communicate with them. If I had someone to visit with, my days would certainly be more pleasant. But how could I meet anyone cooped up at home all the time?

I'd enjoyed socializing with my Shanghai language school classmates. Perhaps America also offered such programs. Justifying it to Dave would be no problem; I was still nearly illiterate. Searching online, I discovered that a public library in nearby Buckhead offered free classes for immigrants. I couldn't believe America had so many benefits for its people.

"GuoGuo, why is there a grocery cart in our garage?" Dave asked, tossing his computer bag onto our purple striped chair.

"I needed groceries," I replied. "I have exciting news, and I'm cooking a special dinner to celebrate."

"Awesome. But how did you—wait, you *walked* to the store?"

"It's not far."

"It's, like, two miles from here!"

"So?"

Dave ran his hands through his hair in typical fashion, but then stopped and grinned. "So, you walked home pushing a grocery cart?"

"Yes."

He fell onto our couch, laughing. "Oh my God, you are so funny." When he sat up again, he said, "You know, I could have driven you there when I got home."

"Dumplings take time. But that doesn't matter," I said, smiling up at him. "Ask me what we're celebrating."

Dave was very supportive when I explained how important the class was to me, but when I told him the details, he said, "Honey, I can't take you there during the day. I'm really sorry."

"It's no problem," I said, channeling Madame Li. "I'll take your car."

He raised his eyebrows. "Have you driven a car before?"

"I have a Chinese driver's license," I replied smugly.

One of the many things I'd done while waiting for my visa was take driving lessons. The car had been manual transmission and difficult to drive, and I'd failed my driving test several times before finally passing. Dave didn't need to know the details.

He looked at me skeptically, but then said, "Okay, we'll go out tomorrow, so you can get used to it."

If I could drive a golf cart, then his car would surely be no different. I went to bed that night feeling confident.

郭

Dave's car was not easy to drive. At first, we just went around the neighborhood. A short person, even after adjusting the seat, I had trouble seeing over the steering wheel. His sedan was also very large. And while I enjoyed riding in it, driving it was a different story.

Over the weekend, Dave and I mapped out the route to the library, and then Monday morning, I rode with him to his office.

"Are you sure you're okay doing this?" Dave said, parking in his office lot.

"I'm very okay," I said, kissing him. In truth, I was nervous. There'd been a lot more traffic on the road this morning than on Sunday afternoon.

Class was wonderful, and I met many interesting people. Unfortunately, my tires met many curbs as I drove around town. By week's end, I'd backed into a fire hydrant and sideswiped a telephone pole.

"I'm sorry," I said, hopping out of the driver's seat. "That shopping cart was closer than I thought."

Dave's eyes traveled down the passenger's side door panel, and then he walked to the back, rubbing the bumper. "It's fine," he said, sighing. "We'll have Jonathan's crew give us an estimate."

Jonathan managed the dealership where Dave had purchased his car. Both new to Atlanta, they'd become fast friends, and at this point, there was little they wouldn't do for each other.

"He'll give us a good deal," I said confidently.

By month's end, I'd become better at driving—only taking the car back to Jonathan's dealership once more.

"This morning, I'm driving you to work," I announced over breakfast. "I want to show you how good I am."

The Atlanta beltway was busy at any time of the day, and people drove really fast. Morning rush hour was the worst time of all because everyone was trying to get somewhere in a hurry.

"Okay, GuoGuo, now merge in," Dave instructed as I neared the end of the entrance ramp.

There were cars everywhere, all cutting in front of one another. "I am," I said, panicking when I saw no opportunity.

"Merge faster," he said, clenching his teeth.

Horns blew loudly behind me. I'd never driven the car faster than thirty-five miles per hour, and the faster I accelerated, the more out of control I felt. "What if I wreck?" I choked out, suddenly terrified.

Dave blanched, his face pale even for a white person's, and my scalp began tingling.

"You've got to press the accelerator harder, or we'll be hit!" he yelled, pushing my leg down. "Stomp on the pedal. Use more gas!"

When the giant truck barreling towards us blew its deafening horn, I screamed.

Parking in a UPS visitor's space, I turned off the engine, and we sat in silence. As the minutes ticked by, tears slid down my cheeks, one after the other. Finally, Dave snatched up my trembling hand and kissed it. "You did great."

"I'm a terrible driver," I sniffed.

"We should have practiced more on the highway."

"I'm never driving on that road again!" And then, in Chinese, I cursed the car, the beltway, and all humankind.

"Okay," he breathed.

郭

"Jonathan and I need to do some guy stuff," Dave announced, Saturday morning. Assuming that meant drinking beer and watching a televised ballgame, I was happy not to go; I hadn't learned to love football yet.

Morning turned into late afternoon. Hungry and unable to go anywhere, after doing my homework, I started dinner.

"We're home," Dave announced. "Mm, whatcha cooking?"

"Fried noodles. I was hungry and tired of waiting for you. Did you watch two games?"

"Nope," Jonathan replied, coming in behind him. His smile was one I didn't trust.

"I have a surprise for you," Dave said, kissing my cheek.

"Yeah. A big surprise," Jonathan added, nodding.

"Close your eyes," Dave instructed, slowly leading me outside. The October day had cooled off, and I was looking forward to going back inside as soon as possible. "Okay, open!"

Jonathan was standing in front of a shiny car I didn't recognize. "Who's here?" I asked, looking around for its driver.

"No one."

"Whose car is that?"

Jonathan said, "Ta da!"

"Ta da, what?" I asked.

"It's yours, GuoGuo. Your very own," Dave murmured into my hair.

"Don't you love it?" Jonathan said, opening the driver's door for me. "It's loaded."

Climbing into the passenger seat, he began animatedly speaking a language I didn't understand; power this, automatic that... Of course, Jonathan was always excited when he talked about cars.

When I looked up at Dave, he gave me the sweetest smile. "I love you," he mouthed.

Stunned that he'd bought me such an extravagant gift, I mouthed back, "I love you, too."

"Want to take it for a spin?" Jonathan asked. "I'll show you all the features."

This car was smaller than Dave's, which made me feel better, but all the buttons Jonathan kept pushing confused me. My confusion turned to fear when I realized where I had to park it.

I thought our garage was big, but the first time I pulled into it, I ended up mere inches from Dave's car. He groaned from the back seat, but then calmly said, "Pull out and try again, honey."

Assaulted by Jonathan's Asian-driver jokes, it took me four tries to get it right.

"Red is a lucky color," I told Dave that night in bed.

"Why do you think I chose it?"

"Because I'm a lucky girl?"

"Yes, and because we'll be lucky if you don't wreck it."

I smacked his head. "No more massages for you."

44

Complicated

Christmas was a thrilling time. Dave and I enjoyed all sorts of festivities: the tree lighting in Lenox Square, a celebration at Olympic Park, music at the zoo. We even erected a plastic tree in our living room. That red was a traditional Christmas color warmed my soul. I hung red lights and decorations all over the house, and Dave helped me garnish the outside with red bows. The pinnacle event was meeting Dave's family.

China and America are nearly the same size, and crossing from one side to the other takes many hours. As we neared Washington, we flew over great, snow-covered mountains poking up through thick clouds. A huge bay dotted with boats came into view as we landed.

I'd been in the US nearly a year now and had yet to meet his family. Secretly, I worried that he was embarrassed by me, but every time I brought up his parents, he just sighed and gave the same explanation: it's complicated.

Dave's mother had given birth to three boys. After divorcing his father when Dave was six, she married a man named Gary. Three years later, Dave's mother died, and Gary legally adopted the boys.

When Dave was thirteen, Gary married a woman named Dahlia,

334 • Virginia Gray

who decided two years later that she didn't like being a mother. After their divorce, Gary married a woman named Cassandra, who was only ten years older than Dave. When that didn't work out, he married his current wife, Marie.

"You don't need to call her Mom or anything," Dave murmured, waving to an older couple at baggage claim.

"So good to see you, son," the man said, hugging Dave and slapping his back. "And you must be GuoGuo. Am I saying that right, honey?"

"Yes, perfectly," I replied.

Gary pulled me into a big hug, and I liked him instantly. "This is Dave's stepmother, Marie," he then said.

She smiled tightly as we formally shook hands. "Nice to see you." She offered Dave the same greeting.

Seattle was a hilly place, and every time we crested another peak, I saw the distant high rises.

"We'll go downtown later in the week to see the sights," Gary said, the corners of his eyes crinkling in the rearview mirror.

Gary's house was very beautiful, but it was not the house in which Dave had grown up. Rather than red, their scant Christmas decorations were pink and white. Marie dressed in white as well.

"I don't remember this sunroom," Dave remarked, patting the doorframe. "Was it here last time I visited?"

"No, we added it four years ago," he responded jovially.

"Five," Marie corrected coolly.

郭

Atlanta and Seattle were different in many ways. The most significant to me was the prevalence of Asians; the airport had been filled with them. Entranced by young, fashionable Chinese women conversing in perfect English, I wondered if Dave might find a way to transfer to this city, if for no other reason than to stave off my growing loneliness.

After visiting the Space Needle, Gary took us to Chinatown. With its Asian grocery stores, gift shops, and eateries, I was thrilled to learn such neighborhoods existed.

"Most major cities have them," Gary assured me.

"What about Atlanta?" I asked, hope flaring.

Dave shook his head. "Sorry, honey."

Passing a park teeming with old men huddled around mahjong games, Gary pulled to the curb in front of a restaurant called Mike's Noodle House. Grabbing the only empty table, I glanced around the crowded room, and then smiled hugely; Gary and Dave were the only white people in the place. Studying a menu written in Mandarin, I ordered steamed tripe for myself and chicken noodle soup for them. It was the first time I'd eaten anything truly authentic since moving to this country.

Sipping jasmine tea while Gary paid the check, I listened to the sweet sounds of Mandarin spilling from the kitchen. It was painful to leave this place.

On Christmas Day, Dave's brothers came to celebrate. Dave's oldest brother, Scott, brought his wife and grown daughter. They were kind to me, and it was clear they loved Dave very much. Dave's middle brother, Bruce, was also a pleasant person, though he seemed to make Marie nervous.

Marie served a variety of dishes on Christmas day. Thinking of Chinese New Year and the symbolism of every food we ate, I asked about the significance of the ham, the potatoes, and the beans. Marie shook her head. Both Gary and Dave shrugged.

336 • Virginia Gray

"I'll tell you the symbolism," Bruce said, his plate overflowing with food. "The end of the world is coming. Any meal could be your last."

I laughed. "Dave said you were funny. That's a good joke."

Suddenly, Dave reached under the table and pinched my knee.

"You'd better take this seriously, GuoGuo. You should stockpile food like me. Right, Dave?"

Dave smiled indulgently, but Scott and Gary cleared their throats.

"Who wants coffee?" Marie interrupted, jumping up and scurrying to the kitchen.

After dessert, we moved to the living room, claiming seats around a tree seemingly grown from decorative boxes. Dave and I had purchased a sweater for Gary and perfume for Marie; claiming he didn't know her well enough to pick a fragrance, he let me choose. I hoped I'd gotten it right.

Gary gave an emotional speech about having his family reunited after so long and then welcomed me into the "brood". Afterward, he handed Dave a small red box with both our names on it.

"It's for a belated honeymoon trip, or whatever you need," he said earnestly.

Inside, we found a gift card for one-thousand dollars.

"Dad…" Dave said thickly.

"This is very generous. Thank you," I added.

I watched in fascination as the brothers exchanged gifts. This was neither my family nor my home, and the significance of the holiday itself was lost on me, but the sentiment was real. I'd never felt more homesick.

郭

Bolstered by my Chinatown visit, when I returned to Atlanta, I began seeking out Chinese people. Using the WeChat app, I filled out my profile in Mandarin and then searched "people nearby", looking for anyone who identified themselves similarly.

Within a few short hours, I discovered three women. We arranged to meet in Lenox Square Mall's food court.

"Hunan girl!" a voice yelled.

My head whipped around, and I hurried over to a willowy Asian woman. "Ahsha?"

"I can't believe we're from the place," she said excitedly, gripping my arms.

"I can't either. Changsha! Who could have guessed?"

"Oh, this is Meredith," she then said, introducing the short-haired woman who'd appeared beside her. "We already know each other, so we rode together."

Meredith smiled brightly. "I'm so glad we found each other!"

A third Chinese woman with long shiny hair and a large purse walked with purpose towards us. "GuoGuo?" she asked.

"Yes. Tina?" I said.

We became fast friends and began meeting weekly for tea and mahjong. All three had married American men, and all three were miserable.

"Mark is fine, but I'm divorcing him as soon as I get my green card," Ahsha said.

"I can't wait to divorce mine, either," Meredith spat. "He's a pig."

"How did you meet your husbands?" I asked, somewhat shocked.

"Online," all three women said at once, breaking into giggles.

"What about you?" Tina asked.

"I met Dave in Shanghai. We fell in love."

"*Love?*" Ahsha sneered. "I don't believe it."

When it was my turn to host, the girls studied my house with interest. "This is nice," Meredith said.

"Very nice," Ahsha added.

In 2008, Chinese New Year came in February. Because I finally had friends to celebrate with, I invited the girls, their husbands, Jonathan, and my English teacher and classmates to a third-day feast—the time for visiting friends.

The girls spent the morning helping me put together dumplings and spring rolls, and each planned to bring a traditional dish from their region. Hoping she was a good cook, I especially looked forward to Ahsha's fish in chili sauce.

After the other girls left to get ready, Ahsha said, "I need something to wear tonight."

"Oh, sure," I said, wiping my hands. "Let's go upstairs."

Ahsha rummaged through my closet, trying on three different dresses before deciding on a fancy pink one.

"That's one of my favorites. Dave bought it for me in Las Vegas. You can borrow it. And these shoes, too," I said. "They go well together."

郭

My classmates were from all over the world: Russia, Peru, Mexico, Malaysia. Each brought their partners and a dish from their country. I spent a lot of time talking to a Haitian man named Emmanuel. Before moving to Atlanta, I'd never seen anyone with dark skin, and though I'd grown accustomed to the sight over time, Emmanuel's was the blackest I'd ever seen.

"Can I touch your arm?" I asked timidly.

He laughed. "Sure. Can I touch yours?"

Ahsha looked especially nice in my dress. Ignoring her husband, she flirted with many men at the party, including Dave, which displeased me greatly.

The following week, Ahsha hosted our mahjong game. "Could I have my dress back?" I asked when the game broke up. "Dave's taking me out for Valentine's, and I want to wear it."

"Oh, I'm keeping it," she said flippantly.

"What? I loaned it to you. I told you it was a gift from my husband."

"Look at this place!" she suddenly snarled, sweeping out her arms. "You have a nice house, and I live in this ugly, cramped apartment. You drive an expensive car and have plenty of clothes. My husband gives me nothing. You should be more generous, GuoGuo. Let Dave buy you another dress."

"No," I said, marching into her bedroom and pulling the dress from its hanger. I didn't want to ruin our friendship over a dress, but this one was special. I found a reasonable voice. "Look, Ahsha, keep the shoes. I loaned them to you, but you can keep them if you want. And I'm happy for you to borrow any of the clothes in my closet as long as you return them."

"Fine," she said, glowering.

At Meredith's house the following week, Ahsha barely spoke to me. Meredith was distant as well, and when I returned from the bathroom, I caught them whispering about me.

Tina called me that evening. "Ahsha and Meredith asked me to uninvite you to my house next week."

"Why?"

"They don't want to play mahjong with you anymore. They want me to ask one of my American friends instead."

"But I've done nothing wrong."

"I know. I'm not happy about it either, and I still want us to have a good relationship, but I have too few Chinese friends to lose any of them. You understand, right?"

I was heartbroken. So desperate for Chinese companionship, I considered buying Ahsha's friendship with the dress. But I knew that one dress wouldn't be enough for her. And if Meredith was so quick to turn against me, there was little to salvage.

Tina and I remained on good terms, occasionally having lunch, but having been burned once, I kept her at a cautious distance. To fill the new, and seemingly deeper void, I shopped often, indulged in expensive spa services, and picked up a second English class at a recreation center. And simply to see Asian faces—still a rarity in this city—I had my nails done in a Vietnamese-owned salon and bought bad egg rolls from the Laotian family who owned the nearby Chinese restaurant.

I missed home more with each passing day.

45

A Stab To The Heart

One of my marriage conditions was returning to China at least once a year. While Dave had immediately agreed, neither of us realized the impossibility of keeping that promise.

At this time, an immigrant was required to remain in America for two years before he or she qualified for Green Card status. Since my three-month visa had long ago expired, if I were to travel home, I would have to secure a new visa before re-entering the US. This was terribly frustrating and difficult to explain to my family.

The travel restriction's sting magnified tenfold when I received Jin's wedding invitation; she wanted me to be a bridesmaid! Saying no left me inconsolable for days. Dave couldn't understand why missing a wedding was so tragic, and I couldn't understand his blindness to the chains binding me here.

On the two-year anniversary of stepping onto US soil, I submitted my green card paperwork, and on the day the card was issued, we made plans to visit my family. Dave was excited to return to China. *Excited* was not a strong enough word to describe my feelings.

Our trip still two weeks away, I'd only begun shopping for gifts. Ting's frantic call changed everything.

郭

Racing through the Changsha airport, I threw myself into the waiting arms of Ting and Jin. From there, we hurried to Yang's apartment.

Sorrow hung over the building like a heavy cloud. We were shown to Yang's small bedroom, where she lay on a thin mat, holding her squirming baby. Her eyes traveled to our faces in vague recognition.

"She's been this way since receiving the news," Ting murmured.

On the street outside their apartment, Yang's husband had gotten into a disagreement with a stranger. In the middle of the dispute, the man stabbed him in the heart; Yang's husband did not survive. My thoughts went to Xian, the crazed man who'd attacked Ming and Chen so long ago. And just like Xian, Yang's assailant had government connections.

Neither Yang's nor her husband's family had any such relationships, so there'd been no punishment for this crime. There would also be no burial ceremony while the families petitioned the government for justice and reparations.

The three of us visited Yang daily, encouraging her to eat and entertaining her child. Despondent, eventually, her mother took her back to their village.

Dave and I weren't scheduled to arrive in Hunan for a few more days. When I told Ming I was in Changsha, he insisted on coming to get me. Powerfully angry when he learned of the injustice, he said, "Chen still knows people. I can talk to them if she'd like."

I thought of the suffering Yang's family would endure if things went badly. "Thank you, but they need no more trouble."

Bursting into my parent's kitchen, Ming said, "Mama, I have a surprise for you!"

Mama stared at me as if I were an apparition. Silent tears wet her cheeks as she touched my face and hair, cataloging my appendages to make certain I wasn't missing any. Surely, the strong hug I gave her proved I was healthy and well-fed.

Baba went through a similar inspection. Perhaps it was good fortune that Dave's arrival was staggered. My parents' animosity towards him for keeping me away so long would surely be lessened by then.

"I've made congee for WeiWei. You will have some."

"I'm not hungry, Mama," I said.

"You will have some," she repeated sternly, setting a bowl in front of me.

郭

Mama was not overly warm to Dave when he arrived, but Ming and Chen both treated him as a brother, even getting drunk with him one night.

"You will bring Mei Zi home more often," Baba said, glaring at Dave.

"Yes, sir. We didn't know about the rule, but now that GuoGuo has her green card, she can come anytime she wants."

"It's America's fault, Baba," I added.

Flying to Shanghai with Dave, I saw him off. His job at UPS had changed, and he no longer worked on Asian projects. Without paid business trips, he was required to use his limited vacation days for the trip. He was not pleased with the situation.

"Wish me luck on my annual review," he said, giving me one last kiss before boarding the plane. "I'm demanding China back."

"Good luck," I said. "You'll be great."

Leaving the airport, I went directly to Nancy's, immersing myself in all things Shanghai. We shopped and ate our way through the city. When I wasn't with Nancy, I traveled with Xiao and Ning.

"We should go to the Gobi Desert," Xiao said, lounging by my hotel's indoor pool.

"I've never been. Have you?" Ning asked.

Chuckling, I said, "I could never have afforded something so exotic."

"You can now," Xiao said, flagging down the bartender. "You're a rich American."

I thought of all the times these two wonderful women had taken care of me when I could afford little more than a cup of rice. "We're going to the Gobi Desert, ladies! My treat," I said, wondering what Dave would say when he saw the credit card bill.

Before returning to Atlanta, I visited Hunan once more. Jin had long since gone back to Guangzhou, which saddened me. What saddened me far more, though, was Yang's situation. It had been over two months since the tragedy, and her husband had yet to be buried; nothing had come of her family's petitions. It seemed as if, in the eyes of the government, the life of Yang's husband was worth no more than a dog's.

Yang had returned to Changsha by now—even going back to work at her sister's spa, but it was clear that she was deeply depressed. After one dinner together, I knew that the smiling, happy dreamer I'd once known had died on the street with her husband that day.

46

Notice

Seeing Dave's face at the airport was a thrilling thing. Though we'd talked often, touching him was another matter entirely.

"Oh, I've missed you," he said, breathing me in.

Once the joy of reuniting waned, and we settled back into our old routine, I noticed that Dave was not himself.

"You seem distracted," I said the following weekend.

"I'm just working on something," he replied, mostly to his computer screen.

Along with his attention, his patience soon fled, and the easygoing person I'd fallen in love with became increasingly disagreeable. We began arguing, often about nothing of significance.

"I don't want to watch CNN," he snarled.

"Well, I don't want to watch baseball," I returned.

"Whatever. I'm going out."

In the aftermath of a particularly unpleasant fight, I thought of Fu. Could Dave have found a girlfriend while I was gone? This wasn't something I could bear to think about.

Reasoning that his dark mood would improve if I were more submissive, I prepared his favorite dishes, agreed with whatever he said, and encouraged him to play golf with friends. Unfortunately, the easier I made his life, the sullener he became.

郭

Dave's expression was grim when he walked through the door on my birthday. The flowers in his hand were beautiful, and he kissed me sweetly, but there was no joy in his eyes—no light. He took me to a fancy restaurant downtown, which was also a nice gesture, but when I asked about work, he said he didn't want to talk about it. Then again, he didn't really want to talk about anything anymore.

That changed after dinner.

Dave parked in our garage but made no move to get out of the car. "GuoGuo, we need to talk," he said.

My heart hammering in my chest, I blurted out, "Why don't you love me anymore?"

"What?" he said, seeming confused. "I do love you." Grabbing my hand, he kissed it. "Of course, I love you."

"Then why are you so miserable?"

"It shows?"

I raised my eyebrows and stared at him. "I am your wife."

"That's what I want to talk about. This is a big decision, and you should have a say in it."

Looking so unsure of himself, so anxious, so unlike the confident man I'd always known, he began turning the wedding band around his finger. "I haven't enjoyed work since I moved to Atlanta. The company's changing, and the promotion they promised me didn't happen." He dropped his eyes. "They passed me over."

"So, they'll give it to you next time," I said.

Twisting his ring again, he let out a long breath. "The thing is, I don't think they will. I've been with the company for over twenty years, and based on my review, it looks like I've moved up as far as I'm going to. I always planned on retiring at fifty-five, but I don't want to spend the rest of my time there spinning my wheels." He took a deep breath and then looked deeply into my eyes. "I want to start a sign company."

I waited for the rest. As time stretched, I finally asked, "That's it?"

"This is a big deal, honey. I want to quit UPS."

"Do you know anything about signs?"

"I've been doing a lot of research. Every company needs them. I'm talking about the directional signs, like the plastic ones in hospitals pointing to x-ray and surgery rooms, signs for bathrooms, numbers for apartment complexes. Those kinds of signs."

"Okay. If that will make you happy, we'll have a sign company." Honestly, at this point, I would have agreed to anything to get him back.

"You need to understand that money will be tight for a while. We'll have to pay more for health insurance, and I'll forfeit my retirement benefits. But this business could be big." His newfound excitement was thrilling.

Insurance was an alien concept to me, and retirement benefits that much more so. "I've lived with nothing. I've starved. This is no problem," I said eagerly.

Dave looked at me oddly for a moment, but then shook his head and smiled. "I can't believe you're okay with this. I expected a big fight." Leaning over the console, he kissed me. "God, I love you, GuoGuo."

The smile I'd missed so desperately came through the door the following evening. "I did it," he said. "I turned in my notice."

郭

While I was in China, Dave had contacted a broker to help him find a business to buy. A handyman by nature, he decided that owning a company that made things would give him a deeper sense of accomplishment.

The broker had put him in touch with an old man named Bill, who was ready to sell his sign business. The company offered established suppliers and clients, and Bill assured Dave that his profits would easily exceed his investment in the very first year.

Bill owned the company's building and offered to rent it to us for a good price. Since Dave had no design experience, Bill even agreed to stay on an extra year to teach him the craft. In return, Dave offered him a nice salary, even promising a large bonus if he doubled sales before retiring.

郭

The next nine months were wonderful, Dave came home every evening with exciting news; he'd made a sign, he'd won a new client—always something to celebrate. When he worked late, I took him dinner, and on weekends we dreamed of the things we'd do when we were rich.

"I'll buy you a lake house," he said, after watching a television commercial advertising property.

"We'll need a boat then," I said, laughing.

"Two boats!"

In the evenings we walked through the gated neighborhood, discussing which mansion we wanted to buy. This reminded me of our carefree time in Shanghai, and I relished it.

47

A White Dress

"Hey Dave, do you want to get married again?" I asked, crawling into bed after ending a call with my mother.

"Anything you want," he replied, pulling me into his arms.

Shortly after my village's destruction, the government began paying restitution for displacing its residents. Every few months, they sent money to each individual, including me. The payments began while I was waiting for my visa, and once I moved to the US, my mother, claiming I was an unmarried student there, continued collecting my remittance. In her mind, this was nearly true; my marriage wasn't legitimate to her.

Considering I'd barely completed the eighth grade, I found her claim wildly amusing, though I could see her point; learning to live in another culture was very much like being a student. Regardless, my family's heritage and livelihood were worth far more than the paltry sum they were being paid, so I was happy to help.

As soon as the government had disbursed all the money it was going to, Mama began making plans. My blind uncle informed her that May 23rd was an especially auspicious day for a wedding, and since we didn't care all that much, we agreed.

郭

In many ways, our wedding would be similar to every other village ceremony I'd ever attended; in some ways, it would not. Because Black Village's farmland and barren country roads had been demolished, many of our special traditions, including the wedding parade, were no longer feasible. This saddened me—saddened everyone.

My parents invited their entire community to the celebration, and I invited Gary and Marie, who politely declined. Jonathan was very excited about coming until he discovered he needed a US passport, which he did not have, and special vaccinations, which he did not want.

I sent invitations to my Shanghai friends, as well as my Hunan friends and their families. I was both surprised and delighted that everyone responded with a yes, even Yang and her little son. With so many coming, I was never happier that my brother ran a hotel.

Pulling into the village compound, we were met with a giant, red inflatable arch, decorated with yellow dragons. Two accompanying golden lion statues, much taller than me, stood on either side of our building's entrance. It secretly thrilled me that my parents had gone to such trouble.

"Mama!" I squealed, jumping out of the rental car before Dave had turned off the engine.

The caterers commissioned to cook every meal for the next three-days arrived later that day, bringing with them a variety of livestock: pigs, lambs, even turtles and snakes. Since Mama's kitchen was small and on the top floor of the building, the cooks set up their operation outside, using propane stoves and meat-hanging racks. Having never seen animals slaughtered and prepared before, Dave seemed fascinated by the process.

While working for Genji, I'd entertained fantasies of my own lavish Shanghai wedding, complete with an array of extraordinary dresses. Age and experience had reshaped those dreams. Forgoing the traditional qipao, I wore a white American-style gown to symbolize my future. Ming served as my photographer. This would not have been a good career for him, I learned belatedly.

Over two-hundred people attended our celebration. Everyone in the village came except for Baba's dysfunctional family. This troubled him, but after a lifetime of being shunned, I was secretly pleased.

Looking out over the mass of revelers, I thought of our living room ceremony with its single guest. In my ignorance of all things American, I'd accepted our tiny ceremony as the norm. Knowing differently now, I realized how much I'd been cheated, and I was grateful that my parents had done this grand thing for me, had made this monetary sacrifice.

As we repeated words that Dave didn't understand, I considered the unknowing promises I'd made. For better or worse had been easy to keep thus far. Aside from the tiniest of bumps, our marriage had been all for the better.

郭

"Now that you're married, you can give me a grandson," Baba said the following evening.

"What, honey?" Dave asked, noting my shocked expression. I translated for him, and a huge smile claimed his features. "We'll get right on that, sir," he said.

"No, we won't," I replied, gawking at him.

"Did I say something wrong?" he asked, confused.

"I don't want children, Dave. I'll never want children."

"You won't?" he said, his face falling. "GuoGuo, I want them. I really do. I just thought we were waiting awhile—until we were wealthier."

"We're waiting forever," I said, rising from the table. "I'm tired and I'm going to bed."

I'd never imagined being a mother. Mine was so capable, so superior, so willing to sacrifice for us. I knew I could never measure up, and I wasn't interested in trying. Perhaps selfishness had as much to do with it as my fear of inadequacy. Life had never been easy until now, and I wasn't ready to give it up or, after watching JiaoJiao attend to her children's every need, have that kind of responsibility.

Dave didn't broach the subject again, though his spirits were subdued for the rest of the trip.

With Bill set to retire at the end of June, Dave needed to get back to begin the transition. Forgoing an expensive Chinese honeymoon, I saw him to the airport and then returned to my village complex for another week.

"I want to talk to you," Mama said as I packed my suitcase. Following her past her little garden, with its flowering herbs and climbing bean vines, I was reminded of the last time she'd brought me here.

"What is it, Mama?" I asked.

"I've been saving your restitution money."

"Good. You'll need it one day," I said, patting her shoulder.

"No, you'll need it."

"We have enough money, and as soon as the business takes off, we'll have even more. You keep it."

"I won't take what's yours. But you must promise to keep this money a secret from Dave. Put in somewhere safe. Otherwise, he will take it from you."

Dave had long ago proven himself a kind and generous husband. Had her grave expression not reminded me so much of a lioness intent on protecting her cubs, I would have laughed.

"Really, Mama, it's okay."

"Use it for your spa. Then if his company fails, you'll have something of your own. Do this for me."

Early in our marriage, Dave had explained how proud it made him to provide for me. And though the easy life he'd given was a lonely one, if he didn't want me working, I would honor his wishes. Besides, we'd be rich soon; I could have a spa then.

"Okay, Mama," I said, sighing.

48

Empty Bed

Bill was ahead of schedule in fulfilling his end of the bargain; he'd doubled the number of sales. Unfortunately, the orders were rarely large, and it was becoming clear that many of these new customers were onetime shoppers. The cost of supplies and raw materials was also very high, and after paying employee salaries, rent, and loan payments, finding enough for the large bonus Dave had promised him was challenging. To come up with the money, Dave skipped paying himself for three months straight.

"It's going to be tight, honey," he said. "No more shopping for a while, okay?"

郭

Dave decided that the best way to increase profits was to expand. Cashing in his IRA, he hired several more employees and rented a warehouse four times larger than the old one. I was quick with my hands and had experience working on assembly lines, so I insisted on helping as well; it was the first time I'd felt productive since moving to America.

The company quickly took over our lives. We left for work before the sun rose and returned home well after dark, falling into bed each night exhausted. On weekends, Dave did paperwork, and if we had the energy, we went out with Jonathan and his work friends.

My husband knew how to manage enormous projects with big budgets, where someone else paid all the bills. Managing small projects on a limited budget turned out to be a completely different experience. We didn't have departments or divisions in our company, so Dave was forced to handle payroll, taxes, sales, and anything else required.

Used to working on teams, Dave had a gentle managing style, and I noticed some of his employees were beginning to take advantage of him. Two of them were Bill's men, who seemed to have no loyalty to their new boss. They came in late, left early, and took long lunch and smoking breaks.

In Chinese factories, bosses have strong personalities and don't hesitate to punish lazy workers. If they quit, there are always others begging to replace them. Had I not once stood in mile-long lines with that same desire?

"You should work faster," I told the men as orders began piling up. "You should care about your job."

When I noticed they were throwing away only partially used materials, such as the expensive plastic sheets Dave and I had driven all the way to Texas to buy, I pointed that out to them. In China, we wasted nothing, but these men didn't get why I was upset. Did they not understand conservation at all?

"You need to fire these guys," I told Dave on the way home from work one night.

"Honey, skilled workers are hard to find, and I don't have time to search and train new ones right now."

I refused to hold my tongue with these men, especially the one Dave had promoted to manager after Bill retired. Nearly every week, this guy had some excuse for not coming in: family emergency, a sick wife, a death. At first, I felt sorry for his bad fortune, but as time passed, and these events always occurred on Fridays, I stopped believing his stories.

When he left for a smoke break and returned an hour later, I stormed into Dave's office. "The manager is terrible! Be a tough boss and fire him."

Dave huffed. "We've been over this. I can't afford to lose him right now—any of them. And besides, they've all got families to feed. Look, the guys are starting to complain about you. They say you're harassing them. Maybe you should start working in payroll instead of the line."

"I know nothing about payroll," I said, shocked. Outside of using them socially, I wasn't good with computers and worse with math. Payroll was a terrible job for me, and it was no surprise that I began making mistakes.

On my six-month anniversary of working for the company, Dave called me into his office. "We need to talk."

"What did I do wrong now?" I grumped.

"Nothing. You're doing fine, but… I just don't have any work for you now."

My jaw dropped. "What do you mean? You have too much work! You pulled me off the assembly line, and now your production is down. Then you give me jobs I don't know how to do. You won't let me talk to customers because I negotiate Chinese-style. You are not a good boss to me."

"That's the problem," he said, raking his hands through his hair. "I don't want to *be* your boss. Look, it's taking everything to run this business, and I don't have time to fight with you or to teach you things." He looked out his small window. "I think you should stop coming in."

"What do you mean, stop coming in? Are you firing me?"

"No, honey, I'm not firing you. We'll just both be happier if you stay home. It's hard for couples to work together," he said gently. "The lines get blurred. That's why I never dated women at UPS."

"But—"

"Just stay home. Okay?"

We were partners in this company, and I was doing everything I knew to make it successful. It was clear he needed me. But needing me and wanting me were two different things. Completely crushed, I went home.

That night, I slept in the guest room.

49

Broke

The business was a sieve, with money running out in all directions. Dave couldn't afford to pay himself for months on end, and by the following year, we'd spent most of our savings. I came to dread the droning sound of the afternoon mail truck, knowing that among the advertisements I would find past due bills, some marked "final notice"; those were the only ones Dave cared about.

I began lying to the utility companies when they called, and once, when a bill collector knocked on our door, I spoke only in Chinese. With no money, I was forced to postpone my annual trip home.

Denying myself all forms of luxury and finding ways to spend less on food—*I discovered the wonder of coupons*—I kept our home bills to a minimum. With little to do other than watch the news and worry, I'd never felt more abandoned. Worse, Dave's confidence was slipping away. It was painful to watch, but by insisting I not come into work, he'd rendered me helpless.

郭

Dave's Lexus was parked in the garage when I returned from

grocery shopping one afternoon. Worried that he'd been injured or become sick, I left my bags in the trunk and hurried inside.

"Are you okay?"

Seated on the couch, his lips pressed into a grim line, Dave looked up at me and shook his head.

"What's wrong?" I asked, assessing him. He didn't look sick. "Why are you home?"

"We need to talk," he said, patting the cushion beside him. "The accountant called. I don't know how to say this, but… well, the company is almost bankrupt. I can't order supplies, and I'm going to have to let some guys go. If we don't find money from somewhere, we're going under."

"Can't you get more from the bank?"

"I've already tried." Dropping his face into his hands, he said, "I don't know how to fix this."

In predicting this day, it was as if my blind uncle had lent Mama his fortune-telling gift. Weighing her warnings against this impending reality, I felt I had no choice. Though I was betraying her, and myself to a degree, I had to help my husband.

"I have money," I said, in a small voice.

In addition to the restitution settlement, the investments I'd made, thanks to my Singapore friend, had grown remarkably. I'd amassed over fifty-thousand US dollars. I'd never in my wildest dreams imagined owning such a sum.

Shock claimed his features as I explained this. "Wow, honey. That's… that's a lot of money."

"I've been saving it to open a spa one day."

"And you will. I promise. The nicest one in town. But right now, my company needs it. Call it a short-term loan," he quickly added. "I'll pay you back as soon as my business is in the black again, okay?"

I felt a stab of pain when I realized he'd called the company *his* instead of *ours*. "How much do you need?" I said dispassionately.

"Thirty-thousand. Don't worry, it's just for now."

Living comfortably had never made starting my spa an urgent thing. However, giving him over half of my savings would remove that dream from reach. But had he not provided for me, rented and furnished a nice Shanghai apartment for me, given me a shiny new car and a lovely home? Loaning him this money seemed a small price in return.

"If that's what you need, I'll go to China and get it. But I think making signs is not a good business for you."

Pulling me into his arms, he held me tightly. "Thank you," he whispered.

"Do you need me to come back to work?" I asked hopefully.

"Not just yet."

50

Stupid Girl

As Chinese citizens had once dutifully followed Chairman Mao's proclamation to have more babies, they now embraced Deng Xiaoping's slogan "To get rich is glorious." Money was pouring into my country, and my friends and even my family were trying to claim their stake.

Though I knew no truly rich people, I felt shame that I could no longer spend money as if I were one. When Xiao and Ning asked me to take them on trips, I made excuses. When Nancy wanted to go shopping, I made more excuses. When Ming demanded a Rolex watch, I laughed outright.

Mama was not pleased that I'd stayed away for so long again, and even less so when I explained why I'd come. It was the first time she'd ever called me "stupid girl."

I needed the love and support of my family and my friends, and an escape from Dave's misery and my growing despair. Could they not see this?

Well, Jin saw it. After a brief reunion in Changsha with my oldest girlfriends, she asked me to return with her to Guangzhou. She and her husband were doing remarkably well and had just purchased a luxury apartment with a sweeping view.

"Gorgeous," I said, peering out the bank of floor-to-ceiling windows.

"As nice as yours?" she asked smugly.

"Nicer," I replied. "Definitely."

I realized at that moment that I truly missed urban life. Though the Sandy Springs suburb was pretty enough, it couldn't seem to make up its mind whether it was city or country.

After an exceptional meal at the White Swan Hotel, which her husband insisted on paying for, Jin and I wandered the boardwalk. This part of the city had a distinctly Western flavor, the buildings reminiscent of those I'd seen in New Orleans when Dave, Jonathan, and I had gone to Mardi gras.

"Tell me," she said, stopping suddenly. "Something's wrong. What is it?"

Sighing, I slumped onto a nearby bench. "Our finances are in awful shape, Jin. Dave's not the businessman he thought he was, and it won't be long until we're poor."

Watching a boatman scoop garbage from the wide Pearl River below, we sat quietly. A woman offered us coupons for a nearby restaurant. Another, selling low-quality pearls, promised us a good deal. A boy stopped his ice cream cart in front of us expectantly.

Jin waved him away and then turned to me. "So, what are you going to do about it?"

"There's nothing I can do. He won't let me help him, and when I give him advice, he doesn't listen."

"Are you no longer Chinese?" she said, scoffing.

"What?"

"Look around you. Here, everyone works. Everyone has a job. Are you so spoiled that you've forgotten how to feed yourself?"

"Of course not, but—"

"But what? Are you forbidden to work in America?"

I laughed at my friend, who'd never hesitated to speak her mind. And I laughed at myself for being as stupid as Mama had suggested. It had simply never occurred to me to get a job.

郭

I'd never been so sad to see China fall away. The warm hugs, the simple joy of friendship, Mama's cooking… It was as if, oxygen-deprived, I'd finally filled my lungs with air, only to hold my breath again as I returned to America.

Surveying the landscape below as we circled Hartsfield-Jackson Airport for final approach, I felt a pang of regret for hurrying back. Atlanta held no magic for me.

When I shared my employment plans with Dave, his lack of enthusiasm was disheartening. "Honey, you really don't need to work. Thanks to your loan, I can get what I need. Don't worry. We're in good shape again," he said, smiling.

"Good shape?" Picking up the thick stack of bills on the counter, I waved them in front of him. "This is not what 'good shape' looks like, Dave. We need money."

Sighing heavily, he said, "Alright, fine. Get a job if that's what you want."

郭

Getting a job in the "Land of Opportunity" was not as simple as

I'd imagined. Yes, I was adept at grocery shopping, buying clothes, and driving a car, but there was a big difference between getting by in America and being successful, especially when it came to employment.

Companies didn't post vacancy notices on their doors like Chinese merchants so often did. And going from business to business inquiring about jobs only got me the occasional application form. What were forms to someone who couldn't understand them?

Since moving to America, Dave had been my English crutch, just as I was his Chinese one back home. At restaurants, when confronted with menus lacking pictures, Dave either read them to me or ordered based on my meat preference. Reading complicated instructions, ingredients, or medicine bottles was nearly impossible. This impediment rendered me unqualified for every job I managed to apply for, including UPS, where I had contacts.

Steeped in defeat, I drifted back to watching television. While listlessly flipping through channels one afternoon, I came across an infomercial promising easy money. The job required no experience, I could work from home, and the employee testimonials promised tremendous sums. This was exactly what Dave and I needed. I called the toll-free number immediately and spoke with a representative.

Failing to ask about my educational background or reading level during our brief phone interview, they hired me. I was ecstatic. Finally, someone was taking a chance on me.

The job entailed calling strangers and convincing them to buy timeshares, though I wasn't certain what they were. My salary was commission-based, which meant the more I sold, the more I made.

"Hello, this is Gloria, your travel expert!" I parroted, following the script. "Do you want to vacation like a pro?"

"I'm not interested," a grumpy voice interrupted.

This became the general direction of every call. No one wanted to buy these fabulous-sounding timeshares. In the first week, I made over five-hundred calls, and by month's end, two-thousand. Few were willing to talk to me, and none were willing to buy. Though I had nothing better to do with my time, I would not work for free, and even though the company encouraged me to keep trying, I finally quit.

That following Monday, I slipped on a nice dress, pinned up my hair, and applied a lovely shade of blush to my cheeks and eyelids. The palette was wearing thin. Shaking my head, I sighed. My replacement would have to come from a drugstore rather than an expensive makeup counter.

The one thing in life I was extremely qualified for was spa work. This profession required very little reading, and no one knew a woman's face better than I. And if I couldn't start my own spa at present, well, I could certainly work for someone else's.

Atlanta was rife with spas—some very elegant. Back when we'd had money, I'd frequented several salons, enjoying a wide variety of facial services. I drove to the first of those.

"Are you hiring?" I asked the reservationist.

Recognizing me, she smiled brightly. "Sure, Mrs. Wiseman. We're looking for a facialist, actually. Do you know anyone?"

"I am one," I said. "A good one."

"I didn't know that. Please have a seat while I get the manager. Would you like something to drink while you wait?"

With its cucumber flavored water and excellent coffee, I'd always enjoyed this particular salon.

"No, just the manager," I replied.

She warmly greeted me and invited me back to her office. "I

haven't seen you in a while, Mrs. Wiseman. You haven't found another spa, have you?"

I wanted to laugh. In our current financial situation, the thought of spending money on services I could easily perform myself seemed a ridiculous notion.

"No, I'm loyal only to you," I lied, smiling.

Dave had created a professional-looking resume for me. Having scoffed at my telemarketing job, at least he supported me in this endeavor.

The manager uttered nice comments as she read through the extensive list of services I'd been trained for. "Your experience is very impressive," she said. "I'd be delighted to have you join the team. Do you have a copy of your license handy?"

Feeling both elated and curious, I pulled out my wallet and handed her my driver's license.

She laughed pleasantly. "No, your esthetician's license."

"This is the only license I have," I said, confused.

She glanced back at my resume again. "Did you not attend beauty school in the US?"

"No, in China."

Her smile faded, and she bit her lip. "I don't know what to say, Mrs. Wiseman. You can't legally work in Georgia without a license."

"How do I get one?" I asked.

"You've got to complete training at a certified school. It should be no trouble for you at all, based on your resume."

I felt tears welling. Why was everything in this country so difficult?

"Listen," she said. "As soon as you get it, please come back. You'd be a fantastic addition to our team."

Once home, I called the school she'd recommended. If my only obstacle was getting this piece of paper, then that's what I would do. The director explained that Georgia required fifteen-hundred training hours before granting a license and that this school had an accelerated nine-month program.

What was nine more months, I thought.

"How much is tuition?" I asked.

"Sixteen-thousand, plus supplies," she said.

While the sign company was no longer headed for bankruptcy, Dave still could not pay himself regularly. I'd taken to dipping into my money to help with the mortgage and bills when there seemed no other way to pay them. Tears ran down my face when I checked my account; I didn't have enough.

"When business turns around, money won't be an issue anymore," Dave said after I told him. "You can do your training then, okay?"

At this point, I doubted the business was ever going to turn around, but for once, I didn't argue. In fact, I stopped arguing about anything.

51

Monkey Business

About this time, Jonathan received a big promotion. I was very happy for him until I learned he'd have to move to South Carolina; this was no time to lose my only American friend. His new position demanded all of his time, so phone calls soon became as rare as his visits.

Increasingly overwhelmed by loneliness and despair, I sank into depression. When my friends and family left messages, I was slow to respond. Sometimes I let weeks slip by without talking to Mama. At Christmas, I didn't bother putting up the beautiful red lights I'd once enjoyed so much. What was the point?

I was a prisoner in chains, trapped in a place surrounded by invisible mountains too steep to climb—mountains of education I could never obtain, rules I didn't understand, and procedures I couldn't guess at. My warden was rarely present anymore, and when he was, we barely spoke.

In many ways, I'd become Yang. Though Dave hadn't been lost in a single stab to the heart, I was losing him piece by piece. Yes, he was still living and breathing, and he still wanted to make love, though I wasn't interested anymore, but the man I'd traveled across the planet for had disappeared.

Staring at the gray landscape of my bleak existence days before yet another Chinese New Year without my family, I considered killing myself.

郭

Brilliant light broke through a slit in the guest room curtains the following morning, wrenching me from black dreams. Dave was long gone, of course, so I crawled downstairs to make tea. While waiting for the water to boil, an unexpected sense of optimism suffused me. Had I not lived through miserable conditions before—through miserable times? Nothing had been taken from me that I hadn't freely given. And giving up was not the Chinese way.

Donning a warm sweater and fuzzy hat, I set out to walk the neighborhood—something I'd altogether stopped doing. My mind worked especially well during exercise, and the cold, clean breeze and uncompromising sun did wonders to burn away the grim cloud that had made my heart its home.

I thought about my life in China. When one door closed, I'd always pushed through another. Surely other Chinese who'd moved to this country had been in similar situations to mine, and they'd found other doors. I needed to do the same.

After my early misfortune, I'd abandoned all attempts at connecting with compatriots. Because Atlanta didn't have a Chinatown, Asians were not a common sight, but they were definitely out there, scattered around this city. Perhaps one could help me.

My walk became a run as I hurried back home to get my phone.

郭

WeChat had been useful before, so I searched again for people near me—and those not so near. This time, I attached a message to my profile: esthetician with green card needs work.

I heard nothing back right away, of course, but I continued checking throughout the day, my heart sinking as the silence stretched. Near midnight, my phone finally buzzed.

I need a masseuse. Come by tomorrow.

Delirious with joy, I burst into the master bedroom and jumped onto the bed, waking Dave. "I have an interview!"

"That's great, honey," he mumbled, rolling over.

Snuggling under the covers, I draped my arm over his chest and nestled against him. Sleeping with Dave felt odd after so much time in separation. He responded as I knew he would, pressing me into the pillow and leisurely kissing me.

郭

Bankhead was not an affluent area. Older-looking, one-story buildings and dingy strip malls, housing anything from pawnshops to discount clothing outlets, lined both sides of the street. Past a grimy convenience store, where several poorly dressed men loitered, I found the address.

Golden dragon statues guarded the entrance to Lotus Oriental Massage Parlor's red brick building. Walking past the flashing neon sign, I opened the bright yellow door. I needed a job, and I was not taking no for an answer. And if they asked for a license, well, I would lie and tell them it was on the way; I'd certainly had enough practice doing that.

When I stepped inside, and the blond-haired receptionist greeted me, I cursed under my breath. The only thing Asian about her was the cheap qipao she wore. Perhaps I'd come to the wrong place.

Mustering a smile, I asked, "Is your boss here?"

She looked me over and said, "Sure. Are you one of her friends?"

"Yes," I said immediately.

The imposing Chinese woman who emerged through the beaded curtain rendered me speechless. She could have been Madame Li's twin.

"May I help you?" she said pleasantly, her shrewd eyes assessing me.

"I need a job," I replied.

Motioning to me, I followed her through the curtain to a small, messy office.

"I'm Lily," she said, taking a seat.

"Hong Bo, but I go by GuoGuo," I replied.

"You said you had experience. Do you?"

I pulled out the now wrinkled resume Dave had drafted for me so long ago. Her eyes traveled over it quickly, and then her head snapped up. Shanghai Theatre Academy?"

"Yes. Makeup certificate."

A slow smile unfurled across her face, and she spoke beautiful words. "Can you start now?"

"Absolutely," I said, wanting to sing.

This was not a beautiful facility with expensive products lining glass shelves. The tan carpet was worn, and the walls begged for fresh paint. It didn't matter, though. Only the money did.

"Do you know American massage techniques?" she asked as I followed her to a dimly lit room scented with jasmine.

372 • Virginia Gray

"Chinese is my specialty," I replied.

Massage in my country is about pressure points. People expect pain. With years of practice in this technique, my hands had become strong.

"We offer Thai and Swedish massages here. I'll show you. Take off your shirt and lie on the table."

There are two types of massage places in China: legitimate houses and places for monkey business. In legitimate spas, clients wear soft, loose-fitting outfits similar to doctor's scrubs or pajamas during services. In the other type, clothes are an inconvenience.

It's also easy to distinguish between the two types based on appearance. Those nasty ones are open at night and have pink and blue lights above the doors. The middle of the afternoon here, I hadn't noticed such lights outside this shop, but I'd been mission-focused.

"Why do you want my shirt off?" I asked, eying her suspiciously.

Her eyes filled with humor. "We do Swedish massage on bare skin. That's what Americans expect."

I'd noticed men in the lobby. "What else do they expect?"

"This isn't that kind of place," she chided. "You'll wear a proper uniform when you work."

I nodded, and then reluctantly removed my top.

When Lily began the Swedish-style massage, I could barely feel it.

"Americans like slow rubbing movements down the lengths of their muscles. Be gentle. If you do acupressure, do it lightly."

If I'd paid for a massage and hadn't come away sore, I would feel cheated. But if this method was legitimate and would get me good tips, I could easily perform it.

"Do you have an American name?" she asked.

I thought back to my early Shanghai days. "Stephanie," I replied.

"That's a good one. Use that."

郭

Using the gentle strokes Lily had demonstrated, I performed my first massage on a middle-aged woman. When I applied a little pressure to her knotted neck, she hissed and told me it was too hard. After that, my touches were like a butterfly's wings. Pleased at the end of the session, she gave me a nice tip.

Lily next appeared with a young woman, introducing me as her very best masseuse.

"Okay, you've proven yourself," she said after escorting my smiling client to the front. She handed me sixty dollars, cash. "You get fifty percent plus tips. We open at ten o'clock tomorrow. Don't be late."

At this point, making sixty dollars in a day was more than I could hope for. But fifty percent? I calculated my earnings if I were to give five massages tomorrow. That was real money! This job would help our finances significantly and give me a small measure of security. Moreover, in time, I could earn enough for beauty school tuition, and one day my own spa.

Giddy, I raced back to the warehouse to share the good news.

"I'm happy you found a job. What's this place called?" Dave asked.

"Lotus Oriental Massage Parlor."

He raised his eyebrows. "An *oriental* massage parlor?"

"It's legitimate."

"Are you sure about that, honey?"

"I work on women, Dave. Do you think I'm stupid?"

"No, of course not, but some of those places have bad reputations."

"Can't you just be happy for me?" I felt as though I were arguing with my father.

"I am. Just… be safe, okay?"

郭

I knew how to make women feel special, and I earned good tips that first week.

"China called in sick," Lily said. "You can have her clients today."

China wasn't her actual name, and with her ebony skin, large round eyes, and wide hips, she could never hope to pass for Asian.

"Thanks," I said, pleased to have the extra work.

With hungry eyes and the ghost of a smile, the large man began undressing. "Face down," I said, slipping out. I hustled to Lily's office to protest. On her phone, she waved me away.

Pacing back and forth in the hall outside the massage room, I reminded myself that we needed the money—*I* needed it—and that this place was respectable. It shouldn't surprise me that American men enjoyed legitimate massages; this culture was so different from mine.

Rubbing my damp palms against my smock, I quietly opened the door. The room was not a large one, and he seemed to fill it.

When I peeled back the sheet, my jaw dropped; there was a lot of him. Folding it neatly at his waist, I rubbed scented oil on my hands and then slid them across his hairy back in a slow, measured way. He groaned in pleasure with each stroke, the sound making my stomach clench. This felt wrong.

If he were simply a very large woman, this wouldn't bother me at all, so I conjured that image to calm myself as I moved to work on his shoulder blades. His dangling hand brushed against my leg. Massage was a physical activity, and I thought little of it at first, but when his arm pressed against my thigh a few moments later, I knew it wasn't an accident.

Reminded of Fu and his unwanted touches, I scooted out of his casual reach, positioning myself at his head. With his face buried in the support ring, I began kneading his scalp and then neck.

"That feels so good," he moaned.

Suddenly, he grasped the backs of my thighs and pulled me against the table. His hands ran up my legs before firmly squeezing my bottom.

"Stop! What are you doing?" I shrieked, struggling from his grip.

"I want the China special," he said, confused.

"You want sex," I said.

"Of course, I do. How much?"

"This isn't that kind of place!"

He chuckled. "I'll give you seventy-five extra for the full body massage."

"No."

"Aw darlin', I love that you're playin' hard to get. One-hundred then. Hand me my wallet."

"I'm not a prostitute," I screeched. "Get out!"

When he climbed off the table, the sheet skidded to the floor. I'd seen only two naked men in my adult life, and even so, this one was not impressive. Turning, I stormed out of the room and into Lily's office.

"My client wants sex," I seethed.

She shrugged. "How much did he offer?"

"He could offer one-thousand dollars, and I still wouldn't do it. You said this place was legit. Is it or isn't it?"

"It's legit, of course. But any service you provide past the standard massage is your own business."

"I do this job professionally, or I quit."

"Stay. Just tell him I'll fire you if I find out."

"Fine. But I want only women from now on."

"That I can't promise you."

"How was work?" Dave murmured when I climbed into bed.

Disturbed by the day's events, I'd wrestled with quitting during the long drive home. But what were my alternatives? Lying on the couch all day depressed—or worse? At least when I was out of the house, I felt alive.

"Fine," I said.

"I'm proud of you, honey," he said, wrapping his arm around my waist. When he pulled me against his body, I squirmed away.

"I'm tired."

郭

Though my salary was helping pay the bills, as the months went by, and the propositions continued, I became increasingly ashamed of my job. I refused to tell my friends or family what I was doing and only mentioned my female clients to Dave. It was fortunate in some respects that we didn't spend much time together; my acting skills weren't that good.

Beauty school would be my salvation, so I made earning tuition my singular goal. Taking on as many clients as possible, I worked eight to ten hours every day. The sheer time on my feet began taking its toll, and before long, my back ached, my legs and ankles swelled noticeably, and my elbows throbbed incessantly. Pushing a grocery cart became torture. I took lots of pain medicine and covered myself with ice packs at night.

"I want to open my own spa one day," I told Lily as I quickly shoveled dinner into my mouth.

"I knew you didn't want to do this for the rest of your life. Especially with your training. How can I help?"

"I need an American license," I said thoughtlessly. My chopsticks hovering in midair, I met her eyes. She'd never asked about my license. Had I just said too much?

Her lips formed a sly smile. "Of course, you do. I'm opening a second shop. A smaller one. Would you like to manage it for me? Fewer hours on your feet, higher pay." She cocked her head. "I've seen you limping."

郭

Managing was far better than massaging, which I only did when one of the two girls working for me called in sick. I was far happier than I'd been in a long time. At least at work. Home was a different story.

Dave's management skills had not improved, and profits had taken a downturn again. When he asked me for another loan, I became incensed.

"You forget my birthday two years in a row, you're never home, and then you ask for money? Do you want a wife or an ATM?"

"That's not fair, GuoGuo. If you knew how hard running a company is, you'd understand."

I had every intention of finding out, and even though much of my earnings went towards bills, I'd saved nearly enough for tuition. I thought of my mother's advice and finally took it.

"I don't have much. I can only give you two-thousand."

"What about your stock money?"

"I've spent it paying our mortgage." This was true. My massage savings, on the other hand, were hidden in a box in the guestroom closet.

"I'll take it," he said, his eyes sad.

"Be a better husband to me," I retorted.

Sighing heavily, he said, "I'll try to get home earlier. I promise."

52

Charity

"You do make-up, right?" Lily asked while looking over her books one afternoon.

"Of course," I said. She'd seen my resume. Did she not believe I'd attended the STA?

"An acquaintance's daughter needs hair and make-up for an upcoming dance. She's looking for someone to do it. If you want the job, you can have it. She'll pay fifty dollars."

"I'll do it," I said gratefully. At this point, no sum was too small.

郭

Located in an expensive Buckhead neighborhood, the sprawling ranch was not difficult to find. A lovely Asian face met me at the door.

"Thank you so much for coming. I'm Caihong Martin. Please come in," she said in perfect English.

Chinese objects—vases, jade statues, a rice-paper scroll, were quietly tucked here and there in the otherwise American decor. Pictured in the large portrait over her sofa, this fine-featured woman stood behind a seated blond-haired man, a lovely child on either side. Though her girls retained our race's black hair, their noses and eyes were not Chinese.

Nearly silent during makeup application, when Caihong's daughter, Emma, finally turned to me, her smile was brilliant.

"Oh, she's beautiful," Caihong whispered, entering the bathroom.

I nodded, pleased to know I hadn't lost my touch.

"I've made tea," she said as I packed up my supplies. "Won't you join me?"

Sitting in her sunroom, nibbling ginger cookies, she explained that she'd come to the US on a student visa and fallen in love with an American during graduate school. After earning her Ph.D., she'd secured a government position at the CDC. Though China and America were run differently, I was secretly pleased to have this new government connection.

"My parents were so upset when I married an American," she said, laughing.

"Mine, too." Thinking of Mama's response, I rolled my eyes.

"And then when I became Christian..." Shaking her head, she smiled ruefully. "Baba's afraid I'll get arrested every time I come home." While the US government promoted religion to the point of printing it on their money, the communist party aggressively frowned upon it. "Do you have a church home?" she asked.

"I don't go to church," I replied.

"I attend a Chinese church. I'd love for you to meet my friends."

"A Chinese church?" I asked, astonished.

"Oh yes. The sermons are in Mandarin, and the people are wonderful. Come back tomorrow morning, and we'll go together."

I had little free time, but I decided to humor her. If nothing else, other churchgoers might have daughters with dances to attend.

郭

The building was not large, but sure enough, the sign out front displayed Chinese characters. The interior was simple, with pale walls and a dark wooden cross behind a small stage. Caihong introduced me to so many people that I lost track. Eventually, she led me to the pew where her family sat. I noted that her husband's face was not the only white one in the congregation.

I was unfamiliar with the music, and the sermon meant little since the religious concepts were alien to me, but it was such a joy to hear my native language that I listened, rapt. The prayers spoke of kindness, love, and forgiveness, and by the end of the service, I felt a surprising sense of peace.

Wu Ling, the minister's wife, introduced herself and invited me to have lunch with her family. The Martins agreed to come as well. During our meal, which was Lu cuisine and very good, the preacher and his wife shared their coming to America story.

Meeting missionaries in Fuzhou, they'd become Christian. When the government learned that they were preaching to a village, officials came to arrest them. The secret church there helped them escape persecution and get to America. Their courage was moving.

"How did the dance go, Emma?" Wu Ling asked over dessert.

"You should have seen how lovely she looked," Caihong gushed when her daughter's beet-red face was accompanied only by silence. Emma's father raised his eyebrows.

Pulling a packet of photos from her purse, Caihong passed them around the table. "GuoGuo did her makeup."

"Really?" Wu Ling exclaimed. "She looks amazing."

Caihong beamed. "GuoGuo is a graduate of Shanghai Theatre

Academy. She's worked on famous actors. How fortunate we are to know her."

Wu Ling's eyes became speculative. "You know, my niece has a dance next weekend. I would consider it an honor if you would do her makeup. My sister will pay you well for your time."

"Sure," I said, grateful for Caihong's gift.

郭

Two jobs turned into three and then to four, and as I got to know these church women, I learned their stories as well. Some had been students like Caihong. Others had relatives here, and for a variety of reasons, from the need for political asylum to relief from religious intolerance, chose to join them. A surprising number had fled China in order to keep second children. Of those, one had even worked for the government. Her husband, who also held a government position, had chosen to remain in Beijing rather than follow her. Their professions, provinces, and education levels were as varied as their reasons for coming to Atlanta, but one trait they all shared was genuine compassion.

The church supported several outreach programs. While I wasn't able to contribute financially to any of them, one in particular called to me.

To survive in America, arriving immigrants needed money. Many of these people were poorly educated and had no connections, so finding jobs was difficult; I understood their helpless frustration all too well.

The church was currently sponsoring two Burmese families who'd escaped labor camps and found their way to Atlanta. Their horrible experiences made me grateful that I'd been born in China instead.

"You're going to do something nice that will profit us," I announced, walking towards the large table where Dave sat sketching designs. The sound of my pointy church shoes echoed eerily in the cavernous warehouse.

"What am I going to do now?" he asked, looking up after a moment.

"You're going to hire some new workers."

"Honey, I only have a few guys left. You know I can't afford to hire more."

I told him about the plight of these Burmese and how they didn't even know where their next meal was coming from.

"I'd love to help them. I really would, but…"

Crossing my arms, I glared at him, channeling my mother. "You will do this for me."

Dave ran his hands through his hair as he so often did when frustrated. Silver glinted in the overhead lights; this job was aging him. "Do they even speak English?"

"Does it matter?" I retorted. "They work with their hands, not their mouths. Just show them what to do."

"GuoGuo—"

"Let them work for free then!" I said, exasperated. "Put them on the line for two weeks. If they prove themselves, hire them—part-time if you can't afford more. Dave, these people are cheap and they'll work twice as hard as any of your other employees. Pay them with the money I loaned you." Narrowing my eyes, I glared at him.

郭

Using a translation app to communicate, three seized the opportunity: two men and one woman. Because of my job, I had little time to help further, so the church agreed to provide them with transportation.

My estimate of their capabilities had been wrong; they didn't work twice as fast as Dave's American workers, they worked three times as fast.

"Oh my God," Dave said a few days later. "These guys are amazing. They barely even take bathroom breaks." Dave may have been astonished, but I knew these people. I'd been them once.

At the end of the first week, Dave hired all three. With quick Asian hands on the line, production began increasing, and soon Dave could pay himself consistently.

This pleased me because I could keep more of my own earnings—finally crossing the fifteen-thousand-dollar mark that December. What didn't please me was Dave's continued inattention. I hadn't expected a miracle, but without the oppressive weight of failure, I'd hoped he would make more time for us. But hope can be a fleeting thing.

53

Packed Bags

Being frugal is being Chinese. Rather than getting restaurant reservations for this special night, I cooked a lovely meal, going to great pains to make Dave's favorite dishes. We had much to celebrate, and I had news; I'd enrolled in beauty school!

Expecting him home early, I hurried through my shower and then shimmied into the complicated pink dress I'd painstakingly ironed. With the table set, I sipped a glass of wine, waiting for the sound of the rising garage door.

I'm not sure what time that event actually occurred, but the bottle of wine had long been emptied, the food put away, and my dress hung back in the closet. When Dave fell into bed without so much as a kiss, my anguish turned into anger. I was alone in a country that wasn't mine, relegated to a life I'd only chosen for love, and I was living that life by myself. Well, no more!

郭

"I'm going home," I announced the following morning.

"We don't have the money right now," he replied, buttoning his cuffs.

"I don't care."

Huffing, he dropped his shoulders. "Honey, be realistic."

"No."

Following as he hurried down the stairs, I collided with him when he stopped short in the foyer. His wary eyes traveled over the row of bags lining the wall and then met mine. Using every suitcase we owned, I'd spent the night quietly packing my clothing, jewelry, pictures, and anything else of personal importance.

"GuoGuo, are you leaving me?" he whispered.

"Would you notice if I did?"

"What? Of course, I would!" Seemingly lost, he began walking in circles. "Honey, don't do this. I love you."

I snorted. "Do you know what yesterday was?"

"Um…"

"Yes, um." I turned my back on him.

"Oh God, our anniversary!" he said after a moment. "I'm so sorry. I'll make it up to you tonight. I'll leave work early." He tried to wrap his arms around me, but I struggled, finally kicking him until he let go.

"Look, you miss home. Go see your friends and have a good time. Spend all the money you want. I don't care. Just… please come back to me." When I didn't respond, he said, "I know I've been a crappy husband lately, and I'm sorry that things haven't gone exactly as planned, but you mean everything to me."

"Your company means everything to you. Go," I growled, pointing at the door.

郭

Leaning against a column near my designated baggage carousel, Nancy checked her phone.

"Hi," I said, coming up beside her.

"GuoGuo!" she cried, engulfing me in a full-body hug. Pulling back after a moment, she looked into my eyes. "You okay?"

My lips quivering, I simply shook my head no.

"Oh, sweetie. Let's drop your stuff off at my place and go get drunk."

"That's how I got into this mess to begin with," I sniffed.

Cataloging my ever-increasing mound of bags, Nancy gave her husband, Wang Wei, a meaningful look, and he disappeared to get a cart.

Seated across from one another during the train ride back from my Hunan wedding, Nancy and Wang Wei had spent those long hours getting to know one another. After disembarking, he'd insisted on seeing her home safely, even though he lived in the opposite direction. Ever impressed by a chivalrous act, it wasn't long before Nancy fell head over heels in love with him. Like so many other important things, I'd missed her wedding.

Sighing, I shook my head.

郭

I'd like to say my mother was shocked—or at least surprised, when I showed up at her door bedraggled after a straight week of mixed advice and wicked hangovers. She did have sympathy for me, however, and in one of those rare instances, she reached out and embraced me.

After New Year's celebrations ended, I immersed myself in my family's world, working the front desk of Ming's small hotel, helping Mama prep her little garden for spring, and waitressing for Chen. But with each passing week, I became more aware that life here no longer felt as it once had.

China's metamorphosis continued. Great sums of money were flowing into the country, and some of its wealthiest citizens were even finding their voices, but the quality of life for those living in rural areas had improved little. In fact, the divide between the poor and rich seemed greater than I ever remembered.

The indifference was profound as well. With no welfare system in place, many had little access to food, medicine, or good-paying jobs. I thought about the assistance programs most Americans took for granted and the generosity of organizations like the Chinese church.

There were kind people in my country, too, and I imagined how they would thrive in a caring environment. Perhaps living so long in a country with different priorities had reshaped my worldview, because the life my family was now forced to lead bothered me like never before, the mass grave containing my ancestors' salvaged bones a testament to my government's callousness.

My wedding ring was another reminder of loss. Dave's apathy had laid waste to our marriage, forcing me into this state of limbo.

Whenever despair threatened to overwhelm me, I visited my Changsha friends. Still working for the same flourishing spa, Ting and Yang had mastered an array of innovative techniques, including eyebrow and lip tattooing and laser ablation. Fascinated, I convinced Yang's sister to train me, spending weekdays at her spa and weekends with my family. I practiced on JiaoJiao, my cousins, and even Wai po, and as my skills improved, the neighbors. Surely, these poor mountain women had the nicest looking eyebrows in all of Hunan.

These distractions kept my mind off my larger problems, but they did little to lessen my increasing loneliness and sense of estrangement.

郭

On a warm afternoon, I set out to find my lost self. Fighting a strong sense of foreboding, I merged onto the formidable highway winding through what was once Black Village. Pulling into a scenic overlook lot, I parked JiaoJiao's little blue car and walked to the railing.

Gazing out at the lush and rolling hillside, tourists would never know that the valley below had been anything other than pretty landscape. Nor could they guess that generations of farmers had worked that soil, raised families, eked out livelihoods... and buried their dead. The erasure was unforgivable.

The only monuments to my beloved birthplace were the high mountains surrounding it. Scrubbing away my tears, I climbed over the fence and picked my way down an overgrown path towards them.

Ambling through the stiff grass, my mind was a whirl of decades and thousands of miles. Past a mulberry bush bursting with brilliant jade leaves, I discovered a familiar trailhead. Surely, this was the one I'd used throughout elementary school. In search of that mud-caked little girl, a torch in one hand, a rusty lunch tin in the other, I began trekking up the hillside.

The day I'd used that torch in self-defense popped into my mind. A branch cracked, and on instinct, I froze. Shaking my head then, a chuckle escaped my lips; that particular beast was long dead, and besides, I wasn't afraid anymore.

When I came to the place where Chang had first kissed me, a

wave of tenderness swept over me. Pushing past the overgrown rhododendron, I scooted out onto the rocky ledge, my mind wading into pleasant memories. The difference between that bubbling teenage infatuation and the rushing roar of adult love was as deep and wide as the eight-thousand-mile chasm separating Dave and me.

Hunan was a wonderful refuge—a place to lick my wounds, but could I live in China again? More importantly, did I want a divorce? I thought about my marriage and the life I'd envisioned. Some of it—at first, anyway, had been very good. I'd been privileged. I'd been loved. But over time, Dave had built for me a mountain of broken promises, and it was difficult to see past it to the happiness we'd once shared.

To be fair, I shared some blame for my unhappiness—or at least I'd been an unwitting accomplice. In my ready willingness to give Dave the reins, I'd gotten lost along the way, forgotten who I really was—my tenacity, my resilience. But couldn't I reinvent myself wherever I lived?

Though I'd lose the hefty deposit I'd put down for beauty school, the remainder of my money would adequately cover basic equipment and supplies here in China. And if I were willing to live cheaply—even with my family, to begin with, I could start a small spa. In America, my funds would be exhausted simply gaining a license. But what did a heart know of logic?

In the distance, I heard a growling engine, the squealing of tires, and moments later, a loud horn. So much traffic in a place where no cars had once dared venture.

"Mei Zi!" When Ming's voice rang out a few minutes later, all the blood drained from my face. *Was Mama okay?* Jumping to my feet, I tore down the path.

"GuoGuo, honey, where are you?" a second voice sounded.

"Dave?" I said, skidding to a halt.

"GuoGuo!" The relief in his voice was palpable.

Far below Ming's lanky form came into view, followed closely behind by the taller frame of my husband. When our eyes met, Dave started running. Slipping on rocks and uneven ruts, I hurried to meet him.

Grabbing me up in his arms, he hugged me tightly. In that moment, my face pressed against his warm chest, I forgot to be mad at him. I forgot everything bad.

"What are you doing here?" I said, gasping.

"Coming to bring you home."

His failure to apologize meant that nothing had changed. "What if I don't want to come home?" I said, stepping back and crossing my arms. "What if I want to stay here?"

"Give him a break, Mei Zi," Ming groaned, finally catching up. "The guy's just flown across the world for you."

"This is not your concern," I barked.

Rolling his eyes, he patted Dave's shoulder and said, "Good luck, brother." And with that, he retreated down the path.

"Can we talk?" Dave said.

Nodding, I turned and began climbing the hill once more. He followed wordlessly, and when we got to the big rhododendron, I ducked under its branches.

"This is beautiful," he said, settling beside me.

"There's my house," I murmured after a moment, pointing at the grassy meadow. "And our rice paddy terrace there, and our pond stocked with fat carp and turtles. See how it reflects the orange sky just like a mirror? See the cattails and the large lacy willow at the far end?"

Leaning over, he kissed my cheek. "I'm sorry, GuoGuo. About so many things."

Neither responding nor looking at him, I continued to stare out at my invisible world. I needed more from him than this.

When one moment of silence became two, and then three, he inhaled deeply. "I have news."

"Oh?" I murmured.

"Good news. We got that hospital contract."

This was big news. Dave had applied for several contracts, but he'd been unsuccessful on all fronts. The new hospital under construction required every kind of sign imaginable. That project alone could occupy Dave's company for six months or more.

"Yeah, the group who underbid us backed out at the last minute, and we were next in line. I still can't believe it," he said, softly chuckling. "I used the advance to buy a couple of cutting machines and a 3D printer, which'll make production go even faster. And I hired a sales guy Jonathan recommended. Honey, he's already gotten us two more clients. One's a cute historic town outside of Macon. They want neighborhood signs with their new logo on them. A town? How crazy is that?"

I was happy enough for him, but it changed nothing as far as our marriage was concerned. Stoically, I watched the sun silently slip behind the next mountain range.

"What I'm trying to say is we have money again. You don't have to work anymore. And I want you to go to school and make your dream happen," he said, nodding emphatically. "I want that more than anything."

"If I come back, school isn't all I want," I whispered.

"Name it. What can I give you?"

"Your time. I want a husband again. I don't want to be alone."

"Me either." His voice dropped to a hoarse whisper. "You don't know how I've missed you. I'm lost. I'm absolutely useless without you."

I didn't want him to know how badly I ached—how lost I'd been as well. Turning back to the darkening purple mountains, I said, "Well, you found me."

His voice took on an edge of desperation when I refused to look at him. "GuoGuo, please. Will you come back with me? Be my wife again? Forgive me?"

Thawing a little, I said, "The first two. I'm not sure about the last."

"I'll do everything in my power to earn your forgiveness," he said earnestly. "Everything."

A ghostly mist floated down the hillside, settling in the valley below. "We'd better go if we hope to find our way back," I said.

"Yeah, about that," he said, smiling. "I think I'm going to need a ride."

54

Baby Buddies

Having long missed the start date for beauty school, I had two months to wait until the next term began. Refusing to sit idly at home, I contacted Lily and went back to work at the massage parlor.

The first week of class was pleasant enough, but not terribly interesting. Few of the students—most of whom were teenage girls—had any actual work experience, so we started with the basics: scrubbing floors, washing towels, and prepping rooms. Fighting the bitterness of wasting my spa money in this way, I reminded myself that like working in Lily's massage parlor, school was merely a means to an end.

The second week was a vastly different story. After lunch, most girls took cigarette breaks. Not a smoker, I stayed inside and folded towels. Without warning, my stomach heaved, and I raced to the bathroom, barely reaching the toilet in time.

That evening, I was sick again.

"Do I have a fever?" I asked Dave.

Kissing my forehead, he said, "Nope. Why?"

"I think your cooking made me sick," I said, smiling.

"Hey, I'm still learning."

Dave in the kitchen was humorous. Without the existence of takeout menus, he would surely have starved before we married. Two nights a week, he was home by six to prepare dinner. Though some of his concoctions were nearly inedible, he was trying, which is all I could ask for.

The following morning, I hopped up from my chair and fled class. The most terrifying thought crossed my mind as I wiped my mouth; what if the tuberculosis disease had come back? I might be spreading it to these unsuspecting girls right now. I checked the tissue for blood.

"Are you preggers, too?" the blond, waif-like girl named Kaeley asked, smacking her gum as I emerged from the stall. "I've been puking for weeks. So gross, right?"

The concept defied words. I couldn't be pregnant. Not now. Not when my dreams were within reach.

"Hey, you need to sit down or somethin'?" she asked. "You don't look so good."

郭

Reading the pregnancy test instructions was impossible, but I refused to ask Dave for help; I hadn't decided what to do if the answer was yes. TB might kill me, but right now, having a baby seemed worse.

Yes, I was thrilled that Dave's company was doing well, and that money flowed into our accounts more freely, but years of failure had taught me that success could be a fleeting thing. Once this hospital contract was fulfilled, would there be another, or would we go back to a trickle of small orders? If I didn't get this license now, I wasn't sure when I would have another chance. Giving up on the confusing words, I pulled up a YouTube video.

"Are you still feeling sick, honey?" Dave asked as I ghosted into the living room.

"I'm fine," I said absently.

Pondering my situation the following day as I mindlessly washed one head of hair after another, I considered abortion. Not only was this practice common in my country, the government actively endorsed it. In fact, practically every woman I'd ever known had had one at some point or another. Everyone, except Mama.

In all regards, my fear of inadequacy was her fault. How could I forget her endless years of struggle just to feed and clothe us and her determination that we be educated no matter the cost? How could I endure the exhaustion that had so often plagued her, her frail smiles, her whispers that we were worth it? No, I lacked her mettle.

Risking everything just to have me, I could only imagine her grave disappointment and utter sense of betrayal if she learned that I'd given up so easily. And without a doubt, I knew what Dave would want—had always wanted. To take that joy from him seemed cruel.

There's an old Chinese saying: "Everything bitter is good for you." I'd come to believe it was true. Had I not been attacked at the fabric factory, I would never have found spa work. Had I not been tricked and then molested by Fu, I would never have returned to Shanghai to exact vengeance. And had my wicked roommates not stolen my money and kicked me out of their apartment, I would never have met Dave.

After a great deal of soul-searching, I decided that if this pregnancy made me feel bitter, well, there must be good to come. There had to be.

郭

"We can be baby buddies!" Kaeley squealed when I grudgingly admitted my condition. "When you need to puke, I'll cover for you, and when I do, you can cover for me. How far are you along, anyway?"

I thought back to the night after Dave had found me on the mountain; we'd barely slept. The next night had been much the same. "Three months, I think."

The news overjoyed Mama and my friends. But for some reason I couldn't seem to tell Dave. Perhaps his knowing meant no turning back.

"You need to sit down," I said softly.

Dave's expression turned serious. "Sure, honey. What is it?"

"I'm pregnant," I breathed.

Dave gasped, his shock quickly exploding into elation. "That's the best news I've ever heard. Oh, my God!" he said, pulling me into his arms. "I'd totally given up on being a dad."

"I'm afraid," I whispered.

"I've got you. I promise," he said, kissing me.

"I'm finishing school," I added.

"Of course, you are." His eyebrows knitted together. "Why shouldn't you?"

Pregnant Americans exercise and do anything they want. Celebrities even pose bare-bellied on magazine covers. In China, it's common practice to treat pregnant women as if they're sick. They don't travel or go outside. Rather, they're expected to lie in bed all day, eating and eating until they become fat.

I sighed in relief. At least I didn't need to fight this battle with him.

"And I'll need help."

"Anything you want," he said earnestly.

"I want Mama."

Dave began the paperwork for my mother's travel visa that very night. I prayed to whomever was listening that she hadn't been exposed to TB at any point.

55

Superwoman

If flying across the world had been daunting for an adventurer like me, I could only imagine what Mama was feeling. Of course, I had no choice but to imagine it, because regardless of never having flown before, or even traveled far from our village, she showed little emotion during what was surely an extraordinary experience. Any fear she harbored, she bravely held inside herself; this had always been her way. The only time her emotions betrayed her was during take-off when she squeezed my hand.

"What do you think, Mama?" I finally asked, exasperated by her stoicism. I'd given her the window seat, and I knew what she was seeing: China falling away, staying behind to tend to the earth.

Her eyes flicking from my face to my swollen belly, she smiled tightly and then returned her attention to the scene outside.

Though the obstetrician had assured me that flying at seven months was perfectly fine, it had horrified my family and the village at large. If her behavior was any indication, I wasn't sure Mama was planning to forgive me. Unbuckling the seatbelt, I shifted again. Flying safely and flying comfortably were two different stories.

郭

Bizarrely, it was people rather than the magnificent feat of flying that most fascinated her. Her eyes never stopped roaming around Atlanta's airport. "Look at all the white people," she remarked. And then when she saw her first black face: "Oh!"

"Mama, don't point," I hissed.

My house was similarly absorbing. She touched the walls, the art, the appliances, pressing buttons, feeling material.

"Do you want to help me cook dinner?" I asked, handing her a knife and an onion. She needed something to do that made sense to her.

I spent the weekend helping her acclimate. She'd taken her surroundings—the grocery store, the pharmacy, Walmart—and even the time shift in stride. Awed by her indomitable spirit, I hoped my child would inherit it from her.

"You should be in bed, Mei Zi," Mama scolded when I came downstairs dressed and ready for school Monday morning.

"I have to work. If I don't, I won't graduate before Arthur is born."

We'd decided to name our son after Dave's uncle. Since American names didn't have any real meaning, Arthur was as good to me as any other. And it was fitting that he should have an American name; he would be a child of this country.

"He needs a proper Chinese name. Gang," she said. "Because he will be stubborn like you. Sit, I'll make you congee."

"That'll take too long, Mama. I'll just have an egg."

"The baby won't come out right if you run around like this. Go, go, go. It's not healthy," she said, tsking me.

Transferring my tea to an insulated cup, I grabbed my purse. "You worked in the fields until the day I was born," I said. "And I came out just fine. Arthur will be fine, too. You'll see."

郭

Grateful that I'd stockpiled hours prior to leaving for China, by the middle of my eighth month, the demands of school had become overwhelming. I felt swollen and achy all the time, and picking up dirty towels from the salon floor was a chore I came to dread. I lay in bed each night with my feet propped up on pillows.

"Want a foot rub?" Dave asked, breezing into the room.

"For hours and hours," I said, smiling up at him. He hadn't slipped back into his old habits as I feared he might once Mama took over. He seemed committed to preserving our marriage, and I loved him even more for it.

Mama and Dave attended the little graduation ceremony held in the back room of the beauty school. It lacked the grandeur of my STA graduation, but it was equally meaningful since Mama was there to watch.

"I can't believe you did this, honey," Dave said, kissing my cheek. "You amaze me."

I'd amazed myself as well. Perhaps I had more of Mama's will in me than I thought.

We turned Dave's home office into a nursery. Though blue is the boy color in America, I'd always loved purple. On the day my contractions began, I was just finishing the lilac trim.

The three of us went to the hospital that evening. The birthing room had only one reclining chair, so I decided Mama should wait at home until the baby was born. Of course, convincing her that this was a good idea was like negotiating with a water buffalo.

"I'm staying," she said.

"You'd be much more comfortable at home, Mrs. Guo," Dave explained through translation. "I promise to bring you back as soon as Arthur's born."

"I'm staying," she repeated, crossing her arms.

"Seriously, Mama, I'm in a hospital full of doctors. We can pay for any medical treatment I need, no problem. Please let Dave take you home."

"You make no sense, Mei Zi," she said, glancing at the scattered equipment surrounding me. "Chinese women have been delivering babies forever—the right way." Picking up a blood pressure cuff as if it were a decaying carcass, she examined it briefly and then dropped it back onto the counter in disgust. "Why do you think our country has the largest population? No, these American doctors will thank me for teaching them proper methods."

"What did she say?" Dave asked.

"She said, she'll be happy to go home and wait."

郭

Morning brought stronger contractions. It felt like the baby was clawing my skin open from the inside. Between contractions, I had fitful dreams, often hearing Mama's voice. Sometimes she sounded far away, other times nearby. I thought of my childhood fever and her search for me.

"Mei Zi?" she shouted.

My eyes flipped open, and Dave, who was holding hand, said, "Is that your mom?"

"You can hear it, too?" I asked, bewildered.

"Mei Zi!"

Dave stuck his head into the hallway. "Oh my God, it *is* your mom! Mrs. Guo," he shouted, waving.

Suddenly, Mama was standing beside my bed, drenched in sweat.

"How did you get here?" I asked, stunned.

"I walked."

"Ten miles?" I said.

She shrugged. "Not so far."

"What did she say?" Dave asked.

When I told him, his eyes grew wide, and his mouth popped open. "You walked from our *house*? In this heat? It's, like, ninety outside. Mrs. Guo, I would have come and gotten you."

Ignoring him, she felt my forehead. "You need me."

I couldn't wrap my mind around the concept. This tiny woman, who could only read a few words in Chinese and certainly none in English, had somehow found her way back to me. I don't know how she remembered the roads, and it wasn't as if she could ask for directions. Still, she was here.

I'd always believed my mother was Superwoman. She'd overcome so many obstacles in her life. And now, in a country so foreign it seemed the very opposite of China, she was ready to take charge of this modern hospital. I was so touched that I began to cry.

郭

"Do you have a name?" the nurse asked a little while after putting the baby in my arms.

"Arthur," Dave responded, unable to take his eyes off of our son.

"And the middle name?" she asked. Dave's face lost all expression.

"Ji Tao," I said.

"Okay. How do you spell that?"

Mama nodded her head in approval. "That's a good one."

"What does it mean?" Dave asked.

I'd been pondering names ever since Mama had insisted I give him one. She was right; this child was both American and Chinese, and he should have something to remind him of both heritages. "*Ji* is the god of grain," I said. "I never want Arthur to be hungry like my parents were." Mama smiled, though she had no idea what I was saying. "*Tao* means humility. Arthur will have everything this rich country can offer, but I want him to appreciate it."

"Ji Tao," Dave reverently said. Taking our son into his arms, his eyes roamed Arthur's face and then mine. "It's perfect."

56

Epilogue

Three years have passed since Arthur's birth. Motherhood has not come easily for me, and bringing my spa vision to life has taken more time than I'd hoped. When I felt Arthur was old enough to travel, I took him home to meet my family—a twenty-hour airplane ride with a screaming baby is not for the faint of heart. While there, I attended a beauty industry trade show in Guangzhou. Ordering the bounty of equipment and furniture necessary to create the perfect spa experience was a thrilling thing. More thrilling is the space it's destined for.

One of my church friends is a doctor. Through her connections, I was able to purchase space in a lovely medical office building before it went on the market. The white stone and stucco structure, which resembles a mansion, houses a cosmetic dermatology group on its second floor, and an orthodontist practice on its third. With my spa taking up the entire first level, it's a true house of beauty.

As I walk through the rooms of this space, the contractor at my side taking notes, I tell him which walls to tear down, the dimensions of the treatment rooms, how I want the back wall to be nothing but windows so my clients can enjoy the elegant Asian garden outside.

A child's delighted squeal interrupts our conversation.

"Over here," Dave calls out in a singsong voice.

"Da!" Arthur replies, toddling across a linoleum floor that slate will soon replace.

"There's my big boy," Dave says, scooping him up and turning in circles. I can't imagine anyone being a better father. He may even be better than Baba. Certainly, he's more patient.

The key slips from my hand as I lock up the building. When I bend down to pick it up, I'm distracted by my reflection in the shiny gold sign Dave's company has made for me. *Far East Spa*.

Running my fingers over the logo that spells my name in Qing Dynasty characters, I lose myself in the vision of a little girl—a dirty and coatless urchin, her face smeared with dried egg yolk, picking up garbage by the side of the road. How cold she is, how hungry, how unsure of her place in the world.

I glance over at Arthur, the very picture of contentment, and I swear an oath that I will never allow him to be hungry, that I'll do everything in my power to keep him healthy and safe, and that no matter what it takes, I'll ensure he has the best education possible.

My sight clearing, I shake my head and smile. I've become my mother.

The End

Afterword

Mrs. Guo and I met one suffocating morning in Negril, Jamaica. Over tea, we struck up a conversation. Having seen my Chinese-adopted daughters running around the resort, she seemed as eager to talk to me as I was to her.

Beyond her fiery spunk and straightforward manner, what I found particularly interesting was her use of American slang. Though her speech was heavily accented, she tossed in terms such as "like" and "you guys" with abandon and in all the right places. I found it difficult to separate the two visions of her: the mainstream American and the Chinese national.

When I asked how she'd ended up in Atlanta, she pointed to a sandy-haired man furiously writing a best man's speech. (Jonathan's destination wedding). "My husband and I met in Shanghai when he worked for UPS."

That's all an author suffering from writer's block needed to jerk herself right out of it. Envisioning a multiracial romantic comedy rife with cultural faux pas, I asked, "Would you let me write a book about you?"

We began emailing, but this proved difficult for her, so we moved to WeChat, an app that allowed her to record her answers. Not long after, she took her son back to China for an extended visit, propelling me into a state of sleep-deprivation as we negotiated the twelve-hour time difference.

I'm not sure what I expected when she began reminiscing, but her life had been far from comedic. No matter, the details were so interesting that I was hooked and more driven by the day to craft a story around them.

Though this is predominantly fiction, I will say that I've developed a newfound appreciation for memoir writers. Every question I asked led me down a branched path requiring a barrage of follow-ups, and I never knew which direction those would take me. I also discovered how difficult it is for a person to chronologically recite their rich and ever-evolving personal history. How can one be expected to recall their worldview at, say, age ten? Try it!

Her explanation of cultural issues meshed with some of what I'd learned through the adoption process, but China was rapidly changing. In fact, the version I'd first experienced was obsolete several years later. Poverty had not been eliminated during that time-span, but the towering skyscrapers and the shocking sight of sports cars zipping through city traffic certainly masked it (until you got to the orphanages). Mrs. Guo lived through those light-speed changes, and it was fascinating to experience them through her eyes.

The writing of this book has been an emotional journey for me. I could go on for pages about international adoption and the experiences the families I've known have had; hundreds of books have been written on the subject. Instead, I want to share one story.

During a trip, we visited the Stone Forest, a national park in the Yunnan Province. While there, an old man came up to us and pointed to our baby. Speaking quickly and ardently, he broke into tears. We couldn't understand his words—we only have a rudimentary grasp of Mandarin—but sometimes understanding the words isn't necessary to understand their meaning.

Thank you for sharing this journey with me. If you are able, please leave a review so others can walk in your footsteps.

Acknowledgements

VIRGINIA GRAY

I offer a universe of thanks to my family and friends for their unerring support during this labor of love. Thank you, Barbara, Pat, Elaine, and Audrey for your brilliant insight, and to my editor Bob Atkinson, whose eagle eyes searched every single line of this manuscript for errors and misplaced commas. Special thanks to Amy for her insight, and to Geoff of Toaster Shock Designs for his patience. Finally, thanks to Ms. Guo for sharing your story with me, even though you believe it is nothing special. The opportunity to work with you has been an extraordinary gift that I will cherish always.

About the Author

Award-winning Author Virginia Gray is a graduate of Wake Forest University. A former college professor, she stepped away from academics to pursue a career in writing. She lives in the Midwest with her wonderful family and far too many pets.

For more, please visit virginiagray.com

Made in the USA
Columbia, SC
15 December 2020